Born in 1943, in the midst of the Second World War, W J Roberts grew up in Birmingham where he still resides. At 15, he trained as an electrician, he met Veronica at 18, married her in 1964 and they are still happily married. After writing a series of amusing rhymes for his grandchildren, Lewis and Lydia, Roberts went on to write a series of short stories. This led to his passion for writing, which fills his retirement. After publishing his first book, *Distance is Our Enemy*, his passion for writing flourished.

I would like to dedicate this book to my daughter, Deborah, who listens to my ideas and helps with the editing and on this occasion designed the cover.

W J Roberts

A Family Unravelled

AUSTIN MACAULEY PUBLISHERS™

LONDON ★ CAMBRIDGE ★ NEW YORK ★ SHARJAH

A CIP catalogue record for this title is available from the British Library.

ISBN 9781035810109 (Paperback)
ISBN 9781035810116 (ePub e-book)

www.austinmacauley.com

First Published 2024
Austin Macauley Publishers Ltd®
1 Canada Square
Canary Wharf
London
E14 5AA

For my beautiful and caring wife, Veronica.

Chapter 1

Henry Swan Jenson surveyed the sombre expressions etched on the faces of the extraordinary large cortege of friends and family attending the funeral of his father, Frank Jenson. As the mourners gathered around the grave, one particular vexatious thought crossed Henry's mind, whereby all those so-called friends, business colleagues and even some of their so-called family had deserted him when he became ill. Henry's anger had begun to germinate soon after his father's illness was diagnosed as terminal. Anger engendered by what he considered an appallingly uncompassionate lack of empathy shown by those, who in his opinion should have been there for him.

As Frank's health declined, it furthered Henry's anger to bourgeon like a volcano with its seething cauldron of magna lying beneath the surface waiting to erupt. It was during Frank's final weeks as he lay on the cusp of death writhing in pain from the cancer, (eased only by the introduction of a syringe driver to administer morphine to that pernicious malignancy which had invaded thus consumed and ultimately his frail body) succumbed to. Some of those so-called friends and business colleagues had not ventured near.

His immediate family had rallied round, Henry's younger sister Caro Swan Dean, his mother Mary Swan Mathew and her husband Mathew, Elaine Frank's new wife Mary's best friend and friends Cherry stone and her partner Barney Phillips. His other half-sister Lindy the product of Mary and Mathew was desperately upset at losing the man she called Granddad therefore considered it far too distressed to attend those undoubtably harrowing, sombre proceedings. Throughout those final distressing weeks Henry, with help from those close to him had nursed his dad, but the stress had transgressed his usual calmness and pragmatism. Diametrically the consequence of watching his dad's suffering proliferate left him emotionally drained. He was virtually unable to apply his mind to anything else, reducing him to the point of physical exhaustion. Deeply depressed, distressed and close to an emotional breakdown the finality of Frank's demise came as something of a relief, though it must be said Henry would never concur with that exposition.

Henry recalled the last words his dad voiced at the point he miraculously came out of his morphine induced coma minutes before he passed away, offering a heartfelt apology and an ingenuous plea, "Henry son with all my heart I'm sorry for the pain I've caused you, Corrina Jade and my grandson Denni, can you ever forgive me?"

Thereby a duality prevailed, Henry loved, even lionised his dad as a son should, nevertheless, bastardised him in equal measures; without realising it, Frank had unintentionally broken his heart. At first, Henry had found it difficult to reconcile his feelings towards his father because of the hurt he had inadvertently inflicted on him. Nonetheless, Henry's compassion for his father outweighed his rancour, thereby acquiescing to his father's sincere adjuration exercising his pragmatic approach to life giving an antapology, "You're my dad and I love you; we all make mistakes. Dad there is nothing to forgive."

Frank was a charismatic man who could charm the birds out of the trees, not to mention the knickers of practically every woman he came into contact with testified by the number of women who were in attendance. Two of them present to the family's certain knowledge, had born him children. One of them Frank's long-time live-in partner and now wife Elaine, the mother of his son Jude. Also attending was Cherry Stone who had been an under manager of one of his shops with whom he had a short fling; Cherry had borne him another son Myles. There were another half a dozen people who the family could only assume as to their own reasons why they were there.

Henry over time had grown to accept Jude and Myles as his brothers, and to like and love both of them but unfortunately neither of them were able to attend the doleful proceedings. The youngest, Myles, couldn't make it back from a school skiing trip to Canada in time, and Jude suffered from an acute fear of cemetery's, a phobia that goes by the grand, almost unpronounceable name of coimetrophobia. Sadly, no amount of persuasion could induce Jude to attend, however he was quite happy to be present at the reception.

There was a third child, a girl, whom Henry hadn't known existed until he reached his mid-twenties. She was one child his dad had never spoken about, although Henry suspected he was well aware of her existence. To all who knew Frank it was a question or supposition as to just how many more offspring there might be. Indeed, it had been rumoured there might be at least another three, however, it was pure conjecture; no further women or siblings ever did come forward. Frank's philandering and outright devil may care attitude to everybody and everything apart from business, had been the cause of the break-up of his marriage and subsequent divorce from Henry and his sister Caro's mother: Mary. Frank a self-made man could be classed as very wealthy, in fact by the time of his death he had achieved millionaire status. Born and bred on an ageing housing estate in the Aston district of Birmingham, right on the doorstep of Villa Park and the Jacobean country house 'Aston Hall' to which Frank always aspired to owning a house of the same magnitude. Humble beginnings for a man who went on to live a very affluent lifestyle. He was born the second son of a bricklayer, his mum a machinist in the local screw manufacturing company and they still reside in the same house. Frank had not seen his older brother Stanley since he had migrated with his family to Australia.

However, ambitious Frank was endowed with an astute business brain, his keenness, insight and judgment added to his resourcefulness made him stand out among his peers. He never quite attained his dream of a country mansion but came very close when he moved to the leafy suburbs of Sutton Coldfield where his neighbours were luminaries of the same high-octane personas as himself. It was one of the few times in his life Frank felt satisfied with his endeavours as he collected the keys to an enormous Bungalow composing of six bedrooms, each with en suite bathrooms. There were three reception rooms, a man cave or study and a kitchen large enough to fuel a restaurant. The house also accommodated a small heated indoor swimming pool complete with a Jacuzzi. The house was so large Frank gave it the name, "High Chaparral" after one of his favourite television shows.

To his credit as a young man struggling to build a business, he always made sure as a family, they never wanted for anything. Henry and Caro when youngsters, their dad would never miss any opportunity to be with them, despite his work ethic. Each year as his fortune increased, he would take them both and their two half-brothers on holiday, always venturing to foreign climes; once, he took them on the holiday of lifetime to Florida.

As the pallbearers lowered the casket into the ground, despite the pale early morning spring sun it gave little warmth or comfort to Henry, he was visibly shaking. This was a direct result of his sadness combined with the growing anger of which he was attempting to keep locked inside. His sister Caro sobbing, gripped his arm struggling to hold herself together such, was her grief, her husband Lindsay wrapped a loving arm around her shoulders in an attempt to comfort her.

After the Minister had finished reciting the committal prays, Henry threw a handful of muddy earth onto the casket, declaring beneath his breath, "Thank you for everything Dad and thank you for nothing DAD!"

Caro added a single red Rose, the flower Frank would always buy for the most important women in his life. Divorced from Mary for more than fifteen years but never withstanding her remarrying, always on the anniversary of their marriage he continued to send a bouquet of Red Roses; it was his way of showing he cared for her.

Henry stepped back, somehow managing with great difficulty to contain the anger broiling within. Once again, he surveyed the many sad faces of the mourners, who one by one were throwing a handful of muddy earth onto the casket. Out of the corner of his eye he observed a young blonde-haired woman. She stood a little further away, behind the main cortege, her presence immediately brought a smile to his face, setting his heart racing; in an instance his anger subsided, whispering to Caro, "Corrina Jade is here I need to speak to her."

Still tearful, Caro nodded an understanding smile, replying, "Go on while you can, say hello from me and Lindsay," advising, "ask her to stay for a while but if she can't we will understand."

Henry made his way towards the young woman, as he did so, she started to walk away, Henry quickened his step calling out her name, "Corrina, Corrina Jade" catching up with her, he pulled her back. As she turned round he noted how tired she looked, her soft blue eyes sad, woebegone and red from crying, her soft pink Rose petal cheeks all puffy and streaked with mascara. Grasping her by the hand he too felt tears begin to moisten his eyes, whilst offering a heartfelt greeting. "Hello Corrina Jade, my darling, it's lovely to see you."

"Awright Hendrie." She whispered shaking with emotion which seemed to accentuate the soft Scottish accent she had acquired (as a child her family had moved to Edinburgh). During the four years they had been together, allied to the two years working in Edinburgh, Henry had learned to understand her and was quite fluid in the Scottish vernacular she would slip into when she felt comfortable with someone. Gently stroking her cheek, he offered his thoughts, "I really didn't expect you to be here but I'm so glad you came, you've raised my spirits."

"Hendrie twas a prnickety decision bit twas achance tae be able tae see ye again wioot faimly 'n' neighbours comin tae ony wrong conclusions aboot us."

"Corrina, where have you left your car?"

"Ah didn't fancy driving a' this wey sae ah git th' train."

Henry's next question moistened his eyes further to the point where a tear began to trickle down his cheek, "How is Denni?"

"Missing his daddy terribly as a'm."

"Corrina Jade, I'm missing him and his mum just as much, but I'm afraid there's no answer to our pain without bringing the whole of the dammed establishment and it's laws crashing down on us."

"Henry we had such a verra bonnie lec thegither, we wur so happy, how come och how come wur we cursed wi such afowk?"

"Corrina Jade, we did have a lovely life together so when I say I'm missing you, it's an illimitable understatement. My darling there's a country song called (Once a day) a song that expresses exactly how I feel. Ironically it was the favourite of the man who gave rise to all the heartache we have had to endure over the last couple of years. The words are quite unambiguous, proclaiming (I'm down to hurting once a day, every day, all day long). Corrina Jade I'm hurting more than I could ever give voice to, but whatever happens nobody can ever take away the love I have shared with you."

"Hendrie. I'm aff tae stairt greetin again I'd better gang."

"Can't you stay just for a little while? And maybe join us for something to eat? Say hello to Caro and Mum?"

"Na ah wish I cuid bit ah hae a train tae catch a'm needin tae get back hame tae the bairn 'n' forby if ah bide yer mither micht git pure upset."

"Corrina my darling, I'm sure Mum will want to talk to you, she loves you, as do all the rest of the family."

"Na Hendrie a mist git back tae Denni."

"Corrina Jade, give Denni a big hug and a kiss, tell him Daddy loves him, as soon as I have completed my duties as executer of Dad's estate I'll be up to see you both."

"I'd better gang, see yer later Hendrie ah aye loue n' wull aye loue ye."

Kissing her softly on the cheek, he reiterated her words, "Bye Corrina Jade, I still and will always love you too."

With a heavy heart, Henry watched as Corrina Jade turned to walk away from him, yet again he tried to persuade her to stay a little longer asking, "Corrina

Jade are you sure you won't stay just for a little while? I don't care what people will think of us, they can take a running jump."

"Hendrier a'm waantin tae bit ah can't, me 'n' Denni wull see ye whin you've th' time, we'll keek tae th future tae it till then I'll dream."

"Can I at least drive you back to the station?"

"Dae nae palaver yerself I'll git a bus or you'll neer hear th' lest o' it us gaun aff th'gither anyway ye hae th' reception tae host you can throw a handful o' soil on th' greve fur me if ye wid?"

"I'll do that for you my darling, bye."

"See you later Hendrie mah special man."

Henry walked Corrina Jade to the cemetery gates, gazing into her eyes he gave her another soft kiss on the cheek. Feeling sad, he watched her as she walk down the street to catch a bus into town, she turned to wave goodbye, his initial excitement, was usurped by melancholia. Wiping the tear from his eyes he turned to rejoin the cortege and realised everyone had been staring, He could almost hear their moral outrage. The sadness drained from him to be replaced with an outpouring of vitriolic anger he could no longer contain, grimacing, he let fly with rancorous rhetoric which he directed at them.

"What are you all looking at? You fucking nosey fucking bastards mind your fucking own business, if you don't like it then just piss off!"

His mum Mary, who only once before heard him express such a vehemently caustic declamation, joined him by putting an arm round him, calming him down and reasoning with him, "Come on Henry they don't understand I'm sure they're not judging you probably just the opposite."

"I'm sorry Mum, even after two years my emotions are painfully raw and it's all his fault, him! Lying in that box."

"Son, what's done is done, think on how hard his decision must have been to speak up and admit the truth to both of you."

"Mum I know you're right, I loved him, but I hated him for it."

"Henry, I know he was never a full-time father, but he would always go out of his way for all his children, especially for you and Caro. Son you have repaid him in a way he wouldn't have expected, by being a wonderful son, helping to nurse him through his illness to the very end, and taking on the burden of running his business. Considering the situation and pain he caused, you were wonderful, there aren't many sons who would ever have done so."

"Despite everything, he was still my dad, and I loved him, Mum I think we should make a move I've kept everyone waiting long enough."

"Have you calmed down son?"

"I'll be fine no more outbursts I promise."

"Good, Henry I haven't heard you give out such invective in a very long time, I think an apology should be forthcoming don't you?"

"Ok Mum I'll speak to everyone."

Henry took one long last look at the casket, threw another handful of soil on the coffin for Corrina Jade and said, "Good-by Dad" then went back to Frank and Elaine's house for the funeral reception.

Later as the reception began to wind down, Henry gave his apologies to all the mourners for his vitriolic effusion. However, he had to endure the endless anecdotal memories by friends and family alike, all of whom reckoned Frank was a great bloke to spend time with. Henry managed to forbear from asking if he was such a great bloke, why, while he lay dying had they treated him like a leper, a social outcast? Henry wanted to scream out to them his dad hadn't contracted Bubonic plague or Leprosy and he most certainly wasn't contagious. Frank had been struck down with the nightmare of colon cancer, which had spread expeditiously, until savagely reaching its painful conclusion. Surely some of those so-called friends could have taken time out to see him, if only to say goodbye.

The past few weeks had been Gloomy and unhappy, as was the funeral and the sad finality of the day. Today, however, Henry's day lightened somewhat when by chance overhearing part of a conversation between his mum and an erstwhile friend of his mum and dad. During that conversation her friend intimated in a jocular fashion, a sort of impudently bold insinuation that his mum wasn't quite, 'the blushing bride', the day she married Frank. Something had occurred at her hen party, which was obviously embarrassing, nevertheless she countered the accusation well, laughingly telling the friend to behave. Henry wasn't sure whether he had misheard the accusation or could that supposedly throwaway remark possibly be true.

Unlikely as it seemed perhaps there might be a slim possibility there could be some grain of truth contained in those girlish pixilated memories. He was puzzled and unsure what to think nevertheless, it elicited a surge of excitement within him, to find out if there was any truth in those immature tipsy giggling innuendo's and their implications. Henry faced an extremely difficult obstacle which he would need to surmount; how would he confront his mum?

The very nature of what may have been a throwaway remark, he had certainly overheard, made him extremely curious. However, Henry would need to tread warily, because he will have to ask his mum some quite searching intimate questions. She could well be unavailing to the questions because the very nature of them might embarrass her. Nevertheless, he decided once his dad's estate was settled, those questions should and would be asked.

Chapter 2

The story of the duality towards Henry's Father began immediately after Henry's introduction into the world. Within a couple of weeks of their honeymoon a delighted Mary, Henry's mum found out she was pregnant.

Henry was the first born of two children to Mary and Frank, and to be fair to Frank, Henry was the apple of his father's eye. Regrettably, Frank's eye had a wanderlust of its own, most certainly where the opposite sex was concerned. Frank who ran his own chain of stationary shops had a magnetic personality, and was an extremely hard working businessman, tall, good looking, always well dressed, and enjoyed the company of ladies far too much. Unfortunately his predilection towards the opposite sex, I'm afraid, was more often than not reciprocated: Frank was a modern day Don Juan.

Frank's success in business was driven by ambition allied to his steely determination, furthermore his incredible work ethic. With the advent of fatherhood, he felt the need to provide ever more for his family, as his business began to expand, he found himself having to increasingly devote more and more time to his work. Unhappily, the downside of working excessive hours away from the family home, began to affect his relationship with Mary, inevitably putting a huge strain on their marriage. When Henry came along Mary hoped, no expected Frank to rearrange his work schedule thus allowing him more time to embrace his family life. To be fair for a while he did exactly what a young wife would expect of her husband and the Jenson household became a stable and happy family home.

Unfortunately ensuring the success of the business was paramount to Frank, therefore it wasn't long before, and increasingly so, things began to sour between him and Mary and Frank's business took Centre stage with the family taking second place. Mary made allowances because she knew he loved her, Lord knows he told her often enough, and she most certainly loved Frank. To distraction; sadly all that was about to dramatically change for the worst.

Henry's earliest recollections of his dad and his transgressions outside of his marriage, although quite vague, he believed, happened when he was about four years old. On the odd occasion when Frank would take time out from his busy commercial Schedule, he would strap Henry into his buggy ostensibly and take him to the park to play on the swings and roundabouts. However, those excursions to the park would very often entail his dad making a courtesy call to one particular lady, a certain Susan Phillips who lived opposite the park and just happened to be a friend of Frank and Mary. Susan would occasionally act as a babysitter giving Frank and Mary time to enjoy a night out together.

During those so-called visits to the park, Frank's courtesy calls to their friend Susan became more regular and the duration of visits, longer. Whilst there, Henry would have to stay in the lounge with Susan's son Elliot, who was about the same age a child security gate was fitted to the doorway preventing them from straying elsewhere in the house. Quite often they would be left to their own devices for a considerable length of time, while Frank and Susan were delighting in their bedroom assignations.

For some reason, those regular visits to Susan's house mysteriously stopped, along with the babysitting. Susan completely disappeared out of their lives, Henry never saw her again or so he believed. About three years later there was an incident Henry would only come to understand the full significance of many, many years later.

Chapter 3

Seven-year-old Henry, while playing with his friends, fell of his bicycle leaving him gripping his right arm and crying inconsolably. Mary was unable to pacify him because he appeared to be in so much pain, so she called Frank. Frank suspecting he may have broken his arm, took Henry to the local cottage hospital. As luck would have it, by the time they arrived the pain had subsided and Henry had stopped crying, even so, Frank thought it necessary to have the injury checked over.

Once all their details had been given to a receptionist and processed in an exceptionally busy A and E, they were directed to a waiting room to have any possible injury assessed then directed to a different waiting room to have his arm X-rayed. Henry was thirsty and asked his dad for a drink, he said he would get him one but while doing so he insisted that under no circumstances was Henry to move, just in case they missed their place in the queue. Frank also took the added precaution of informing the nursing staff where and why he was leaving Henry on his own. No sooner had Frank left the waiting room, Henry was called in for his X-ray the procedure lasting no more than a few minutes fifteen at the very most.

Henry was sent back to the waiting room to await the result the radiologist who asked to speak to Frank. As he hadn't yet returned, Henry went looking for him. He spotted him in the reception area talking to a woman, she stood with two children by her side, a boy about the same age as himself and a little girl about two years old. Henry thought he recognised the woman but wasn't quite sure, in any event he was more interested in quenching his thirst shouting, "Daddy, Daddy the doctor wants to speak to you, have you got my drink, I'm thirsty?"

Hearing Henry shouting, the woman said something to Frank, then gathering up the little girl and whilst holding the boy's hand, she made a rather hurried exit.

Needless to say, Henry inquisitively asked, "Who was that lady Daddy?"

Dismissive of the question Frank explained, "Just an old friend of your mums, nobody you know son."

It wasn't until Henry had reached his teen years and Mary had divorced Frank that those memories manifested into an awareness of his dad's assignations with Susan. Apparently one fateful afternoon Henry and Eliot managed to escape from the confines off the lounge by climbing over the gate, then scrambling up the stairs: thus walking in on Frank and Susan's tryst in the bedroom. Calamitously for Frank a few days later, Henry, let the cat out of the bag while quite innocently asking, "Mummy why was Daddy kissing Susan?"

Mary who was eight months pregnant at the time with Caro, Henry's Sister, managed to remain quite calm considering the question and the information that had just been imparted to her. Henry didn't remember what her answer was, he could only Imagine it being said through gritted teeth, and surmise it went something on the lines of, "I don't know Henry I'll have to ask him."

Henry's question brought his mum's world crashing down around her which was, I'm afraid, the defining moment in the marriage, the instant when their Idyllic family life all but came to an end.

Despite his insistence, it would never happen again, Mary, never trusted Frank again, try as he might to convince her, he was reaching for an unattainable goal. Everything confirmed when she deserted the marital bed moving into one of the spare bedrooms. From thereon, their once happy home life deteriorated, and became a verbal battle ground, when the slightest misplaced remark would ignite into a venomous free for all slanging match.

Unfortunately, Mary while nursing her new two-month-old daughter Caro, was right to distrust him. Four months after the disclosure of Frank's original indiscretions, it emerged he had been having an affair with his company secretary Elaine, she was someone Mary had never met. In addition to the revelation of his unashamed duplicity, it emerged she was pregnant too, with the first of two half siblings for Henry and Caro, of course, fathered by Frank.

For Mary, it was one humiliation too many, the ultimate perfidy, a calculated violation of trust, one she could not ignore, she vented her raging malevolent vitriol at her husband. After the argument and recriminations had subsided, she asked Frank to leave the family home. Frank taken aback by her explicit invective didn't argue, he left quietly apologising profusely for the hurt he had inflicted on the family, but at the same time promised to look after them financially.

Frank loved his children, therefore keeping his word, he genuinely was constantly available to them. For what it's worth in spite of his never-ending womanising, he always maintained Mary was the love of his life: his one and only true love. He forever regretted the consequence of his actions right to the bitter end. Their divorce was the bitterest of blows, not just to his ego but to him it was like he had been shot through his heart.

When Mary met and subsequently married Mathew, Frank was mortified, for the first time in his life he experienced the emotion of jealousy, because he had such dynamism he had invariably attained all his primary objectives, he still carried a torch and harboured the possibility of winning Mary back. He was beaten when Mary finally turned her back on him by Marrying Mathew it had left him dejected. He never did come to terms with, what he classified quite rightly, as his own stupidity.

Frank never remarried until a week before he died. Leaving him free to indulge in many more elicit liaisons, and so it transpired, even so he would recognise each offspring as his own. But as rumoured there may have been more to which nobody except Frank had the answer.

After Frank had moved out of the family home, Henry age 6, didn't understand why his parents had separated. His dad's continuous absence didn't faze him, and when he collected him for his twice weekly visitations, there was always a treat. Treats included visits to the cinema, or he would take them to Macdonald's for a burger and fries, a big favourite of Henry's. If there were ever any problems concerning the children, he would always take time out from his business to discuss the issues with Mary. Henry had started to ask questions such as, "Mummy why doesn't Daddy come home to stay with us?"

How does a mum tell her offspring that Mummy and Daddy no longer love each other? Avoiding the truth, her answer was to tell him, "Mummy and Daddy both love you and Caro very much, but Daddy is so busy at work he doesn't get much time to be with us."

Children know when things are not right, Henry knew instinctively there was more to the situation than his mum let on, but because he was so young Mary wasn't forthcoming with the real reason. Unfortunately, before Frank moved out of the family home Henry had been at the table when the final verbal assault between his parents began. The angry contentious argument verging on violence, the parental confrontation frightened him sadly adding to the nights he spent covering his head with a pillow to dull the sound. As he progressed into his late teenage years he acknowledged just how frightening the heated aggressive nature of those arguments had been. At such a young age, he had difficulty attuning to the polemic separation of his mum and dad, although, as he got older he did begin to gradually accept and come to terms with the divorce that followed.

Caro on the other hand wasn't used to having her dad around full time, she was too young to understand what had occurred, therefore she was never fazed or upset by the situation. She accepted it as normal. Consequently, she never posed any awkward questions like the ones Henry would often ask.

Sadly, after the separation Henry went through a troubling period of self-doubt believing he was the cause of the unrest and arguments that had blighted the latter part of a once happy relationship between his mum and dad. Frank had increased his son's troubles, having moved in with his secretary Elaine, mother of his new baby son. Henry I'm afraid plunged headlong into the most traumatic epoch of his young life, which began when he was introduced to his new baby, 'half-brother', Jude and unable to understand why his dad wanted to be with Jude and not him and Caro. Sadly, it left him feeling extremely angry and unwanted in short, unloved by his dad. His normal blithesome self, turned inward, he would hide himself in his bedroom, head buried beneath the bed linen crying, refusing to come out from under the covers and refusing to eat or drink, even more worrying slipping into a state of melancholia. Mary genuinely concerned of her son's behaviour was at first unwilling to ask for Frank's help because of her antagonism towards him, nonetheless in desperation she had to call on him for his help. Mary and Frank after a rather lengthy and uncomfortable discourse, and only after some ground rules had been laid down both agreed, for the sake of Henry, the only course of action they could take to alleviate the stress their son was suffering, would be for Frank to move back into the family home albeit on a temporary basis. Hopefully, they could persuade their son that he was really loved by both of them. One of the problems they could not foretell was how, Henry would react when his dad went back to his girlfriend and baby son Jude. Frank and Mary would have to tread warily; nevertheless, while Frank was in residence, they stuck to their promise to be civil to each other refraining from arguing, particularly whilst their son was at home.

Elaine, Frank's girlfriend was none too happy with the outcome of their decision convinced Mary had an ulterior motive, specifically an attempt to regain her husband. Nothing could have been further from the truth, their marriage was defunct, Mary had filed for divorce, it was she who laid down the ground rules expressing Frank would have to sleep in a spare room. Furthermore, he was to spend more time with Henry, no excuses would be tolerated for arriving home after his bedtime. Mary insisted he had to be there to say goodnight and be there in the mornings, until such a time Henry was comfortable enough to accept the situation. What Frank did in between those times was of no concern to Mary, she wasn't interested in the slightest.

Frank was true to his word, Henry responded quickly, his demeanour changing dramatically, precipitated no doubt by his dad's return into his daily life, bringing a smile back to his little face. Strange, but considering the strife and bitterness prevailing before his mum and dad parted, they both kept their promise, never once raising their voices during the four weeks Frank was in full time residence, which at one time would have been deemed implausible. Apart from their obvious differences outwardly they appeared a happy family unit, spending a lot of time talking and explaining to their little boy why Daddy could not always be at home.

Although Frank and Mary felt Henry was again the carefree little boy, he had been before their marriage break up, both had acknowledged from the outset it could never be a permanent solution. Consequently further, and wholly amicable discussions took place, altogether a more adult approach unlike the original extremely uncomfortable, ugly, raucous and abusive exchange of views.

Frank's baby son Jude had to be taken into consideration which could possibly have created further friction, however, Mary seeking the best for all concerned especially for Henry, asked Frank to invite Elaine to conduce her thoughts on how the issue could be resolved. Elaine in the first instance as you would expect was hesitant of the idea, in fact vehement in her opposition to such a meeting, nevertheless Frank used all his persuasive charm and after a lot of heated discourse he succeeded in allaying any apprehension she felt. Elaine eventually agreed to a meeting which would in the long term be good for all concerned, moreover the children.

Mary and Elaine elected to meet on neutral ground in a café located in the local shopping complex. Both women naturally had preconceived ideas about each other, so at the initial meet coldness prevailed, viewing each other with a great deal of suspicion. At first talks were a little stilted but gradually over a period of time the whole aspect of their preconceived ideas of each other changed as they got to know and understand how the situation had affected both of them and unbelievably something totally unexpected arose from their meetings and they both acknowledged their children were of more importance than their feelings. Thus, the beginning of a harmonious relationship began to develop, eventually and incredibly they became not just close friends, but best friends, a friendship that has continued to the present day. Ultimately the wider impact on both women meant they were happy to act when required as babysitters for each other, they also shopped together, even occasionally going out on an evening together, ensuring Frank would be left in charge of his offspring, all three of them! Frank had to start learning about Fatherhood, doing things such as feeding his children and much to his dismay, he was invariably left with the irksome task of changing Jude's nappy. Peace reigned in both households: removing the unpleasantness prevailing, preceding their first meet.

Mary and Elaine's friendship blossomed, a complex arrangement formed and a smooth family life evolved, whereby Frank would stay with Mary and the children, (him sleeping in the spare room) twice, sometimes three times a week so he could be with Henry and Caro. He helped Mary put them to bed, and always took time out each night to read them a story, conversely, Henry and Caro would occasionally stay with their dad, Elaine and baby brother Jude. Those at first, infrequent nights Mary and Elaine ventured out together became a regular weekly Friday night event. Elaine would overnight with Mary because inevitably, both would get legless, intoxicated to the impairment of physical and mental faculties, spawned by the over imbibition of a mixture of intoxicants, whatever they found appealing at the time; invariably followed by a visit to an Indian restaurant. Thence on leaving the restaurant, they would burst into unmelodious screeching, loosely termed as singing, both believing they sounded like a heavenly choir. Usually they gave their rendition of (Nothing compares to you) as a compliment to each other, there would follow raucous laughter interspersed with bad jokes and filthy language. Quite often, one or both of them regularly disgorging the entire night's infusion of intoxicants and hot spicy curry, thereby constituting a recipe requiring them to stay away from their children. It would be polite to call them inglorious nights.

Chapter 4

Much to his mum and dad's relief Henry's melancholia evanesced never to rear its ugly head again, he and Caro loved seeing and being with their dad. Despite his inherent predisposition towards work and the opposite sex, he was a good dad to his three children, all of whom adored him. How he juggled his complicated home life was anyone's guess but juggle it he did, in the same manner as he conducted his business affairs: successfully.

The arrangement strange as It appeared to friends and extended families especially the children's grandparents, suited and worked well for both households, all thanks to the two mothers who had become such close friends and wanted the best for their children. Both sets of Maternal grandparents initially expressed strong disapproval to the ethos of their daughter's family living arrangements, considering the unorthodox situation, to put it in perspective, it was a bit of a tangle, nevertheless, eventually conceding their grandchildren were actually benefitting from the interaction afforded them. Suffice to say complex as it was it had created a very happy environment; therefore they reluctantly gave credence to what they had previously considered rather alien.

However, Granddad Jenson couldn't help quipping, "Frank should change his name to Brigham Young" you can make of that quote as you will. Little did he know the full extent of his son's capacity to put himself about, never dreaming his son's philandering would present him and granny Jenson with a further two grandchildren, their biggest surprise came with the introduction of a fifth grandchild. The surprise being she would be twenty-five years old before she was introduced into their lives. However, they had gotten used to their son's propensity for women, nothing shocked them, not even the unexpected advent of an adult grandchild. By the time they were informed of, furthermore met their second, elder granddaughter, the moment of which should have been particularly Joyful, sadly would later be filled with extreme sadness for all concerned. It was a time when skeletons began to emerge from locked cupboards: hearts were broken and ultimately, lives would be in ruins.

For a number of years life for both of Frank's families, for the most part, was peaceful and happy. Needless to say, as in all domestic situations the odd differences of opinion would arise, usually minor disputes, but whatever the problem Mary and Elaine between them, were able to calm stormy waters. Their friendship became far too strong to allow petty bickering to interrupt the status quo which was usually achieved with a short discourse, eliminating the possibility of any lasting hostilities. Overall, it was an extremely tight knit supportive family group.

By the age of ten, Henry had many of his mum's features, especially her eyes and mouth; there was little of Frank to be seen even their characters differed, Frank's excitable but charmingly gregarious personality in direct contrast to his son. Henry's equable character was quiet, but not introverted more studious, given to moments of introspection often finding it difficult to interact with people outside of his close coterie of friends, nevertheless, when into his mid-teens it was something he would have to, and did overcome. On the other hand, Caro had inherited many of Frank's features, there was no way he could deny her. Three characteristics Henry did share with his dad was his height, (both very tall), both very good looking, both exhibited an inherent work ethic, a driving ambition and an excessively fierce determination to succeed.

Henry was a very bright, intelligent, extremely inquisitive boy, always asking questions then pursuing answers with further questions, always wanting to know more about any and everything of any subject matter into which he delved. Henry as a young boy was simply indefatigable: a trait he has carried to the present day. Like his dad, dilatoriness was something he could never be accused of, a man who never seeks to avoid or neglect his responsibilities.

Henry had the capacity to absorb knowledge which his teachers denoted at a very young age considered him a formidable erudite, advising he was red brick university material, while still at Junior school. Therefore, encouraged by his parents, was advised to take the eleven plus exam with the intention of gaining a place at Grammar school. Expecting him to do well teachers and parents alike were ecstatic when the results were announced, he had attained a rare yet exemplary score of 154. Henry himself certainly happy he had passed couldn't understand what all the fuss was about, affirming he had hoped for better. When Mary asked him what he wanted to do when he left school, his mum shook her head in disbelief at his reply wishing she hadn't bothered. Grinning with his repost, "School crossing patrol officer."

She had to ask, "That's not very ambitious is it, why?"

Chuckling he explained, "You don't start till you're sixty-five."

It was around about that time Henry, then twelve years old had settled nicely into Grammar school when his mum introduced him to the new man in her life, a guy called Marcos Havers whom she had met while on a night out with Elaine. From the moment, Mary had introduced him Henry had taken an instant dislike to him and made his feelings obvious, there was something about him that in his mind didn't sit right, he resented and mistrusted him viewing him with a great deal of suspicion. He wasn't his dad, and try as Marcos did Henry could never warm to him, he felt he was trying to take over. There was something about his demeanour, which in Henry's mind did not gel, suspecting there to be an ulterior motive. Unlikely as it may seem, some children do have an innate ability to see beyond a parent's gullibility, especially when a parent believes they have met someone they consider very special.

For Henry, things were about to take a turn for the worse. One Sunday morning because of business commitments, Frank, unexpectedly took Henry and Caro home early after they had spent the night with him and Elaine. Mary had been out for a night with her new man Marcos, unfortunately Henry, with Caro walked into her bedroom to say hello, only to find her in bed with Marcos. Henry stood agape at the sight before him, unable to articulate his feelings he slammed the door, stamped along the landing and locked himself in his own bedroom, Mary shocked, realised he was distressed followed him desperately trying to placate him, it would be the first time her son had uttered profanities directly aimed at her. Expressing hurtful names and insinuations calling her a dirty slag asking, "How much has he paid you? I hope it was worth it slag."

"Henry, don't you ever talk like that again do you hear."

"Fuck off, you slag."

"Henry, stop it."

"Go away slag, I hate you, I hate you, I hate you!"

That was too much for Mary she broke down sobbing, "Henry please stop it come out, let's talk about it?"

Things suddenly took a considerably bigger turn for the worse when Marcos joined in, "If you don't open this door, when you do come out you'll have me to deal with saying things like that to your mum."

"You can fuck of as well you creepy bastard."

"Talk to me like that again and you won't know what's hit you."

Mary through her tears let rip at Marcos, "You ever so much as look cross eyed or touch a single hair of his head I'll get the police onto you."

"I am trying to help you."

"I think you had better go you're causing more problems."

"Yes fuck of creep," yelled Henry.

"That's enough Henry, I want you to come out now."

"Not until that fucking creepy bastard has gone."

Mary gestured to Marcos to leave.

"Mary you're not going to stand for that nonsense, are you?"

"Marcos he's my son don't ever interfere again, I'll deal with my children the way I see fit, now go I'll speak to you later."

Henry his head troubled and whirling, watched from his bedroom window as an irate Marcos drove away.

Mary quietly asked her son to leave his room, promising, "Henry son, I know you're upset there won't be any shouting, but we do need to talk things over."

"Has he really gone Mum?"

"He has, I promise Henry, now open the door I want to hug you."

There was a pause while he made up his mind, finally he unlocked his bedroom door his head bowed and offered, "I'm sorry Mum I didn't mean those things I said."

Tears in her eyes she wrapped her arms around him kissing his forehead whispering, "I love you and Caro, I would never do anything intentionally to hurt either of you."

"Mum I don't like him he's creepy."

"I don't like him either," Caro agreed with Henry.

"Why don't you like him has he said or done anything I should know about?"

"He doesn't like us Mum and we don't like him, do we Caro?"

"No, he's horrible."

"I'll tell you what you two, shall we go to the pictures this afternoon, what would you like to see?"

"Can I pick the film Mum," yelled an excited Caro.

"Is that all right with you Henry?"

Looking resigned to the prospect of seeing a film Caro chose for them, Henry quietly said, "Yes Mum."

Caro had a question for her mum, guessing it was rude she asked it anyway, "Mummy what's a fucking creepy bastard?"

Keeping calm and smiling she explained, "well Caro my little sweetheart it's not very nice to call someone a name like that, promise me you will never repeat it to or about anyone."

"Okay Mum, except Marcos."

"Not even Marcos, my little darling."

Later in the day Mary spoke to Henry advising him that she never wanted to hear him speak such unpleasant abhorrent and offensive language again. She also made it clear never to hear him cheek his elders no matter what he thought of them, if he ever did, he would be in big trouble. Sunday lunch and a visit to the cinema, treated to ice-cream and popcorn then the whole sordid incident was forgotten that is as far as Henry and Caro were concerned: Mary though, had a lot of thinking to do.

Lying alone in bed Mary had a cry, she liked Marcos a lot, he was courteous, affectionate, treated her like a queen not to mention the fact he was a good lover, but to cause trouble between her and the children she conceded was ever likely and it really troubled her. Henry and Caro had obviously observed something in him that she hadn't. Mary thought long and hard before advising him the next day that she couldn't continue with their relationship, making it clear how his attitude towards Henry appalled her. After Mary had made the decision not to date him, she only came across him one more time, when some weeks later stopping off at a supermarket one lunchtime, she caught sight of him pushing a trolley along one of the aisles with small child seated on the trolley seat, while linking arms with a very good looking dark haired woman.

Humiliated, likewise incensed, she had been duped by this man into thinking she was special. Steeling herself, her face sporting a scowl she walked up the aisle towards him deliberately standing in front of him, she enjoyed watching the colour drain from his face, thence looking him straight in the eyes she sneered, "The kids were right, you are a fucking creepy bastard," before scornfully adding, "you're not even good in bed."

The woman who Mary presumed was his wife, enquired angrily, "Who is she, what's going on Carlos, what is she talking about what's going on, w-w-what kids?"

Feeling justice had been done she left. Once outside looking up at the sky, in her mind she thanked Henry and Caro for a narrow escape. Collecting Henry and

Caro from school that afternoon she gave them both a huge hug, Henry embarrassed whispered through gritted teeth, "Mum stop it my mates are watching."

Laughing she informed them they were going to McDonalds for tea, Henry was curious because his mum hadn't laughed much since the angry exchanges between himself his mum and Carlos, even her Friday night outings with Elaine had been put on hold; he pondered why? Big Mac, fries and cola ordered Henry and queried, "Carlos isn't coming back is he?"

"Henry son I can assure you Carlos will never ever be a part of our family, there is only one man in my life and that is you."

"What about Dad? Caro asked slurping cola through a straw."

"I love your dad as a friend, no more than that."

"I think you need a new boyfriend Mum," was Henry's advice.

"I thought you didn't, want me to have a boyfriend."

"I didn't want creepy Carlos, find somebody nice Mum."

"All in good time son, when I'm ready."

Cheeky grin on his face he chuckled, "You had better get a move on especially if you want to give us a new brother or a sister."

"Henry Swan Jenson are you inferring I'm getting old?"

"Mary Swan Jenson it's time you changed your name," he chortled.

Caro, who up to that point had been gorging on a burger that was nearly as big as she was, added her own thoughts to the converse, "Mummy If you change your name does that mean you have another baby?"

Henry nearly choked on his burger, laughing.

"Henry what's funny, Mummy what's he laughing at?"

"Caro sweetheart it doesn't quite work that way, when you're a little bit older I'll explain."

Mary lay in bed giggling to her-self as she contemplated her revengeful verbal assail on Marcos after she came face to face with him in the supermarket, which left her wondering why, why heretofore, all the men in her life appeared to be libertines, what was it she wondered, that attracted her to them including her husband, the consummate lothario, she was about to divorce. Despite the self-analysis, she concluded any man who might be Mr Right would have to accept that the two most important people in her life were Henry and Caro. Mary at last, felt she was in control of her own destiny, with that in mind, she stretched contentedly, fell to sleep endowed with happy valley dreams.

When Mary told Elaine what had happened in the supermarket, Elaine herself broke down in tears and confided in Mary that she believed Frank was also having an affair. Notwithstanding Elaine had taken Frank from her, Mary had a great deal of sympathy for her, embracing her and softly enquiring, "Elaine what makes you think he's having an affair?"

"I'm sorry Mary, you know him better than I do and he's still your husband."

"Not for long Elaine just for a few weeks, tell me your worries."

"It's the way he behaves, he's been so secretive lately, he tells me he's going out but when I ask where? He just tells me work."

"Elaine, I'm not sticking up for him but he is always at work."

"Mary if you ring him at his office, according to his secretary he's out of the office visiting one of the shops."

"Perhaps he is, have you checked?"

Tears trickling down her cheeks catching her breath before lamenting, "Yesterday I rang all the shops morning and afternoon, no-one had seen him, and he came home late again, very late."

"Did you tell him you had tried to contact him?"

"I asked him outright if he was having an affair obviously, he denied he was doing anything untoward."

"What are you going to do?"

"What did you do after he did it to you, I was part of it?"

"Elaine it was completely different for me, I found out he was playing away well before you came into the picture, sadly and honestly I'm afraid it was all over before his involvement with you came to light. The fact you were pregnant sealed it for me, that's when I asked him to leave."

"I'm sorry."

"Don't be, if he hadn't been with you, I'm sure there most certainly would have been someone else."

Deep down it came as little surprise to Mary that Frank was maybe, up to his old tricks fully knowing his reputation as an incorrigible serial womaniser. She had experienced first-hand the emotional suffering the hurt and the heartache which is the biproduct of those inveterate infractions of love and trust that Frank was capable of. Mary and indeed most people who have loved and trusted in someone faithfully and unquestionably, believe those breaches of trust are a violation of love, they strike like a stab in the back and thus when you are cut, severely you bleed.

Mary's now viewed her own outlook on love and it's fluctuating fortunes with cynicism, however she still managed to elicit a great deal of sympathy for Elaine who was obviously very much in love with Frank, desperate and at her wits end of what to do because she was unable to get any answers from her man. Elaine burst into tears, Mary waited until Elaine had finished crying, quietly expressing her thoughts,

"Elaine I know exactly what you are going through, the pain, the uncertainty and of course the feeling of rejection, I'm sure everything will work out. Whatever happens, please don't let it fester or you'll go mad my best friend, you should ask him again; you do need to know the truth."

The following morning Elaine rang Mary all excited, revealing Frank had arrived home early presenting her with a large bouquet of flowers. "We are going to dinner tonight will you have Jude for me?"

"I'm so pleased for you Elaine of course I'll have Jude."

"Mary, thank you."

"Go on get yourself ready I'll collect the little man."

Whilst looking after and playing with Jude she began reflecting on her life with Frank which had for the most part been good, even exciting at times though she no longer loved her soon to be ex-husband at all: Mary realised she did still miss his company.

When Elaine arrived to collect Jude, she wore a grin as wide as the Atlantic ocean, waving an engagement ring: Frank had proposed. Mary was happy for her friend but later she removed her own engagement and wedding rings placing them in the bottom drawer of her jewellery box, it was finality.

Chapter 5

Life, in both Jenson households returned to normality. Elaine feeling her relationship with Frank was secure, despite their plans of where and when they would jump the broomstick (as Frank joked), had to be delayed because of his business commitments: she was a very happy lady.

Mary's decree absolute came through some weeks later, finalising her divorce from Frank thus inspiring a resumption of her teenage confidence, a confidence she had not experienced since before she was married. She began to wear the latest fashions, wearing makeup all, her monthly visit to the hairdresser's became a weekly visit, she started to look at herself in the mirror and observed quite a good looking woman staring back at her: concluding to herself, Mary Swan you ain't half bad darling. A striking brunette with large dark brown eyes, gracefully slender, urbane with an olive complexion which gave her a soft Mediterranean look, she had retained her slim figure despite having borne two children; she had looked after herself. Thinking out loud she posed and answered her own question, yes, I have two children, but I'm only Just thirty-two years old!

The down side to any possible, favourable romantic interlude could be if she met someone she liked, would they want the problems that come with two children? For that matter would Henry and Caro welcome another man? Considering the problems that had arisen from her involvement with Carlos; she would have to wait and see. First, she had to meet someone, however, the sum total of her social life was going out once a week with Elaine, she surmised the chances of that ever happening would be extremely limiting. She had to be positive, fortune of one sort or another can raise its head in the most outstanding significance, in the most unexpected and unlikely of place.

It did...

One Saturday morning while the children were having a sleep over with Frank and Elaine, Mary paid a visit to her parents and took them to a new, out of town shopping centre. After a lovely day, she set off for home and stopped to refuel the car at the very supermarket where her contretemps with Carlos had taken place. Requiring something for the children's tea she decided to venture inside too. Browsing among the freezer cabinets looking for ideas, she stopped to look at some ready-made Indian meals, unfortunately unlike Henry and herself, Caro didn't like curry, so she needed to look for something else. Just about to move on when one of the cabinet doors suddenly swung open hitting her full in the face, dropping the basket she gasped with pain and instinctively put her hands to her face.

Mary's nose was bleeding profusely; she had a split lip, eyes watering, she was almost crying. As she tried to regain some composure there was an apology being uttered, "I'm so sorry I pulled open the wrong door, here let me have a look, I'm so so very sorry."

Eyes smarting, she let him look, he began dabbing her nose and lip gently with a handkerchief still apologising, "I'm so, so sorry."

Through watery eyes she began to refocus advising him she wasn't badly hurt. As her eyes cleared a worried looking man came into view, a very worried but extremely good-looking man she noted, he continued wiping her eyes and gently dabbing her nose.

"Thank you, I think I'm alright."

"Come and sit down I'll get you a cup of tea or coffee."

"No, I'll be alright honestly."

"I insist, you need to sit down for a few minutes to give you time to recover I gave you quite a bang, it's the least I can do."

Still a little dazed, the man steadied her as they walked slowly to the supermarket coffee bar, he sat her down at a small table and asked, "What can I get you, tea or coffee?"

"Tea please, no sugar."

Mary's nose had stopped bleeding and her eyes back to full focus by the time he returned with two cups of tea.

"I'm Mat aka Mathew, Mathew," he said while offering his hand, "and you are?"

"Mary."

"Mary who?"

"Mary Swan Jenson."

"Nice to meet you, Mary Swan Jenson."

Sore as she was, she started to giggle, "My son calls me that when he's trying to cheer me up."

"Oh, you have a son what's his name?"

"Henry Swan Jenson he is thirteen and my daughter Caro Swan Jenson is nearly ten, and don't try flattering me by saying I look too young to have a thirteen-year-old son."

"Mary Swan Jenson if I had said it, I would have meant it, your husband is a very lucky man."

Looking puzzled he enquired further, "Why have you all got the name Swan?"

Mary explained, "When I married my husband, I wanted to keep my maiden name which is Swan, Mathew, Mathew, that in itself is unusual."

"Yes, my dad is Mathew and his dad before, his dad as well, I don't know how far back they go, probably forever, probably as far back as the stone-age."

Finishing her tea and making her excuses to leave, Mary told him, "By the way I'm divorced and there's no one else except for Henry and Caro."

His eyes lit up responding by way of 'Have another cup of tea unless you're in a hurry'.

"I'm not Mathew, Mathew, in a hurry that is."

There was an instant liking for each other, a sort of love at first sight stone-age style, a club over the head and you're a couple, but in this case a freezer cabinet door. Over the second cup of tea Mary told him about her last inopportune visit and the subsequent encounter in the very same supermarket.

"What was the guy's name?"

"Marcus Havers do you know him?"

"I know of him, I went to school with his older brother Tony, I've heard through the grapevine that Marcus's wife has filed for divorce."

"Blimey I hope I wasn't the reason it's happened."

"Mary Swan Jenson the only one to blame is himself, serves him right for playing away from home, you can't have any sympathy for him."

They were on to their third cup of tea.

"Mathew Mathew, you have managed through cheek and flattery to somehow wheedle a fair bit of my life story out of me, now tell me about you?"

"What do you want to know?"

"Are you married, If so, do you have any children?"

"What do you think?"

"Looking at you very handsome and very cheeky with it, I'd say probably yes."

"Thanks for the complement, but you are wrong on both counts I'm not married nor do I have kids, sorry to disappoint."

"Why, are you gay?"

"No, I'm not, but I am cheeky," he retorted with a grin.

"Well why?"

"Simple answer is I've never found anyone I've liked enough to ask them to marry me, that is until now Mary Swan Jenson, would you like to change your name to Mary Swan Mathew?"

Mary, her mouth full of tea spluttered laughing at the absurdity of the question he had asked. Gaining her repose, she giggled, "Mathew Mathew first you nearly knocked me out, split my lip and blooded my nose then within an hour you're asking me to marry you, nut case!"

"Well will you, I mean it Mary Swan Jenson, marry me?"

"Mathew Mathew don't you think we should have at least one proper date?"

"Isn't this a proper date?"

Mary lost for words searched for an answer, but could only muster.

"Mathew Mathew I don't know what to say you're embarrassing me."

"I'm sorry I didn't mean to embarrass you, I want to marry you."

Beginning to realise her newfound friend might be serious, Mary decided to humour him, "I'll have to ask the committee."

"Who are the committee?" he asked, puzzled by her statement.

"Henry and Caro are the committee, we do need to get to know each other a little better before they are introduced don't you think, I only know your name that you're not married, don't have any children, nevertheless I think I'm entitled to know a little more about you."

"Well Mary Swan Jenson soon to be Mary Swan Mathew, I'm thirty-six years old, unmarried with no kids as you know, and I live on my own in a large four-bedroom house. Work-wise I own a Vauxhall car dealership, Oh and I play golf."

"Oh, you're a golfer?"

"Yes I am, but when we're married I'll have to give up playing golf."

"Why would you do that Mathew Mathew?"

"Because I'll be too busy chasing you round our bedroom."

Giggling, furthermore, blushing like a teenager enjoying her first kiss on her first ever date replied, "Mathew, I wish you would be serious."

"Mary Swan Jenson I have never been more serious in my life, if you won't say yes immediately can we begin our courtship tonight, let me take you out to dinner."

"Mathew Mathew I can't believe I'm saying this, yes I would love to have dinner with you but can we make it for tomorrow? I have to arrange for someone to look after Henry and Caro."

"Mary Swan Jenson yes of course, give me your address and I'll pick you up at seven if it's ok with you?"

"Mathew, Mathew, I look forward to it, thank you."

They were exchanging phone numbers about to go their separate ways when suddenly Mathew wrapped his arms around her, kissing her full on the lips. Mary was startled but for some reason she couldn't help herself falling into his arms, putting up no resistance whatsoever; Mary it seemed, had found the man of her dreams. Outside he walked her to her car kissing her again, this time longer, slower, and sweeter taking her breath away.

"Till tomorrow Mary Swan Jenson, the future Mrs Mary Swan Mathew it can't come soon enough."

"Till tomorrow, Mathew, Mathew."

Mary got back into her car physically shaking, totally bewildered by the events of the past two hours pinching herself to check she wasn't dreaming. Had she really been kissed by a handsome man who two hours ago had been a complete stranger, had he really asked her to marry him? Could this be a wind-up? She hoped not, as her excitement began to rise her heart was beating faster than a jet plane thundering through the sound barrier she wondering, was it possible she had fallen in love with this handsome stranger? Mary decided to calm down, she was being very silly because unfortunately happy endings are only found in fairy tales; he wasn't a frog and she wasn't a fairy-tale princess.

Checking the time, she realised it was nearly four o'clock, if she didn't Hurry she would be late collecting the children, Caro from her gymnastics club and Henry from his friend Charlie's house. Mary had been totally distracted and preoccupied, what's more totally overwhelmed, she realised during the short time she had spent in conversation with Mathew, all thoughts of shopping had flown out the window. What would she do for dinner? Mary concluded a visit to McDonalds or K.F.C seemed the preferential answer. Still feeling quite shaky she inhaled some deep breaths in order to unscramble her confused thoughts, allowing the rising excitement to moderate before driving off to collect her children.

Picking Henry Up first. Mary just made it on time which meant she was a few minutes late collecting Caro, she stood with hands on hips tapping her foot irritably and complained, "Mummy I thought you had forgotten me."

Nevertheless, Caro was all forgiving when hearing where her mum proposed to take them for tea. Henry inquisitive as usual wanted to know what it was they were celebrating?

"Henry, you cheeky beggar we don't have to be celebrating anything for us to go to McDonalds, I have been far too busy today to cook that's why I'm late."

"Mmmm," was Henry's sceptical response.

Little did Mary realise, considering the events of the afternoon at the supermarket, just how Henry's scepticism would be borne out.

At home, whilst Henry did his homework Caro had been forcibly coerced into helping her mum to clean her untidy room or be grounded for a week the doorbell rang. Shouting down the stairs Mary asked Henry to see who it was. Henry called back to his mum, "Mum can you come down its for you?" bewildered she asked, "who is it son?"

"A man, he's asking for you."

"What does he want?"

"Mum if you come down you'll find out."

"Ok wait a minute son I'll come down."

At the door, she was met by a man holding an enormous bouquet of flowers.

"Mrs Jenson," the man enquired.

Puzzled she answered, "Yes that's me."

"These are for you."

Perplexed and wondering who would send her flowers she took them and thanked the man then closed the door.

"Mum who are they from?"

"Henry, I don't know."

"I'll read the card Mum."

If Mary had any doubts about the intentions of Mathew towards her, they were very quickly dispelled by the words written on the attached card, which embarrassingly were read aloud by Henry.

To Mary Swan Jenson, who I hope
will become Mary Swan Mathew.
I will be waiting 'impatiently'
my darling until tomorrow night, Mathew.

As Henry digested the words he had just read, Mary waited hesitantly, expecting a cold reaction from her son, probably one akin to a destructive raging cyclonic storm, however, unbelievably it never materialised. A smile wider, brighter, and warmer than the sun above the Sahara Desert began to spread across his face, before enquiring of his mum, "Mum, when did you meet this Mathew, is he nice?"

"Henry, I only met him today and yes, he does seem very nice."

"Wow today! He must like you a lot, look at all those flowers."

"Henry you don't mind do you?"

"Why should I mind? I want you to be happy Mum, this Mathew seems kind I can tell, when are you seeing him again?"

"Tomorrow evening, He's invited me to dinner."

"Will, me and Caro get to meet him?"

"My darling boy of course you will, you'll meet him tomorrow."

"Good can I get back to my homework now? I have an essay to finish."

Mary had a spring in her step as she arranged the flowers Mathew had sent, she Reflected on the day's events, still in a state of confusion still tingling from the kisses she had shared with him and altogether astounded at the affirmative reaction she had received from her son. She phoned Elaine to ask if she would look after Henry and Caro next evening as she had a date. Elaine obviously wanted to know who with and where she was going and demanded to know all the sordid and hopefully licentious details, Elaine informed Mary she would visit immediately; thus arriving ten minutes later armed with a bottle of red wine.

Chapter 6

As soon as Henry and Caro had retired to their respective bedrooms, Elaine listened intently while Mary recounted in great detail her incredibly exciting but strangely romantic afternoon at the supermarket. As the story unfolded Elaine's Jaw dropped, her mouth got wider and wider, she was totally astonished and wide eyed in disbelief, Mary's narrative completed, Elaine burst out laughing.

Mary excited but unsure proffered her own unconvinced thoughts, "I know, it does sound funny doesn't it? I suppose I'm being naïve to think anything may come of it. I mean two kisses and a proposal in a supermarket within two hours, yes I'm being silly aren't I?"

Giving her a hug, assuring her she wasn't laughing at the situation in a mean way, she was amused by the very lovely romantic story. Elaine cupped Mary's hands in her own opining, "Mary I think you may have fallen head over heels in love with this man, how absolutely wonderful."

Mary tried to deny it saying, "No, it isn't possible in such a short time, I'm not Cinderella, that's Fairy-tale stuff isn't it? Think on, in the real-world romance like this doesn't happen to people like me, and, I have Henry and Caro to consider."

Elaine offered her own observation, "Mary my very best friend it sounds to me that if you hadn't had to collect Henry and Caro, you possibly would have booked a hotel room with him or at the very least ended up in the back seat of his car."

"Oh no, no, no I wouldn't have gone that far, but he did make my spine tingle and I felt so very safe in his arms. I shouldn't have responded to that first kiss so quickly but it melted me, and I didn't want to let him go with the second kiss in the car park, I'm getting excited talking about him Elaine, he is so handsome, so nice."

"You my darling Mary you have definitely fallen in love with what's his name…Mathew Mathew. Mary you shall go to the ball!"

"Hark at you fairy god mother Elaine."

"Mary do you want the kids to stay with me and their dad tomorrow while you're having Dinner?"

"I would rather you stayed here if you don't mind?"

"Ooh that will be good, I might get to meet him."

"Elaine, he might not turn up and I'll look and feel stupid."

"Don't be daft that bouquet and the card say it all, he has fallen in love with you, big time girlie! He will be here for sure, then I can give him the once over for you if you like, you know check out his credentials."

"Elaine Hurst, you cheeky sod."

"Only to make sure you are safe, no other reason."

"I do like him; I like him a lot but I've made too many mistakes in the past so I'm not jumping headlong into a relationship again especially one I may live to regret. I don't want Henry and Caro hurt we've been through all that rubbish before."

"Let's finish the wine and I'll get a taxi home leaving you to dream the night away about Mathew." Elaine chuckled.

Mary stood at the door watching Elaine get into the Taxi, tired but so happy that she had a girlfriend like Elaine to talk to: it was very late her bed beckoned.

Sunday morning rousing out of a pleasant dream about Mathew; two indistinct figures loomed into view of Mary. As her eyes regained some clarity she became aware that Henry and Caro were stood by the side of her bed holding a tray upon which there was tea, a boiled egg and toast. She adjusted her eyes to the light filtering through a small opening between the curtains and asked, "Henry, Caro is that for me? That's very nice of you my darlings, thank you, what time is it?"

"Seven o'clock Mum."

"Seven o'clock, why so early you two?"

"Well Mum you've got a date tonight so we thought you could do with some extra time to get ready." They must have practiced their whimsical little speech because they said it in unison, then proceeded to cackle like demented chickens.

"You cheeky pair of beggars, how old do you think I am?"

"About ninety two? Mum honest we are only joking we just thought it would be nice to do something for you as you do everything for us, this is just a thank you, and...can we meet your date?"

Caro cutely added, "We love you, Mummy."

"Not only cheeky but crafty as well, of course you will meet him, When I've finished this lovely breakfast come and snuggle up with me, something we haven't done for ages we used to do it all the time, I'll do the washing up later."

Mary with her arms wrapped around her two offspring awoke and began to emerge from the cocoon of bed linen where they had snuggled together, it was nearly ten o'clock. Feeling equanimous she sighed contentedly gazing proudly and lovingly at her little brood, heartened by Henry and Caro's positivity towards her forthcoming dinner date with Mathew: Mary was a very happy bunny. She woke her two progeny and euphorically hugged them both telling them how much they were loved.

Henry smiling back iterating her words but adding, "We love you more Mum don't we Caro?"

"Henry, Caro; I love you more than you will ever know."

"Mummy, when is Mathew coming?" Caro asked throwing her arms around her mum's waist and burying her head in her chest.

"This evening my little cherubim, you can say hello to him."

"Mummy is he nice, he's not horrible like Marcus is he? I, didn't like Marcus."

"Caro sweetheart I think he is very nice."

"Mum."

"Yes Henry."

"If you like him we will, no one can be as creepy as Marcus."

"Well my young man I don't know where the creepy bit came from but I trust your instinct, I don't think there is anything creepy about Mathew at all. Now I think it's time for us to get up or I won't have enough time to get ready."

"Mum you are beautiful I don't know why Dad wanted someone else."

"Why thank you kind sir, but unfortunately we drifted apart, now come on its time we got up don't you think?"

As the hour of seven o'clock approached there was no hiding Henry and Caro's excitement, they were itching to meet Mathew. Elaine arrived early helping to calm them and also calm Mary, continually whispering to her, "Calm down he will be here, he's in love with you."

"Elaine, stop saying that."

"Promise me you won't get married tonight."

"Bugger off your making me more nervous."

"I can't wait to hear all the gruesome details."

"Like what."

"How good he is in bed." Elaine whispered.

"Elaine, I don't know whether I'm coming or going, stop it Henry will hear you."

"I am only teasing you but you will tell me, won't you?"

Mary changed the subject by calling, "Henry."

"Yes Mum."

"How do I look, any VPL?" queried Mary.

"Mum you look like a beauty Queen, let's have a look, no there's no VPL," was the assertion from Henry.

Caro who was looking out the dining room window shouted, "Mummy is that him he's got a bunch of flowers and oh, what's VPL?"

Henry smiling broadly explained, "When, you can see the outline of knicker elastic through your clothing."

The doorbell rang, Mary followed by her attendants made up of children and best friend Elaine approached the door nervously. When she opened the door, Mathew's face lit up like a refulgent morning sun rising above the horizon. Thrusting a dozen pink roses into her hand he kissed her on both cheeks while complementing, "Hello Mary swan Jenson you look even more beautiful than you did yesterday if that is possible," then brushing her cheek with his hand he asked, "I hope the pain wasn't too severe I've been worried about you?"

Before she could answer, Henry agreed, "See Mum I was right you do look beautiful."

"Henry, stop it!"

"It's true Mum, I'll put the flowers in water for you."

"Hello Henry and you must be Caro, hello Caro."

"This is Jude Elaine's son."

"Hello Jude."

"And I'm Elaine her best friend, look after her please."

"Elaine I'm not a child nor made of china!" was Mary's assertion.

"Hello Elaine, nice to meet you."

Introductions completed the entourage watching as Mathew escorted her to his jaw dropping car where he opened the door for her, a 1970 E type Jaguar coloured British racing green, "Is this yours?" asked an astonished Mary.

"Mary Swan Jenson nice isn't she, this was my wife until I met you, now it's just another possession, do you want to drive it?"

"Mathew Mathew I would be frightened to death lovely man, just take me to dinner."

Mathew had a quiet unassuming manner which belied his assertiveness, despite his undoubted positiveness she felt he hadn't got a nasty bone in his body, she was very much attracted to him.

"Where are we going Mathew?"

"I've booked a table at the hotel De'Grande' I thought something special for someone special."

"The hotel De'Grande," Mathew you don't have to spend so much money I would be just as happy at K F C or McDonalds, and don't forget you need to drive me home.

"No I've got that sorted I've booked a mini cab, we can drink and dance the night away if you would like to!"

"Not too late I want to be home for Henry and Caro if that's okay with you."

"Mary Swan Jenson when you're ready to leave just say,"

"Thank you Mathew but can I ask you in all honesty do you think I will look out of place?"

"Honestly, Mary Swan Jenson you look beautiful but I wouldn't care if you were wearing flannelette striped pyjamas or a mechanics boiler suit, you could look stunning in anything."

"Awwww Mathew that is the sweetest thing anybody has ever said to me thank you."

"I mean every single word Mary Swan Jenson; you are so beautiful."

Entering the palatial sophisticated country club Hotel De'Grande Mary felt somewhat intimidated by the grandeur of the surroundings in which she found her-self. Frank despite his well-established business and the material possessions it provided him, had never taken anyone to dinner anywhere with the splendour of the Hotel De'Grande. Mathew linked his arm in hers as they were welcomed and escorted by the Maitre d' to their table which was set in a cosy alcove suffused with soft lighting, positioned just a little way from the tiny dance floor, an ice bucket containing a bottle of pink Champagne sat on the table.

Agape at the surroundings Mary asked again, "Mathew I feel out of place here, there are so many beautiful and beautifully dressed women here."

"Mary my darling you are the only beautiful woman in here, truly, now, champagne?"

"You say the sweetest things Mathew thank you for that."

The wine waiter opened the bottle and poured, Mathew proposed a simple toast, "To us."

Mary a little embarrassed because they had only known each other less than thirty-six hours responded, "To us."

The Champagne, moreover the attention Mathew was paying to her began to ease the diffidence which to some extent had overwhelmed her when entering the restaurant. Now far more relaxed her tongue began to loosen, allowing them to get to know more about each other, their likes and dislikes, they talked of family matters and got to know each other better. However, anybody watching them conversing, laughing, enjoying each other's company would have recognised the signs; a natural emanation of magnetism pulling them together: love was definitely, in the air.

From the outset when they first met Mathew told her he wanted to substitute the name of Jenson for Mathew, Mary was embarrassed yet flattered, if not a little unnerved by his forthrightness, but she was definitely not prepared for how the evening would ultimately unfold.

Part way through dinner Mathew took a handkerchief from his pocket and leaning across the table he dabbed her cheeks, as he did so, he spoke quietly and began to express his feelings. "Mary Swan Jenson, it was while doing this in the supermarket yesterday I fell in love with you, for me it was love at first sight."

Mary wasn't sure if he was telling the truth, either way for a moment she couldn't fully comprehend the words he had spoken, she was speechless, her thought processes scrambled, she looked at him open mouthed staring incredulously. Somehow, regaining her composure, she asked him, "Mathew, are you being serious?"

"Mary I have never been more serious in my life I'm in love with you, I have never felt this way about any woman before."

"I don't know what to say Mathew."

"I'm sorry I didn't mean to embarrass you."

"Mathew I'm not embarrassed 'I'm flattered'."

"But you don't, feel the same, is it too much too soon?"

"I didn't say that."

It was Mathew's turn to look bemused, "What are you saying then?"

"I suppose Mathew, I'm saying I've fallen in love with you too lovely man."

"Mary Swan Jenson did I hear you right, would you repeat it?"

Speaking with purpose she repeater her answer, "Mathew, I love you."

A beaming smile lit up his face standing up he produced from his pocket a small black velvet box which he opened. There displayed against the black velvet nestled a ring with three diamonds set in gold, he proceeded to get down on one knee looking her straight into her eyes proposing, "Well Mary Swan Jenson, will you do me the honour of changing your name from Mary Swan Jenson to Mary Swan Mathew?"

Taken aback by the overture Mathew had just propounded, brought tears to her eyes, never before had Mary felt so desired and never before had she, desired with the such extreme desire, as she did for Mathew. Mary realised that despite only forty-eight hours had passed since their first kiss she had fallen head over heels in love. Perhaps she was that fairy tale princess, although conceding she hadn't kissed a frog he was indeed a handsome prince and she was going to marry that handsome prince: she sighed a sigh of inner contentedness. She hadn't had to think, because deep down in her mind if it happened she was always going to accede to his romantic proposal; she was in no doubt Mathew had fallen in love with her and she with him.

Mathew waited patiently for an answer, when Mary finally found her voice it was shaky and cracked but it revealed the words he had hoped to hear, "Mathew Mathew my lovely man of course I will marry you, but you must understand we will have to wait I have Henry and Caro to consider. I'm not sure how to tell them they will be shocked although Elaine won't be surprised she said we had fallen in love."

"Mary my beautiful bride to be I will wait forever."

"My lovely man I don't want to wait forever if circumstances were different I would Marry you here and now, but we have to wait a little while at least."

"You have just made me the happiest of men Mary, I have never felt love as powerful as this, in fact I honestly believe I have never really been in love before, I have waited all my life for you. Will you do me the honour of wearing the ring, while we are here at least, until we leave?"

She held out her hand which he kissed before slipping the ring on to the third finger of her left hand declaring, "I think this calls for some more Champagne I'm in a celebratory mood, but first I need to taste your kiss," holding her tightly in his arms he whispered I love you Mary Swan Jenson. The kiss they shared; ambrosia sweet, spiced with an intensity she had never experienced before, making her go weak at the knees sending wave after wave of spine-tingling sensations coursing through every vein in her body. Unwilling to let go of each other, it was quite some minutes before they managed to drag themselves apart.

Mary spoke first, "Mathew I want you so much but I still have the committee to address I will always put them first, I don't want anything to create discomfort between me and my children."

"My darling I promise whatever happens I will never interfere with your parenting I would like to be friends, no that's wrong I want to be the best of friends with Henry and Caro I want them to trust me."

"Mathew, thank you for that because I want you so much."

"Mary I'll drink to that I'll order some more champagne, we'll finish our dinner then let's dance, a nice slow one so I can hold you close. I want you close for the rest of my life."

"Mathew I do love you."

At four a.m., the mini cab pulled up outside Mary's house, Mathew asked the driver to wait while he walked Mary to the front door.

"Mathew thank you for the most exciting night of my life, I can't believe it but I love you with all my heart."

The mini cab driver had to wait longer while they kissed their good-byes.

"Mary, I'll ring you tomorrow."

"I'll be waiting goodnight my lovely man."

One final kiss when suddenly the door opened and Elaine stood there left hand on left hip wagging a finger, grinning she demanded, "What time do you call this young lady I hope you have behaved yourself."

Mary with her head still in a whirl offered, "Elaine, sadly I have behaved myself, but look at this?" waving her hand showing her the engagement ring, "he asked me to marry him, and I said yes! You were right I have fallen in love with him, he is special, so nice and so handsome, we have been drinking champagne all night, I feel tipsy."

"Let's get you to bed you can tell me all about it tomorrow."

"Oh dear."

"What's the Matter Mary?"

"What, am I going to say to Henry and Caro and when?"

"If I were you girlie the sooner the better, tell them tomorrow but ask Mathew to come over, do it together."

"Do you think I should tell them so soon?"

"To be honest I don't think there will be a problem, they both said they liked him in fact, Henry was of the opinion you will be getting married sooner than later."

"How come? They only met him for a few minutes."

"You only took a few minutes and in less than forty-eight hours you're engaged to him."

"Elaine they are only children."

"Very, very astute children, Henry's perception on life, people, and most of all you his mum masks his tender years. He has a natural keenness, insight and judgment he will definitely be happy for you."

"Do you really think so?"

"Trust me I'm right, now before you go to bed let us have a proper look at the ring, oh Mary it is beautiful, he must have bought it yesterday straight after he met you, he really is serious about you."

"I know, Elaine I'm so happy and so drunk I need my bed, good night Elaine."

"Come on I'll help you up the stairs we don't want you falling and ending up in casualty do we."

"Thank you, my very best friend."

Elaine made sure her friend was safely escorted up the stairs and helped her get undressed.

Chapter 7

Mary hadn't a clue what the time was when she came out of her intoxicated induced stupor, barely able to open her eyes, they were almost glued together.

Her head was thumping, the strident aftermath of too much Champagne and she had difficulty adjusting her eyes as the glare of sun gleaming came through the gap in the undrawn curtains.

Henry, Caro and their half-brother Jude were sat on the bed smiling, "Morning Mum." Henry greeted her.

"Hello, Mummy!" was Caro's welcome.

"Hello, Mary!" added a smiling Jude. Despite sore eyes and a stinging headache, she smiled weakly, enquiring, "Hello you three what are you up too?"

Henry now grinning from ear to ear offered, "Congratulations Mum, when are you getting married, have you fixed a date yet?"

Mary was rendered dumbstruck by Henry's question Her mind scrambled as if it had been sliced, diced, crushed and put through a kitchen blender. She attempted to achieve some sort of coherent reply to the forthright enquiry, with pounding in her head she was totally perplexed, wondering how on earth, did he know.

Caro pleaded, "Mummy can I be a bridesmaid?"

"Can I come to the wedding as well please Mary?" added Jude.

Mary's head began slowly to regenerate and reenergise allowing her to formulate the only answer she could offer, "Who told you I was getting married, was it Elaine, where is she? I wanted to tell you myself."

Henry revealed, "It wasn't Elaine, it was you who told us Mum."

A very confused Mary asked, "When, where, how; I didn't did I?"

"Last night I mean early this morning when you came home you woke us up, you and Elaine were talking in the hall so loud even the neighbours probably heard everything, Me, Caro and Jude were on the landing listening, Mum you were so drunk, Oh, and of course the card pinned to yet another bunch of flowers that came this morning written, to my bride to be, I'm not going to repeat the slushy bits you can read them yourself, and there is something else."

"What?"

"Mum you're wearing an engagement ring."

"I'm really sorry Henry I was going to tell you but only when I thought you were ready I won't marry anyone you don't like."

"Mum we like Mathew, don't we Caro?"

"Mummy he's lovely."

"You have only met him once and then only for a few minutes."

"Mum he loves you like we do; we can tell."

Jude commented, "Mary he really is nice."

Mary felt relieved she would not have to apprise them about her possible intentions; they had it seemed given their approval. For once, everyone was on her side, she lay back happy and contented, her children all lay next to her.

Elaine wandered in still half asleep wondering what all the hullabaloo was that had dragged her out of the comatose dream-state she was enjoying, she flopped down next to Mary and ventured. "What on earth is going on?"

"I'm getting married." Giggled Mary.

Elaine looked quizzically at Mary and the three children sat on the bed beside her. "What did you say?"

"Elaine I'm getting married, my two darlings know all about it apparently, I was drunk and we were so loud in the hall they heard everything we said. Was I really so drunk? Oh, never mind, would you believe I've got their blessing, I am so happy."

"Blimey Mary at this rate you'll be married before me, and yes you were, very drunk. Mary I'm so happy for you, come on let's have a family hug."

All five of them embraced in a family huddle.

The one thing Mary never envisaged was the reaction she would receive from Frank. One morning a few days later while Henry and Caro were at school, he paid her a visit. He was demanding to know who this Mathew was, who she was engaged too, taken aback by his angry tone, she angrily enquired of him,

"What business is it of yours?"

"For a start, you have only just met him, when was it, last Saturday?"

"What's it to you?"

"I'm concerned for you."

"It's a pity you wasn't concerned six years ago when you made your secretary pregnant."

"I made a stupid mistake something I've regretted ever since."

Giving him a look of distain then refuting his argument Mary let him have it with both barrels. "Frank don't make me laugh did you regret your affair with Susan? I wonder how many others there were before and how many since.

You're lucky because if Elaine wasn't my best friend I would tell her about your concern for me, now sod off."

Frank maintained his aggressive stance, "Mary remember there is also Henry and Caro to be considered."

"I repeat, you didn't consider them while you were busy sowing your so called, bleeding wild oats. If you are really interested in how they feel, ask them they will tell you they like Mathew they are happy for me but it is patently obvious you are not!"

Frank continued with his assail, "If he ever hurts one hair of either of their heads I'll swing for him."

"Frank you really are pathetic go away, in fact you can fuck off, yes go and fuck your latest secretary isn't that what they are paid for?"

Their altercation was getting out of control the tirade they were directing at each other was getting more vociferous and more strident in tone, threatening to break the friendship they had rebuilt since their divorce was finalised. Frank stunned by the vitriol and profanities Mary was returning to his assertions, stopped to think for a moment, he could not find a suitable declamation with which to reply. He knew he was never going to get the better of his ex-wife, taking in a deep breath he calmed himself.

"Mary honestly, I don't want to see you get hurt."

"Frank you bastard you must think I'm stupid, you broke my heart while I was expecting Caro, but now you don't want to see me get hurt? My arse! Let me tell you 'O guardian angel' I've waited a long time for a loving man to come into my life, he will never cheat on me like you did!"

Frank knew he was beaten, so he attempted to placate her, "Mary I know you won't believe me but I hope it works out for you especially for the kids."

"Just go will you Frank."

Frank left with a parting verbal assail. "Think on Mary, remember I won't help you if it all goes tits up."

By then, she had taken all she could, shouting after him as he walked to his car, "Fuck of Frank and don't come here unless it's something to do with the kids." After which, she slammed the door.

Alone again, Mary sat on the stairs crying. She revisited memories of contention as their marriage which was once a hotbed of passionate love had suddenly deteriorated into dying embers of smouldering coals which turned to cold grey lifeless ashes, the smoke from those dying embers may have blown away, but she didn't regret marrying Frank. Mary could not forget the good times taking heart from the fact she had birthed two gorgeous children by him. So why what was Frank so angry about meeting someone else? He should have been delighted for her, his outburst disappointed Mary who decided that when Henry and Caro came home she would ask them if they minded if she and Mathew married sooner rather than later. However, she hadn't expected the enquiry Henry gave for an answer, "Why Mum, are you pregnant?"

Swallowing hard, stifling an indignant reply and shaking her head Mary returned an answer with a question of her own. "Henry what made you ask such a question? It's not a very nice thing to ask your mum, and no, I'm not pregnant you cheeky beggar."

"Mum I was only joking honest."

"Well Henry do you mind, what do you think Caro?"

"Mummy, can I be a bridesmaid?"

"My darling I wouldn't have anybody else, oh by the way Henry."

"Yes Mum."

"Would you give me away?"

"Don't give her away Henry I want Mummy to stay with us," Caro protested. Mary kept a straight face, but Henry collapsed laughing at his sister's assertion explaining, "Caro in the wedding ceremony someone has to give the bride away to the groom usually her father."

"Stop laughing Henry, Mum he's always laughing at me, tell him to stop Mummy tell him!"

"Henry, stop it now, she didn't know, I'm asking will you give me away?"

"Mum what about Granddad, he's your dad shouldn't he do it?"

"Granddad won't mind I'm sure."

"I won't have to make a speech will I Mum?"

"Only if you want to son."

"If you really want me to Mum, I will."

"Thank you Henry, I want you by my side my lovely boy."

"Will you invite Dad?"

"I'll ask, but I don't think he will come, Elaine will though."

"Mummy?"

"Yes Caro."

"When is the wedding?"

"As soon as possible that is if Mathew still wants too, if he does we will have to buy you a new dress my darling bridesmaid, Henry, you will need a suit."

Mathew called in to see Mary on his way home from work, he was greeted with an especially long welcome kiss, Henry who was watching declared, "Haven't you two had any dinner?"

Ignoring him Mary gave Mathew the surprise of his life, she took him to one side thereby revealing that if he still wanted to, she was ready to get married; as soon as possible. Mathew though stunned by Mary's surprise proposal was overjoyed and a broad smile spread across his face while wrapping her in his arms. Kissing her affirming, "I've been ready from the moment I met you Mary Swan Jenson, I will love you for eternity," pausing he added, "and a day."

Nestling her head on his shoulder she breathed his name with a sigh, "Mathew. Oh Mathew my lovely man, I love and want you so very much."

Discussing the possible date and venue Mary was quite content to have a civil ceremony. Mathew on the other hand wouldn't hear of it insisting it would be a church wedding. Mary however had her doubts whether it would be possible because she was a divorcee. Mathew though was adamant they could marry in church because she hadn't been the transgressor in her marriage to Frank, expressing to Mary that this is the beginning of a new millennium not the dark ages, ministers were far more liberal in their thinking towards divorcee's marrying in church, so church it would be.

Six weeks later a very happy Mary wore a cream-coloured wedding dress and walked down the aisle of the church holding the arm of her extremely proud son Henry with Caro her bridesmaid and Jude the page boy. Henry conceding he had never seen his mum look as happy in a long time, she was glowing.

Frank was invited and did attend the wedding with Elaine, veritably wishing both Mary and Mathew all the happiness for the future which pleased Mary a great deal. Mary graciously accepted his sudden pleasant and affable disposition with a kiss on the cheek, bringing closure to their rather noisy and hostile disputation of a few weeks earlier.

However, during the proceedings Henry noticed something which made him sad, but he kept his observation to himself: his dad couldn't take his eyes off his mum.

There was more excitement in store for Henry and Caro, just as the Newly Weds were about to leave for the airport for their honeymoon in the Caribbean Island of St Lucia, they presented Henry and Caro with tickets to join them the following week where all four of them would spend two weeks on holiday together. However, seriously strict instructions were explained and demanded of both siblings but especially to Caro who was warned, if she didn't behave, moreover do as Henry told her, she would be grounded for six months, maybe more!

Chapter 8

Back from the honeymoon family life almost certainly changed for the better. Henry and Caro's domestic environment became more stable their mum's marriage to Mathew, fortunately for everyone was a wonderful, as the saying goes their relationship was (a match made in heaven).

Mathew was the consummate stepfather always ready to listen and wherever possible advising Henry and Caro in a friendly way, he never interfered with Mary's parenting, if she had reason to chastise either of them it was her business; occasionally if he felt she had got it wrong he would give his point of view when the children were well out of earshot.

Eighteen months into the marriage Henry and Caro were presented with a new baby sister: Lindy Swan Mathew. Mary and Mathew were aware there could be a problem with the older siblings feeling rejected, which happened to Henry when Jude first came on the scene. Not wishing a recurrence of that rather unquiet period they both made a conscious and determined effort to make sure they felt wanted and loved, ensuring no favouritism and a happy family unit. The approach worked, Henry and Caro adored the little one, Caro in particular was thrilled to have a baby sister, while Henry admitted having another baby around meant they were a proper family.

The family moved into a large six-bedroom house so all three children had their own room.

It was clear Mathew could never take the place of Frank nor would he expect to, but he did become a man Henry could turn to in his teenage years, especially if he had a problem when his dad was not available. Thankfully family life could not be more harmonious for both families, at least for a while...

Unfortunately the status quo was about to be thrown into disarray. One afternoon while Mathew was at work and the children were at school, there was a frantic knocking on the front door, Mary nervously opened it to find Elaine distraught, crying hysterically. Mary managed to calm her enough to elicit the gist of her incoherence, "Frank's in trouble with the police," she sobbed.

"Slow down Elaine what do you mean he's in trouble with the police what's happened what's he done?"

"I'm not sure, all I know is he's at the police station."

"Elaine you must try to calm down, tell me what you know I'll get Mathew to look after Lindy and he can pick the kids up from school, then we can go to the police station and find out what is going on, I'll be surprised if it's serious."

Regrettably, it was far more serious than both women foresaw. Frank had been involved in a fight at one of his shops, with someone they presumed was a customer, Frank apparently hadn't thrown the first punch, but sadly his retaliatory punch left the man badly concussed and bleeding, he had to be ambulanced to hospital. The consequence of which the police were called, as usual Frank's luck held out and he wasn't charged with any misdemeanour. The customer for some reason, chose not to press charges, nevertheless Frank received an official warning from the police.

However, there were far more repercussions to follow from his altercation with the customer as the whole story began to unfold when Frank was released. Elaine emotionally traumatised and concerned by the unsavoury fracas, demanded to know what had caused an argument to escalate into such violence. Frank dismissed the incident in his usual confident manner declaring it was something and nothing, a bit of a kerfuffle, Knowing Frank's ability to whitewash over his escapades, Elaine despite his insistence remained sceptical and she continued to question him about the matter. Unsatisfied with his scant replies she became even more suspicious, guessing there was far more to the story than Frank would have her believe, deciding the only way to find out the real story would be to speak with some of Frank's staff, people she knew and trusted. Although in her heart, she hoped he was telling the truth, sadly Elaine's suspicions were well founded, as she guessed there was far more to the so called 'kerfuffle'. Eventually It emerged the dispute wasn't with an irate customer at all, It was with the husband of an employee who was an assistant manager. Elaine therefore, could only assume the reason for their altercation was that he was having an affair; she needed to know.

The rumour circulating was that Frank had been seen in a restaurant with this assistant manageress, somehow her husband got wind of their assignation so he confronted him, ensuing the contention turned violent. Elaine feeling deeply distressed at the inference, though only hearsay, once again confronted Frank. Frank was very matter of fact in his comments concerning the angry discord with the woman's husband, but did confirm he had taken the woman to dinner, he explained, "Yes I took her to dinner but to offer her a promotion to manager because she had given notice to leave, she is very good at her job and I don't want to lose her, does that answer your question? I can assure you there is nothing else going on."

"Frank," she implored him. "I wish you would tell me what you're doing, all this secrecy worries me I feel left out."

"Elaine love, it was spur of the moment."

"Well, who is she, did she accept your offer?"

"Her name is D'arcy Rhodes, I'm still waiting for an answer though her husband might not be too fond of the idea after our unfortunate dustup."

Elaine still unsure of whether he was telling the truth, had to concede she may have let her imagination run wild. She decided it would be better to let sleeping dogs lie; putting her suspicions to the back of her mind. For a while, all seemed hunky-dory in the Jenson household, Frank and Elaine's relationship seemed to have weathered the storm. However, chaos was about to befall, a domestic storm of tropical proportions...

Trouble really raised its ugly persona when late one evening, Mary answered the phone to a sobbing Elaine who had obviously been drinking and was so distressed she had difficulty speaking, garbling unnervingly, "Frank, work, police, hospital, Jude." Mary tried to make sense of Elaine's disjointed ramblings nevertheless she recognised through the desultory effusion something unsavoury had occurred involving Frank at one of his shops. Unable to mollify her best friend she advised, "Elaine I'm coming over right now try to calm down I'll be with you in ten minutes."

Mathew drove her to Frank and Elaine's house and waited outside, just in case he was required to help out in some way.

When Mary arrived Elaine was hysterical, Jude was crying and clinging to his mum because she was so upset. Quietly Mary managed to calm her down which calmed Jude enough for Mathew to take him to be with Henry Caro and Lindy. However, it took a while before Mary, in-between Elaine's fitful incoherence was able to apprehend the reason for her friends state of distress. Elaine finally composed herself so she could explicate the reason for her anguish. Mary was surprised but not really shocked by her friend's fraught outpourings concerning Elaine's relationship with ex-husband Frank she too had been through the mill with him, nevertheless, she was more than shocked by Elaine's further revelations.

"Mary, Frank is hurt, he's in hospital."

Aghast at the news she proffered the question, "Oh my god in hospital why, what's happened, is it serious?"

"All I know is he's been badly beaten, and the Police have arrested someone."

"Who the bloody hell would want to attack Frank, and why?"

"Who knows he never tells me anything."

"Come on Elaine I'll phone for a taxi we'll go to the hospital."

The duty doctor attending to Frank took the two women to one side to give them a gentle warning, he advised that Frank had taken a heavy beating and though his injuries were not life threatening, he was very poorly. Despite the warning, on entering the side ward they were horrified by the sight that filled their eyes. Frank was unrecognisable his face was a mixture of black, blue and purple bruises, his eyes and mouth were just slits amongst the swelling. Such was the gravity of the injuries, Frank's broken nose was hardly discernible from the rest of his facial Distortions. His left arm was in plaster and both hands were bruised and badly grazed; he must have been in one hell of a fight.

Both women were severely distressed, but Elaine disintegrated into a shaking sobbing wreck, Mary escorted her friend into the corridor to calm her down, however Elaine was in such a state the doctor who was helping Frank had to dispense a mild sedative. Thankfully, half an hour later the sedative calmed her sufficiently, making it possible for her to return to the ward.

Because Frank was so poorly the consultant felt it was in his best interest to administer a strong tranquiliser to Frank which fortunately induced a much needed sleep. Unable to talk to him, Mary managed to persuade Elaine to go home and get some rest, return in the morning in the hope he would be well enough to talk to them. There was a further problem, having to tell the children their dad was unwell and the hardest part, informing them he was in hospital and why.

Mary phoned Mathew to explain the exact nature of Frank's injuries, adding they were still none the wiser as to the why's and wherefores surrounding his admittance to hospital, apart from the fact he had been given a severe beating so they would be going to the police station in the morning. Tired and worried they headed home, understandably Elaine was far too upset to go back to an empty house, so at Mary's suggestion, she decided to stay with her and Mathew so she could be there for Jude when he woke up.

Mathew had put the three younger children to bed but allowed a very worried Henry to wait up until his mum came home, assuring him his dad would be okay. However, Henry was like a cat on a hot tin roof, only the reassurance from his mum that his dad would be okay would suffice. Once home, Mary, because of her son's age decided she could not give him all the facts, at least not until, she was fully aware of how his dad came to be in such an awful state. However, considering Frank's ability to gloss over any given situation; they might still not ever be sure of the truth.

When Henry had gone to bed, all the two women could do was speculate as to the reasons why Frank had bought about such a pernicious outcome, was it a robbery? They could not conceive of anything, to give rise to such malicious violent beating. Frank was no shrinking Violet and could handle himself in any situation; even so it seemed like overkill. They were determined to visit Frank first, and hopefully he could shed some light on how the situation evolved; then a visit to the police station to find out the real truth.

On visiting the hospital, they found Frank sat up in bed supported by pillows looking worse than he did the previous evening, if that was possible. Nevertheless, the medical staff attending to him were pleased with his progress elucidating it would take time for the bruising and swelling to go down, Sadly, he still wasn't well enough to acknowledge his visitors.

The following morning Mary and Elaine visited the Police armed with questions, the police officer dealing with the case declined to give any details but confirmed they had two men in custody assisting them with their enquiries, however he did divulge, the two men in custody also required hospital treatment. He advised he would inform Elaine and Mary once those enquiries were concluded and promised to enlighten them as to what those findings would be. Perplexed and disquieted they went home. The two friends could only assume it may have been a robbery gone wrong, nevertheless it was self-evident Frank had put up one hell of a fight and Mary had a sneaking suspicion there would be a woman involved somewhere along the line, however; she did not voice her thoughts to Elaine, she, was upset enough: it was all very worrying.

Four days passed before the bruising showed signs of healing and the swelling reduced somewhat; giving definition back to Frank's features at last he was cohesive enough to recognise and converse with his visitors.

Another worrying aspect for Elaine arising from Frank's incapacity and subsequent sojourn in hospital was, who would look after his business interests. Mathew offered his time and with the help of Frank's secretary Imelda took temporary charge until Frank recovered enough to return.

There was a twist to the story, in fact there were a number of twists relating to that sorry episode when Frank was attacked; anything involving Frank would have to be complicated. With Police enquiries concluded, Elaine was informed that the two men in custody were to be charged with grievous bodily harm. Such was the severity of the assault it was expected Frank's stay in hospital would be lengthy, nevertheless somewhat surprisingly within four weeks Frank was considered fit enough to be discharged from hospital. He still retained a lot of bruising to his body, his face was still puffy however his features were once again fully recognisable. Miraculously his broken nose had sustained only a hairline fracture which had healed by itself. His left arm was still cocooned in plaster, fortunately he was right-handed. Despite his injuries, he remained upbeat, the ebullient irrepressible side of Frank's character returned within a few days with him joking, "You should see the state of the other fella." He apparently had no recollection of the assault or the two assailants, furthermore he hadn't a clue why he had been given such a savage beating; or so he said. Both Elaine and Mary were unconvinced by his lack of memory; they knew him too well, but they would have to wait and see.

Elaine although pleased with the speed of his recovery had many questions for her fiancée to which she wanted truthful answers. He was still unable to concentrate on anything for any length of time and his memory remained vague, however, Elaine had her misgivings or was he was purposely avoiding her questions? Elaine opted for patience; at least for a couple of weeks until he hopefully regained all his mental faculties.

Elaine knew Frank was on the mend when he began to worry about his business, believing she had held her peace for long enough, she decided it was time to get to the bottom of the circumstances relating to the beating. Calmly and quietly she began her opening salvo of questions, questions that she considered obvious where her man was concerned, "Frank what is going on I'm sure there is something you're not telling me, whatever it is, I will find out you can be sure of that! Is there a woman involved somewhere?"

Unusually laconic with his answer, made her even more suspicious, dismissing her questions, "Elaine don't be so silly there isn't any woman, now leave it."

Elaine's voice began rising irritably, "Me silly? You've been beaten almost senseless, almost killed and you won't tell me the reason why, Frank I want to know, I want to know everything no matter how serious a problem or problems you have, you're the man I love and you're supposed to love me."

"I've told you to leave it I'm not in the mood."

Elaine frustrated, her anger growing. "Frank you have to tell me this time, you can't fob me off I won't let you, whatever you've been up to, one thing for sure I'll get to the bottom of it."

"Elaine I'm too tired for all this leave me alone."

Shouting in desperation she pleaded, "If you don't tell me I'll leave you, alone for good! We can't go on like this I'm at my wit's end worrying about you."

Frank began to get angry, testily replying, "There's no need to get uppity I'm perfectly capable of taking care of myself thank you."

"Look at you Frank is that what you call capable of looking after yourself, I don't think so, have you forgotten Henry, Caro, Jude even Mary your ex-wife, just like me they are all distraught. How do you think the kids feel, their dad badly injured, how are you going to explain to them! When you can't or won't even give me an answer?"

"The children are too young to understand."

"Henry isn't; are you going ignore his questions? There's Mathew too he's taken time out from his own business to help your secretary run your business! Henry helps out every spare minute and Mary has been a Rock to me I can understand why she divorced you."

"I think you had something to do with that particular matter."

"Yes I'm a bigger fool than her, but I still love you It's about time you sorted yourself out. The ones I feel sorry for are the kids, you have scared them stiff you're like Mr Punch, Frankenstein's monster and the Elephant man rolled into one; not a pretty sight."

Frank ever the joker quipped, "That good! I've improved then."

Nonetheless Elaine's angry testament concerning the children had its effect, Frank went quiet; replying in a pensive, reflective tone offering, "I know it looks bad, but I will sort it out I promise."

"You could start by telling the truth for once."

"Elaine it's difficult you're right but you're not going to like it."

"Just tell me Frank."

She waited expecting the worst, and it could not have been worse.

A rather chastened Frank despite his initial denials and subsequent explanations, head bowed, eyes on the floor, laid his cards on the table 'so to speak' finally admitting to having an affair with another member of his staff: Infidelity and Frank it seemed went hand in hand. Elaine gasped; a tear trickled down her cheek as his confession began to unfold. "Honesty Elaine it didn't mean anything it was a fling. I know I've hurt you I'm sorry but honestly it was over almost before it began. I love you I never want to hurt you."

"Who is this woman? Why, did it become so violent?"

"It's quite a story but I'll answer truthfully."

"I want and expect you to tell me the truth for once!"

"Elaine, I will tell you everything."

Chapter 9

It was a complex story, the narrative of which took some time for him to orate.

The woman in question was Cherry Stone, who, it transpired was the girlfriend of one Barney Phillips, a man Frank knew from his teen years when they had an altercation effecting bad blood between them since their schooldays. To add further spice to the mix he was the ex-husband of Frank and Mary's friend Susan who had been one of Frank's previous extra marital transgressions. Barney's character was at best splenetic and choleric, grown from a narcissistic school bully: graduating to a degenerate sadistic thug with a taste for beating his wife. After one of his alcoholic binges Susan badly beaten, she walked out on him taking their son with her, divorcing him before disappearing with no trace; such was her fear of him.

Barney and Frank were enemies. Both had attended the same senior school, Frank a year younger than Barney knew and was well aware of his arrogant overbearing vindictive nature as one day on the way home from school Frank saw Barney demand money from a younger pupil. Frank stepped in to help the boy which angered Barney who had the temerity to tell him to fuck off and mind his own business or he would punch his lights out, 'OUCH!' red rag to a bull, red mist descended and Barney received a pasting. Barney was man enough to accept being beaten in a fight but losing to a boy younger than him meant losing face in front of his friends, that was hard to swallow. Realising he could never get the better of Frank in a fair fight he raged menacingly, making it clear by hook or by crook he would one day get his revenge. Frank exacerbated the situation as only he could, when laughing at him derisively taunting, "You and whose army, bully boy?"

So it came to pass one of Frank's multifarious extramarital liaisons, lamentably, had finally caught up with him: the chickens had come home to roost. Barney had somehow found out about Frank and Cherry's tryst: thus, exacting revenge for all the latest and previous humiliation he had suffered.

Frank continued his story of the attack, he remembered locking up his office to go home he walked to his car where he was confronted by two men, one of whom attacked him with an iron bar, Frank no slouch with his fists defended himself aggressively, However Barney and his sidekick eventually overwhelmed his defiance, forcing him to the ground; kicking him unmercifully until he succumbed to unconsciousness. Nonetheless as the attack had progressed Frank had managed to inflict some serious damage to both of his assailants, Barney received a broken jaw the other received a serious head wound earned from cracking his skull against a kerbstone. Luckily Frank was saved from further punishment as a brave young woman passing by used her umbrella to intercept the two assailants shouting and screaming, they ran off: she called for an ambulance and the police. If she had not got involved, he may well have died.

Frank's long-time adversary from schooldays, Barney Phillips, the man Frank had cuckolded twice. Barney, assisted by his brother Chad had been determined to get revenge for all the past humiliations. Prior to the attack such was his anger because of Cherry's involvement with Frank, he had beaten her severely: whilst threatening to put Frank six foot under. Cherry badly bruised and angry decided enough was enough regardless of Barney's threat, as he succinctly put it, "Knock her into the back of beyond if she called the police."

Cherry extremely frightened for her own safety but extremely angry called the police. As the police began to interview Cherry, she received a call from Barneys brother Chad informing her Barney was having surgery to a broken Jaw. He and his brother were arrested in the A& E department of Heartlands Hospital. Barney was charged with grievous bodily harm with intent, against Cherry, but both brothers were indicted on the charges of grievous bodily harm with intent against Frank. After evidence given by Cherry, Barney was further charged with attempted murder, which luckily for him was again reduced to grievous bodily harm with intent. Cherry herself later decided through fear, against pressing charges. She still had to be a witness for the prosecution for the charges relating to the attack on Frank.

Chapter 10

Elaine listened grim faced whilst staring at the man she loved, her thoughts raging with hurt and disappointment, a tear trickling down one cheek of her face; a face becoming more haggard with every syllable he spoke. She remained calm despite the inner pain and torment she was suffering, she waited patiently until he finished his admission. Collecting her thoughts she began her reply quietly, "Frank I don't know what to say or do you've knifed me in the back and it hurts, Don't forget this isn't the first time you have played away?"

"Elaine there has never been anyone else."

Elaine's voice began to ascend becoming more strident, "What about D'arcy what's her name?"

"I told you that was business nothing more."

"I'm not sure whether you told me the truth, come on Frank, come on Frank there must have been some sort of provocation, you must have been screwing her why don't you admit it Frank, admit it! How many more flings have there been?"

"Elaine, I never touched her; I promise you there was nothing between us, she is still working for me remember, in fact her husband Roger has become a friend, it was all a terrible misunderstanding."

"Whatever, it doesn't detract from the fact this time you have caused mayhem, you bloody fool you could have been killed, it frightened me."

Frank could not help himself, he had to make light of the situation, "Do I detect a note of disdain from my beautiful fiancée?"

Elaine was not in kilter with his humour, she exploded, "You bastard I've cried myself to sleep every night since it happened and all you can do is make fun of me. Frank you have hurt me, I trusted you I don't know if I ever will again."

"Elaine I'm sorry I know I've been stupid believe me I won't stray again."

"What's happened to this fling of yours?"

"I don't know, I haven't given any thought to her, it's done with, finished, over, something we can put behind us."

Elaine still seething but slowly regaining her composure spoke an assertive response, "Do you honestly think we can put it behind us, you want me to forget it ever happened? I don't think so, I need to get away, to find myself, think things over and clear my mind; I need some space of my own."

"Elaine I couldn't be sorrier, it will never happen again I promise you."

"Your promises are like pebbles on the beach they break down and turn to sand."

Frank, with his pride and bloody mindedness refused to beg, throughout his adult life he was in control of all things pertaining to his life, except of course his propensity for the opposite se. He struggled to voice the words and express how much he needed, wanted, and most of all how much he loved Elaine, instead, he subscribed to monetary bribery assuring her, "Elaine I will make it up to you, you can have whatever you want, new clothes, a car, holiday, maybe a cruise, yes we could go on a cruise what do you think?"

"Oh Frank you are hopeless, the only thing I want is you but I need to be able to trust you, being frightened to answer the phone in case it's the police or the hospital, isn't what I want. Frank I love you but I can't live like this, something has got to change, I need to get away: I need to think."

"Where are you going; what about Jude?"

"Right now I don't know, but I'll take him with me."

Frank still couldn't bring himself to acknowledge his true feelings preferred to say, "I'll wait until you've decided but I will miss you."

"Frank I'm confused do you love me or not, I thought you did but you're not expressing the words I need to hear."

"What do you want me to say?"

"Forget it Frank I'll go and pack, maybe take Jude on a holiday somewhere."

By then, Frank was feeling irked because the situation wasn't going his way thus responding wearily, "Whatever."

Elaine needed someone to talk to, especially the one person she knew had been through the same experience as herself, so, she turned to her best friend Mary who would lend a sympathetic ear to her troubled mind. Sat in Mary's kitchen, Elaine sobbed uncontrollably and related the whole sordid episode, "What am I to do Mary?"

Mary did her best to console her; she had a deep awareness of the distress her best friend was suffering, she had lived through the nightmare that envelopes you, when your heartstrings are savagely scythed: precipitated by the perfidious actions of the one you love. She remembered vividly how she cried herself to sleep night after night, the hurt, the frustration engendered by the feeling of rejection.

"You still love him, don't you?"

"Stupidly yes, but I don't know what to do, I'm not sure I will ever trust him again, Mary I'm scared."

"He's a lucky man to have you so If you still love and want to be with him tell him, but lay down some ground rules, and I stress this point, whatever you do, do not give in to him!"

"Mary I now recognise the heartache you must have gone through when you found out about me, I'm so sorry."

"Elaine it's in the past and of no consequence, trust me our marriage was on the road to disaster before you came on the scene, but isn't it strange how things work out, look at us now, If Frank hadn't employed you we wouldn't be best friends, so best friend what are you going to do about your man Frank?"

"I'm going away for a few days to think it over I'll take Jude with me, Frank still needs some time to fully recover he won't be able to cope with looking after Jude."

"If you prefer Jude can stay with us for a few days, give you time on your own to think?"

"Thanks Mary that will be good."

Elaine departed for a few days alone to file her thoughts; the whole disastrous episode had not really shown its true razor edge. An edge that could not so much slice and dice their relationship but shred and blitz what remained in a liquidiser: the residue to be poured down the drain.

When Elaine returned from her short unplanned but necessary furlough; all contradictory thoughts were settled and calmed, she attempted a softly, softly approach towards Frank and his affair with Cherry Stone. Their discourse began amicably, he welcomed her with an embrace strong enough to crush her ribs, affirming how empty his life would be without her. However, she suspected something was amiss; his demeanour was lacking his customary self-confidence. With his head bowed, eyes fixed to the floor there appeared to be an air of resignation; she observed a distinct undertone to his voice, there was something troubling him. Concerned for him, despite all the problems that had gone before, she still loved him. She questioned him.

"Frank what's wrong?"

Grim faced; for the first time in his life he spoke with despondency and contrition, visibly shaking Frank asked her to sit down, which worried her even more, she waited for his reply, "Elaine I don't think there is an easy way to tell you, to be honest you will probably leave again and I won't blame you if you do."

"Frank for God's sake what on earth is the matter are you ill?"

"No Elaine that would be an easy option."

"Are Mary and the kids alright?"

"Yes they are fine, please let me explain."

"Please Frank, tell me what is going on?"

Frank took her by the hand looking into her eyes in a hushed tone he started haltingly, "Elaine, oh fucking hell I'm so fucking stupid."

"Frank what is it, if you're not ill and the kids are ok, what the bloody hell is going on?"

When he did eventually proffer an admission, his articulation slowed down as if he was searching for a way to express his thoughts, although curious, Elaine was totally unprepared for its content. "Cherry stone came to see me yesterday."

"SHE CAME HERE, WHAT DID SHE WANT?"

Frank was still trying to find the right words, his voice got quieter almost hoarse, finally in a tired barely audible whisper he voiced, "She came to tell me she was pregnant." His voice almost disappearing he added, "She is claiming that I am the father." As it unfolded the blood drained from her face, she was floored her head spinning trying to digest the information he was imparting to her.

Elaine her face contorted with restrained anger, shaking her head in disbelief, could only summon up a hushed tone, "Why do you do this to me Frank, WHY?"

Elaine stood up, walked across the room to stare out of the window her thought processes confused crashing through her mind like a stampeding heard of migrating Wildebeest, continuing to stare out of the window, her head scrambling to assimilate the totality of Frank's violation of trust, nevertheless fatherhood, was ultimately a more troublesome, awkward, embarrassing state of affairs for her emulsified brain to contend with. While she continued to stare, Frank's voice fluttered, she was unaware of its substance or who had spoken: It wouldn't coalesce with the emotional quagmire besetting her mind. Frank spoke again only louder.

"Elaine."

She remained in a state of flux, her glassy eyes observing nothing; the profound silence unnerved him. Frank tapped Elaine on the shoulder startling her snapping her from the clouded abstraction she had lapsed into. He spoke quietly, "Elaine."

"Yes!" turning to face him again she asked, "why Frank why?"

Frank normally in complete control of any given situation, this time was at a loss, unable to vocalise the true depth of his feelings. He looked directly and deep into her eyes, sadly for Frank he could draw from her demeanour any excuse or apology, would be ineffective, but he had an overriding need to show his remorse for the hurt he had inflicted. Despite his outward cavalier approach to life, he didn't want to lose Elaine: he loved her. Frank began his entreaty with a simple, "I love you, Elaine."

Staring at him with empty eyes unconvinced by his adjuration she scornfully rejected his declaration, sneering, "Frank you have a funny way of showing it."

He tried again, "I know I've hurt you and let you down but it's true I love you."

"How can you say that when you've been having an affair and what else was it? Oh Yes the woman is pregnant!"

"I know I've been an idiot but it doesn't detract from the fact I love you and want to be with you always."

"How can that be when you're having a child with someone else, Frank it just doesn't gel how can I believe anything you say ever?"

"It will never happen again I promise."

"Frank at this moment I don't think we can be together."

"I love you Elaine and I can tell you still love me; we can work this out I'm sure we can."

Elaine's rhetoric became more forcefully assertive as did her animated body language, displaying rancid anger she was vehement and vociferous in her reply, "You really are a fucking bastard, what's going to happen when this child decides to put in an appearance, have you thought about that? Knowing you, Frank, probably fucking not."

Explicating quietly, he tried to avert further conflict, "Elaine obviously as far as the child is concerned, I have an obligation to be part of its life but not part of its mother's life, you are the one I love, the only person I want to be with."

"Frank, I do love you but how the fucking hell can I trust you? Every time your late home from work I'll be wondering who the fucking hell you're screwing."

It wasn't in his makeup to beg, however what he said next would be the nearest he would ever walk down that path of begging, but he was desperate, keeping calm he continued, "Listen and understand, there will never be another woman in my life, I can't impress on you enough how much I want you to stay."

Elaine's demeanour softened, "Frank I want to be with you, but for God's sake how is it going to work? There's another child to worry about and I don't really believe you have thought this through."

Frank iterated his thoughts imploring If you give me another chance I'm sure we can work things out, "I'm sure of it," inhaling deeply he promised, "I know I've been selfish and unfair all because of my egotistical attitude, it will never happen again."

Elaine relented, softening her tone while shaking her head she voiced her own thoughts. "I do love you, but I'm not sure what to do however, we can talk if you mean what you say, maybe just maybe we can work it out."

Charismatic Frank had worked his persuasive powers to good effect consequently winning over Elaine, she offered to give him another chance to prove he meant what he was proposing but obviously there would be conditions, to which, without argument, he agreed to.

Later on she rang Mary, who was not surprised by Elaine's headline news concerning Frank and the backwash derived from his extra sexual curricular activities. Mary commented, "Elaine to give him another chance you're either very foolish or you must be very much in love. I gave him a chance the first time he played away, like you I was in love but thankfully there wasn't a child added to the equation, there, I'll say no more."

"Mary I know I'm being foolish, trouble is, I do love him, believe me he won't get a second chance. If there is even a hint he's playing away again, that will be the end. He will be on his own!"

After giving Frank the benefit of doubt, Elaine's attitude towards Frank wasn't conflictual or antagonistic, more strained; nonetheless, gradually they began to find solutions to their problems. However, one very large problem lay at their door; looming menacingly, threatening to derail any progressive accord they had reached, the new addition to Frank's ever extending ménage, the consequence of his liaison with Cherry Stone.

All supposition regarding his erstwhile dalliances with the ladies aside, he remained espoused to the idea of family life; his previous perfidious behaviour locked away, never again to escape from its confinement. Frank, to all intents and purposes had seen the light, that said, Frank would never be the model husband, or the so-called modern man. Helping with the housework never entered his head, if left to cook he couldn't even toast bread properly but he remained a hard worker in business. Business was his energy outlet nevertheless he changed his attitude towards his female employees, remaining friendly but distancing himself from contact during out of office unless it became absolutely necessary. He was always helpful but expected his staff to be as hard working as he was, and one can only guess that the thought fathering four children by three different mothers was enough for any man, despite the fact he could afford to give them the best of everything; even a wealthy man had to curb his libido.

Frank must have had a celestial being hiding behind the storm clouds which had been shrouding his life watching over him. No-one could have forecast or even imagined what, or how the outcome of his affair with Cherry Stone would plan out; to most people really quite extraordinary in fact it was singularly bizarre.

Chapter 11

Cherry Stone, although carrying Frank's child did not want him or anything from him other than to keep her job, obviously she expected him to be a proper father and for the child to be part of his family. Elaine bearing in mind how her own relationship had developed with Mary, was able to understand Cherry's mind set however, she had strong misgivings concerning her continued close association with Frank at work. She continued expounding quite forcibly that being close was the very reason their own relationship had almost reached breaking point. After a few more heated discussions, Elaine reluctantly relented, accepting it would be in the best interests of the child to be part of the family, Frank felt the only option open to him, was to agree to her behest considering the circumstances.

There was more than a touch of irony about the situation after Cherry had given birth to a boy named Myles, because of the need to accommodate the new infant into the family, Elaine approached Cherry just as Mary had approached her. Conversations were at first laboured but gradually their exchanges became more informal, they became friends. As their tete-a-tetes mellowed further, Cherry made it clear the so called affair was an unfortunate one off Wednesday afternoon, stupid mistake, which she whole heartedly regretted; apart from her baby son Myles.

There would be a further irony to the whole Frank and Cherry episode which from an outsider's view point was nothing short of unbelievable…

Chapter 12

Barney Phillips who had held a grudge against Frank since schooldays received a five-year prison sentence for the brutal beating he and his brother Chad had inflicted upon Frank, Chad received two years' probation. Barney served Just short of three years of his sentence, who on his release made contact with Frank. Suspicious of his motive he invited Barney to his office making sure there were plenty of witnesses. Frank was taken aback, Barney looked a shadow of the arrogant bully he had known, he stood pale and gaunt his eyes sunken above his hollow cheeks. It was obvious to Frank, Barney's incarceration had not settled easy on his pride, his self-respect had plunged to an all-time low; he seemed broken. There was a further surprise when a contrite Barney offered his hand, giving a profound apology explaining his three years in prison had given him time to reflect on his wasted years.

Frank, bemused by Barneys apparent character metamorphosis, graciously accepted his hand; for the first time ever, their thoughts were expressed openly and amicably. Three years confined to a prison cell meant Barney's previously inherent antagonism towards Frank had evanesced, a feeling Frank recognised and reciprocated. Then the improbable happened, Frank offered him a Job on a six-month trial, but only on the understanding that his ex-partner Cherry, agreed and was convinced he was a reformed character. Patently it was an important factor in any discussion as they would ultimately be workplace colleagues.

Frank tentatively broached the subject with Cherry, who at first refused point-blank to even consider the question, ruefully expressing, "Are you mad? No way, absolutely not I'm still feeling the bruises from the last time we were together. I'm amazed you're even considering such a possibility remembering, the beating he and his brother gave you; they almost killed you."

Despite her angry protestations, Frank using all his persuasive charms managed to convince her to at least listen to what he had to say. Knowing how scared she was of him, he offered to act as chaperone, making sure in the event of anything more than an angry slanging match whereby words became overheated; he would be there to calm the situation. Nonetheless she was adamant if Barney became aggressive in the slightest way she would say no, emphasising NO! Frank made a promise, he would abide by her decision explaining that he himself had left their past differences behind; it was time to move forward. Barney needed a job, so he was willing to let bygones be bygones. Their meeting at times had its dark moments with all the antagonism coming from Cherry, but as it came to an end and the atmosphere lightened because Barney never once raised his voice. Nevertheless, Cherry still unsure, informed Barney if you so much as looks at me cross eyed you will be out, notwithstanding she needed to think it over…

Think it over she did, experiencing a few sleepless nights, certainly worried because she was frightened for her son Myles, hers and Frank's issue from their one and only Wednesday afternoon encounter. She had a few more discussions with Frank and even though she had serious doubts, his persuasive assurances won the day, she acceded to his promises that any problems of concern, Frank would have to let him go.

Human nature is a strange beast, the qualities and traits bestowed on us which we believe are programmed by and handed down via our forebears can, and often do play tricks. Barney's narcissistic antisocial demeanour was certainly not culled from his parents, they were caring, loving and hard-working parents who doted on both of their offspring, indulging them in whatever they wanted, yet they always wanted more: Barney in particular, by whichever means possible. When Barney went to prison if they hadn't been such loving parents they would have disowned him, it was another reason he wanted to transform his way of life: Hence his meet with Frank.

Over a period of time, what was to follow would seem to most observers Implausible, inconceivable, a more apt expression would be incredulity of the situation.

Chapter 13

One week later, Barney started work for Frank driving one of the company vans. Cherry received a bouquet of flowers from Barney with a card saying, "Thank you." However, when he had to deliver or collect from the shop managed by Cherry, one would say at the very least, the genus loci towards him could be characterised as decidedly frosty, to be honest, the atmosphere between them was colder than the bitterest of Antarctic storms. There were days when Barney thought he had inadvertently entered the South Frigid Pole. Realising he had gained nothing from being as he called himself, a total twat, saphead, jackass, idiot, bozo, thug; it was a complete waste of his life. He had to change he was fast approaching the end of the line; he was on course for a crash more explosive than two express trains colliding head on. If he didn't change, the prognosis would probably be further, longer spells of mind numbing, enervating, imprisonment. Nevertheless, trying to be optimistic he hoped someday, Cherry might stop being afraid of him, however; she had her son Myles to think about and Frank was his father. Cherry's maternal instincts he believed would not countenance him having anything to do with him, which could make communication for both of them, difficult.

Barney stuck to the pledge he had made to both Frank and Cherry therefore always acquitted himself in a manner unlikely to cause offence, ergo, would ask politely what it was she required of him, Cherry would grimace whilst deliberately avoiding direct eye contact and turn her back on him before mumbling her instructions. Barney grateful for the chance given to him understood that he wasn't in a position to address the awkward situation until Cherry defrosted. He couldn't ever visualise a time, unless by some miraculous divine intervention, if and when a friendship would sometime begin to develop.

Barney, from an early age was taller and heavier than most of the other kids, at school he had been a violent bully, it became only a matter of time before his caustic egotistical intimidating mien landed him in trouble, notably his prison sentence. Throughout his teenage years he possessed an almost obsessional opinion of himself. Here, I will offer you a quote from the pen of George Eliot, "He was like a cock who thought the sun had risen to hear him crow." When it came to women, he had an obsessive need to exert control over them.

If anyone was intrepid enough to have the audacity to question his actions, they were put down verbally and quite often with his fists. Reaching his thirties alcohol began to play a big part of his aggressiveness, most of his friends, if you can call them friends, disowned him, wishing to distance themselves from his wildly irresponsible and downright seditious behaviour, he was lonely, hence the drink became his only friend.

His time with Cherry came to an abrupt end the night he found out about her affair with Frank, the man he hated at school because he had handed him a severe beating. It was too much for Barney to accept, especially when learning Cherry was pregnant.

Throughout their relationship Barney had been the dominant partner, she had endured numerous acrimonious slanging matches which would be a precursor to a beating: she was terrified of him. He at last understood that during their previous life together he had been a pernicious destructive force for which he took full responsibility.

As a guest of her Majesty for nearly three years, his incarceration had completely changed his perception of life, giving him time to reflect on the vile lurid, furthermore negative aspects of the behaviour which had landed him in jail. Bored to tears he read a lot and one quote by Thomas Huxley struck a chord changing his whole perspective on his expectations for the future, "Veracity is the heart of morality."

Out of prison Barney began to focus on giving some meaning to his life, there were other people to win over, not just Cherry, but people he used and most certainly abused. He lost his family because of his inability to accept they needed love and care; his focus was always about looking after himself. Susan his ex-wife had escaped the continuous verbal rancour and violence by divorcing him and took their son away and disappeared, to all intense and purposes off the face of the earth. He very much wanted to find his ex-wife to apologise and desperately wanted to see his son and be part of his life. During his confinement he had thought about them often, which only served to make him determined that if by some chance he found them, it might be possible for him to make some sort of reparation. Reawakened from despair Barney took a pragmatic view because he was fully cognisant of his situation, he needed to establish himself as a positive member of society, which meant not just moderating but curbing his anger totally. Barney's determination to succeed emboldened by Frank's hand of friendship did what would have been unthinkable previous to his term of imprisonment; he enrolled on an anger management course. Slowly his narcissistic temperament, vexations, and petulance towards people who had more possessions than him, reversed. Driven by his firmness of purpose he began to appreciate you only get out of life, what you put into life. From behind the dark cloud of ugliness, there began to emerge a lighter personality, a man who's Idea of a joke Heretofore, was either dredged from the bottom of a sewer, usually caustic, vindictive, sarcastic and always structured to decry, or to embarrass and inflict emotional pain and distress. Slowly he settled into a life devoid of violent conduct and disagreements. Degree by degree the blackout curtain drawn across his mind opened to a brighter consciousness.

Sadly Barney could never foresee a time in the future Cherry might allow him to make reparation; the essence of which was all too obvious; he still loved her. However, six months down the line, the unwelcoming, dispiriting cold atmosphere which usually greeted him when in the company of Cherry, unexpectedly brightened. One evening he was running late when delivering an order to the shop when to his utmost astonishment she spoke in a comparatively civil manner asking, "Barney?" He was taken aback because she spoke while looking directly at him, stunned he replied with a, quizzical look on his face, stuttering, "Ye-e-e-s."

"How are you, I understand you're managing to stay out of trouble these days?"

His answer shocked her, "Cherry, trouble has been my middle name, making so many poor decisions and so many stupid mistakes which has left me with so many regrets. To be honest if I'd used half the brains God gave me who knows where I'd be, or what I may have become. I want to make up for lost time, I know I can't alter the past but truly, I am desperate to put my house in order and if possible put some of those decisions and mistakes right."

Something else he hadn't anticipated, She looked at him smiling and said, "I'm glad things are on the up."

"Cherry, I'm getting there but it doesn't make up for the years I've wasted on booze and drugs, which I have given up, I am clean, my stupidity has been costly, especially when my wife divorced me and took my son away with her. I haven't a clue where they are. You would have thought losing them would have been a reality check but no, pig headed and slow to learn, I did it all again resulting in losing you, not to mention three years in prison."

"Barney I'm sure things will work I can see you appear to be on the right track."

"Cherry thanks."

"What for?"

"Just for asking how I am."

"Barney, you hurt me badly emotionally and physically but it's in the past I can forgive but I can't forget."

"I can only apologise even so I know it can never be enough I'm so, so sorry."

"Barney It's a start."

"Enough of me and my problems, you're a single mother now, how are you keeping?"

"Well everything is good, Myles is growing up fast and I have a lot of help from Frank, his fiancée and his ex-wife, we are all friends, in fact we are one big family, it's good."

"Cherry I'm happy for you if I hadn't been such a prat I could have had all those things I missed out on, a home, wife, kids. Don't get me wrong, feeling sorry for myself isn't what I'm about, however it makes you think what if, who knows."

"I know I shouldn't really ask but have you got a man in your life? God knows you deserve someone nice after the awful time I gave you."

"Barney no, there isn't anybody I've got Myles which makes me happy."

"I take it there isn't someone in your life either Barney, mind you the way things are going all those things will come your way, I'm sure of that."

"I doubt it, time is running out and none of us are getting any younger anyway, I've delayed you enough, its time I went home as Chad's wife is doing dinner for me, so I'll say good night and thanks again Cherry."

"Goodnight Barney take care."

That half an hour of casual, amicable discourse with Cherry lifted his spirits higher than the clouds leaving him in a bright sunlit space, he derived from their converse she wasn't in fear of him anymore. Nonetheless he was fully aware of the hurt he had inflicted on her in the past, accordingly under the prevailing circumstances he still believed there would never be a time when they might be true friends again.

Later that evening, lay on his bed in the darkened room, Barney not one to show his emotions, despite the sense of cheerfulness gained from the lack of animosity from Cherry received during their first conversation they have had since he joined Jenson's. Sadness befell him when the light from a street lamp shone through a small interstice between the curtains, illuminating a picture of his ex-wife Susan and his toddler son positioned on the bedside cabinet, suddenly tears trickled down his cheeks; for the first time since childhood.

Barney's horizons widened, his aspirations began to climb, sunlight began to radiate from his face. It was Inconceivable that six months previously, Cherry who had refused to have anything to do with him began to feel at ease in Barney's company, their verbal exchanges were cosy, cosy enough for them to not exactly make fun of each other but share the odd witticism. Despite the undoubted acceptance from Cherry, he still believed it was only a friendly working relationship, nothing more. Being her friend was very important to Barney, it was encouraging giving him confidence to open out to others his newfound cheerful sociable side of his face. The old defiant hostile confrontational face of Barney had begun to disassemble, those people who knew and were wary of him before he went to prison, were for the most part very circumspect of his apparent change of personality. Others however, did perceive a genuine transformation from an angry scornful, menacing, resentful thug, into a respectful calmer man, free of turmoil and agitation: a man with a smile.

Chance encounters can undoubtably have an effect on our lives, one such encounter occurred to Barney, the consequence of which would have a profound effect on him, whereby it would quite dramatically transform his life…

One Sunday lunchtime while out shopping Barney checked if he had won anything the on the lotto, as usual disappointingly, checked out negative. Barney felt ravenous, he stopped off at a local K.F.C intending to treat himself to a take-away meal. He stood in a queue waiting to order when someone gently nudged his arm, on turning round he met eyes with a smiling Cherry holding the hand of her son Myles, jokingly she proposed, "I'll have a bucketful for, me and a bucketful for Myles."

An astonished Barney laughed and replied, "I'll get three buckets! Find a table what would you like to drink tea, coffee or soft drink?"

"Honestly Barney I was only joking."

"Cherry I'm not joking find a table what would you like."

"That's nice of you, thanks Barney. Myles will have a chicken burger and fries. I'll have the same please."

"What about drinks?"

"Coffee and a cola please."

Barney returned with a loaded tray in a state of bewilderment, it had been nearly five years since he had enjoyed any genuine pleasurable time with someone he liked.

"Barney this is my son Myles, Myles this is a man from work, Myles, say hello then."

"Hello Barney, that's a funny name."

"Hello Myles, I'm very pleased to meet you, Barney is a short name for Bartholomew."

"Why do they call you Barney then?"

"Myles don't be so cheeky." His mum gently scolding him.

"It's alright Cherry, erm, it's because I don't like the name Bartholomew it's daft, you wouldn't like it would you?"

"I like my name Myles."

"Myles, eat the burger Barney has kindly bought you."

"Cherry what brings you into town today?"

"Nuisance here needs new shoes for school, what about you?"

"I just like being able to walk where I want and when I want, nobody watching me every minute of the day."

"Bad as that?"

"You wouldn't believe it. I considered myself as a hard person, but I was nothing compared to some of the animals I came up against. They were evil and when they knew I was in for GBH they assumed I was one of their ilk, they were absolute Bastards. Sorry Cherry I forgot Myles is here, honestly, I never want to see the inside of a prison again."

Myles who was listening, with a mouth full of chicken asked. "what's prison?"

Quick as a flash Cherry answered, "It's where Barney used to work."

"Is that why you work with Mum now?"

"Yes, it's much nicer."

"Come on Myles finish your lunch we need to get your shoes."

Before leaving, Barney said, "This lunchtime has been the best time I've had since leaving prison, thank you."

"Yes I've enjoyed our chat too, thanks for lunch, say thank you Myles."

For a fleeting moment, Barney was on the verge of asking Cherry if they could do it again sometime. However, recalling their lamentable history, regrettably because of that troubled past, he deemed such an idea as a negative proposition. However, he took solace from the fact Cherry had clearly shown a willingness to step aside from the past whether it was forgiveness, he could not tell. With a heavy heart, but with smile on his face he bade them good afternoon.

Driving home Barney felt an intangible surge of warmth sweeping through him, suddenly the endorphins were running wild, euphoria lifted his spirits, all the pain of the last few years disappeared. There glowed a rainbow, which after so many years of a gale force storm beclouding his innermost thoughts, had relented. For the first time ever, everything seemed right with his world.

For once in his life, optimism invaded his whole entity, a simple lunch with Cherry and her little one, where they talked freely and openly considering their forgoing turbulent often tempestuous association. The repercussions of which ultimately without qualification led to his lengthy sojourn as a reluctant guest of Her Majesties Prison service. His body language began to display a certain confidence, regaining his pride, at last able to hold his head up high. His true friends of whom you could count on one hand stood by him offering him encouragement plus he was gaining new friends. Despite his buoyancy, he precluded any thoughts of him and Cherry ever actually being more than friends; just friends would be good enough.

It Is really quite mind-boggling when you have accepted the possible is impossible, then something unplanned happens to contradict those convictions; making the impossible: possible. Three unforeseen occurrences all of which Barney, only in his wildest dreams could conceivably hope for, opened his horizon even further. The first significant event happened the following Friday after taking Sunday lunch with Cherry and toddler Myles…

Barney on release from prison had vowed never to partake of drink or drugs again viewing them as the devil incarnate strangling the very lifeblood out of him, personifying the reasons why his spirit became seriously disabled. So, when two of his work colleagues Jack and Sam invited him to a night out, initially he refused as he did not need, nor want, to revisit his former degenerate self when after a few beers his antagonistic character would want to fight the world.

Nonetheless he decided in the affirmative, and he found himself in a pub for the first time in nearly five years. Enjoying the atmosphere generated by the warmth of his friends, he continued to stick to his pledge by drinking non-alcohol lager beers. All three of them made fun of each other, a measure of how comfortable Barney felt, never once taking offence. Leaning back and laughing out loud at some typical male obscene jokes, Barney looked up and nearly choked. Three women stood in front of him and would you believe one of them was Cherry? "I thought you had taken the pledge" she offered scornfully.

Waving the bottle in his hand replied. "Cherry I'm beginning to make a life for myself I don't need the aid of alcohol."

The other two women moved away.

"Barney I'm sorry, I didn't mean…"

Barney interjected before she could finish, "There's no need to apologise I know what it looks like, anyway you're all dressed up are you out on a date?"

"No I'm on girls night out with Elaine and Mary."

"Oh hell I had better scarper fast."

"Why?"

"After the hurt, I caused them I'd better go."

"Don't be daft I'll introduce you to them."

She called them over, as she did so Barney's stomach felt like a cement mixer needing water as the gravel was about to disgorge.

Thankfully all was well, he apologised to them they in turn admitted at one time both of them could and probably would have killed him, but the past is the past, he introduced them to Sam and Jack, it turned into a lovely evening. Too much wine and vodka was imbibed by the women by the end of the evening all three of them were in a state of disrepair, Barney being the only one sober offered to take them home, for which they were only too grateful. On the way home, Barney nearly had a coronary, when Cherry who was sat in the front passenger seat draped her head on his shoulder, Mary and Elaine spark out on the rear seat. All three of them were bedding down at Mary's place, because usually, after a night imbibing too many intoxicants they are physically and mentally unable to hold a conversation let alone get home alone. Getting three drunken women out of the car was difficult but with Mathew's help they manage. With all three of them safely in the front lounge, Mathew commented, "At least, they're not puking up tonight, thank you for bringing them home, the buggers."

"Do it often do they?"

"Every Friday, it's a ritual but I don't mind as long as they get home safe."

The evening for Barney was about to be star studded, Cherry helplessly inebriated somehow rose unsteadily to her feet reaching for him, gently kissing him on the cheek and slurring, "Thanks Barney see you on Monday."

He drove the rest of the short journey home intoxicated by that kiss, but unable to apprehend whether or not it would be deemed romantic or influenced by her lack of sobriety, he wasn't even sure if she would remember. A kiss can be so overwhelming it can scare you, yet similarly it can inflame your senses. Cherry had unwittingly administered the ultimate ambiguous kiss. Barney lay on his bed awake into the early hours, trying to grasp the implication of what that kiss offered, only slipping into a happy dream-state through sheer exhaustion.

By Sunday, Barney had determined he shouldn't put too much store by that kiss even so it still played on his mind. With a weekly shop on the agenda, he headed for the supermarket, shopping completed he went to get his lotto tickets checked, after Scanning the first ticket, the machine buzzed ejecting a winning ticket, he questioned, "How much is it?" expecting a minimal sum, he noticed the assistant looking perplexed and explained. "I have never seen this before it says you should check online or ring the lotto office."

"I wonder why? "asked Barney Grinning she joked. "Perhaps you've won the Jackpot."

"I don't think so I'm not that lucky."

Still grinning she replied, "You never know someone has to, perhaps it's you."

"If I have, I'll send you a bunch of flowers what's your name."

Giggling she answered, "That would be nice I'll hold you to that, I'm Penny."

Barney didn't think too much of it and went for some lunch at McDonalds, resisting the temptation to visit KFC (just in case Cherry was there, although unlikely), preferring under no circumstances, to be accused of stalking her.

We have all experienced a strange impalpable awareness that someone is for whatever reason observing you, which gives you an uneasy feeling…

Barney while tucking into a double quarter pounder could actually feel that uncomfortable chilly sensation surrounding him, raising the hairs on the back of his neck, he couldn't resist turning round and the sight before him took him aback, there was Cherry with Myles sat at a small table by the window façade. Taking a deep breath, he went to speak to her. "Hello Cherry hello Myles I didn't notice you two, have you been here long?"

"Just before you, I thought you were avoiding me."

"Honest, I didn't see you, good job, as you may have thought I was stalking you."

"Why would I think that?" Before he could answer she gently admonished her son, "Myles eat your nuggets I won't tell you again."

Barney laughing admitted, "Well we have been bumping into each other quite often haven't we."

"Does it bother you?"

"No but I thought it might bother you."

"Barney all our past is past, I've seen the change in you and on Friday you were a perfect gentleman, I liked it."

Barney shell shocked by her comments asked cautiously, "Does that mean you are not afraid of me anymore?"

"I'm not, but Barney please don't give me any reason to be in the future."

"Cherry I promise never again, I have turned my life around, I've found my feet and everything is working out."

"I'm really pleased for you."

A rush of blood to Barney's head resulted in stuttering a question, "I-I-I, err, err, wo-o-ondered if, no I shouldn't put you on the spot."

Looking puzzled Cherry asked, "Barney what are you trying to say?"

Mindful he might jeopardise the friendly relationship they had rebuilt over recent months, shakily gave his sceptical question, "I'm not expecting you to accept but I'll ask anyway, would you join me for dinner one night?"

Cherry screwed up her face disdainfully, her response, "Barney some months ago that question would have received short shrift." Continuing, but with a smile, she added, "You are a different man now, so Barney yes, I would like that, but," emphasising the but she added, "don't get any Ideas we are not an Item."

"Cherry honestly on the contrary I wouldn't be so presumptuous I am just delighted you have said yes, now then where and when would you like to go? You know I've always been a pub man, so I'll leave you to choose a nice restaurant."

"I'll have a think tonight," Myles caught her attention.

"Mum, can I have an ice-cream?"

Barney took his hand, "Come on Myles let's see what they've got, Cherry do you fancy one I'm going to have one."

"Yes please, that would be nice."

All enjoying their Ice-creams together finished of Barneys Sunday on a high, except for a brief moment when a cloud hovered over his felicity reminding him of his past being a self-seeking ungenerous husband and a niggardly inadequate Father, In the past this might have been the norm.

At home in his flat, he reflected on the moment when the eerie sound of prison gates slammed loudly behind him shutting out the world: the thought still made him shudder. Shaking off those thoughts of the past, he was excited, inwardly smiling because despite the past he would be having dinner with Cherry. Conscience stricken, he vowed never to subject her or anybody else to any form of physical or emotional pain ever again.

What happened Monday lunchtime left him stupefied, delving into his wallet for money to pay for a sandwich he found the lottery ticket, the one he was advised to ring the lottery office. When he did get round to phoning the lotto office, they asked for the ticket number and to his utter amazement he was informed he had won £40, 041-90 then they gave him details of how to claim it. Unable to apprehend of what to do, Barney finished his day's labour and waited for Cherry to lock up the shop, he needed to tell someone and she was the only one he trusted.

She looked surprised when she saw him, he reassured her, "Honestly Cherry I'm not stalking you, I need to tell someone what has happened."

"Why what's wrong?"

"That's it, there is nothing wrong I'm excited, have you got a few minutes?"

Unlocking the shop she said, "Come in I can't stay long so what's happened."

His excitement was so intense he blurted out, "Cherry I've won just over forty grand on the lottery."

"Honestly, you've won how much, £40,000? Wow fantastic."

"Cherry, I can't believe it."

"What are you going to do with that amount of money?"

"First up, I'm going to take you to the best restaurant in town as a thank you for being so forgiving, the rest of it I'm not sure, but I'm thinking a deposit on a house, I've never had my own place."

"Barney really I'm so pleased for you but I need to get home to Myles."

"Sorry, of course."

"We'll talk tomorrow."

Locking up the shop again her smile as wide as the ocean repeating, "I am really pleased for you Barney," adding, "I'll see you tomorrow."

Barney watched her drive off, on his way home he determined the money would be used as the deposit on a house: at last, he was going to lay down his own roots.

That weekend, life and its possibilities Barney adjudged that given the present circumstances, it to be the start of something special. His perspective on life had changed dramatically, his preceding faults of principles and malevolence, now thrown into the garbage, his horizons carried a vista of sun and expectation, lustrously shining down, warming his very being. He hoped but in fact more than hoped, dreamed his feelings for Cherry would one day be returned. However, it was a dream he discounted because there had been too much friction between them in the past, still he was taking her to dinner, reasoning from little acorns; oak trees grow.

The following week Barney received even more good news, he took a call from Frank requiring him to go to the office that evening. Barney curious, finished his last delivery for the day, and made his way to the office. Frank and Barney, despite all the outright contempt and dislike of each other that pre-existed between them over many years, incredibly, had become friends. Barney was even beginning to be included into Frank's social circle, therefore he didn't really feel particularly anxious about the unexpected request for a meet, just a little puzzled.

Barney's thoughts were justified when Frank smiled broadly, welcomed with a handshake and proceeded to enlighten him as to why he had been summoned. "Barney, after speaking to your colleagues within the company they all expressed how well you are doing and that includes Cherry, So the reason I asked you to come into the office this evening is to offer you a job as a trainee manager if you are interested."

Barney's mouth wide open was so surprised it took him a few minutes to grasp the reality of the opportunity Frank had presented to him. Gobsmacked is an adjective that best describes the sensation ripping through his thoughts, "Frank what, can I say is someone leaving?"

"Ah now, you see, I have this Idea to have someone always available to take charge of any of the shops anywhere in the UK."

"Frank I'm not sure I get the drift of this conversation."

"I want someone who is prepared to go anywhere when a manager leaves or goes on holiday, to take charge until a replacement can be found, it will mean working in any of the shops, are you interested?"

Barney's retort came quickly. "Can I think about it?" adding immediately. "Frank I've thought about it YES Please!"

"Barney I'm glad, so if it's alright with you as soon as we can find a new driver you will start, I think the best place will be in Cherry's shop, it's easier if you know the people you will be working with."

Still dazed by the offer but sceptical as to whether he would be welcomed full time by Cherry. He shook Frank's hand warmly. "Thank you for the opportunity Frank," and adding, "however has Cherry been told I might be working alongside of her, more importantly will she accept me considering all that has gone before; I was a bastard to her."

"Barney, I can assure you I have spoken to Cherry and she doesn't foresee a problem with the situation, by the way obviously there will be a suitable salary increment befitting your new appointment."

"Frank I never even thought about money thank you."

Two weeks after his appointment on Barney's first day in his new job, he stood waiting for the shop to be opened, clutching a huge bunch of flowers for Cherry, to his astonishment she kissed him on his cheek, only this time alcohol played no part in its bestowal, but she made it obvious, it was just a thank you for the flowers.

Chapter 14

Although Henry grew up in an idiosyncratic family environment, it was to all intents and purposes a deconstructed family relationship: ravelled would be the easiest way to describe it. Despite the unconventional aspect of family life, for Henry, and all his siblings including Lindy, it was a very happy environment.

The three women that had children all fathered by his dad Frank, remarkably had all become good friends.

Henry however, as he journeyed through and beyond his teens never subscribed to or condoned the lifestyle adopted by his dad, who he thought of as not exactly a libertine more of a happy go lucky philanderer: but it was not for Henry. As he made that journey into manhood there came a defining moment in his approach to love, likewise to all aspects of his life. Like many teenage boys before him his first girlfriend unceremoniously dumped him, initially hurt and disquieted by her rejection moreover, infinitely more distressed to discover she had dumped him for his best friend Charlie: that hurt. Still, being so young he soon overcame his disappointment especially when Charlie was also dumped by the same girl. He viewed positively the obvious happiness his mum shared with her husband Mathew, determining when the right girl came along whatever happened and under any circumstances, he would never be unfaithful to any girl, he desired the same stability and required the same unambiguous love his mum and Mathew shared.

Henry chose to follow a different path in life to his dad, even though there were many things about his dad he wanted to, and did aspire to. One of those things without doubt was, self-belief, Frank's character was the personification of; if anything was possible, he could and would find the means by which to achieve his objective. Whatever life threw at him, he would ride the storm and sail into calmer waters and his gift for overcoming any adversity he might encounter, held his son in total admiration. He was a man who could talk his way out of any awkward situation, given the chance his cogent reasoning would nearly always be enough to settle any disputation amicably, except in his love life. Despite his lacklustre academic achievements at school, his astute eye for business allied to his work ethic, had brought him success monetarily and sociably. He treated his staff with the utmost respect, to which in the main part it was reciprocated, there were a few exceptions of course: you can't please everyone.

Henry, had a much more serious character than his dad and was far brighter academically. From the time he started primary school, his teachers recognised his undoubted capacity, not just to learn but to absorb and grasp the concept of the many subjects they tutored. He had a remarkable ability to assimilate language's, by the time he left senior school he was not only fluent in French Spanish and German but he could also adopt the everyday language spoken by people distinguished in the literary language. His teachers Recognised from an early age his potential believing he would almost certainly gain a place in university, which he did, with ease. His progress through school amazed everyone, Frank often joked, "I don't know where he gets it from it certainly isn't me he must be the milkman's." As predicted by everyone involved in his schooling, Henry easily achieved the entry criterion required to gain a place at university to study economics and management, but first, like a lot of young people he took a year-long sabbatical back packing across Australia with his friend Charlie.

Henry and Charlie's year-long vacation in Australia taught Henry life wasn't all about academia, at home and school he had been cloistered from the wider world, his intellectual faculties perceiving there was more expansive avenues to pursue. One of them exploring and enjoying different cultures, absorbing their ideas, their attitudes their differences their political agendas and of course their sexual orientations, all of which gave him an insight into how best to be involved with others, he realised the best way forward was to accept people for what they were not for what you wanted or expected from or of them. Understanding his own and other peoples limitations gave him a whole new subjective evaluation of humanity, he needed to enhance his social skills if he were ever to forge a successful future. He finally stepped out from his sheltered life into a more demanding and intimidating world.

Henry unlike most of his peers found academic life easy, the end of his three years of studying resulted in a BSC First Class Honours degree, the world was his oyster; the world of business beckoned; he was ready to take on that business world. Henry's horizon however lay across the pond in the America's setting his sights westward to North America; notably the Big Apple: New York, New York, he was almost twenty-two years old and felt he was more than ready to face the real world: the corporate world.

Frank wanted: furthermore, expected him to join the family business, initially Henry rejecting the idea out of hand, young, intelligent, and ambitious, he like his dad preferring to be the architect of his own destiny: to be his own man. Nevertheless, Frank persisted with his inductive reasoning, hoping to convince him to at least listen to his proposition first, then maybe wait for a while before he headed west. For once, Frank had the full backing of Mary, although she wanted Henry to make his own way in life she was equally concerned that at the age of twenty-two he was too young to fly the nest. Although air travel was easy, she was concerned, and the thought filled her with dread that she might never see her son again because Henry's preferred destination of New York lay some three and a half thousand miles from home. Both Mary and Frank expressed their genuine concerns to Henry over his proposed venture across the pond, explicating he should gain some experience in business and life, before relocating halfway across the world. Initially Henry refused to accept his dad's proposal but as always Frank got his way, especially when Mary with tears in her eyes and a fervent motherly entreaty turned the tide in Frank's favour.

Negotiations were drawn out over a period of weeks, whereby different options were laid out as to what Henry's role within the company would be, eventually to Mary's welcome relief an amicable settlement was reached. Henry agreed to join the family business, pledging to stay for one year only, however, if things didn't work out he would follow his dream and try his luck in America.

The outcome was Henry would expand 'Jenson Office Supplies' first into the Principality of Wales where he would establish an office in Cardiff, the capital, If successful then further expansion into Scotland. The main sticking point during those protracted discussions had been Henry's refusal to accept interference from the CEO: his dad, but Frank recognising Henry's potential was keen to have him on board so he acceded to his sons demand, giving him carte blanch to conduct business as he saw fit. Frank insisting he started at the bottom he also made It clear if he needed assistance or guidance no matter what problems may hinder or frustrate him he only had to pick up the phone, and insisted he gained experience in all departments within the company.

On his first day in employment, Henry was completely taken aback, expecting to start at the bottom yes; however, he had not expected to start, as he called it, down in the basement: making tea for everyone, Nevertheless, such was his determination to succeed, he did as he was asked without complaint. There was another shock waiting for him, he was introduced to Barney Phillips the man Henry knew some years previously who had hospitalised his dad. Henry disquieted by the introduction, was at first reluctant to work with him. Barney sensing the diffidence shown by Henry, explained, "Henry I know what you're thinking but honestly your dad gave me a chance, for which I am eternally grateful. Me and your dad from an early age were sworn enemies, but he has helped me turn my life around, I just can't thank him enough, I hope you and I can someday be friends."

Henry stood listening to Barney's sincere adjuration, believing his words he shook his hand. Over time they did indeed become very good friends.

From then on, it was onward and upward almost six months of intensive training from making tea, to having to manage one of the shops for five weeks, while the usual manageress was on sick leave, which was enough for Frank to judge that Henry had gained the necessary astuteness and judgment, allied to his visionary and foresight he possessed. Shaking his hand Frank gave him the necessary wherewithal to hopefully make a success of their venture, into the Principality. Henry thanked his dad for having faith in him to deliver results which he understood: the venture had to make a profit Henry, determined to achieve success, unbeknown to Frank would drive to Cardiff every Sunday in order to acquaint himself with the city centre where he began to shape his future in the world of business. Little did he know it but the next few years would bring success on a scale he dreamed and hoped for; but never imagined would come so, quickly…

Within eight weeks of settling in the Welsh capital his vision of building, a successful, and more importantly sustainable business began to evolve. Working tirelessly, he found suitable premises which required very little attention, situated on the outskirts of the city centre with an added bonus of its own car park with enough space to accommodate upwards of twelve cars.

After receiving the keys, he immediately posted an advert in the South Wales Echo for three new staff, he spent five days conducting interviews, subsequently employing two young women, Jane and Cathy to assist him in the showroom, and a middle-aged man Emile to help with the heavier work and deliveries. All three staff started the following Monday to help put the place in order and get ready to receive the stock for opening day. Henry had set his sights on selling anything and everything required to run an efficient office from, paper clips to furniture and electronic goods such as computers and printers.

As Frank never interfered, despite some misgivings he harboured, he was amazed, moreover, proud at the speed with which his son had accomplished the project he had been employed to do; he couldn't have done any better himself. He asked Henry if he could be there for the opening of the shop, which was fast approaching, to which Henry gave him the green light.

Henry feeling tired and decidedly lonely left the shop to walk back to his Hotel late on Thursday evening, just one week before the opening of the shop. On an impulse, he decided to have dinner in the local hostelry for a change, after dinner he relaxed and enjoyed a drink musing over the past couple of months. Leaning back in his seat, tired but quite mellow he surveyed the crowded bar. Over the far side a noisy group of girls behaving outrageously, caught his attention making him smile and lightened his mood further. It was Obvious they were out on a hen night and were loud enough for him to hear their squealing laugher, their ribald jokes and indelicate language. Part way through the evening two of the girls from the hen party sat down next to him, one of them was a pretty blue-eyed blonde girl who wore a red and green floral summer dress, he noted by her accent, to be Scottish. Henry who by then was fully relaxed; his mind free of tension engaged both girls in conversation which before he went to Australia would have been unthinkable and feeling really pleasantly intoxicated, but not drunk, asked when their friend was getting married.

The blonde girl answered in a soft Scottish accent, "Saturday but sadly I won't be here to enjoy the day."

"That's a shame why?"

"I've got to go home tomorrow."

"I take it by home, you mean Bonnie Scotland?"

"Yes Edinburgh I've got work on Saturday."

"Do you always work on Saturdays?"

"No not always, it depends where I'm going."

Henry curious enquired, "Intriguing, why, what is it you do?"

"I'm part of the Cabin crew, don't you dare call me a trolley-dolly."

"I wouldn't be so cheeky anyway it's exciting erm, er, can I ask you your name."

"Corrina, Corrina Jade Phelps, and you are?"

"Henry, Henry Swan Jenson, I'm pleased to meet you Corrina Jade Phelps."

"Pleased to meet you too Henry Swan Jenson."

Corrina's friend who had not contributed much to their conversation decided to rejoin the main party leaving Henry and Corrina chatting.

"Where are you off to on Saturday then, somewhere exciting I guess?"

"Tenerife, there and back in a day."

"Nice part of the world, The Canary's."

"Honestly, we never get to see anywhere, I'm looking to do long haul flights like New York, you get to stay overnight sometimes longer, which allows you more time to do some sight-seeing: far more interesting."

"Corrina, New York is the place where I've always wanted to live."

"Why haven't you, is it because you are you in a relationship?"

"No not at all I didn't go because my dad, allied to a worried mother, offered me an opportunity I could not refuse, so I agreed to stay for a year, then we'll see what transpires."

"I'm curious what was this offer you couldn't refuse?"

By the time Henry had finished relating his story of the past year, it was eleven thirty, Corrina's friends took their leave and headed for a night club she declined because she had an early train to catch the following morning.

"Henry, it has been really nice talking to you but I do have to go."

"Have you far to go? Where, are you staying?"

"The Ramada, do you know it?"

"Blimey, I should do, it's been my home for the last two months, I'll walk back with you, that's if you don't mind?"

"I would like that, thank you."

"It will be my pleasure."

They said their good-byes in the reception area, Henry watched Corrina whose room was on the fourth floor enter the lift, she turned and waved goodnight.

He hadn't enjoyed himself as much in a long time, she would be a lasting memory of his time in Cardiff, he liked her a lot, in fact he felt drawn to her in a way he didn't quite apprehend. He surmised he would never see her again; he turned a pleasant page in his book of life, and, he had a business to run, but it still didn't stop him thinking about her while he lay in bed.

When the shop had its formal opening proud parents, Frank and Mary made the Journey to give support. Opening day disappointed on the commercial front; there was more staff than customers but as luck would have it, it coincided with end of school summer holidays which proved to be invaluable. The first three weeks custom was mainly Mum's and Dad's dragging their disinterested offspring with them to buy educational materials, Emile suggested maybe they should explore the possibility of stocking children's educational books if they could find space. It was an idea Henry was quite taken with; however, they needed to get established before venturing directly into a more academic and instructive library department. Slowly the commercial element began to gather apace when a number of company's began placing orders to supply new office furniture: Jenson's Office Solutions of Wales had arrived in the beautiful capital city of Wales. Henry's year stretched into eighteen months and using Cardiff as his base, he opened two more shops, the second in Swansea southwest Wales and the third in Bangor in Northeast Wales. He liked Wales and the Welsh people and he was about to find one Welsh person he liked even more...

Chapter 15

Five weeks after opening the first shop business was booming, sales had gone through the roof, so much so Henry decided to extend opening hours by an extra half hour each day Monday to Thursday for prospective customers, during the rush hour. Thursday evening by fortunate happenstance when locking the shop and rechecking to make sure all was well, Henry heard a voice from behind, Turning round he faced a young girl, not blonde, nor dark, fairer she queried, "yduch chi newydd gau?"

Henry smiling responded, "Sorry love I don't speak Welsh it is Welsh isn't it?"

The woman smiled back and replied, "I beg your pardon I was asking if you have just closed?"

"I have but I will open up for you, what is it you're after?"

"I need some copy paper."

"No problem, give me a minute and we'll sort something out."

Shop unlocked Henry was surprised when he asked her how much she required, "I want 40 reams of 80gms A4 multi-purpose copy paper please."

Henry looked her up and down she was wearing skin tight jeans and a black leather Jacket over a black crop top he couldn't resist, "It's a good order but where are you going to put them all? Your pockets aren't big enough in those jeans."

She started to laugh, "Well I thought you might do me the honours."

"My pockets ain't that big either."

"Well let me see can you deliver young man."

"Yus milady, when would you like to take delivery?"

She was now joining in with his patter, "My good man, tomorrow would be wonderful if that is possible?"

"Yus milady where is this delivery to take place?"

"Begin Hill School, if that would be possible my good man."

"Any particular time, milady?"

"As early as possible please, my good man."

"There is one problem milady."

"And what would that be my good man?"

"Money milady."

"Oh of course, silly me, the school will pay you on delivery."

Henry suddenly remembered Emile had booked that day off so realising he would have to do it himself, impudently asked her, "Will 8.30 be soon enough."

"That will do nicely my good man."

"You understand there will be an extra charge milady."

Looking a little shocked she asked, "How much?"

"Let me see now, early morning delivery? That will require, tea with milk no sugar."

"You're a cheeky one I meant how much will the paper cost."

"Well milady 40 reams at £3.25 a ream is £130, don't forget the tea."

"You really are a cheeky young man, but thank you for opening up the shop I'll see you tomorrow at 8.30, Bye."

"Bye milady."

As she walked down the road she turned, smiled again and waved, returning the wave all Henry could think was how beautiful she was, she had made a distinct impression on him.

Finally he was able to close the shop for the evening, much later than usual, but the important thing was he had made a sale, Henry loaded the twenty reams of paper into his car ready for the morning delivery.

Before he took his sabbatical to Australia, Henry never had the wherewithal to engage in a conversation with someone he had only just met. Australia broadened his perspective on life, happily his confidence grew, whereby his academic knowledge of most subject matter gave him a solid platform from which he could initiate a conversation with anybody, including children. Henry phoned one of his assistants Jane, who had a spare set of keys and explained he would be late in the morning because of the delivery he had to make and asked would she open the shop up for him, she agreed.

Friday morning ever punctual, he delivered the 20 reams of paper to the school at 8.30 on the dot. The same young woman who had given him the order was waiting, still smiling with the tea in hand, he had cheekily asked for, along with the cheque for payment. She spoke, "bore du fy dyn da."

Grinning Henry proffered, "bore da."

Cainwan? Returning the grin, riposted back in English, "Hmmm, not only cheeky but a show-off as well."

"To be honest it's the only Welsh I know."

"It's a start, here's your tea."

"Why thank you milady."

Neither of them had noticed another young woman stood at the door who spoke in Welsh, "Wow Mae e'n edrch yn pwy ydy e a ble wnes I ddod o hyd iddo."

Giggling, the first young woman's reply came, "Gwelais ef yn gyntaf fel galwych chi bugger off."

They both burst out laughing, the second young woman hardly able to catch her breath replying, "Rydych yn gdyyu warchen ac roeddwn In meddwl mai fi oedd fy ffrind."

There came another retort, from the first young woman, "Gallwch ei gael pan fyddaf wedi gorffen gydag ef," adding, "Hwyl fawr."

Henry a little irritated they had ignored him, made a request with a question to the first young woman. "I haven't a clue what you've been talking about; is it possible you could interpret for me? You seem to find it extremely funny."

Reverting back to English, she offered an apology, "Oh I'm sorry, we speak Welsh all the time so the kids don't know what we are talking about."

"What were you laughing at, or is it a secret?"

Her answer caught him unawares, "If you fancy going for a drink later I'll tell you then."

"Milady I would be honoured, where, and what time would you like to meet?"

"How about I meet you at the shop after school?"

"Ok, we can have dinner if you would like."

"That would be very nice, er?"

"Henry, and you are?"

"Ceinwen."

"I take it it's a Welsh name, what does it mean?"

"Fair and blessed."

"Well Ceinwen, I'll see you this evening Hwyl fawre."

"Hwyl fawre Henry."

For once, Henry couldn't wait for the days labour to end, a normal day now looked anything but normal. He was locking up the shop and as his usual routine rechecking the locks when from behind he heard Ceinwen.

"Hello Henry."

Continuing his checks, "Noswaith dda fair and blessed."

Giggling she reminded him, "You told me you didn't speak Welsh."

"I don't, my assistant Jane taught it me."

"We'll make a Welshman of you yet."

"Ceinwen you must be endowed with some extraordinary intellectual creative powers to understand the linguistics of the Welsh language, you are a veritable genius I'm in total awe of you."

"Thank s for the compliment."

"I think I should at least try and learn a few more words it's very remiss if me."

"Here's another one for you to learn diolch, which means thank you."

"Diolch."

"Milady Ceinwen, is there anywhere particular you have in mind for dinner?"

"I quite like the Ramada hotel but it is expensive, do you know it?"

Smiling to himself but keeping a straight face, "I know where you mean; it's that big hotel in the town centre, I've seen it, let's go."

"Henry I was only joking about going there, look at the way I'm dressed."

"Don't be daft you look beautiful come on let's go to the restaurant I'm hungry and you can tell me what you and your colleague were laughing about this morning."

Entering through the revolving doors of the Ramada, the duty receptionist called, "Mr Jenson will you be having dinner tonight?"

Henry replied, "Yes please, dinner for two tonight."

Ceinwen with a puzzled expression on her face asked, "How do they know your name?"

Starting to laugh he admitted, "Ceinwen I should have said, I've been living here for the past ten months, the food is special though, you'll like it."

Over dinner she explained, "Basically, my friend Ruth fancies you,
I told her, she could only have you when I was finished with you."

"Cainwen, we have one dinner date and you're already shipping me out."

"Henry I'm hoping there will be many more dinners?"

"Me too, how about tomorrow?"

Henry was beginning to warm to her admiring her intelligence and her sense of humour which harmonised with his own, she had a presence that excited him, which he felt extremely comfortable with. Another aspect of her character he liked he would get to find out in the future he would find out about at a later date was that she could stand her ground in any argument; she was nobody's fool. Another factor drawing him to her was that she was extremely pretty and he was fascinated by her huge hazel brown eyes which emitted a rich warm radiance complimented by very long eyelashes, accentuated by her fair hair and pale skin tone.

Romantically, things moved quickly between them, Ceinwen had her own flat and within six weeks Henry had moved in, at last he was able to enjoy some scintillating conversation with someone who was his intellectual equal. He and Ceinwen had a spark which ignited his appetite for life outside of business albeit quite limited, he considered her very special however, he was never quite sure if he was In love but he was extremely fond of her, he wasn't sure of her true feelings towards him either, but he did understand he liked being in her life.

Chapter 16

Henry had not taken a holiday throughout those eighteen months in Cardiff apart from weekends when he would go home to see the family. Work was paramount to Henry his achievements in Wales, in all respects he was undoubtably a resounding success in such a short space of time. He amazed everybody especially his dad; his mum was just glad he had remained in the UK, nevertheless, he felt his time in the principality had come to an end it was time to move on: Scotland beckoned…

Before, effecting his move to Scotland, Henry and his girlfriend Ceinwen took a much needed break; their destination the beautiful Greek Island of Rhodes. One particularly hot day while enjoying a beer at a bar in Rhodes old town they chatted about what the future may hold for them. Henry outlining his plans to Ceinwen pointing out he would like her to be with him when he moved to Scotland, she was seriously taken aback, Henry had spoken about Scotland when they first met but because everything had gone so smoothly and as he seemed settled, moreover happy, she had put Scotland to the back of her mind, although at first tentative with her answer, she eventually answered in the affirmative. Obviously, there were obstacles because Ceinwen, a newly qualified primary school teacher would need to find another teaching pos. One particular barrier was she needed to complete the school year, two full terms before she would be able to join Henry, the upshot of which; meant, they would only see each other for the odd weekend or during school holidays. Notwithstanding that, she felt she should give a move to Scotland a try.

Chapter 17

The holiday over, Henry began to formulate his proposed move from Cardiff to Edinburgh, the elements of which would be of the same configuration and strategy he employed when first moving to Cardiff. However, the transition did not go as planned, the first difficulty he encountered started before he left as Jane, his general manager was taken ill, Henry was the only replacement so his proposed segue was put on hold for two weeks. Further disruption came via some hard bargaining, pertaining to a possible, large order of Furniture and general office supplies for the British Steel Company, which he successfully completed. When he finally managed to travel, albeit five weeks late, he thankfully found Edinburgh very much to his liking; vibrant, exciting, beautiful and clean, everything he had been led to believe it would b, and he was determined to emulate all the success he had achieved in Cardiff.

Given the experience and business acumen accumulated during his rather longer than anticipated sojourn in the Welsh capital, he determined his stay in the Scottish Capital would be shorter. Once (Jenson's office supplies Scotland) was established and running smoothly with the aid of staff he could trust, he would then follow his dreams and aspirations across the Atlantic to the East coast of America: New York.

This time, rather than stay in a hotel for too long, he found a small cottage to rent in Juniper Green, a village situated a short distance from Edinburgh city centre, hoping that though temporary, it was somewhere he and Ceinwen would make their home.

One of the difficulties he encountered in his new project came from not understanding the Edinburgh dialect. He found the locals to be friendly, endowed with a wicked sense of humour and they could understand him, however, he struggled with the linguistic nuances of their speech pattern. Over time, because of his ability to absorb local dialects, he learned to understand the regional parlance and used it, when in the company of his own family members to annoy them. Henry in furtherance of his objectives required some assistance at the shop, thus ever resourceful he employed a young woman Ellie Crane, as a part time interpreter who gently guided him through the puzzling, Edinburgh vernacular. She impressed him so much he invited her to become his full-time assistant, the offer of which she accepted. Ellie was exceptionally bright; industrious and full of exciting ideas which Henry was quick to seize upon, moreover he began to realise she was someone he could trust: they quickly becoming a formidable management team.

Ceinwen was due to join him over the half term school holidays, allowing her to get to know Edinburgh a little more before she moved permanently from Cardiff. Extremely busy as he was Henry began to feel excited at the prospect of their reunion, even though he was still unsure of his feelings towards her. Ceinwen arrived a day later than expected Henry sensing immediately there was something amiss, their welcome embrace somehow didn't feel as warm or thrilling as it should have been considering they had been apart for the best part of six weeks. During the week he began to think that possibly, there wasn't the strength of feeling from either of them required to sustain a lasting relationship and towards the end of the week, it became apparent she did not like Edinburgh.

Sat in an Italian restaurant for dinner the day before Ceinwen was due to go back to Cardiff, they talked about her proposed move to join Henry in Edinburgh, Henry broached the subject of their 'affaire de coeur' as tactfully as he could asking her, "Ceinwen what is worrying you?"

"Why do you ask?"

"You seem distracted, as the week has progressed you've become distant."

"Henry, I want to be with you, but I don't like it here, can't you move back to Cardiff? The flat is lonely without you, I'm lonely without you."

"Ceinwen I've missed you but I'm surprised at your response you knew all about my plans for the future from our very first meet and again while we were in Rhodes, I outlined exactly what my goals in life were. *When my job is done here, I'm off to New York,* I thought, actually hoped, you might like to make that journey with me."

"So, what are you telling me?"

"I'm saying I set out to make something of myself, I won't be going back to Cardiff, my work is done there but it's obvious you don't want to be part of it."

"I'm so sad, it's not what I wanted to hear."

"Ceinwen I'm sorry but if you can't see that we should call it a day."

"Just like that?"

"If we are only going to see each other once in a blue moon, I see no other option open to us, if both of us are unwilling to compromise, sadly, it's not a solid foundation for a relationship."

Ceinwen had tears in her eyes, as she said goodbye, she kissed Henry gently on the cheek before she began the drive back home to Cardiff; nevertheless, Henry remained obdurate, disappointed, the final outcome was not what he had hoped for, but he could not let a long distant, emotional attachment, distract him from his chosen path. He waved goodbye, sadly it was over. Despite his seemingly cold manner Henry missed her, in fact, he missed her more than he expected, but it was time to put it behind him, it was over, there would be no going back.

Henry's experience with women was somewhat minimal, Ceinwen was his first serious relationship since leaving university, where previously he had been involved in a couple of relationships, albeit brief affairs. Despite his outward intense demeanour which belied his sense of humour, girls were attracted to him, furthermore, he enjoyed the company of the opposite sex. Preoccupation with his business life left him very little time for affairs of the heart, Henry like his dad had the gift of the gab; nevertheless, unlike his dad his communicative skills were restricted mainly to commerce: his direction to conquer the world of business. For the time being, he was not looking for romance, he believed it would come to him; he would know instinctively when the right person came along.

From the onset, Henry found Edinburgh a far more difficult project to establish than he had encountered in the Welsh capital, but thankfully he had Ellie, his new personal assistant who made life in the Scottish capital appreciably easier for him to manage. The first hurdle to overcome was to find premises in the centre of the city, large enough to accommodate the quantity of stock required; easier said than done. Obtaining a lease for a large floor area at a reasonable rate proved almost impossible which worried him. They searched for two months, eventually a suitable premises was found, albeit a little further out from the city than he originally hoped. From then on, it was all systems go, he and Ellie worked nonstop for a further two months, liaising with shop fitters, hiring two more staff and ordering and installing stock ready for opening. Ready at last, the opening date was set, so two weeks before the opening, in order to let people of Edinburg know what 'Jenson office supplies Scotland' were about, they invested heavily in an advertising campaign using papers and local radio, Henry had considered TV advertising however, the cost was unsupportable on the budget he had allowed. Opening day as you would expect was quite fraught, and what they hadn't bargained for was the success of the advertising, which attracted an extraordinary amount of customers.

At closing time, Henry took his staff out for a celebratory dinner to thank them for their efforts.

With the success of the first shop, added to the experience he had garnered in Cardiff, it gave Henry the impetus to establish a further three stores in Scotland. First in Aberdeen on the north east coast, Dundee, on the Firth of Tay estuary, the eastern North Sea coast and of course Glasgow. The Glasgow site, in the long term, became the most valuable asset they held in Scotland. Henry was endowed with an aptitude for finding suitable sites with easy access and parking for prospective customers, however, problems he faced was finding staff. He was looking for people with the right personal qualities, which included experience but more importantly he required enthusiasm from staff with a wholehearted commitment to the new company, especially if they were to be promoted to manager.

Before each store was opened, he enlisted the help of his capable assistant Ellie to facilitate her thoughts on any possible prospective staff. Using her female intuitive apprehensions or assurances she might identify necessary requisites for each position. He trusted her implicitly, he admired her drive and work ethic, something which was always important to him. He had already set plans ready to reward her, making her an offer which he hoped she couldn't refuse.

Opening four stores in such a short period of time created serious problems. Henry had to borrow far more money from the bank than he originally anticipated stretching his budget which for a time put one hell of a strain on the whole operation; nonetheless he held his nerve. One afternoon, he was returning from a particular uneasy and tense meet with his bank and headed down a traffic laden Queen Street, looking through the traffic on the opposite side, a young blonde woman caught his eye. She immediately distracted him from his business problems as she reminded him of someone, though he was not quite sure who. He stared across at her and to his surprise she smiled and waved to him, before disappointingly she turned into Hanover Street. He wracked his brain, he knew her from somewhere, but for the life of him he couldn't think where or when, she had a familiarity about her and because she had waved, he was certain they must have met sometime in the past. Unable to remember he concentrated on his business monetary problems.

While relaxing with one of his neighbours in the Railway Inn, his local pub, to relieve his mind of his problems, a noisy group of girls out partying gave him the answer as to who the girl was, he had noticed in Queen Street and more to the point where he knew her from; furthermore, who she was. He had enjoyed a pleasant couple of hours in her company the week before the opening of the first shop In Cardiff. His cerebrum suddenly coming into focus, he remembered her name Corrina Jade Phelps, was it? He wasn't certain if she was the same person, nonetheless the more he delved into his memory he began to believe it was her. Despite his business worries when they first met regarding his first shop, her looks and personality had contrived to make an indelible impression on him.

Chapter 18

Opening four stores so quickly extended Henry's stay in Scotland by two months, making certain each store would hold their own; In short making a profit. By the time he was ready to leave Scotland, he was exhausted, he had worked upwards of twelve-hour days for over three years. Everything was running smoothly except for the odd, unexpected hiccup. He Needed to find a replacement for himself, the one person that impressed him by her willingness and earnest application to accomplish whatever was undertaken, so despite her young age, he asked his assistant Ellie Crane if she would be prepared to take over, when he was ready to relinquish control, not as manager but general manager of all four stores.

Though flattered at his offer, she was at first very reluctant to accept, However, Henry knew full well her capabilities so he offered to stay another month to watch and assist with the day to day strains and politics of running such a large enterprise. Ellie, much to Henry's delight, after the month ended, accepted the position of general manager. If everything planned out how he envisaged with Ellie he would recommend in an Email to Frank, she be made chief executive. Frank agreed. His job completed; he immediately resigned his position as Chief Executive from 'Jensen's Office Supplies Scotland'.

On his return from Edinburgh exhausted but proud of his achievements first in Wales then Scotland, he felt liberated from the pressure placed upon him implementing the expansion of the family business, at last, he was able to relax, he had never envisaged or planned to spend more than one year working for Jenson's, which was his original agreement with his parents. He drove home determined he would never go back, he was done with Jenson's believing it was his time to do what he wanted: win or lose.

Home at last doing nothing but enjoying family life, the very substance of which he had avoided over the previous three years, as he dismissed anything which would distract him from the goals he had set himself. Over those three years he had only been home for three Christmas holidays and a total of five weekends and the odd day, he needed a complete rest from anything business related so he decided to stay with his family reacquainting to family life, for a couple of months before planning his move to America. Two months relaxing in the bosom of the family, without the intensity of being a CEO somehow stretched to six, during which time, his sister Caro got engaged to her boyfriend Lindsay which pleased him.

Time passes so quickly; especially when you are enjoying yourself, yet all too soon Henry's short hiatus from the work a day world, concluded. His decision to move to America was final he knew it would be difficult for his mum to accept his move nevertheless, she knew he had to follow his dream, she recognised she might not see her eldest for many years, if ever again, but she genuinely wanted him to be happy so graciously but with a very heavy heart she gave her blessing.

Henry meticulously planned his proposed adventure down to the last detail, leaving nothing to chance. Before he left, he contacted a number of American companies via the internet, to his surprise every one of them replied, which much to his astonishment within two hours receiving offers from three American recruitment companies, courtesy was, and still is the watch word in One in particular caught his eye representing a large corporation whose head office was located in New York, MSIA, full title (Mighty Sales Incorporated of America), coincidently their operations extended into Europe where they had an office on Henry's doorstep too, situated just outside Birmingham located in West Bromwich in the West Midlands. The British arm of the company was run by an outlandish American who went by the bizarre name of 'Dusty J. Upthegrove the 3rd' a good-looking, hard-bitten Texan who invariably wore a cowboy hat and boots, always set off with a western dress bow, or Bollo tie. He may have dressed like a cowboy, he was anything but a cowboy, he was a very astute businessman who to some extent reminded Henry of his dad. Henry, like his dad though ambitious to the point of obsession, understood that in business he had to remain calm particularly when a client was giving him a hard time: remaining courteous. Dusty was equally charismatic and shared the same work ethic and Henry's dad undoubted had the ability to charm anyone especially any and every woman who came near to him. However, Dusty's charm reflected friendliness not lasciviousness, he put everyone at ease, there was never any ulterior motive.

Henry's interviews were conducted over a period of four weeks via the internet using Skype, including a couple of searching conversations with the said, Dusty J Upthegrove the 3rd. Ultimately when concluded, he was offered a job which was where Dusty J Upthegrove the 3rd really came into the equation as it was his responsibility to obtain the green card which would enable Henry the right to live and work in the USA. He joined the company in West Bromwich working as an assistant alongside Dusty while waiting for his green card, a delay in the green card application was one of the reasons why his original plan of two months stretched to six, it was one of those periods when nothing seemed to be happening. Henry's pragmatism at times would desert him getting discouraged; however, Dusty would assure him it as he put it in his Southern Drawl, "Dusty J Upthegrove the 3rd is on the case boy and I never fail." True to his word the Green-card was duly approved, thus Henry began to make final plans for his departure to New York.

When the day came for him to start his life in the whole family were at the airport to wave goodbye, his mum could not stem the flow of tears even his dad shed a tear. Carro gave him a silver dollar as a good luck charm hugging him, she whispered, "Go and kick some ass, Henry, me and Lindsay will come over and see you when you get settled, you can show us the sights."

The moment for take-off had arrived, he inhaled a deep breath and for the first-time anxiety commixed with his excitement was something he had never experienced before, an uneasy feeling of insecurity coursed through his body. He was on his own. Strapped into his seat his thoughts floated between his future in America and how he would miss the love and support from his family, they were and always had been the cornerstone, the very bedrock of his life, now he was leaving them behind. Regardless of any reservations about leaving which to be honest were few, Henry was steadfast in his determination to succeed nothing would distract him from his chosen path.

Chapter 19

Filled with excitement and a fair amount of apprehension, Henry flew to New York arriving ten days before he was due to begin his employment. At last, he was fulfilling the dreams he held since a young boy and he was ready to explore the new exciting world to which he had aspired. His aspirations derived from watching cowboy films as a child to marvelling as a teenager at rockets launched into space from Cape Kennedy: he had always known where his ambitions, moreover, his destiny lay.

Landing at J.F Kennedy airport early afternoon, he waited patiently until he had negotiated all the security checks imposed since the 9/11, heartrending, murderous terrorist attack on the world trade centre. Eventually he stepped out from the air-conditioned airport terminal to be greeted by a hot sunny day and a young man who Henry perceived to be in his mid-twenty's holding, a board with his name written on it.

As Henry approached the young man he grinned holding his hand out to Henry's, he said, "Hi I'm Walter Williams, nice to meet you, we are going to be working together, I've come to escort you to your apartment."

"Walter, I'm Henry Swan Jenson it's nice to meet you, I wasn't expecting anybody to be here to greet me."

"Why?"

"To be honest in Britain we are not so accommodating, cordiality is not for the most part the nature of business life, unless of course they want something from you, If you're going to make anything of yourself you have to do it yourself."

"Henry, we have a lot of hard-nosed business people in this company so you will have to watch your back."

"Walter my friend, I'm honestly not blowing my own trumpet when I say I can handle competition; but thanks for the warning."

Introductions completed they got into one of the renown New York yellow taxis, to take him to the apartment he had rented on the west side of Lower Manhattan New York City. Another place he had read about and admired from afar was Greenwich Village. Henry's excitement grew as he travelled the twenty-five km to Greenwich Village, he could feel and smell the bohemian atmosphere for which it was famous. Everything he had read and looked forward to, lay before him, it was as if his imagination had come to life: he felt at home.

His apartment compared to British standards was enormous, consisting of two bedrooms both with en-suite bathrooms, each with a walk-in shower, a huge living room and an equally large fully fitted kitchen which contained gadgets he had never seen before, one being a tap supplying instant boiling water making the use of a kettle redundant: he was excited.

Henry wasted no time in getting to know his new surroundings, it didn't take long for him to realise Greenwich Village's ultra-convenient location. It accommodated a varied mix of college students, artists and inquisitive visitors who at times could be intrusive. However, there were warm-hearted local residents exhibiting the qualities of friendly neighbours and like himself, motivated ambitious professionals, frequenting its cosy tree-lined streets. Greenwich village boasts sidewalk cafes, brewpubs, fine dining eateries and flower boxes on every corner giving a feeling of warmth and friendliness. Unusually, the neighbourhood managed to project an intimate feel whereby you can enjoy life amid a quiet unruffled village atmosphere yet still it retains the characteristics of a metropolitan city, if you want to remain anonymous you can take advantage of and lose yourself in the crowds. Even the local proprietors of grocery and bakery stores were on first name terms their affability welcoming locals and newcomer's alike.

Henry had allowed himself ten days to see as much of his adopted city as possible, eagerly exploring the sights of his new home. Beginning the day after he arrived, his first port of call a trip to the magnificent awe inspiring and welcoming arms of America, the Statue of Liberty, aka Lady Liberty or the green lady, whatever you call her she stands beckoning anyone and everyone into the bosom of American life: the American dream. Standing on Liberty Island overlooking New York harbour she rises majestically three hundred and five feet one inch from the ground to the tip of the torch, Henry climbed the one hundred and fifty-four steps to the viewing platform in the lady's crown, from where he viewed the city; he was overwhelmed by the whole experience Henry did not know what to expect when he paid a visit to Ground Zero he like most people in the free world had witnessed the tragic events unfold, when in the space of less than two hours in the early morning of September the eleventh 2001 Islamic fundamentalist terrorists destroyed the twin towers of the world trade centre. He stood staring at the new, One World Trade centre also known as Freedom Tower, sadness befell him as he tried to understand why or what could possibly give rise to such intensive anger, incurring such hate which in turn would allow fellow human beings to inflict such extreme pain, misery and devastation. The very fabric on which democracy is founded was destroyed. Henry shed a tear for the 2977 innocent people who died that morning and the 6,000 injured.

During those ten days he managed visits to just about every iconic sight in New York he had ever heard or read about. From Lady Liberty to the empire state building, Coney and Ellis Island, he relaxed in the various parks including the Highline Pan and of course Central Park. Each day increased his delight and enthusiasm for his new surroundings.

Three days into his exploration in the symbolic heart of Greenwich Village, moreover one of New York City's most recognisable public spaces Henry marvelled at all the sights in Washington Square Park. Henry lay back on the lawn basking in the sun absorbing the energy that makes the place so special, while listening to musicians sat on benches strumming guitars and watching chess players battling over built-in chess tables and watched a large number of people he perceived as NYU students forgathered around a central fountain. Smiling inwardly as he lay back, enamoured by the enthusiasm of all who were there, inhaling the undoubted provocative atmosphere, Henry felt a sense that anything and everything was possible; the world was his oyster. Henry closed his eyes to the warmth of the afternoon sun and slowly slipped into a happy state of contemplation, true he missed his family and he understood it might be some time before he embraced family life again, Nevertheless, he knew where his destiny lay as his new environs totally beguile him. He was excited and stimulated to give his all, which he felt in turn would bring success. Lucy Maud Montgomery wrote (while solitude with dreams is glorious, without them it has few charms) While he was enjoying a couple of hours of quiet contemplation relaxing in the warmth of the evening sunshine after a day of sightseeing, strangely, something occurred which left him quite perplexed and completely unbelieving of his eyes. He shook himself from his musings just as a group of six or seven people who had been stretched out on the lawn a little further back from him, decided to move on. Sitting up as they passed him by, one of them a young, blonde, blue-eyed woman stopped for a second as if she was about to speak. However, the group of people she was with appeared to be in a hurry, called to her, as they did she smiled at him; involuntarily he smiled back, for some reason she looked vaguely familiar, he knew her from somewhere, but how could he? It seemed Impossible, because during his residency of a mere three days he hadn't spoken to anyone he knew, apart from local shop proprietors and total strangers. He sat back down searching deep into his memory bank, the only person he could possibly connect her to, outlandish as it seemed, was the blonde girl who smiled at him in Edinburgh as he walked down Queen Street, the same girl he believed he had met in Cardiff: Corrina Jade. He quickly dismissed the idea, conceding certainly she did look like her, but it couldn't be her, it was far too much of a coincidence, as a distance of three and a half thousand miles lay between those smiles, not to mention the time span between those smiles, nevertheless the smiles intrigued him to such an extent he could not get her out of his thoughts he was convinced she was the very same girl, Corrina Jade or was his mind playing tricks.

Henry used evenings to find out the best nightspots, pubs, bars and restaurants, he was astounded by the diversity of entertainment that was on offer, a cultural montage of entertainment resonating from the many Greenwich Village locales. If anyone from anywhere in the world, walked down those streets they are bombarded with a variety and composite choice of music and food to titillate both ears and taste buds. York and Greenwich Village night life far exceeded and excited him more than any of the places he had enjoyed anywhere he had ventured before. Another, aspect of his evening explorations which added to his enjoyment and gave him much pleasure came from the friendliness of the local people, from the moment he arrived he never felt alone, there was always a friendly face and someone interesting to talk to. Henry had never considered himself to be handsome, to his surprise and unbelievably the local girls seemed to be drawn to him, for which reason Henry had a theory, maybe his English accent had something to do with it, any young man could have their head turned with the attention he seemed to attract but the truth of the matter was, he had always been more interested in being successful like his dad; yet, unlike his dad he did not have the same wherewithal with the ladies.

Henry though flattered by the attention received from the ladies, was resolute in his determination to remain focused having set himself two years in which to accomplish his ambition and attain success in his adopted country: the ladies would have to wait. America and lady liberty had opened their welcoming arms to him. He was following many millions of likeminded people who had migrated from all over the world with exactly the same dreams and aspirations: he was determined to succeed.

Each evening while alone in his apartment, his crowded contemplations of each day's sight-seeing would inevitably stray back to the blonde-blue eyed girl whom he believed to be Corrina Jade. Despite his firmness of purpose regarding his work ambitions; furthermore, his rejection of any amatory diversion he may incur with the opposite sex up to this time he refused to be distracted from his chosen path throughout his working career. However, this particular young woman sporadically crossing his path, for some unknown reason captured his attention. True, he had dallied for a few short months and been fond of Ceinwen when he worked in Cardiff but unusually, the more he thought about Corrina Jade the more he wanted to speak to her, the more he was attracted to her. For some extraordinary reason, he felt there was a connection, a genuine affinity. Thereby lay a problem, he was sure their paths had crossed in two different continents; would they ever cross again: highly unlikely…

Henry believed the possibility of their paths ever crossing again was highly unlikely so. Once again put any thoughts of the young woman and for that matter any other potential amatory liaisons he relegated to the back of his mind, unusually for Henry, in his mind, he might just be tempted to stray a little from his dedicated quest to succeed in his pursuit of the American dream. There was something about the young woman which seriously courted his attention, thereby restricting him from completely dismissing her from his mind.

Henry had enjoyed every minute of his time exploring New York but his holiday. The ten days he had allowed himself to get acquainted with his new surroundings had flown therefor with mixed feelings he ended. He would have the rest of his time in New York to range over his adopted home: work beckoned.

Chapter 20

Time to start the next chapter of his working life, time to prove to himself he had the wherewithal to make it on his own, away from his family particularly the family business. The initial welcome to his new job by the CEO Mr Cy Sanchez was extremely warm, who took time to Introduce him to each of the team he would be leading. However, the first couple of weeks he began to question himself as to whether he had made the right decision. His new colleagues some of whom had been loyal employees for several years did not exactly warm to him viewing his appointment with a degree of suspicion, Henry noted there was a distinct frostiness towards him. It became more apparent when one afternoon he overheard a conversation between two of them, both bemoaning why they had been overlooked for the position Henry had taken, adding to the insult, the company had employed a foreigner thereby they offered their idea of a derogatory expression: calling Henry a Limey.

Henry to date, always had a good relationship with his staff, so it came as quite a shock to discover his new colleagues did not warm to him. Joining this company meant he had not been party to recruiting his staff, whereas previously he had always conducted interviews and selected people who he thought were suited to his work ethic, thereby capable of driving his business ideas forward. Therefore, being made unintentionally aware of their obvious disappointment he fully understood their frustrations, his resolve was to overcome any resentment his colleagues may hold. Thankfully, within a couple of months of his introduction of new working practices, their bonuses increased as a result of an increase in productivity brought about by the changes Henry made: attitudes appeared to change. Slowly, Henry detected a warmth in the demeanour of his staff, they began to talk to him even shared the odd joke. Eventually the difference in their attitude towards him was infinitely more relaxed the frostiness that had greeted him on his arrival completely evanesced as if there had never been a problem. Henry knew he had succeeded In winning them over when much to his surprise and delight, one of his colleagues, a guy of mixed race, an African American man called Cornelius, who previously had complained about his appointment, asked Henry to accompany him and the rest of the staff to an evening out. That had been arranged before Henry joined MSAI. That evening was a turning point in his working life as Cornelius eventually became his best friend, spending a lot of time together, Cornelius introduced Henry to American football a game he came to enjoy, becoming an avid supporter of The New York Giants.

Cornelius was single and had been through a short but turbulent marriage which ended in divorce. He advised Henry never to rush into marriage as he had done, he explained having met and married within a month, three months later it was all over, luckily there was no issue from the marriage and as he put it, "Thank god there was nothing else to share." Cornelius loved life and his attitude began to attach itself to Henry, for the first time in his life, since leaving school, Henry began to relax in his down time away from the workplace particularly American football.

Henry had begun to realise how good his colleagues were at their chosen profession, the consequents of which he would only occasionally go home to dwell on his day's labour, unless there had been a problem that required a solution, quickly. Most nights and weekends he was out and about town with Cornelius enjoying the social side of what America had to offer. Before migrating to America, his social life had never been exactly extensive, truthfully it had been decidedly narrow, but America and his American friends changed his view on life. He was happy, his social life was more expansive, he made a lot of friends a lot of them girlfriends, but they were just that, friends, one or two of them he liked and dated; however as nice as they were for some reason none of them really floated his boat. Henry wanted to emulate the beautiful warm and loving relationship his mum enjoyed with his stepdad Mathew, something that had not been evident between his mum and dad. Sadly, when it came to loyalty his dad was a maverick or as his mum dubbed him, morally dissolute.

Henry and Cornelius felt good after an afternoon watching the Giants beat the Cleveland Browns, usually they would head to one bar which they frequented quite often, The Shade Bar located in Greenwich Village a small very intimate bar who served up crepe's savoury and sweet, where they were on first name terms with the staff. Unusually that particular evening, they decided to patronise another of their favourite establishments, deciding they fancied something with a more local flavour and more substantial to eat. Thus, they made their way to The White Oak tavern, an establishment priding itself on the quality of its rustic tradition, which they preserved through forgotten cooking techniques. They offered locally sourced ingredients for their rich and unique food menu, and of course more importantly for Henry and Cornelius their craft beers. Henry was particularly fond of the bangers and mash, not quite the same as his mum made, but still delicious, he ordered them and likewise did Cornelius. Dinner eaten quickly, they sat at the bar enjoying a beer chatting with the barman about the game they had just watched.

It Is widely suggested everything happens for a reason and part of that philosophy is coincidence, whether you believe in such things is not of importance, nonetheless neither of them would ever have dreamt of just how the decision to eat at the White Oak Tavern would dramatically affect both of their lives...

Chapter 21

They were in the mood to party, the Giants had won, celebration is what they were about. Henry was relaxed enjoying his drink having banter with a jets supporter when someone tapped him on the shoulder turning round he was astounded, smiling at him was Corrina Jade, laughing she remarked, "I thought it was you, hello Henry Swan Jenson are you stalking me?"

Gobsmacked, he stuttered back, "Corrina Jade it, it, it, it, is you."

"Oh, you haven't forgotten me then?"

"How could I forget those beautiful blue eyes, anyway I think you must be stalking me, you cheeky sod, everywhere I go you turn up flashing that smile."

There came a nudge and a cough from Cornelius, "Aren't you going to introduce me to your friend then?"

"Oh I'm sorry Cornelius this is Corrina Jade, Corrina this is my very good friend Cornelius."

"Corrina Jade are you on your own?" enquired Henry.

"No, I'm with the crew."

Cornelius interjected, "What do you mean by the crew?"

"I work for BA, they are the people I work with, you know, cabin crew."

"So, where are the crew?"

"They are sat over the back of the room deciding if they want anything to eat."

"I recommend the bangers and mash," Cornelius prompted.

Henry smiling, asked her, "Corrina can I get you a drink?"

"Oh thank you Henry, if you don't mind I'll have a Bud please."

"You said you wanted to do long haul, it's obvious you got your wish then, how often are you over here?"

"This is a regular trip for me, now you know why I'm here, tell me what you are doing here so far from home?"

Henry had a moment when he remembered how his mum had met his stepdad Mathew, forgetting his diffidence of the past he explicated, "Well Corrina Jade you may have guessed I have left the family business, like you I'm following my dream and you know what; she is sitting beside me."

"Behave yourself, silly bugger tell me what you are really doing here?"

"I've told you I'm here to follow my dream Corrina Jade, and you know what, I really have found my dream."

"In what way?"

"I'm looking at her."

She looked at him steadfastly before breaking into a smile, "Henry I'm flattered but you're embarrassing me."

"Corrina Jade, I don't mean to embarrass you however I have thought about you and the first time we met, since then, we have been ships that pass in the night, so to speak."

"Henry this is only the second time we have spoken to each other; it seems as though you are making fun of me, I think you should tell me the real reason you are sitting in a bar three and a half thousand miles from home."

"First things first, I have to say you look even more beautiful than you did when we first met in Cardiff."

"Henry are you telling me I didn't look too good that night?"

"Oh Corrina, I did not say that at all, no way, I wouldn't be so rude."

"I know you wouldn't, thanks for the complement, now tell me what you really are doing in New York?"

"Corrina before I do, I must reiterate how beautiful you look."

"Henry stop it you silly bugger, I want to know how come you're here, tell me?"

Henry couldn't remember if on the night they first met in Cardiff if he actually told her his plans for the future, thus he quietly outlined what had gone before.

"Do you remember when we first met in Cardiff the week before opening day of the first shop? I'm not sure whether I told you my dream was to live in America, anyway in Wales I opened another two shops before moving on to Scotland. There, I spent a further eighteen months based in Edinburgh, which is where I saw you in Queen Street. I went on to open a total of four shops there, Job finally achieved, I resigned from the family business to follow my dream, and here you are."

"Stop it, you nut case."

"I am only saying it as I see it."

Blushing again because she was a little discomfited by his boldness she answered, "This is amazing you lived in Edinburgh for eighteen months and we only saw each other once, and yet here we are in New York and we have seen each other twice."

"Edinburgh is a big city it's unbelievable that we actually caught sight of each other at all."

"Yes, I suppose you're right, it's even more amazing how we have come across each other twice, in this even bigger city."

A young woman came over to speak to Corrina, "Corrina, the crew are thinking of going somewhere else to eat, are you coming or are you staying with your newfound friends?"

"Jesse this is Henry, someone would you believe, the first and last time was in Cardiff, where Henry kindly walked me back to my hotel."

"Hello Henry, I'm Jesse, blimey Corrina what were you doing in Cardiff. You have to tell me more I'm all ears?"

"Hello, pleased to meet you Jesse, this is my best friend Cornelius can I get you a drink?"

"Hi Cornelius, nice to meet you and thank you Henry I'll have a bud please."

The four of them chatted for about an hour, during which time more than a couple more Buds were consumed before the girls and the other crew members, who were intent on doing a pub crawl, moved on. Before they left, Henry took Corrina to one side, "Corrina Jade here's my number, next time you are here phone me and perhaps we can meet up again, obviously, only if you would like to."

"Henry I would like that very much."

She kept looking back, her smile lighting up her face waving as she walked away, Henry could not take his eyes of her until she was out of sight.

Cornelius watched his friend staring down the street asking him, "You like her don't you? I would say a lot, I'll tell you something else, she likes you a lot."

"What gave you that impression?"

"I saw the way she looked at you."

Henry never prone to counting his chickens admitted he did like her, however; he brushed aside the comment made by Cornelius, believing he may have frightened her away because of his own comments about her being the one he had been waiting for, his dream for the future.

Chapter 22

Henry never was the type of man who let his feelings overtake his thought processes, nonetheless, his unexpected meeting with Corrina held a profound effect within him, deeply penetrating his innermost emotions, previously his amatory interludes had never even scratched the surface of his feelings, due to his hard bitten enamelled attitude towards anything that would interfere with the goals he had set for himself. Certainly, any possible worthwhile romantic notions, except for one, had been of a cursory nature which never tested his resolve or moved him enough, to deter him from his chosen path.

Until now, the one truly romantic part of his life was when he met his Welsh girlfriend Ceinwen. He was attracted to her because of her obvious good looks in fact she was beautiful and she allied to a similar outlook on life as him-self, she was strong minded and ambitious she knew exactly what she wanted out of life: and was prepared to work hard for it. At the time, he believed he had fallen in love, however when the issue of Ceinwen joining him in Edinburgh arose, she declined, in fact she hoped to persuade Henry to return to Cardiff. Within a couple of weeks of Ceinwen returning to Cardiff, she disappeared from his thoughts completely.

Meeting Corrina again unsettled Henry in a way he had never before experienced. He began to think about her at odd times, for no apparent reason she would just enter his thoughts especially while alone during his more reflective moments, when problems which had beset him during the day began to relinquish their strangle-hold on his tired mind. Before going their separate ways, he had given Corrina his phone number on the off chance she might contact him next time she was in town, he was also disappointed with himself because he had not taken the opportunity to make a definite arrangement to meet up with her. Surprise had been the element that had caught him unaware, never expecting to get the opportunity to speak to her again.

Once again Henry tried to put aside any thoughts of a romance, preferring to stay focused on his work, but thereby lay a problem as Corrina became a constant companion in those thoughts. Nevertheless, His thoughts were quite often negative, believing she would be having too much of a good time with her friends and probably wouldn't bother to make contact with him, again why should she? Despite the misgivings and contradictory thoughts he was experiencing deep down he knew she was the special one, the one he had always hoped would one day be a permanent fixture in his life, nevertheless for the time being, he understood their paths might never cross again though he hoped their paths would cross again for the meantime he would attempt to place all those thoughts on the back burner of his mind.

Henry needed something to take his mind off Corrina, from a very young age he had been able to focus on the goals he had set for himself, however, now he was finding it extremely difficult to direct his thoughts and attention on the things that he should have been concentrating on. Four weeks went by and despite not hearing from Corrina she remained very much in the forefront of his thoughts always the optimist given the circumstances of their first meeting allied to the more transitory sightings and subsequent meetings, Henry really hoped she might at some point get in touch. Another four weeks drifted by, Henry was beginning to give up on ever seeing Corrina, to some extent it depressed him. Eventually three more months had evanesced, Henry had all but given up on ever meeting up with Corrina, at least by then he was able to put her to the back of his thoughts, that is, if you consider thinking about her only when he wasn't working, was putting her to the back of his mind. However, in his more pensive reflective and lonely hours at night his thoughts of her were an irreversible surging cascade of hostile raging river water, crashing down a steep waterfall creating a vortex of confused notions of possibilities and potentialities commixed with the likely ever-expanding improbabilities of which Henry had difficulty unscrambling from his mind.

Henry was desperate to meet up with her, so much so, he even made enquiries with the airline she worked for but unfortunately their company policy would not allow them to disclose any personal information concerning one of their employees. Henry was at that point determined, enough was enough, he would have to forget she ever existed: however difficult. Nevertheless, he resolved Corrina would have be stored permanently in the vaults of his memory bank, because of this his best friend Cornelius advised that they should both take a vacation. Although initially reluctant to the idea, he wasn't offered an option to refuse, Cornelius in his wisdom booked two rooms at the Embassy Suites on International Drive in Florida. They were going to Disney world, Henry couldn't argue, thus a two week break to visit Disney World was booked. Renting a car they shared the driving, covering two thousand kilometres from New York in three days. They were determined to fly back to New York which would allow them time to enjoy their vacation until the last possible moment. Henry at last, had to admit he seriously needed this holiday to get away from every-day life for a while. During their time in Florida both he and Cornelius had a whale of a time, daylight hours spent in the various parks followed by evenings visiting the hottest nightspots and of course overindulging in the delights of local alcoholic beverages. The vacation was never going to be a complete panacea for Henry but it's therapeutic value was invaluable, by the time he managed to crawl into his bed each night tiredness and or intoxication dulled his mental faculties, making what little sleep he managed was deep and Corrina free. Each morning he could feel the crunching sound crashing like thunder through his brain as he ate his breakfast cereal, each mouthful sounded like a car being driven over a gravel pit. Two Paracetamol would follow.

We have all been there, the vacation its expectations and excitement begins, then in the blink of an eye, you are homeward bound. For most people back to the routinely traffic laden banal daily schlep to an equally mundane humdrum workaday, completed with a mind-numbing commute home, usually to the warmth of a family: Sadly Henry's family consisted of an empty apartment.

At Miami international airport, Henry and Cornelius stood waiting in a queue at the check-in desk for their flight home to New York. Henry watching idly at the throngs of passengers milling around, in what appeared to be chaotic disorder. He drifted into a sort of mesmeric daydream, probably the result of two weeks where sleep had been a commodity in short supply, the result of consuming vast quantities of alcoholic beverages. Both men badly needed sleep. Something suddenly jolted him from his soporific state, his eyes attempted to focus through the chaotic crowded airport entrance hall as a group of people in flight uniforms walked towards the exit, he couldn't quite make out for certain who they were but he was positive Corrina was one of them. He tried to make his way across the busy departure lounge, desperately hoping it was her and hoping to speak to her, sadly he was too late, whoever it was disappeared with the rest of the crew into the crew lounge. Cornelius pulled him back informing him they were required to board the plane for their flight back to New York. Though feeling doleful, Henry ever a pragmatist believed there is a reason for everything, he understood there would never be a future for him and Corrina: she had obviously forgotten all about him. To be fair why would she be bothered? Henry had enjoyed her company for a just five precious hours, *Mistakenly,* he thought, no hoped, Corrina also enjoyed those five hours.

During the flight home to New York, despite his disappointment he and Cornelius drank a bottle of champagne; however, Henry's mind drifted back to Miami airport his matter-of-fact approach to life began to desert him, his thoughts vacillating, maybe Corrina had not had the time, perhaps she had encountered problems, some difficulties preventing her return to New York. Of course, there was always the possibility she had been transferred to the Miami flight, so maybe, just maybe he was misinterpreting the reason she hadn't been in touch. Feeling more reposed pushing himself back into his seat, slowly sipping his champagne from a red 16 oz solo-cup through his clouded thoughts he reasoned, hopefully, maybe, he was mistaken concluding the girl who had caught his attention in the airport was probably a complete stranger. Reaching that conclusion permitted him to relax enjoy the flight. His pragmatism took over again, why or what, when and if, whatever the reason he would accept. What will be, will be; his pragmatism had effectively won through.

Chapter 23

When he moved to America, he never realised, or envisaged how once the initial euphoria of his boyhood dream commixed with excitement of new surroundings inviting him to new a way of life and it's rich culture would affect him. He completely embraced Americans and their way of life.

His days were extremely busy; however, evenings once he closed the door to his apartment were filled with loneliness, homesickness besetting him quite severely: he missed his family. Wheresoever and whenever he had been away from his family for any length of time previously, if he felt the need of emotional sustenance, his remedy would be to get in his car and drive home. One welcoming hug from his mum, a home cooked meal and an evening with his siblings was the panacea that filled him with warmth, mentally, physically and emotionally. Sadly, living three and a half thousand miles away travelling back every time he felt lonely, realistically, was impossible in agreement. Cornelius would often use an American colloquialism which determined it would be like trying to (Scratch your ear with your elbow.)

The vacation thanks to his best friend Cornelius had been a welcome distraction, back home in New York he felt refreshed, stronger, mentally he was in a better place. For him to succeed in his quest to be part of the American dream, any thoughts of Corrina must take a back seat and he could concentrate solely on his career. Henry reconciled himself to the fact it was highly improbable he would ever meet Corrina again, there was a tinge of sadness to his thoughts, nevertheless, despite knowing very little about her he knew instinctively they shared an affinity. It was uncanny because that affinity had drawn him to her, therefore, he would never be able To completely eradicate Corrina from his mind; she had turned his head. Occasionally in his more reflective moments his musings would entertain thoughts of what might have been had Corrina, contacted him.

Henry kept in touch with his family via the wonders of face time, he had only been home a week when he received a call from Caro asking if she and her husband to be Lindsey could visit him, she was keeping her promise made at the airport just before he boarded his flight to New York. Henry could not contain his delight he and Caro were very close, he adored his younger sister, his reply obviously in the affirmative. The silver dollar she had given him as a good luck charm before he boarded his flight to New York, was always in his pocket.

The day of the visit arrived, Henry was waiting for them at the airport, I have chosen Mark Twain's analogy to describe Henry's emotions, at that time whereby he expounded, (his heart was light and his anticipations high). Having Caro and Lindsey visit, would completely dominate Henry's attention eclipsing any thoughts of Corrina Jade, at least for the two weeks.

Holding the position of vice president in the vast organisation MSCI, afforded Henry many privileges, of which he had used very little till now, he made full use of them to give Caro and Lindsey not just a good time, he gave them a wonderful time. He could not have been more excited having them in his new home, showing them the sights of New York and his beloved Greenwich Village. He could not do enough for them, wining and dining in his favourite hostelries, introducing them to American football by going to the game, buying them New York Giants shirts and caps, he also bought them for Jude, Myles and Lindy; the sizing he left to Caro.

Henry had started to acquire an American accent which was immediately seized upon by Caro calling him cowboy. Caro wanted to know everything about his life in America and how he was coping without the family, however she offered him one question he wasn't expecting that concerned his love life, had he got himself a girlfriend? He would only admit to her that although he enjoyed time with a lot of girlfriends, they were just that, friends, there was no one special. He deliberately refrained from mentioning Corrina Jade because he had given up any hope, he would ever see her again. Despite his dubiety, he still thought about her; however unlikely he still hoped she would call. Caro looked him In the eyes. She knew there was something he wasn't admitting to, growing up they had forged a very close sibling relationship. She didn't delve deeply by asking too many questions of her older brother and his romantic attachments, however his denial and his lowered eyes indicated tacit untruth. Caro was certain there was someone he liked she wondered why he behaved so recondite, what had gone before to make him so guarded. She had to steel herself to hide her concern for him, sadness engulfing her—for him.

During the nine months Henry had resided in his adopted homeland feeling alien had never been a problem, America was his home, the home he loved he had no intention of moving back to England, nevertheless, the time he enjoyed with Caro and Lindsey brought home to him, how much he missed his family. One evening before a night of wining and dining they talked a lot about their younger days; many memories were shared. Within all families, there are good and bad times, in that respect they were no different to any other family, only the Swan Jenson family more exaggerated. Caro had silhouetted in passing one or two episodes which had occurred but she never gave full testament, preferring to divulge the family history a little at time when reasons demanded. Lindsey listened in disbelief at some of the exploits attributed to his future father in-law, but there he was listening to a saga one which would read like episodes written for an Australian soap, completely unbelievable…

Happily, Henry and Caro were old enough to see the lighter side of family life, mainly because their mum Mary was happy, having found a man who adored her, adoration she reciprocated, a love completed with the arrival of baby sister Lindy. Nevertheless, there was always the possibility something would occur to disrupt the status quo, namely their dad Frank who was the cause of many; actually, most of, no all of the family problems but they had to admit; a very good father to all his children.

Henry noted, "We haven't heard anything untoward in the last couple of years have we? How long is it four, five years maybe, longer?"

Caro with a grin on her face explicating, "Perhaps he's grown up at last."

"Mmmm, we can only hope."

Although Peace reigned within the Swan Jenson family, Caro laughingly offered.

"Yes, but I wonder how long it's going to last."

Henry knowing full well what she meant replied with a hint of sarcasm, "Who knows, but you do have to wonder if there are any more surprises likely to rise to the surface, you know brothers and sisters we don't know about, not to mention angry husbands or boyfriends knocking on the door."

Caro, replying, "Blimey, no, I hope not but I wouldn't be a bit surprised if someone did arrive on the doorstep purporting to be another of his children."

"To be honest Caro I think by now we would have known if there was any more don't you? It has been quite a few years since the last incident."

"Mmmm, Maybe, maybe not, let's hope the latter, talking about Dad do you remember Barney Phillips?"

"How could I forget after what he did to Dad, strangely he became a friend, he was very helpful to me while I was working for Jenson's what's he up to?"

"Well here's a shock for you, him and Cherry are an item again, they have even bought a house together."

Astonished Henry spluttered, "You've got to be Joking, she didn't want him anywhere near her, didn't she threaten him when Dad gave him a job that if he ever looked at her sideways he was out?"

"She did but apparently he has completely changed, Dad has even made him a roving manager."

"A roving manager what's that?"

"If a manager leaves or goes on holiday, he fills in, according to Dad it's working a treat, he goes everywhere, all of the shops."

"Wales and Scotland, does he go there?"

"Anywhere."

"Wow how's he coping with Myles?"

"He treats him like his own, a second dad, you wouldn't believe the difference in the man."

"Blimey I'm glad things have worked out for him."

"You know it's surreal, when you think of what happened five years ago they were enemy's, now he's one of Dad's most trusted employee's, and not only that, he's become part of the family."

"Caro, Lindsey, lets enjoy the rest of the evening, enough is enough we'll put the family to bed for tonight, finish your drinks and I'll take you for dinner, two more days and you will be homeward bound, I'm going to miss you both."

"We all miss you Henry especially me, don't forget I'm getting married next March, you will be there won't you?"

"Baby sister of course I'll be there, I wouldn't miss it for the world."

"Mum and Dad were worried you might not have the time, plus considering the distance you will have to travel."

"Caro if you were getting married in the Antarctic, I would be there with my snowshoes polished, I won't get back for Christmas though, we will be too busy at work, but never fear I'll be back for your big day."

"Henry I'm chuffed to bits and it will come as a relief to all the family, especially Mum."

"Come on you two drink up, let's go to dinner," Henry encouraged.

Henry loved having his sister Caro and her intended Lindsey, sadly their stay came to an end far too quickly, it seemed the two weeks were over before they had started.

With a heavy heart, Henry watched them go through to the departure lounge at the airport. He loved his sister believing she had found a man who he knew would look after her, furthermore an added bonus Henry and Lindsey liked each other. The next time he would see them would be when he was home for Caro's wedding. Chapter 25 Once Caro and Lindsey had returned home it took some time for Henry to acclimatise to being on his own again, his recipe for negating the feeling of loneliness, as always was to immerse himself into his work and enjoy the things his adopted home offered. He was popular amongst his peers accruing a wide circle of friends who made it easy for him to feel at home and be a part of the American culture.

He fulfilled another of his American dreams he decided to buy an American classic car. Tired of continually using cabs he searched through the used car columns of various papers for a suitable model, however over a working lunch talking to Cornelius about his preferred car, Cornelius astounded him remarking, "If you want a classic, I have a 1957 Ford Fairlane I rarely use mainly because it's always in the garage being repaired if you are interested I'm sure we can come to an arrangement."

"Wow! Really you have a Fairlane?"

"Come and look if you like we can do a deal, but I'll warn you the engine often needs some TLC."

"Cornelius, when?"

"This evening after work?"

"Is it in working order at the moment?"

"Put it this way, maybe, we shall see."

Later that evening, Henry as arranged met with Cornelius to take a look at his Fairlane and if possible, take it for a test drive. He took one look, it was almost a love at first sight story, there before him was Henry's idea of the perfect American classic car turning to Cornelius he advised, "I'll take it how much do you want?"

"Henry are you sure, you really should test drive it?"

"Cornelius how much do you want for it, it's perfect?"

The price was no problem, they shook hands; deal done Cornelius was glad to be rid of it, stating, "It's had been a millstone round my neck."

Occasionally there would be mechanical problems, Henry could cope with its idiosyncratic variances of the engine he didn't care how many times it had to be garaged, it was his pride and joy believing it Americanised him even more.

Chapter 24

After living in New York for ten months, Henry felt his adjustment to American life was complete when he met a talented aspiring young actress, twenty-year-old New Yorker Heidi Swan; her stage name, she was working with a local theatre company, a woman who without doubt rang his bell very loudly. She was very pretty with hazel brown eyes, he never knew the real colour of her hair as she changed it every week blue, green, orange, red you name it, she would wear it. Her outgoing character was the very antithesis of his own attracted him to her, he loved her flamboyant nature, her spontaneity and she was endowed with a wicked sense of humour which most people would, if they didn't know her personality, could and sometimes did, take offense; nonetheless she was fun to be with, their dispositions may have been at odds, but Heidi made him laugh. Meeting her affected him to such an extent any thoughts of Corrina Jade attenuated almost disappearing, from his mind.

Henry's romance with Heidi blossomed rapidly and energetically from a quiet first date into a destructive fireball of dust, gas and vapor that could be akin to splitting of the atom; a nuclear explosion. Two months into their relationship Heidi agreed to move into his flat. It was then that their traits of personality started and begun to get the better of them.

Heidi liked to party, party a lot, Henry found her boundless energy exciting he fully enjoyed the razzmatazz life style she embraced. Her attitudes were very direct, though some kind people would say candid, others downright rude, nevertheless her avant-garde friends were mostly of the same ilk, interesting, amusing, provocative, self-indulgent or as he preferred to describe them, eccentric. The whole thespian ethos to which Heidi subscribed was new, furthermore, strange to him, Initially he was exhilarated by the boisterous over the top characters, she associated with, most nights after the curtain came down at the theatre company where she worked, she would go for a drink because Heidi was often buzzing after the evening's performance needed to wind down, inevitably there would be other cast members joining her, each and every one of whom would be on an adrenalin fuelled high. Invariably their conversation would turn to how they perceived the evening performance had been received by their audience. Understandably after a while, he found her constant partying tiresome and the whole thespian circus irksome, wishing he and Heidi could spend some quality time alone. His love for Heidi was obvious to everyone who knew him, strangely though he never felt the love he gave her, was fully returned. Henry began to realise her dreams and ambitions were far removed from the small theatre company she worked for, he recognised him-self in her when he was the same age, completing his studies at university to follow his own dreams and ambitions which, he was now fulfilling. Always remembering his dad's analogy for hard work (if you don't dig the well you never get to drink the water) thus he had dug his own well; deep.

His love for Heidi was intense, but he began to tire of the continual helter-skelter lifestyle she followed, they never seemed to be alone except in their bedroom or on a Sunday. On a typical day, Henry would rise early, Heidi on the other hand stayed abed till mid-afternoon, leaving for the theatre early evening to get ready for the later performance, often as late as twelve o'clock before she emerged from the stage door. On Saturdays, Heidi had a matinee which meant two performances followed by the usual party, hence the reason Henry loved Sundays, he and Heidi would breakfast together, then enjoy an afternoon at the ball game if the Giants were at home, followed by quiet dinner together, Heidi was usually too tired by then to party so an evening cosying up on the sofa watching television would be the order of the day, while enjoying a few glasses of wine.

Henry Knew in his heart their affair was not a forever kind of love, thus, it came as no surprise when Heidi accepted an offer to take the lead role in a romantic comedy, sadly for him she would be touring for six months across a large number of states. Henry, though extremely pleased for her, ultimately found it difficult to accept the idea, he believed, he would never see her again.

Before she left, she had three solid weeks rehearsing in preparation for the tour she was about to embark on, during which time she became a stranger. Henry's dogged outlook on life once again took over, he helped Heidi on to the bus and waved her good-by; watching the bus disappear down the road. Before she left, they had spoken at length Heidi insisting she loved him and would write every week. Henry just knew deep down in his heart it was a chapter in his life completed, the last page had been turned. As he watched her leave, looking up to the sky shaking his head, "Alone again," went through his mind. Nevertheless, despite the unrelenting partying and incessant noise and of course the multitude of her histrionic friends, he would miss Heidi a lot: but life goes on as they say. In spite of her promises to write every week to keep him in the loop with her progress, Henry received only one letter from Heidi, the contents read.

Henry I'm having a great time the tour is going well, we are getting wonderful reviews so more dates have been added, we could be on the road for a year or maybe even more. Hope you are well, Heidi.

The last sentence appeared to be an afterthought making it very clear to him there was nothing to indicate she would be returning.

Christmas day arrived, Cornelius invited him to have Christmas Lunch with his family which Henry accepted and enjoyed immensely, Cornelius and his family welcomed him into their home as if Henry was one of their own. The rest of the Christmas period came and went, the loneliest time he ever experienced since arriving in New York, he missed Heidi, but Skype and face time eased the loneliness a little, allowing him to speak with all his family especially his mum and Caro. He received a card from Heidi postmarked Lincoln Nebraska just wishing him the usual happy Christmas and good luck for the New Year, that was the last communication he received from her.

Chapter 25

Late March, Henry flew home to be with the family for the wedding of his sister Caro to her fiancé Lindsey, there had always been a very close brother and sister relationship between them, their mental capacities and ideas were not just similar; almost conjoined: twin like. She like Henry had excelled at school and likewise university she was now a very successful accountant. As soon as she saw her brother, Caro knew instinctively that despite his outwardly carefree mien, hiding under it lay a tired sadness, she believed something had gone wrong in his American life, she took him to one side asking, "Henry, I think you should tell your little sister what it is that's troubling you?"

"What makes you think something is wrong?"

"Henry, we have laughed and cried together, I think I know you better than anybody else, what is wrong? Tell me?"

"I don't know why you're asking, but honestly, there really isn't anything wrong in fact generally life in New York couldn't be better."

"Come on Henry something has happened, tell me, if you can't tell me, who can you tell?"

Henry pulled her to him, arms wrapped around her, explaining softly, "Caro my lovely baby sister, I promise you everything is tickety-boo, honest injun."

"I take it, what you said, honest-injun is an American expression?"

"Yer darn tootin it is."

"Stop it, you barmy bugger."

"Caro little Sis, I'm still wondering, why you asked me such a question?"

"Brother because you seem preoccupied, distant even, it's not like you."

Henry again reassured her he was on top of the world he was problem free, Caro answered, "Honest-Injun."

"Sis, where on earth did you get that expression from?"

Shaking her head she replied, "Okay, okay I believe you."

The conversation with Caro had the desired affect dragging him from his self-induced morbidity, Henry had a wonderful time during the ten days he spent with his family, a distraction which came at the right time facilitating the elimination of all thoughts of Heidi.

On his return to New York rejuvenated, Henry was completely free of any romantic interest. He put what little personal items and clothes Heidi had left behind into a case, assigning it to a closet in the spare bedroom for now, knowing full well he would eventually have to dispose of them: she was never coming back. He was back to his best, able to concentrate on matters of more importance to focus on.

Cornelius, sad, felt for Henry, he understood the heartache of lost love and was more than happy to see his best friend back in circulation. Best friends back on the town and boy did they rip it up as neither of them were attached romantically, they played the field, enjoying relaxing, fun evenings.

The unexpected can be wondrous phenomena, which can change your life out of all recognition, altering your whole perspective on disappointments and, or perceived victories and failures…

It was during one of those warm early summer evenings, while Henry and Cornelius sat on high stools against a hotel bar, sipping refreshing mint juleps, their favourite summertime drinks, they chatted with friends, quietly putting the world to rights and shared anecdotes, interspersed with a few rather unsavoury jokes, when the unexpected occurred. Cornelius suddenly stopped laughing, his face wide eyed with a look you could only describe as amazement, pointed to something over Henry's shoulder. Henry half turned on his stool to see what Cornelius was gawping at, he had to take a second look to apprehend the sight before him, when he grasped the situation, he was stunned, his eyes opened wider than the Atlantic Ocean, his jaw dropped, his heart racing faster than a F1 racing car speeding round Silverstone race circuit. He felt like his blood pressure was blowing off the scale, the one person he never ever expected to see stood before him, wearing her flight attendants uniform smiling, her smile lit up the room, "Hello Henry, hello Cornelius."

Stuttering an answer, "H-h-hello Corrina Jade," Henry's face creased into the widest smile, "how are you, where have you been?"

"I'm good and it's a long story how are you?"

"I'm really good, but even better for seeing you again."

"Awwww that's nice of you."

"Corrina, you look more beautiful each time we meet."

"Henry you say the nicest things."

"Your beauty captured me way back when we first met in Cardiff and nothing has changed, your blue eyes and smile still lights up the room, I mean it."

"Thank you for the compliment, kind sir."

"Corrina, I mean every word, can I get you a drink?"

"Yes please, I'll have the same as you, whatever it is, it looks nice."

Cornelius ordered them all another mint Julep, asking, "Are you on your own."

Just then another young woman came over, also wearing her uniform, "No I'm not, meet my new best friend Maggie."

"Hello Maggie," Cornelius enquired, "where's Jesse and the crew?"

"The crew have gone up to their rooms, but they will be down when they have showered as for Jess she has left, she's getting married."

Henry couldn't catch his breath he just kept staring at her, his heart beating at a pace, it's a wonder he didn't have a coronary.

"Henry what's the matter is there something wrong? you look as if you're about to blow a fuse."

"Corrina Jade you really do look beautiful and I have to admit you've been constantly in my thoughts, I can't believe you're here, I honestly believed I would never see you again."

"To be honest I wasn't sure when or if I would ever be back."

Henry managed to take control of his excitement, enough to let his brain and his mouth function properly to ask, "Why is there something wrong?"

"Henry I'll tell you later I need to get out of this uniform, look after my drink please." Then she asked Maggie who was talking to Cornelius, "Are you coming with me to get changed."

"Yes, I could do with a shower, let's go and get changed."

They made their way up to their room. Henry, still somewhat in a state of shock though extremely happy, chugged down his drink urging Cornelius to do the same. Cornelius remarked, "Are we in for a night of celebration? If we are slow down, we don't want to crash to early, you'll be fit for nothing calm down."

"Okay point taken, I'll take it easy from now on."

Staring at the bottom of his empty glass, Henry Inhaled deeply, half a dozen times until he felt more settled and calmer, he began to reflect, absorbing the surprise of the preceding half hour. Only three times had he held conversations with Corrina Jade over a period of four years, yet, he felt a natural force of nature instinctively and inherently passionate, binding him to her. Recollecting those previous two meetings realisation dawned on him, from the moment they first met in Cardiff, love had brushed gently into his thoughts, he was aware that even the occasional sightings of Corrina had unwittingly inflicted a state of abstraction, which occupied his late-night contemplations of her. Still sat on a high stool, and oblivious to the noise emanating from friends and other hotel patrons his head reeling in a state of confusion, he began meandering through recollections of those meeting and occasional sightings he enkindled a conclusion. A conclusion that since that first meeting lain lodged but shrouded in the back of his mind was now obvious, from their first hello, love had begun to unconsciously grow, with each subsequent meeting serving as a fertiliser: he was in love.

"Hello where were you then Henry?" the question snapped him sharply out of his reverie. Stood smiling in front of him was Corrina.

"Sorry, I didn't mean to be rude."

"You were miles away, penny for them unless you think I'm nosey?"

Remembering the story of how his mum and her husband Mathew's first meeting happened, again inhaling deeply, he summoned up enough courage to venture his thoughts, "I think I should tell you something important?"

"Mmmmm, I'm intrigued nothing bad I hope?"

"Corrina Jade, you might not like it."

"Henry unless you tell me, how can I judge?"

"I not sure, I might embarrass you; I might embarrass myself, promise me you won't laugh?"

"Oh, Henry what on earth can it be, it can't be that bad, can it?"

"Corrina I think, no, that's not true I don't think, I know and it might come as a surprise, shock even," drawing in another deep breath he continued, "I've fallen in love with you."

"Henry are you serious or are you making fun of me?"

"Corrina I would never make fun of you, it hit me tonight, I actually fell in love with you when we first met in Cardiff."

"But we have never been out together you know, dinner, dancing, cinema?"

"Let's call tonight our first a date."

"I don't know what to say."

"At least, you haven't turned me down, or laughed at me."

"Why would I laugh, I'm flattered beyond belief but it is quite a shock."

"I'm sorry if I've been too forward, too overpowering, it's probably too much for you to take in."

She went quiet, Henry could almost hear her cerebrum attempting to absorb the speech he had advanced, once again he apologised. "I'm really sorry if I have embarrassed you, I know we have only spoken to each other for a couple of hours, but I am in love with you, I want to marry you?"

Before he could finish, she put her finger to his lips whispering, "Shusssh."

"Have I upset you, if I have I'm sorry Corrina?"

Again she put her finger to his lips whispering, "Henry shusssh."

He waited for an acrid response something that might belittle him but it never came, instead she leaned forward gently kissing him on his cheek, "Henry I'm not embarrassed just the opposite, I'm really happy because I've fallen in love with you."

Henry was dumbfounded his heart racing faster than a runaway steam train blowing its quill and louder than the drum section of a heavy metal rock band, he was sure it could be heard above the noise in the bar, stammering a reply he asked, "Corrina did you say you…?"

Before he could complete the, sentence she offered again, "Yes Henry I'm in love with you and I'm so happy you feel the same about me."

Henry still in a state of shock and confusion by her admission volunteered, "Corrina I have had girlfriends but never before considered being close enough to anyone of them to even consider marriage, I know I've found the right person." Corrina reached across took him by both hands, with a tear in her eye softly she reaffirmed her feelings, extolling, "Henry I love you too."

Taking a silk handkerchief from the top pocket of his suit, he gently wiped away the tear, "Corrina we could find a justice and get married tonight."

"I want and would love to get married tonight but I would like my brother Elliot to give me away."

"Whatever you want my darling."

"Trouble is he will never be able to afford the cost of the flight over here."

"Don't worry about the cost I'll pay for him."

"He's married with a daughter."

"Corrina Jade all your family can come, I'll pay for them all, I'm not letting you go again."

"Henry you really are in love with me."

"Corrina I have never felt so alive, I want you so much, anyway what about your dad?"

"I don't know or want to know who or where he is, Mum didn't say much about him, I do know from Elliot he was prone to violence beating her regularly, which is the reason we moved to Edinburgh and changed the family name to Phelps."

"Blimey my dad is a bit of a rogue always seems to be in trouble despite that he never abused any of the family, what about your mum?"

Suddenly she began crying tears rolling down her cheeks, explaining, "Mum died of breast cancer eight months ago, that is why until now I haven't been back, this is my first trip."

Henry, first wiping away her tears gently coaxed her into telling him her sad story, he found a table away from the bar, where she could recount her story in private. Tears dried, she smiled and revisited the past year. "Henry it was the last time we met, I knew Mum hadn't been feeling well for some time, she had found a lump in her breast stupidly refusing to go to the doctor, eventually after me and Elliot badgered her to see a doctor she agreed but I'm afraid her diagnosis came too late. The medical staff at the hospital did everything possible, first operating to remove the lump but it had already spread into her spine, she was in a lot of pain chemo and radiotherapy only made her feel worse."

As she spoke the tears ran down her face again, "Henry the last few weeks were hell, fortunately the powers that be found a place in a hospice. At the end she was so full of drugs, she was barely awake, Henry I watched her die, she didn't know I was there, it was awful I'm only just beginning to accept she's gone forever," Again the tears flooded down her cheeks, she was inconsolable adding, "Mum did everything for me and Elliot, she had a tough time, we were her world and she ours, she gave us love and stability, only to be struck down by that insidious disease, she didn't deserve any of it."

Corrina was heart-broken, obviously hurt by the memory tears again cascaded down her face, the memory as vivid as the day her mum passed away. Henry again wiped the tears from her eyes offering what little comfort he could.

Maggie and Cornelius joined them, wondering why Corrina was so distressed, thankfully they calmed her, slowly the smile returned to her face, "I'm okay now, honest I'm okay."

Maggie gave her a quizzical look, asking, "Are you sure?"

"Honest Maggie, I'm good, I'm really good thanks."

"That's alright then, are you two coming with us and the rest of the crew we're going to a club."

Corrina shook her head, "Maggie I'd rather stay here with Henry."

"If you're sure you're ok, I'll see you later bye."

"Have fun all of you, bye for now."

As they left Corrina reached across holding Henry's hands gently squeezing them she queried, "Did you want to go with them?"

"Why would I? I'm with the one person I want to be with."

"Henry my stomach is churning with butterflies just holding hands is giving me goose bumps, I have never felt this way before, I'm walking on air, trouble is I'm sharing a room with Maggie."

Henry answered quite diplomatically, "If you mean what I think you mean there's no problem we can go to my apartment, I'll bring you back in the morning. Ring Maggie, give her my address and phone numbers."

Corrina leaned across the small table kissing him with such intensity their lips almost fused together, such was their desire; neither of them wanted to let go.

Corrina made the call and collected her overnight bag from the hotel room she shared with Maggie. Stepping out into a warm sultry night Henry hailed a taxi.

Chapter 26

Corrina stared incredulously at the apartment, "Wow this is some flat Henry it's beautiful, how much does it cost?"

"Corrina I can easily afford it, but when it comes to beauty you are the one and only thing of beauty here."

"Awwww Henry, you say the most loveliest of things."

"Just look in a mirror, you will see what I see, beauty staring back at you."

"Henry I love you."

Ten minutes after they entered the apartment Henry's cell phone rang it was Maggie looking out for her friend, checking all was well, "Is Corrina ok, she is my best friend don't you dare hurt or upset her in any shape."

Henry interrupted her antagonistic verbalising, "Maggie I won't hurt her or do anything to upset her, ok, I love her."

Two minutes later she rang Corrina's cell phone, to ask her directly if she was safe encouraging her, "If you feel you're in trouble give him kick him in the balls."

Corrina burst out laughing at Maggie's suggestion, "Maggie Henry will never hurt me, he loves me."

"Ok if you say so but if anything goes wrong if he tries it on, do as I told you kick him in the balls and pull his knob off."

Trying to suppress her mirth at Maggie's obvious concern and disapproval Corrina explained sternly, "Maggie I know you mean well but I'm am happy to be with him, okay let's leave it at that, yes? now say goodnight."

"If you're sure but it won't stop me worrying, it's all happened so quickly, goodnight Corrina?"

Corrina laughing, began relating the conversation she had just held with Maggie when Henrys land line rang, it was Maggie again, "Henry please be careful, remember she is still very raw, still grieving for her mum." Her voice getting more strident as she spoke, threatening, "If you do upset her I'll kick you in the balls myself, is that understood?"

"Maggie, I assure you she is in safe hands, she won't have to kick me in the balls and neither will you honest, she's going to be my wife."

"Be your wife! that's a bit premature isn't it?"

"Watch this space, Maggie May."

"Cheeky bastard, Maggie May indeed."

"Say it as you see it Maggie, goodnight."

Corrina grinning, knowing what her friend might have said, erupted into hysterical laughing mode as Henry recounted the full text of their converse.

Slowly managing to compose herself despite gasping with mirth, she made an attempt to excuse her friend's aggressive vocal attack construing it was her way of displaying concern for her wellbeing.

Henry gently stroking her face spoke softly affirming, "Corrina my darling I understand and I'm glad she cares so much, she is a good friend there's absolutely no reason to defend her. Cornelius would do the same for me given similar circumstances."

Corrina grinning, explicated, "You would have a problem trying to kick Maggie in the balls."

"I could give her a kick up her fanny."

Sporting a quizzical face, she asked, "Henry, what did you say?"

I mean the American version of arse, not what you're thinking, "I'm not prone to cheap or crude expressions."

Grinning, she offered, "I see, but somehow I think she would kick you in the balls before you managed to lift your foot of the ground."

The banter between them, bearing in mind their earlier rather brief encounters, had begun to flower, highlighting and enriching unrecognised emotions which now exposed their obvious intense love for each other. They spoke words of love, yet an embrace had never been forthcoming; all was about to change, Henry pulled Corrina to him engulfing her in his arms enclosing her lovingly, just firmly enough to make her feel safe. The kiss that followed manifested the profound expression of their love their mouths glued by a passionate indulgence which neither of whom wanted to relinquish. Eventually with great difficulty disengaging, Henry reaffirmed his love, "Corrina I have never experienced the sensations that are penetrating my entire body at this moment, I am so in love with you; a love for all time, I want to marry you."

"Henry I love you so much too, if those sensations are like the fiery ones shooting through my veins, we need to do something about it."

Neither one hesitating, another embrace and another kiss of undiluted sweetness, pure nectar, hand in hand they walked to the bedroom.

Love can blossom in the most unlikely situations; however, Henry and Corrina's story deriving from five hours talking and a couple of smiles spanning two continents, three countries, and bridged an ocean, over four years, takes some believing. It was slow combustion which is how their lovemaking began, Slowly with passionate intimate tenderness commingled with a yearning that had gathered unsuspectingly over time. It was just a precursor building into an explosive mix of fervour, lust and desire to be shared, each touch gave a message of the love both of them had been searching for, in their hearts they had found the person with whom they would spend the rest of their lives with: true unfettered love in body and mind they would give totally.

Early hours of the morning they were awakened by yet another call from Maggie checking Corrina was still in one piece furthermore unharmed in anyway. "Corrina you're ok, you didn't have to kick him in the balls then?"

Corrina giggling, advanced her own thoughts, "Maggie I'm safe and you should be the first to know Henry has said he wants to marry me."

"I beg your Pardon?"

"He's said he wants to marry me."

"You must be joking tell me you didn't say yes you've only just met?"

"Maggie that doesn't matter, I haven't said yes, but I'm sure I will, Maggie I love him."

"Wow I'm gobsmacked are you doing the right thing? I would be very wary."

"Maggie to be honest I want to be with him more than anything."

"I'm not being a wet blanket, but you should stop and think things over before diving headlong into marriage to someone you hardly know."

"I know you mean well Maggie, I understand, but honestly I have never felt so happy," just then she heard Henry calling from the bedroom, continuing she added, "Henry is calling. I'm going back to bed."

"Corrina Jade you're sex mad!"

"Maggie, I need him so much, I'll see you later bye."

Lay back in bed they chatted for a few minutes, Corrina drifted into the soft Scottish vernacular she adopted when she felt happy and comfortable with someone, likewise Henry was able to respond, eighteen months of living in

Edinburgh, accepted him as an Edinburgh local. Turning to look at Corrina, he noticed her blonde hair shimmering, her soft blue eyes glistening in the dimness, the happiness in her smile reflected his own inner thoughts, out of the softness of the shadows Corrina giggled to herself, Henry reached over querying what it was amusing her.

"I've got to tell Elliot I'm merrit, 'n' yer the foemaist Jimmy tae see me in the nood."

"I am honoured my future wife to be, but why?"

"Efter ma maws dowi time wi may sae cried faither, th' truth is ae hae neer felt comfy wi' ony Jimmy, neer allowing masel tae fall in loue let ainle see me in the nood."

"Corrina Jade you are beautiful so much so every time I look at you the sap begins to rise."

"Oooooh is it rising noo?"

"It hasn't subsided come here and I'll show you how much?"

"If this is bein in loue ah hae misse oot muckle time."

"Stop talking blue eyes, unless you're going to tell me you love me?"

"Henry Swan Jenson, a loue ye sae muckle."

This time unhindered by first time nerves sensuality prevailed, still tender but the need to fulfil their carnality created an explosive mix of unadulterated animalism. The desire converging into a maelstrom of heightened passionate eroticism defusing only when their bodies were completely satiated.

They rose from the fierceness of their amatory union, awakened by the shrill tones of phone located in the hallway. Henry got out of bed to answer it, the caller was Maggie asking to speak to Corrina, "Are you coming back to the Hotel? we have a flight back to Edinburgh tonight."

"I know I'll be with you as soon as we've had breakfast."

"Breakfast! its nearly five o'clock in the afternoon, what have you been doing?"

"Well Maggie if you don't know I ain't telling you remember I'm with the man I love."

"You greedy Bugger."

While eating a late breakfast in a Diner local to his apartment, Henry gave Corrina a set of keys, "These are for the apartment, it is now your home, our home, it will feel like an eternity until you walk back through the door, my beautiful blue-eyed lover." Corrina's eyes clouded over moistened with tears of happiness, responding softly her voice quivering dropping the Scottish dialect, "Henry I don't want to go I'm missing you before we even say goodbye, but it's my job and It's a job I love doing, my love I can't wait until we are in our home again." Henry's normal, rational approach to life changed dramatically concerning his love life, whereby, whenever a relationship he had previously enjoyed came to a conclusion, his attitude was (que sera sera.) However, on this occasion at the airport saying their goodbyes to each other both distressed at their imminent parting, Henry wiped a tear from his eyes, something he had previously deliberately refrained from with all previous relationships, always holding a stoic calmness which had served him well. He watched Corrina enter the crew lounge, he found himself wiping another tear from his eyes, she turned to wave, forcing a smile she mouthed, "Bye Henry, I love you."

Henry reciprocated by mouthing in return, "Bye Corrina Jade I love you." Maggie had to have her comical input; if you didn't know her you would be inclined to think she was unfriendly as she waved two fingers in his direction, obviously not denoting a victory sign, Henry understood she was attempting to be funny which made him smile.

That same evening, he spoke to Caro and told her he had met someone he liked he enthused about her so much, Caro commented, "You sound as if you've met someone special, how long have you known her?"

"Four years, we met when I was working in Cardiff, and she is very special."

"Oh she's Welsh?"

"No she's Scottish, don't ask, it's an unusual story I'll tell you when I've got more time, I need to phone Mum and let her know?"

"Hang on what's her name?"

"Corrina Jade."

"When are we likely meet her?"

"It's a bit difficult, she is cabin crew member for BA which means she never really knows when she will be home next."

"Oh, moved in has she?"

"When she's in New York yes, does that offend you."

"Henry don't be daft, I can't wait to meet her, I'm really happy for you."

"Thanks Caro, I'll say goodnight, I'm going to speak to Mum now, bye."

Henry rang his mum and went through the same story he had told Caro, only Mary wanted to know more of who she was, asking where and when they would be meeting her, adding, "Henry if she is as loving as Mathew and she makes you happy then I'm extra happy for you."

Henry and Corrina conversed daily via face time, sometimes three or four times such was their certainty of each other. During those conversations they would both declare in no uncertain terms how that love would be fulfilled when they were in the bedroom. Henry's coarse narrative made Corrina blush and squeal with sensual expectancy with Maggie earwigging overhearing one of his indelicate propositions, intervened, she advanced one of her own unedited homespun coarse remarks holding nothing back, her offering, "Henry if you don't stop that dirty mouth of yours, you'll have her playing with herself and for that matter you'll have me at it as well."

Corrina screeching with laughter, "Henry don't take any notice of Maggie, she's jealous, I like what you're telling me I can't wait."

For the next two months in-between Corrina's flights to and from Edinburgh they enjoyed an almost paradisal aliveness, Henry constantly telling Corrina being with her was Edenic, he believed she was his Eve, their apartment the garden of Eden. Like all new young lovers, they rode on cloud nine while drinking love potion number nine, cupid's arrow struck gold—dead centre.

Some weeks later Cornelius and Maggie who were themselves getting very close, discussed how close their friend's relationship had blossomed so quickly. Cornelius made an innocent comment, "Whatever there is between them It's a potent force."

Maggie with her usual colourful, moreover immodest rhetoric offered her own postulation, "Cornelius it's called sex, you know, hanky-panky, coitus, copulation, nooky, screwing, shagging or just plain fucking whatever handle you attach to it, that's your potent force. Corrina walks round wearing the widest smile after a night at home with Henry."

"Come on Maggie, there must be more to it than sex?" he reasoned.

Maggie launched into a contemptuous riposte, advising, "Cornelius I'm joking, you should realise they are in love. I can't see anything ever coming between them, they have become one and the same person, inseparable. I don't know, men; they can't see further than the end of their noses when it comes to romanticism; you're all blind, well mostly."

Cornelius's comment had been nothing but of a friendly nature so it took him by surprise to receive such a berating. He refuted Maggie's vocal attack insisting he had not said anything disparaging. "All I said was they must have something special between them."

Maggie grinning, put her arms around him, "I think you and I have something special don't you?"

"Wow Maggie I like you a lot, but I didn't think you liked me in the same way?"

"See what I mean, romance, you can't see it even when it's staring you in the face waving a fifty foot banner saying, I love you."

Cornelius astounded, at first not fully apprehending what Maggie was admitting, suddenly understood the unambiguous offering, smiling from ear to ear made his own unambiguous reply, "Don't you realise Maggie, I love you too?"

That was the beginning of their own love story, though wonderful it would never attain the roller coaster ride of expectancy and ecstasy, furthermore, overwhelming anguish and despair that would eventually befall Henry and Corrina's love story...

Chapter 27

Henry for the first time in his adult life was able to identify true happiness. Corrina stirred emotions he never imagined were possible, in comparison previous relationships were negative, nothing could shake the fruit off the tree of happiness; he felt blessed to have Corrina's love. If ever he would be subjected to the pain of total severance or long-term separation from her, his feelings were so strong he feared he would be a broken man.

Henry believed they would never be parted so one night when he awoke about two in the morning and reached out to Corrina, she wasn't lay next to him, rubbing his eyes he called out, "Corrina where are you?"

Whispering she said, "I'm over here at the window."

"Why, what's the matter?"

Beckoning him to her she told him, "Nothing. I need to show you something."

Getting out of bed a little bemused, especially when he realised she was stood at the window, completely naked looking up to the night sky, he wondered what it was she wanted to show him. "My blue-eyed darling what am I looking at?"

"Look up there into the sky, what do you see?"

"Stars."

"Yes stars, I feel Mum is one of them, I feel she is looking down on me smiling at my happiness, my happiness is making her happy."

"Which star do you recognise, which one do you think is your mum?"

"It doesn't matter, I feel at peace as if Mum owns the sky, she is watching over me, watching over both of us smiling, she will never allow us to be parted."

They remained for a while, arms around each other watching the night sky, their naked bodies pressed tightly together until the day began to creep over the horizon, filling the room with dazzling sunlight.

"Corrina Jade my blue-eyed beautiful lover, it's time we said goodnight to your mum, I will look up to every night sky from now on, even when your back in Edinburgh and thank her for allowing me to receive so much love."

"Henry my love, I miss these nights they are so precious, when I'm away I think about you all day and dream about you at night, I can't imagine not having you in my life."

"One day I will make an honest woman of you."

"Ooooh Henry, but I like being naughty with you."

"Come here let's see how naughty you can be."

Henry watched Corrina go through to the crew lounge for the flight back to Edinburgh, while doing so he remembered, how his mum loved to narrate the story of the night Mathew had proposed. He knew how much Corrina loved him, over the four years since they met his thoughts and feelings had begun to proliferate, slowly his cognitive processes emerged from his descrambled brain finally aware he had fallen in love.

While she was away, work took precedence over anything and everything, it was the only way he managed to put her out of his thoughts, nevertheless evenings were a time when he felt the full force of loneliness, unable to relax until via face time, they would talk for lengthy periods.

Not a person who was prone to spontaneity unless in business needing a quick decision, he knew instinctively just like his dad when a project or idea would be beneficial commercially. However, affairs of the heart were a different matter he made plans to propose to Corrina properly next time she was home. Leaving the airport he made his way to fifth avenue number 727, the iconic building holding the most famous jewellers in the world, "Tiffany's." Totally out of his depth he took advice from a Tiffany sales professional who took the trouble to educate him in the finer points of diamond engagement rings. After much deliberation, he chose a diamond with a blue sapphires mounted either side of the diamond set in eighteen carat gold; he put the blue box in his pocket, he was set to make his proposal.

In the event, he would either lose his nerve or Corrina would turn him down he never disclosed his plans to anyone not even Cornelius. Henry meticulously planned everything. He booked a room at the New York Edition hotel Madison Avenue, where over dinner he intended to propose hoping to replicate Mathew's proposal to his mum. Strangely the day before Corrina's expected arrival, unlikely as it seemed and despite his careful aforethought, butterfly's began bestirring in his stomach. Throughout life nerves had never interfered in his pragmatic approach to anything; nevertheless, his nerves began to get the better of him. He stood with Cornelius in arrivals, who was there to meet Maggie. Henry not a person who was given to spontaneity, his usual reserved self, began to give way, by the time Corrina's flight landed his excitement had reached fever pitch, his stomach churning to the point of nausea, his nerves were stretched to the limit, like a bow with its arrow waiting to be released to its target.

Corrina eventually emerged from passport control into the arrivals area, he had worked himself into such a frenzy, he couldn't wait any longer, for once spontaneously, despite the crowds and the embarrassment he was about to inflict on himself, not to mention Corrina, his face crimson, shaking like a leaf he stepped forward got down on one knee before her and presented her with the blue box. He began stuttering his oration, "Corrina Jade Phelps, would you please do me the honour of becoming my wife? I love you so much."

His sudden rush of blood, brought the 'rrivals area to an amused standstill as Henry down on one knee waited for the reply he was longing to hear.

Corrina was shocked and somewhat bemused by the reaction of the crowd who all watched and like Henry waited for her answer. She stopped, eyes wide in bewilderment took the blue box, thereupon opening it, she needed a few seconds to assimilate the situation that lay before her, respiring deeply she looked at the ring, her eyes wide with amazement her face efflorescing a smile that gave Henry the answer, whoops, clapping and cheers came from the very large crowd gathered around, all eager to witness the outcome.

Corrina voicing, "Henry Swan Jenson, yes, yes my special man I am honoured to be your wife. I love you so much!"

To more whooping and cheering they kissed, Corrina staring at the ring queried, "Henry my god its beautiful, it must have cost a fortune?"

"Hey blue eyes you are worth a king's ransom, I would give you the moon if I could," then quizzically asking, "lover aren't you going to put the ring on?"

"Oh Henry I am so silly, I forgot."

"If it doesn't fit or you don't like it, we can change it?"

"No way It's beautiful, I would have picked it myself."

As the crowd began to disperse complete strangers offered their congratulations to them. Cornelius shook his hand and gave him a man hug, commenting, "Boy, are you becoming Americanised, you wouldn't have done that six months ago."

"I don't know what came over me, I'm still shaking, I was going to propose tonight when we were alone, but when I saw her coming through passport control I just knew the time was right."

Maggie tearful, hugged them both, only her annotation was more direct.

"Blimey Corrina, it's a good job you didn't listen to my advice to kick him in the balls, you would be still looking for a man, show us the rock then?"

Corrina held out her hand, Maggie for once refraining from a trite platitude sighed, "Corrina it is beautiful, look Cornelius isn't it gorgeous?"

The rest of the crew all expressed their congratulations and the pilot, a guy named Peter propounding they should all celebrate in the nearest bar.

Henry and Corrina sat quietly talking about the future while the crew revelled loudly in glorious gluttony most of them indulging in too many tipples. There would be few sore heads in the morning, thankfully, they were not due to fly back to Edinburgh until late evening the following day. The newly engaged couple slipped quietly away from the tumult of the party to enjoy a champagne dinner at the New York Edition Hotel where Henry had originally planned to propose. Over dinner, Corrina her face still beaming with an incandescent glow stroked Henry's face, "Henry mum will be so happy tonight, I can't wait to look out of our window and tell her."

"My blue eyed darling, when we get home I will thank her again and again for giving me her daughter to love, then I'm going to make love to you all night long."

Henry and Corrina wrapped tightly together woke from the warmth of the cocoon they had created in the bedding, in the early but still dark hours of the morning: It had been a long day. With daybreak still a couple of hours away, they enjoyed more loving when sharing a bath, Corrina was now completely free of any diffidence she possessed before falling in love with Henry; her inhibitions consigned to the waste bin forever. Bathing together attested to their total love for each other they experienced an intimacy of the most indulgent erotic sensual delights, touching and stimulating erogenous zones, coalesced and heightened by the hedonistic desire to pleasure. Drying with soft towels reawakened the need to reconjoin their bodies, returning to bed they reinforced their love with delicate sensorial tenderness admixed with softly spoken seductive words, they reached the ultimate quintessence of love. Both laying back exhausted but contented after their coupling Corrina sighed and sleepily remarked, "Henry if this is love I'm sad."

Puzzled by her observation, Henry whispered, "My darling blue eyed sweetheart why sad?"

"Henry my special man I'm only sad because it's taken four years for us to find each other, the nights of love we share are so special I wish it had happened when we first met in Cardiff, I never realised love could be so wonderful."

"Corrina Jade, we have the rest of our lives to make up for those four years, looking back when we first met the blue touch paper must have been lit enkindling a slow burning fuse and sweetheart each meet has ignited and aroused our passions into an incendiary ball of love nothing will ever extinguish."

"My special man I feel exactly the same, I feel we are one, I feel safe, happiness fills my whole body."

Stepping out of bed Corrina moved to the window to look into the night sky gesturing towards Henry for him to join her, stood naked side by side arms around each other's waists, wrapped in the warmth of the emotions they had just shared, Corrina laid her head on Henry's shoulder, she continued.

"Henry, look into the night see how bright the stars are?"

Kissing her gently he expressed his own thoughts, "Corrina Jade Phelps my darling wife to be, it probably means your mum is showing her approval of me, she is watching over us understanding that although we have a long road to travel she knows we are going to be together for life."

"Oooooh Henry, I haven't felt so happy in a long time, in fact, I don't think I have ever been this happy before?"

"You were obviously very close to your mum?"

"The heartbreak I felt when losing her floored me totally, she was my best friend, she was my mentor I often think about the chats and the laughs we shared. She was there for us, I miss her so much, I wish she was here to meet you?"

"Blimey, not at this moment flashing my meat and two veg."

"Henry you bugger, you know what I mean."

"Sorry my darling blue eyes I couldn't resist, we never met but I'm going to be part of her family, I hope she is happy because I can't thank her enough for giving me her daughter to love."

They watched the sun rise over the New York horizon, its warmth streaming through the glass window.

"Come on blue eyes let's go back to bed, time for some sleep."

"Oh must we?"

"What do you mean must we?"

"Nothing I just thought must we get some sleep."

"Well Corrina Jade Phelps what would your mum say."

"Mum didn't get much loving in her life apart from the love she shared with me and Elliot, I think she's watching and clapping her hands?"

Looking at Henry's nakedness she guessed he was about to deliver another facetious remark, wagging her finger she proffered, "Henry Swan Jenson I didn't say applauding so don't you dare say anymore."

While sporting a wide grin on his face, he replied. "For a minute, I thought I had received a compliment."

"Henry I love you, that's the compliment, let's go back to bed?"

"If we must."

"Stop it you sod."

Chapter 28

Henry to be honest had enjoyed his fair share of successes in business but none of which could possibly compare with its significance, or the pleasurable feeling that overwhelmed him when Corrina accepted his rather theatrical, moreover, flamboyant proposal to become his wife, the most momentous beautiful night Henry ever lived through. Corrina an extremely happy but tearful young woman clung to him like a limpet affixed to the hull of a fishing smack. Painful as it was, they said their goodbyes for another five days or so, she had to work. Looking dreamy eyed at the ring on her finger she asked. "Henry we may have to get married in Edinburgh?"

A little surprised he queried. "Blue eyes why, Edinburgh?"

"I want Elliot to give me away, but he will never be able to afford to come all this way he has his wife Sadie and their little girl Becky they're my family, my only family, It'll break my heart if they're not with me."

"Corrina Jade, whatever it takes or costs I will pay for them all, tell him."

"I don't know, to be honest I think he would be too embarrassed to accept such an offer."

"Ask him, see what he has to say, try and persuade him, give him the excuse that it would be difficult for me to get time off work to travel to Edinburgh, explain that I want him to be involved with all the arrangements, say you'll be disappointed if he doesn't come, say we'll make it a special holiday for Becky, if that doesn't work we will have to think of some other way."

"Mmmmm, I'll give it a try, Henry I'm desperate to make sure they are part of our plans."

"If for any reason, he can't come over here, I will be happy to marry you in Edinburgh."

"Wherever we get married, it will be the happiest day of my life."

"My darling blue eyes wherever we marry, it will be special, I promise."

Before she left for the airport, Corrina ensconced in Henry's arms, cried some more, reiterating she was very happy but very sad to be leaving him albeit temporary.

Bearing in mind Henry's realistic, some would say hard-headed approach to life, tried desperately to contain his feeling as Corrina was about to depart, nevertheless a teardrop trickled slowly down his face. He held her tightly to his chest, whilst gazing lovingly, his eyes clouded with moisture, choked with emotion telling her. "Blue eyes I'm going to miss you dreadfully, I'll be counting the minutes till your home, tonight I'm going to stand in the window, talk to your mum and thank her for allowing me to love you."

"Oh stop it please, I won't go if you keep talking like that."

"Blue eyes I don't ever want you to go, but I know you have things to sort out back in Edinburgh, use your little sister charm to persuade big brother Elliot to come here and give you away, to me."

A doleful cloud befell them when the car to take Corrina to the airport arrived, a long lingering kiss testified their innermost emotions, providing some relief from the pain engulfing them, Henry shed another tear. Corrina wiped it gently away with her thumb whispering. "I love you so much my special man I'll speak to you when I get to Edinburgh."

"Thank god for face time, I'll be by the phone no matter what time you ring I want to see those blue eyes glowing when we say hello."

Waving goodbye as the car drove down the road Henry heaved a heavy melancholy sigh, love had never felt so wonderful, he was missing her before the car disappeared out of sight, it was going to be a long day depressingly, they would all be long day until she was back in his arms.

Henry for the first time in his life understood the emotional turmoil love can inflict on someone's self-determined life, when love hits you right between the eyes. True love is in part hypnotic, mesmeric and truly mysterious in its formulation, transcending anything you may have experienced before; For Henry, true love had arrived.

At work, his concentration deserted him so much Cornelius had to take him to one side and remind him of his responsibilities towards his colleagues who were expecting him to be aware of what was happening in the office. Cornelius explicating. "You have a good job and are the best at that job don't spoil it."

The quiet reasoning offered by his best friend came as a shock to Henry without realising he was putting his job in jeopardy, he acknowledged the advice

Cornelius had given, putting all his energy into his workday which was actually remedial. That remedy took his mind off Corrina until he left his office for home, each evening Henry and Cornelius both required something to soften the loneliness while the girls were the other side of the Atlantic. They chose to visit, thus sample the different craft beers on offer at local hostelries.

One evening while waiting for the phone to ring he lay on the bed staring up at the ceiling unable to apprehend the feelings invading his body and mind, love had hit him like a force ten cyclonic, powerful enough to bring down the New York skyscrapers. He couldn't sleep as the line in Alan Jackson's song advocates, (the workday passes like molasses in wintertime) likewise, his evenings stretched longer and longer and seemingly even longer. He looked up at the night sky. His mood lightened when a shooting star blazed across the sky, he believed Corrina's mum was giving her approval of him. Thankfully, just after five o'clock his cell phone flickered, he answered to Corrina's refulgent smile, her soft blue eyes emitting a resplendence which set his heart pulsating. Blowing a kiss, she giggled.

"Hello my special man did you stand up at the window?"

"Blue eyes I did, I stood as naked as a Jay bird thanking your mum again for allowing you to love me, and would you believe a shooting star scorched across the New York skyline, I understood then she had given her blessing."

"She was probably telling you to stop flashing your bits."

"Nah, she was having a good look checking whether they were good enough for her beautiful daughter."

"My special man she would agree with me they are more than good enough."

"Blue eyes you have made my day, anyway, talking of sex."

Before he could say anymore, a giggling Corrina interrupted. "Don't start I know what you're about to say but Maggie is in the room, she gets all moody when she hears your dirty mouth, she misses Cornelius the same way I miss you."

"I haven't got a dirty mouth."

"you know you have, but I love it."

"Right where shall I begin?"

"Don't you dare it's for my ears only."

"I'll let you get some rest, cos you're not going to get any when you get home."

"Henry stop it I'm getting hot and sweaty."

Maggie interjected, "Yes stop it she'll need a cold shower and I'll need one as well you mucky pup."

"My extra special man, I need some sleep I'll speak to you tomorrow after I've spoken to Elliot, good night and sleep tight lover."

"Good night blue eyes."

The following evening Corrina's face lit up his I Pad, her soft blue eyes spotlighting her vivacity, coruscating a radiance which informed him without asking she was extremely happy. Her opening words proved his thoughts to be correct. "Henry, I'm so happy, Elliot was chuffed when I asked him to give me away, until he realised we would be getting married in New York."

"From your tone, I take it there is a problem?"

"He was at first reluctant to commit because he was worried about the financial implications."

"So what convinced him?"

"I was about to offer to pay as you suggested, when suddenly and I'll tell you in his words, he said, "Sod it we haven't had a holiday since Becky was born this is too important I don't want to miss my little sister getting married I'll find the money from somewhere."

"From what you've said, do you honestly think he will manage; I hope he doesn't go into debt?"

"Well I've told him because I work for BA I can get a good discount on the tickets."

"What did he say?"

"His face lit up asking how much of a discount."

"I had to think quickly without making it too obvious, I said probably 50%."

"Was he happy with that?"

"To be honest he didn't believe me giving me a quizzical sort of look, then informing me in no uncertain terms I don't think so, 50%, no way but if you can get any sort of discount I will grateful."

"Corrina Jade my darling, tell him we can get even better reduced rates through the company I work for."

"I'll give it a try but I know he won't let us pay for all of it."

Henry fell silent for a few minutes to which a concerned Corrina enquired, "is there something wrong you look worried?"

Still looking bewildered he shook his head before suddenly erupting and loudly expelling an afterthought which was unexpectedly employing his mind.

"Oh bloody, bloody sodding hell."

"Henry what on earth is the matter?"

"I haven't told my family I'm getting married, I completely forgot I was so wrapped up in everything, all my friends know but I haven't told my own family how stupid am I!"

"Henry Swan Jenson my special man you have never been and never will be stupid, everybody forgets things occasionally, you should speak to them after we say goodnight, by the way Maggie's not here to interfere so you can talk to me as dirty as you like, I'm all ears my lover."

A further ten minutes of Henry's descriptive love making; the chemical effect of which, had Corrina sighing dreamy eyed and sweating eventually insisting,

"Oooooh Henry please, please stop, I don't want you to but I won't be able to sleep tonight thinking how much I'm going to miss being wrapped in your arms in that king size bed of ours."

"Ok if I must, to be honest I won't be able to sleep myself, I'm going to stand in the window again to thank your mum and watch the sun sink down over the water."

"Henry I miss you so much."

"My darling blue eyes I'll dream the night through as if you are with me."

"Goodnight Henry, you must speak to your mum."

"Goodnight, Blue eyes."

Henry spoke to his mum via facetime, her opening obiter dictum, "Hello Henry, I can see you've got something exciting to tell me, don't keep me suspended in mid-air."

"Mum what makes you think I've got something to tell you, especially something exciting?"

"Henry Swan Jenson, I gave birth to you, I know every expression that emanates from your face, so go on tell me this exciting news?"

"Mum I've asked Corrina to marry me."

Mary squealing with delight asked, "And?"

"Mum, she said yes."

"Wow I said you were excited, I'm excited for you too, so when is this going to happen?"

"We haven't set a date because there is so much to sort out, but, hopefully as soon as possible, It's difficult because of Corrina's work, but I'll keep you in the loop of all the arrangements."

"Son I can't wait to meet her, I can see in your eyes how much you love her."

"Mum you're embarrassing me it's not that obvious, is it?"

"No need to be embarrassed I'm your mum I can just tell these things and if your half as happy as I am with Mathew and Caro is with Lindsay then I'm chuffed for you, wow, wow, I'll have to by a new outfit or two."

"Mum I have some bad news."

"What's the problem?"

"I forgot to tell you that the wedding will be in New York."

"I don't care where it is, me and Mathew will be there, your dad and Elaine too, we will all be there I promise you."

"Phew I thought it might be a problem."

"Son set the date and I'll be there with my boots blacked, actually would you mind if me and Mathew came over sooner, we could meet Corrina before, you as your dad would say, jump the broomstick?"

"Mum you can come anytime, but I'll let you know when she is next home, you can stay in the spare bedroom."

"Good the sooner the better I can't wait."

"Mum thank you, Corrina will be overjoyed when she knows, oh I haven't told Dad yet, it's late, I'll do it tomorrow."

"Henry tell me more tomorrow, I'm going to ring Caro before I go to bed, love you good night Henry."

"Goodnight Mum goodnight."

Henry spoke to Frank the following evening, who showed his delight when promulgating. "I was beginning to think you were gay."

"Why on earth would you think that?"

"Well, you have never brought a girl home, have you?"

"Bloody hell Dad I was busy! first uni, then Cardiff and then Edinburgh I never had time, you worked my balls off! have you forgotten I lived with Cainwen in Cardiff too?"

"We never met her, did we?"

"Dad I still don't get why you thought I might be gay."

"I wouldn't have cared son; I just want you to be happy."

"Thanks Dad, you don't mind travelling to New York then for the ceremony?"

"No problem, let me know when, me, Elaine and Jude will be there with our boots blacked."

"Mum gave exactly the same response, thanks Dad, good night."

Hasty arrangements were made for Mary, Mathew and Lindy to fly out when Henry knew for certain Corrina would be back in New York. To make the arrangement definite Corrina decided to take one week of annual leave to meet with Henry's family. When the arrangements were made, Corrina was excited but extremely worried remarking, "I hope she likes me, some mothers get arsey when their little boys meet a girl."

"Corrina she is not like that, she will adore you as I do."

"Henry I'm going to ask your mum if she will come with me and Maggie to help choose my wedding dress, do you think she might?"

"Blue eyes she will be blown away, in fact she will probably be more excited than you."

"Do you really think so?"

"I'm certain, in fact, unquestionably she will."

"I'm so nervous I hope you're right Henry?"

Mary, Mathew and Henry's youngest sister Lindy, arrived in New York one hour before Corrina was due to arrive from Edinburgh. To say it was an exciting furthermore, emotional experience for them as family underplays the quintessence of joy coursing through his mum's body. Mary, had very little difficulty acclimatising to the fact her son was on the cusp of getting married, she didn't feel 'arsey' as Corrina intimated, she might, but thrilled to be with him, to see the world he had built for himself and of course delighted because he was happy. However, like Corrina worried about meeting her future mother-in-law, Mary was more than a little nervous at the prospect of meeting with her future daughter-in-law.

Nerves were at breaking point for both women when Corrina's plane eventually touched down two hours late. Despite their unease, it was ill-founded, when Henry introduced them, they embraced, Mary held both her hands in hers, looked her up and down then voiced, "I'm Mary Henry's mum this is Mathew my Husband and this Lindy, Henry's sister."

Corrina her voice quavering replied, "Hello Mary, hello Mathew, Hello Lindy this is my best friend Maggie and Henry's best friend Cornelius."

"Oh hello Maggie, Cornelius it's very nice to meet you both."

In unison, they answered, "Lovely to meet you too Mrs Mathew."

Mary continued, "Corrina, now I understand why Henry fell in love with you, you are beautiful. It's so lovely to meet my future daughter-in-law, welcome to the family."

Corrina had gotten so worked up at the thought of how Mary might perceive her, yet overwhelmed by the genuine warmth and affection she felt coming from Mary, she burst into tears. Henry wrapped her in his arms to comfort her, Mary very concerned, questioned. "Corrina why the tears?"

"I'm sorry, I just didn't expect the warm welcome you gave me, I'm so happy to meet you all, thank you."

Mathew added his welcome, "Corrina we are all delighted to meet you, I concur with Mary's felicitations."

Lindy after watching the proceedings offered her own thoughts with a question, "Dad what's felicitations?"

"It means we are chuffed."

"Why didn't you say that? Corrina, I'm chuffed as well."

Feeling more secure she told Lindy, "Lindy I'm chuffed as well." Adding, "Shall we go home? Henry we need to get a cab."

"No I've brought the car."

Mathew's ears pricked up, "What do you drive?"

Corrina interjected, "He's showing off, look at him he's preening himself, he has a 1957 Ford Fairlane, it's enormous, nice though I love it." Adding, "When it's working."

"Take no notice Mathew, she's a cheeky so and so, it is drivable at the moment, I've parked it outside the office, we'll get a cab there first, it's only a short distance."

Mary commented, "Cab, eh? you really are turning American."

Mathew's eyes nearly came out of his head when he saw the Fairlane. "My word that is some motor you got yourself, it's fantastic."

"You can drive if you like Mathew."

"I would love to, but I'll leave it to you for today."

Chapter 29

New York was the city Henry had spent time as a young teenager reading about and researching, he had fallen in love with its voluminous landscape of outlandishly tall buildings which did as their name indicated, they scraped the sky. Lady Liberty had opened her arms to welcome him, allowing him to follow his dream, a dream that was subsequently fulfilling its promise, he had made it his home: it was his home.

Mary and Mathew within very quickly, became aware of the significance of the life, Henry had built for himself, to say they were impressed would be an unqualified understatement; flabbergasted would be a more appropriate expression. His car, his apartment, his beautiful fiancée Corrina Jade, all the friends he had made and of course his prospects for the future appeared limitless; he certainly was like his dad.

He loved moreover, respected his dad, always aspiring to attain the same level of success. When deciding which particular direction, he would follow; especially in business, he was careful in his approach always heedful of evaluating the benefits and its disadvantages. He would often address to himself a quote by Lucy Maud Montgomery (We pay a price for everything we get or take in this world; and although ambitions are well worth having, they are not to be cheaply won, but exact their duties of work and self-denial anxiety and discouragement). Henry believed in this written principle making the quote his bible. To use an American colloquialism, he never made a (horseback opinion) his business strength lay in finding exciting possibilities, moulding them into actualities, he was well aware of how the difference between success and failure could hinge on the smallest of details if neglected.

Mum and Mathew were proud and looking forward to seeing the sights Henry has made home. The nine-hour flight from London, the five-hour time difference plus the hour-long journey to Henry's apartment left the family shattered. Corrina although tired herself encouraged them if possible to keep awake hopefully avoiding Jet-Lag. Henry had planned to take them out for dinner but unfortunately, they were all too tired, the answer of course takeaway Pizza and burgers with a couple of bottles of wine. While Mathew, Henry and Lindy watched several episodes of Sponge Bob Square Pants, Mary and Corrina talked about wedding finery, by nine o'clock, bed beckoned, they needed to hit the pillows before their bodies collapsed. Mary and Mathew were in the spare bedroom, Henry had bought a single put-you-up bed for Lindy, which after a fraught discussion and much to her disgust, was installed in the spare bedroom with Mary and Mathew. Lindy's argued that she wasn't a baby anymore, she was twelve years old she required privacy, plus, her dad snored when he had partaken in few glasses of wine. Her choice of words, which had Henry laughing was, "When he is influenced by intoxication." Mathew of course denied it, but Mary agreed with her daughter's assessment. The bed was moved into the lounge, much to Lindy's delight.

Corrina threw herself across the bed in their room, smiling a smile so wide, so bright, pleasure and blissfulness radiated from her soft blue eyes. Apprising her thoughts of the afternoon's introduction to Henry's family, she remarked, "Henry my special man I'm knackered but getting off the plane this afternoon I was, to put it as delicately as I can, nearly pooing my pants thinking about meeting your mum."

"Bloody hell I'm glad you didn't she might have thought your after-shave was a bit strong."

"Cheeky sod I don't shave or wear after-shave."

"I'm glad I like your beard."

"Henry you bugger; listen to me?"

"Such language and I thought you were a lady."

"You sod you would make anybody swear; listen to me please?"

He answered imitating Humphrey Bogart, "Ok blue eyes tell it as it is."

"Will you stop it?"

Looking peeved but returning to his not so American accent he responded, "Ok, you were saying?"

"Thank you, your mum is lovely she has made me feel part of the family already."

"Do you think she would mind if I called her mum instead of Mary?"

"My darling Corrina Jade I promise you she will be delighted."

"I'll ask her in the morning then?"

"Corrina I think it's time to use that bed properly don't you?"

"Why are you tired as well?"

"I probably will be in a couple of hours."

"Two hours, is that all! are you going off me?"

"You little minx, come here I'll show you."

When two people with an intense emotional attachment are frequently separated for whatever reason, their coming together is often mystical, otherworldly created by a drug known to the human race as Love. Love is the medicinal substance which is the fundamental intrinsic quantity that binds two people together emotionally: harmoniously. Each time Henry and Corrina reunited, their first romantic intoxicating kiss was effused with soft sweet tenderness rising gently to an intemperate passionate state of restless excitement. Each declarative softly spoken word, each intimate touch releasing ethereal sensations consuming their bodies, both fully yielding to rapturous abandon. That night was no exception, wrapped in each other's arms sleep invaded their satiated body's into a dream world.

Corrina waking from a serenely blissful sleep nudged Henry, was already awake, looking up at the ceiling. Feeling snug, warm, soothingly tranquil, she drowsily whispered, "Wow Henry my body is still tingling I've missed you so much."

"Corrina My Blue-eyed, blonde-haired picture of loveliness I'm feeling the same tingling, however; the night is young I think it's time to make our bodies tingle even more."

"Ooooh Henry, you know how to sweet talk a girl."

Contentment pervaded the room, the intensity of which reverberated off the walls and ceiling rousing and inflaming their emotional fervour. Their bodies conjoining, addressing their procreative needs to the full. Lord Byron wrote (could love run forever like a river) Henry and Corrina's love was a fast flowing torrent of a river, rushing inexorably to the ocean, whatever they would face in the future, the river could never run dry.

Later as they always did, they, stood naked at the window of their bedroom clinging to each other looking out at the starry night sky thanking Corrina's mum for bringing them together. Corrina lay her head on Henry's shoulder sighing, "I have never been so happy, I'm in love with the most wonderful man."

"Who's that then do I know him?"

Their love had blossomed, they could engage in humour without taking offence, Henry enjoyed teasing her, "Henry Swan Jenson behave yourself, cheeky sod."

"Swearing Again! you naughty girl Corrina Jade Phelps?"

"Will you behave?"

"I don't want to behave, I want to be naughty with you," he spoke with a salacious look and seductive tone to his voice.

Corrina coquettishly responding, "Hmmm Henry, I have to admit you're good when you're naughty."

"Let's play another good naughty game then."

"And what would that be?"

"If we get back into bed, I'll show you."

"I love you but don't you think it's time we got some sleep, I've been on the go for twenty-four hours, it's been a long day I'm bushed?"

"Spoil-sport, I'm sorry though, I know how tired you must be, it has been a long day for you."

"Thank you my special man, when I'm asleep I dream of you even, it will be no different tonight."

"Corrina Jade every time I have you near, I am elated, every time you're away I miss you, every time I'm in this bed alone I dream of you, every waking moment I think of you', every time I look in the mirror I see your face, every song from the radio echoes your voice. My love is unambiguously incapable of being doubted, if anything was to prevent us being the single entity we are, my life would be unbearable; it wouldn't be worth living."

"Oh Henry, why oh why, do you do this to me?"

"Do what, have I upset you?"

"Don't be Silly. Absolutely not."

"What then?"

"Henry what you just told me has got me all hot and bothered how can I sleep, as far as I'm concerned the day can go on forever; make love to me my special man." It was another hour before they were bestowed with sleep.

They got up later than intended luckily Mathew and Mary were still abed, Lindy sat watching television, protested, "You two, I couldn't sleep last night what were you doing, it went on for hours, blooming-heck I couldn't sleep through all the noise you were you making?"

Both Henry and Corrina were bemused at her question also embarrassed guessed what she was referring to, in unison queried, "Why, what do you mean?"

"The noise you were making! You sounded like Mum and Dad do sometimes only louder, all that ooohing and aahhing."

Children of a much less tender age than Lindy are taught the facts about human reproduction at school, Henry's twelve-year-old mischievous sibling, absolutely knew the reason for all the oohing and aahhing, as she called it. Henry looked at Corrina who was beetroot red with embarrassment, he in a state of confusion his mind struggling to assemble some an answer to placate his twelve-year-old sister. "I'm sorry Lindy I had cramp in my leg, it wouldn't go away and it really hurt."

However, preadolescent Lindy didn't stop there impudently giving more weight to her question she expressed flirtatiously, "I hope that cramp isn't too painful, Corrina might get pregnant."

Henry had to laugh which set Corrina off, he had never been introduced to the malapert character of his little sister. Although he loved her, since leaving school, there had been very little correlation between them, she was just his baby sister, suddenly she was not a baby anymore she was growing up, womanhood had begun to blossom. Realising it was her idea of a wind-up Henry wrapped her in his arms voicing, "Lindy Swan Mathew you're a cheeky minx, in future be careful what you are saying others might get the wrong impression of you, if Mum hears you she won't be very pleased."

"Honestly Henry, who do you think you are kidding, cramp hee, hee, hee, I'm not a baby anymore."

"You're not, are you? Cheeky sod but remember what I told you."

By the time Mary and Mathew engineered enough energy to drag themselves out of bed, Lindy had forgotten all about her lack of sleep or so, Henry and Corrina thought.

Henry wanted to show his family as much of New York and more importantly Greenwich Village. First things first, breakfast, he chose a Diner he and Corrina used frequently, Maggie and Cornelius had also prearranged to join them. Mary and Mathew were impressed with the menu, opting for bacon with eggs over easy, Mathew added hash browns, mushrooms and grits. Lindy ordered pancakes with blueberries, strawberries and syrup with heavy cream, when served she gulped, the stack was almost as big as her. Embarrassment followed, while she was eating, in a very matter of fact manner she asked, "Dad do you get cramp in bed?"

"I do sometimes, why do you ask?"

Corrina's face went ashen she bent forward clutching her head in her hands, a low utterance escaping from her lips, wondering what else would be forthcoming from Lindy's preteen mouth.

Out of the mouths of babes comes to mind but when a nearly twelve-year old girl is a considerably more world widely than her parents were at that age, one might despair at the prospect of being humiliated...

"Henry had it last night, you should have heard him moaning and groaning he kept me awake all night like you and Mum do?"

Her mum realising where the conversation was heading, stepped in telling her, "It's very, very, painful Lindy."

Set with a mischievous glint in her eye, she knew she was treading dangerous waters, but continued, "Nobody has cramp, all night long."

Her dad offered his advice, "Lindy I think you should shut up immediately otherwise you will be grounded for a month, I don't want to hear anymore from you do you hear me?"

"Dad I was only saying?"

"Well don't say anymore."

"But Dad?"

Mary quietly chided, "Lindy I think you had better stop, NOW!"

Much to Corrina's relief nothing more was forthcoming from the precocious little madam nonetheless; Lindy grinned inwardly, she knew she had got away with her little wind up.

A late breakfast enjoyed without any further, uneasy imprudently bold questions offered by Lindy. Thereafter bordering on lunch time, Corrina accompanied by her future mother-in-law Mary and best friend Maggie went searching for a wedding dress and made arrangements to go out to dinner later. Meanwhile Henry took Mathew, with little minx Lindy in the ford Fairlane, to do some sightseeing in New York. Mathew being something of a petrol head marvelled at its red and white livery, all complete with white walled tires, with an all-red leather interior including a covered steering wheel, the seats red and white, the front seat, a bench seat with a column gear change. The boot was big enough to fit a double bed inside, Mathew exuding, "Wow Henry this is special, I would love one of these."

"I know she's lovely isn't she, she's my pride and joy when she isn't in the repair shop."

"What do you do then?"

"I have to go back to using yellow cabs, to be honest It's nice to be able to get up and not think about driving, the traffic is quite formidable at times, I'm lucky the office is only half a mile away, come on then your turn to drive."

Mathew sat behind the steering wheel acknowledged, "Henry It feels like the first time I drove my E Type fantastic."

"Somehow it can't compare to that British beauty, does Mum ever drive it?"

"Once, for about two hundred yards it frightened her, I had to drive it back."

"Corrina won't drive this because she says she feels like Knight-rider, nobody can see her, Okay lets go, have you used a column change before?"

"Of course, hang on to your hats."

Lindy interrupted their male egos, "Dad what do you mean hang on to your hats I'm not wearing one?"

"Henry, give your sister an explanation please."

They concluded the day taking Lindy up Lady Liberty, by the time they got back to Henry's apartment her legs ached, furthermore, ruefully she complained that she had elected to go with the men sightseeing, because she thought it was better than shopping.

The women were out all day, one would assume disquieted having been unsuccessful in their attempt to find Corrina a wedding dress. However, arriving back late evening from their expedition they were giggling like naughty school girls. Mathew shaking his head posed the question, "I take it you enjoyed a liquid lunch then?"

Mary garbled a reply, slurring, "What makes you think that?"

"It could have something to do with your slurred speech."

Maggie due to her ear splitting Scottish accent with speech scrambled, almost incomprehensible, distorted further, "We have only haed a couple."

Corrina just kept giggling, spluttering contentedly she told Henry, "Henry I do love your mum, she is so much fun."

Henry grinning, expressed his thoughts, "Had a good time my darling? It's a good job you're not working tomorrow, and yes she is fun."

Mary still giggling interposed, "I have had a lovely day with my future daughter in-law, and my new friend Maggie."

Lindy just had to voice her own indecorous. Aphorism, "Mum you're pissed, you're all pissed just like you are every Friday night with Elaine and Cherry, I don't know why Dad puts up with it."

Everyone stared not believing the words Lindy had expressed. Maggie and Corrina displayed facial expressions that can only be described as shock, while desperately endeavouring to obviate themselves from exploding into uncontrollable laughter, minimising the possibility of Lindy gaining satisfaction from her obvious attempt of adult humour.

However Mathew looked at her, somehow he managed to restrain his anger but expressed in no uncertain terms, "Lindy if I ever hear you talk about your Mum like that again, you will be grounded for a month do you understand. I never want to hear you use that term again?"

"But Dad she does it every Friday."

"Lindy what your mum does for both of us means she is entitled to go out with her friends to have some fun, and it's none of your business."

"Dad she is pissed, they all are."

Mathew stood his ground, "Lindy I would like you to say sorry to Maggie, Corrina and especially your mum."

"Dad I didn't mean anything nasty."

"Lindy. I'm disappointed now apologise immediately."

She was now resentful towards her dad because of the reprimand administered, which had embarrassed her in front of everyone. Henry aware his little sister was upset, stepped in to hug her, she clung to him tearfully offering her apologies, especially to Mathew, nonetheless, he had chastised her enough, Mathew opened his arms to his little one; smiling inwardly she knew she was forgiven.

Maggie validated Lindy's assertion of the state of the three of them, when Proclaiming, "She's right we are pissed, absolutely steaming, can someone ring Cornelius to collect me before I fall down, mind you I could manage another small one, as long as it's tall and strong."

Her tipsy observation had the aesthetic quality to lighten the mood in the room. All three women laughed. Lindy boosted by Maggie's annotation was about to offer another one of her preteen maxims, thankfully Mathew prevented, any further contention, by placing his finger to Lindy's lips whispering, "Shush remember what I've just said, just because Maggie said the same words it doesn't mean you can copy."

Lindy smiled, eager to append her previous assertions but heedful of the circumstances and potential consequences that may come her way, decided against inviting the wrath of her dad any further.

Cornelius arrived to collect Maggie, Henry helped carry her, she was by then beyond redemption, due to over imbibing a heady mixture of potations, her equilibrium had completely deserted her. It took the two of them with considerable effort to carry her to the car, Cornelius stated, "This is the first time I have seen her, this drunk."

A grinning Henry explained, "She's been out with my mum who likes to party, when women are out on the town they can be way worse than us men, a few drinks they and they forgo their inhibitions, boisterousness prevails, vulgarity raises its head, profanities become the norm and God help anyone who crosses them," he laughed.

Mary incapable of a lucid conversation fell asleep on the Sofa, while Corrina couldn't stop giggling, nonetheless, she staggered unaided to the bedroom.

Henry chuckling enquired, "Did you actually do any shopping; you know for a wedding dress?"

Corrina's bibulous reply was, "I can't remember, but your mum is lovely."

"Corrina Jade sweetheart you have already told me that."

"Henry, my mum would have liked her a lot."

"I'm sure she would have."

"My eyes are getting heavy, I need some sleep, goodnight my special man."

"Goodnight my lover."

Henry covered Corrina with the bed linen, feeling safe, happy and contented, she evanesced into sweet dreams. Henry sat with her for a few minutes then went over to the window. Whispering so as not to wake Corrina he addressed her mum, "Thank you Mrs Phelps for allowing me to love your beautiful loving daughter, thank you so much."

Meanwhile Mathew had carried Mary into their room aided by Lindy who helped her dad as best as she could undress her mum, they both made sure she was comfortable, kissed her gently and told her they loved her, Mary fell asleep happy and secure in the knowledge all her offspring were also happy, she slept the sleep of the blessed deep and mellifluous, peaceful dreams endowing her with total tranquillity.

The following morning Corrina and Mary woke late, both looking like ghosts and nursing sore heads after administering two Paracetamol each, they slowly recovered enough, to rethink where they would begin their shopping again, as neither of them could remember much of the previous day. A crafty move carefully orchestrated by Mathew, would see Lindy accompany the women on their hunt for Corrina's wedding dress, preventing a recurrence of the previous day's fun. Lindy was at first unwilling to be part of the drudge of shopping, she pulled a face and objected strongly, resisting any possibility, she stamped her feet defiantly. That was until Henry explained he and Corrina wanted her to be a bridesmaid, the change in attitude demonstrable, her face lit up with lighthouse power, her smile dazzling asked, "Henry honestly?"

"Lindy, yes honestly."

"I'd better get a shower."

She was ready before Mary and Corrina who were still recovering from the preceding days over enthusiastic intemperateness, eventually they found the wherewithal to embrace the day. Maggie arrived still nursing what she called a dilation of the cerebral arteries, they could only guess she meant, she had a headache, wherever Maggie got such diagnostic information was a mystery to all, even so, she was determined to enjoy the forthcoming day.

Left to their, own devices Henry and Mathew spent a quiet day round the locality enjoying the calm, Cornelius joined them for lunch at the white oak.

Their 'man talk' was all about Henry's Ford Fairlane, Fridays ball game, Mathew's E Type, but the main topic of conversation was the previous day's shopping trip by the women. Mathew smiling broadly, alibied Lindy to Cornelius revealing Mary and her two closest friends Elaine and Cherry did indeed arrive home as he called it blotto most Friday nights. However, it didn't in any shape or form detract from their abilities as home makers; Husbands, partners and children were looked after properly, therefore in his opinion they were entitled to have some fun time together.

Leaving the white oak, Henry and Cornelius introduced Mathew to the iconic Washington Square Park, where they sat for a couple of hours watching the American world go by before heading back to the apartment to await the return of the women from their shopping trip. They didn't have to wait long for an answer when much earlier than expected Lindy, followed by the women all of whom were smiling burst through the door. Lindy grinning, announced, "Corrina has picked three dresses, but she can't make up her mind they are all so beautiful, we are going back tomorrow, I know which one I like, and I've seen the bridesmaids dress."

"You enjoyed it then little one?" asked Henry.

"Fantastic it was great, and we went to McDonalds for lunch and mum bought me some Jeans, they fit perfect, some shoes with heels and some new trainers, then Mum bought herself a dress, Maggie bought some shoes and paid for lunch, Corrina bought some underwear you know knickers, whoo-hoo you wait till you see them Henry, I think they really wanted to go for a drink, but unless you go for a meal children aren't allowed." She spoke without taking of breath.

Mathew smiling, managed to calm her down wrapping her in his arms, quietly told her to take a breath. Corrina waited until Lindy had finished her summary of the day informing everyone that she had actually made her mind up, she was going for the one Lindy favoured.

Henry, asked, "Well are, you going to tell us all about it?"

"Oh Henry it is so beautiful, but it's a lot of money."

Henry, no longer unwilling to voice emotive feelings in company, especially concerning Corrina countered, "Corrina my love you are worth every penny I'm sure the dress will never match your beauty, but I want to see you walk down the aisle in a dress you really want."

The following day Corrina accompanied by her posse of advisers Mary, Maggie and Lindy, ordered the dress every young woman who is in love wants to wear, her wedding dress. Corrina's soft blue eyes glistened like the morning dew, reflecting the early morning summer sun as she explained the dress to Henry, she had chosen.

"Oh Henry, it is beautiful."

Mary, Maggie and Lindy all agreed in unison, Lindy adding, "You wait till you see it and the Bridesmaid dresses are beautiful as well, I can't wait for the wedding so I can—"

Mary interrupting her youngest, suggesting, "Lindy sweetheart, let Corrina tell Henry about her dress if you please."

Corrina glowing with happiness described her dream dress. "Henry, it has a ball-gown skirt layered like a waterfall, a ruched, sweetheart bodice with a delicate low back, it cost a fortune."

"Corrina I'm not interested in the cost; you are worth every penny. When you walk down that aisle to me, I will be the proudest man that ever lived."

Lindy had to interject, evoking a swift, sharp reprimand from her mum when promulgating, "Henry, stop it before I puke."

Chapter 30

A few days after Mary and family returned to Birmingham, Henry received a call from his mum informing him that his dad Frank was unwell, outlining that his doctor had referred him to hospital for further investigation into his obvious ill health. Worried, Henry rang Frank's fiancée Elaine, she was extremely worried too, explaining she had realised something was wrong when she noticed blood in his boxers plus, he was experiencing stomach pains, furthermore his normal bowel habits had changed, she understood he had always been regular now he was continually constipated. Elaine had desperately tried to discuss her worries about the symptoms he was displaying, Frank dismissed any thoughts that there might be anything radically wrong, treating it as a nuisance, an inconvenient diversion from his business life. Reassuring her he had time he would get himself to the hospital when the appointment came through. Elaine at her wits end was not impressed with his assertions, she didn't believe him and was at a loss as to how to persuade him to do as she asked, she felt relieved that Henry was on his case knowing how Frank loved his eldest son.

A concerned Henry rang his dad at the head office of Jenson's, however when he questioned Frank, he received the same response as Elaine, "It's something and nothing, no need to worry."

Henry was acutely disquieted by Frank's patent reluctance to accept that there was anything seriously wrong. "Dad I've asked Elaine to inform me when the appointment comes through, if you find some excuse not to go I'll get the next flight out of here and drag you there."

"Henry there is no need to worry but if you think I should, I will do as Elaine asks."

"Dad you won't let Elaine down, will you? She, like the rest of us, is worried sick, it's time you sorted yourself out, I mean what, I say I will fly back to Birmingham to make sure you go, I want you fit for my wedding."

"Okay son, point taken."

"Thanks Dad you've put my mind at ease; for the time being at least."

Henry spoke to Elaine immediately after ending his converse with his dad, to some extent reassured that Frank would actually keep the appointment, thanking him she laughed nervously, "I want him well, we have a wedding to go to in America."

Henry couldn't resist, "Why, who's getting married am I invited?"

"Henry you silly bugger, I can't wait, I've never been to New York and I want to meet Corrina. I'm so happy for you."

"As long as Dad is fit and well I'll be happy too, I'll keep my fingers crossed, Elaine don't stand any nonsense from him, if he continues to be uncooperative concerning his health, I'll be on the next flight back I promise, It's time he listened to someone else, trouble is he's always been the leader, for once in his life he has to be led."

"Thanks Henry I'll use you as a lever, good night."

"Goodnight Elaine."

Despite the worries, Henry harboured concerning his dad's health he and Corrina were determined they would go ahead with their wedding plans, Henry's Idea was to make it a celebrity style celebration, money would be no object.

Unexpectedly though, while they lay in bed one morning, Corrina surprised Henry by voicing her concerns about their proposed wedding plans, "Henry you know how much I love you but, I don't want a huge over the top ceremony I would prefer a quieter more intimate affair with our families and friends in attendance, not half of New York."

"Corrina Jade, I wanted to show the whole world the beautiful girl I am marrying, but blue eyes if you are uncomfortable with my suggestions then we will do it differently."

"Thank you, my special man, I'm relieved."

"Corrina as long as your happy I am."

"The only thing is I'm Catholic, I've been reluctant to tell you, I must marry in church."

"Don't worry, you should never be scared to tell me anything, I'll ask Cornelius he's sure to know somewhere."

Ten days since he spoke to Elaine Henry received another call from her, "Henry, I'm really worried, the consultant who examined him gave some devastating news, the symptoms show he, could have cancer. They are sending him for a CT scan next week, I'm not sure whether he will go, he can be such an obstinate sod, Caro and your mum have given him some advice but I'm not sure if it did any good."

"I'll speak to him again Elaine, I've already told him I will fly back if he refuses, I'll see if he listens."

"Henry I'm really worried."

"Elaine you must love him a lot to put up with his shenanigans, If I have to, I will fly back, we will get him there by hook or by crook I promise, It's about time he listened to the people who care about him."

"Thanks Henry I am so grateful."

Much to everyone's relief, Henry, over time had acquired the same persuasive qualities as his dad, therefore after talking to him at length Frank accepted his son's advice, eventually conceding it was in his own interest to at least get checked out with the medics; he did keep the appointment. It was a harrowing time waiting for the result, for all who loved Frank, although he himself was completely unfazed by the situation continuing to work, refusing to let the possible diagnosis affect him in anyway.

Despite his worries concerning Frank's health, Henry and Corrina busied themselves planning their nuptials. However, they were in a quandary due to Corrina's preference for a quieter family wedding day, she wanted a church but didn't want a choir, bell tower ringing, or a huge hotel celebration. They looked at dozens of venues, picking out one or two credible locations nonetheless nothing really appealed to either of them.

Henry sat at his desk lost in a ponderance effectuated by the worries of his dad commixed with plans for his forthcoming wedding, all of which addled his brain rendering his thought patterns almost unperceivable. Fortunately, he was dragged out of the quagmire of desperate unease When, out of the blue a knight in shining armour, in the shape of Dusty J Upthe^{gr}ove ^{3r}d, arrived back from the West Midlands, his three-year stint in the UK was complete, furthermore, he had been appointed Executive director of overseas trading. A large hat dropped on Henry's head followed by a bellowing southern drawl; he knew immediately who it was. They had become friends during their on-going series of lengthy discourses while they assessed Henry's character and his qualifications before Dusty offered him the job.

Dusty J Upthe^{gr}ove ^{3r}d slapping him on his back commented, "Henry I knew you would be an asset to the company, how are you?"

"Hello sir I'm well how are you?"

Something Henry adjusted to quite early when arriving in New York was to address older men as sir, out of respect.

"I'm well son, I hear you're getting married."

"Yes sir, when we can find a suitable venue."

"Why, what are you looking for?"

"Well sir, we want something family orientated my Fiancée Corrina, in spite of her job, is really quite shy."

"Leave it to me young man I'll find something suitable, or my name isn't Dusty J Upthegrove 3rd" Initially, Henry was, shall we say, a little perturbed by Dusty J's offer but not wishing to sound pompous or unappreciative he thanked him graciously, accepting his offer, nonetheless, he would prefer it if he and Corrina found a suitable locale for their upcoming nuptials themselves, he needed to share his thoughts and feelings with Corrina.

Henry would never make any decision without consulting Corrina like Barack Obama reached out to all peoples when voicing (our stories are singular, but our destiny is shared). However, he recognised Dusty J's experience, furthermore his intimate knowledge pertaining to all things New York had to offer. Therefore, Corrina and Henry discussed the situation, advancing their thoughts, offering all the possible whys and wherefores and the what ifs. The outcome of which, was both were immensely grateful for Dusty's J's offer. Determining to wait and see what his far reaching tentacular business arms could search out for them, because they had so little time together, by reason of Corrina's flight schedule.

Chapter 31

Henry spoke every day to his family via facetime because he was very worried about his dad, especially Elaine, she was relieved Frank had kept the appointment with his consultant and kept Henry in the loop. Frank remained upbeat but continued his rejection of illness reflected in his thinking that it was something and nothing. However, a few days later amidst the early hours of the morning Henry's house phone rang, its monotonous tone interrupted his dormancy, he answered sleepily, Elaine's distressed voice snapped him sharply out of his quiescence. She was distraught she gave him news none of the family expected; Frank had been diagnosed with Colon cancer. Henry felt his heart sink into the pit of his stomach but he remained calm in a vain attempt to ease Elaine's worries by trying to sound positive; easier said than done she was too distressed, Henry managed to construe that Frank would require another scan to determine if the cancer had spread any further.

When his converse with Elaine concluded, he sat on the edge of the bed and cried, all of a sudden he felt lonely he needed Corrina's shoulder to cry on sadly she wouldn't be home for at least another week, her job was taking her to Australia. He tried to facetime her but she didn't answer, he did the next best thing he left her a text message, he felt even more downcast realising he would have to wait until she was in a position to get in touch with him. For once his pragmatic approach to life had begun to dissipate, sleep did not bless his anxious mind, invaded by the dire consequences of what the possible outcome of his dad's illness could be.

Awake, tired, disquieted, he lay on his and Corrina's bed his mind wandering, lacking any form of clarity of thought, his reasoning a jumblement of disjointed and animated confusion, the turmoil of his reasoning, just added to the perturbations befalling the presentation and elaborations of what he could, or what he should do. He had never faced the prospect of losing someone close, especially his dad, the man he always aspired to be, and to be fair Henry mirrored. The only obvious difference was Henry enjoyed the company and the love of one woman whereas Frank, enjoyed the company of every woman who ever flashed their eyes in his direction, Thankfully, tiredness did eventually persuade equanimity.

A muffled buzzing sound seeped into his melancholic dormancy however his thought processes were unable to assemble a direct assimilation, the buzzing continued, eventually rousing him from his concreted dream-state. Slowly his soporific head cleared when he realised it was his phone was ringing, one look at the screen swiftly marshalled his cohesive senses, Corrina was calling. She had known instinctively something was troubling him, quizzing him in one sentence. "Henry are you ill, in trouble, are your family okay?"

"Oh Blue eyes, I wish you were here."

"Why what's the matter?"

"I've just been told my dad has Colon Cancer."

Corrina went quiet while she contemplated a response, "Oh Henry my special man, what have they actually said?"

"He has to have a PET scan."

"That's to check it hasn't spread further so they can give him the right treatment."

"Did your mum ever require one?"

"Henry despite me Elliot and Sadie encouraging her to visit a doctor by the time she sought help it was too late, so no. She went through all the protocols but maybe if she had listened to the advice we gave her when she first found the lump, she wouldn't be a star looking down on us now. As far as your dad is concerned, we will just have to pray and encourage him to listen to the medics, I know how worrying it is."

"Corrina you understand how I feel, having had the experience of the dread that comes with the word cancer."

Corrina counselled him because he was so worried, "Henry why don't you go and see him, give him some encouragement? It will help the rest of the family if you are there."

"When will you be home?"

"Next Saturday, if you go to Birmingham don't rush back, I'll be okay on my own, do what you have to do, he's your dad you should be there for him, you need to be there, the rest of the family need you as well, go and see how you can help."

"I think I will, if everything turns out okay we should bring the wedding forward, I want to see you in that dress."

"That's unusual, usually you want to strip my dress off me."

"That will come after you have walked down the aisle."

"Henry stop it, I'm getting all flustered."

"Corrina Jade I am getting turned on just thinking about it?"

Giggling she noted. "You seem happier now."

"Blue eyes just hearing your voice has cheered me up, I do miss you so."

"I miss you too my special man, nonetheless I think you should go and see your dad I'm sure he will appreciate your support."

"I will, any problems you encounter while I'm over there call Cornelius, I've had a thought, Maggie could stop with you."

"She'll be too busy getting into Cornelius's trousers."

"Hark at you, I remember when you would have blushed if I had said that you wicked woman."

"Cheeky sod, I have you to blame for that."

"I know I'm a good teacher, mind you you're an enthusiastic student."

"Henry Swan Jenson you bugger I'll sort you out when you get home."

"Oooooh I can't wait, are you going to smack the back of my legs?"

"Will you stop it Henry, put this way you won't get much sleep?"

"Corrina Jade Phelps what am I going to do with this boner?"

"Save it for me."

"Hells bells I can't walk round stiff legged for over a week I'll look like an elephant with his trunk stuck down my trousers."

"I don't really have to tell you what to do with it do I, anyway I've seen your bits fully extended you haven't got Elephantitis, as yours are the only bits I have seen I would guess more like a donkey."

"I'm glad you didn't say tunicate."

Giggling again she asked, "Henry what on earth is a tunicate?"

"Do you really want to know?"

"Well Henry you've inflamed my imagination so, yes I do now?"

Laughing he acquainted her with something that had made him laugh when at school, "It's a minute marine invertebrate, commonly called a sea squirt but I prefer one of its other names sea pork it sounds more manly."

Corrina couldn't contain her hilarity she convulsed into sustained clamorous mirth. In between the gasps as she tried to catch her breath, she asked, "Henry you do come out with some weirdly obscure knowledge where on earth did you dig out information like that? I'll be laughing every time I think of it."

"School, I had a teacher who was into all things pertaining to marine life, as long as you don't laugh when we are in bed."

"Oh Henry my special man, every moment spent with you in bed is blinking wonderful," she again convulsed into exuberant levity commenting, "sea squirt indeed, oh my."

Unfazed, Henry waited until she composed herself, trouble was he couldn't stop laughing himself, therefore every time he spoke the two of them recrudesced into rumbustious guffaws.

Finally, both were able to regain their composure, particularly Henry, because Corrina's call had effected some sensibility to his emotional demeanour. Just talking to her lifted his spirit, she had taken the sting out of his abnormal gloominess. Their frivolous but spontaneous banter contributed to countering the pre call uncertainty he had felt, her concern guiding him in the direction he should take the consequence of which he was able to determine that it was important he should fly back to Birmingham to see his dad and catch up with the family life.

Henry and Corrina expressed their love for each other, as they did when at opposite ends of the world, every time they started and ended a conversation. Their love had an essential nature it was intrinsic; indubitable. If at any-time forces conspired to separate them permanently, which they considered impossible unless God decided otherwise, they believed in the marriage vow, 'until death do us part'.

Chapter 32

As a result of Corrina's phone call, Henry accepted her advice, two days later he flew back to Birmingham. Only after speaking to the company he worked for MSAI who thankfully raised no objections to his request for time to visit his family, in fact they were very supportive of him, wishing him well. The night before he caught his flight discussing the situation with his mum, she advised him to stay with them; his room was always ready.

Upon clearing customs, his mum was waiting for him, embracing him like the prodigal son, "Hello son good flight, I bet you're tired?"

"Hi Mum I'm good, how is Dad?"

"Well he's not well but Elaine will tell you more, let's go home and then we will go and see her, she's in bits, she is so worried as we all are."

"Is he at home?"

"Don't be daft he's working, you know what he's like."

"Surely he should be resting?"

"He won't listen to anyone, perhaps you can talk to him make him see sense."

"I doubt it Mum but I'll try."

"Come on Henry let's get you home."

"Mum?"

"Yes son."

"Don't take offense but home to me is Greenwich Village New York, I am so happy with my American Life and don't forget I have Corrina Jade, she loves our home."

"I know son but to me this is your home, the place where both of you will always be welcome if for some reason things don't work out for you in New York."

"Mum I can't think of anything that will bring me back, I love New York and I love my darling Corrina, as soon as we know Dad is going to be okay, we will fix the date for our wedding I can't wait to see her in that dress."

"Henry son I'm sure Frank will be okay, you'll see, everything will work out for you and Corrina."

Henry didn't exactly stow his suitcase in his bedroom, he dumped it on the bed he was desperate to see his dad. Borrowing Mathews E Type Jaguar, he went round to see Frank's fiancée Elaine. When Elaine saw Henry a torrent of tears cascaded down her cheeks, such outpouring and the embrace she wrapped him in, embarrassed him a little. Luckily younger brother Jude came to his rescue explaining, "Dad isn't very well but he's still gone to work and Mum is upset."

Dismissing his own discomfiture Henry enquired, "Elaine, I take it he'll be in his Office, shall I go to him, or do you think it would be better to wait for him here?"

"Go to the office, we never know when he is going to get home."

"Okay," with that, he made his way to head office. He entered Frank's office Frank was sat behind his desk, head down pouring over some paper-work, looking up a grin spreading across his face, appearing to say the least, chipper to all intents to be his peppiness self, smiling broadly. Hugging Henry he queried, "hello son wonderful to see you but what are you doing here?"

"Dad everybody is worried, because you won't do as the medics are asking of you, I'm staying until you have had that scan."

"Henry I know I've got the dreaded C, however the doctors believe it's contained, the scan is just a precautionary measure so they can decide what treatment I require."

"Dad I will stay until you have had the scan, it'll take some of the burden off Elaine, she is worried sick."

"Son, I'm chuffed you're concerned but honestly there's no need to worry, I'll be fine."

Frank it seemed, did not seem to fully comprehend the seriousness of the situation he might be facing. Henry advancing his thoughts told him, "Dad I don't care what YOU think or say! I am staying to make sure you keep the appointment, in fact I will accompany you and Elaine to the hospital, Remember, it's not just me, the rest of the family Caro, Jude and Myles, and Mum, are just as worried. So here I am and here I stay until you have had that scan."

"Henry son I will keep the appointment so you can go back to the States, don't you have work to do?"

"Dad you are far more important than my work I love you."

"Thanks for that son, I love you too, to be honest I'm really glad you will be here supporting me and Elaine."

Those words uttered by Frank, though not an admittance, indicated to Henry they exposed the fragility of his thinking as usual it was heavily disguised, by his blasé approach to any problem to which he was confronted with. Henry understood his dad was genuinely concerned about his health...

Almost midnight before Corrina's blue eyes illuminated Henry's cell phone screen, brightening his worried mind, her first words, "How is my little sea squirt?"

Attempting to disregard her opening statement and looking imperious, haughtily commenting as disdainfully as he could, given he was trying with difficulty to stifle his amusement, he gave his reply, "Corrina Jade Phelps you cheeky..."

However, he was unable to finish his tongue in cheek verbal assail, exploding into convulsive hilarity.

Corrina giggling, gave her own reply, "Henry Swan Jenson were you going to swear at me you naughty boy?"

Henry still trying to catch his breath, managed to complete his original comment, "Corrina Jade Phelps my blue-eyed beauty you really are a cheeky illegitimate."

Corrina, having difficulty restraining her own mirth retorted, "That's alright then, I thought you were going to call me a cheeky bastard."

Both of them disintegrated into uncontrollable laughing. Henry after a couple of minutes found his voice, "I'm missing you so much Corrina Jade Phelps."

"Henry, I feel as though I have lost my right arm because we are apart, when I wake up in the morning, instinctively I reach out for you, sadly you're not there, that is when I shed a tear, I love you so much, enough of my frustrations, tell me how is your dad, is he going through with the scan?"

"Outwardly he is his normal outgoing self-assured man, nonetheless after talking to him I got the feeling that he is worried, it could be the reason he is playing hardball, so I'll stay here until he's actually gone through with the appointment, I'll come home then, I won't stay any longer than I need too, the consultant reckons it will be another three weeks before Dad receives the results."

"My special man I know what you are going through, I still remember what my mum went through like it was yesterday, we'll keep everything crossed fingers, arms, legs."

Henry suddenly found his humour again advocating, "The latter only till I get home Corrina Jade."

"Henry is that all you think about? Stop it you're getting me all hot and bothered again thinking of when I reach out in the mornings and you are next to me, Oooooh I miss you so."

"Where are you Corrina?"

"I'm at home don't worry, Maggie is staying with me in our apartment."

"What about Cornelius?"

"Don't worry he's here as well, Maggie is not going without, only poor little me I'm so lonely without you."

"I'm going without as well, I have this appendage that keeps rising whenever I think about you."

"Never mind we'll sort it out when you get home."

"Corrina Jade, you won't be able to walk when I finished loving you."

"Shuuush Maggie has just walked in the room, don't start her off."

Too late, something neither of them expected came from Maggie's mouth, she gave her direct observation, "Henry you wait when you get home she won't let your sea squirt go, she's playing with herself now."

"Piss off Maggie," came Corrina's miffed rejoinder. "Henry don't take any notice of her she is a dirty minded bugger," she made Henry laugh again when adding, "that will come later."

"Where did she get the sea squirt information from?"

"She must have been listening when I first called you."

"Bloody hell she'll never let that go."

"I know she's just been shouting to Cornelius, it was time he got his sea squirt out."

"I'm not bothered my blue-eyed sweetheart, I'm more interested in when you are next likely to be home?"

"Well I'm not sure, we might have to do Australia again, I'm really not certain, otherwise probably in about four days depending on where the powers that be decide to send us, which is unfortunate, nonetheless that's the nature of the job."

"Corrina Jade, we might not be together for another couple of weeks what am I going to do with this ever-expanding sea squirt."

"Henry, my special man, take a cold shower."

"Oh well if that's all you can offer, I'll say goodnight blue eyes."

Blowing a kiss she sighed, "What I can tell you is, I will be back in Edinburgh the day after tomorrow, but we will still be apart, I shall hold you in my dreams, good night my very special man, good night."

Henry watched the cell phone picture close down returning him to his previous dolefulness beclouding his thoughts, he was in Sutton Cold field to be with his dad, his regret Corrina was in their home three and a half thousand miles across the Atlantic, he was in dire need of her company; he needed her love. Thinking about their conversation an idea began to percolate through his dysphoria, recalling her words, "I will be in Edinburgh the day after tomorrow."

He had a sudden notionIch filtered froI an idea, evolving to a possibility, thereon to a potentiality, thenceforth transforming to an eventuality. Henry's plan would be to find out her exact flight times from New York, then he would take a flight up to Edinburgh and meet her at the airport, if he could only see her for a couple of hours, to maybe hold her in his arms, would be the one curative analeptic he needed, to drag him out of the anxiety, ergo consequential sadness imposing upon his usual practical mind, It would also give him the opportunity to meet Corrina's family. Excited he called Corrina who had just come out of the shower, standing naked she answered her cell phone giggling.

"Miss me that much do you Henry Swan Jenson, I've just finished showering?"

"Corrina I thank god for facetime, you look beautiful you're giving me a real hard on thinking of you in the shower."

"Well thank you my special man, I wish we had showered together it would have taken much longer and been more fun, mmmmm we could have really eased that problem, but why the call back so soon."

"Did you say you will be in Edinburgh the day after tomorrow?"

"Yes, why do you ask?"

"It's a surprise, one I hope you will like, I'll let you go to bed now, sleep tight my beautiful blue eyes."

"Henry my darling I'm intrigued, it sounds exciting."

"I'm not saying anymore, except goodnight my darling blue eyes."

"Good night, my special man."

The following morning Henry checked with Edinburgh Airport when Corrina's flight from New York was due to arrive, he then booked a flight from Birmingham to Edinburgh, There would be a four hour wait between his flight and the arrival of Corrina's flight, enough time to visit Jenson's of Scotland, head office.

Chapter 33

Entering the shop, Ellie Crain the general manager was talking to a customer, when she was free Henry tapped her on the shoulder, turning round she gave one surprised look before throwing her arms around him squealing, "Henry what are you doing here, I never thought we would see you again, I thought you lived in America?"

"Ellie, I do, I'm here to meet my Fiancée Corrina, but how are you? you look fantastic."

"You look good yourself, America must suit you, and a fiancée eh?"

Henry didn't say anything about Frank, preferring to relate his story of meeting Corrina, the reason why he was there.

"Ellie I hear you run a tight ship, my dad thinks you're wonderful."

"That's nice to know we are appreciated, he comes up quite often, at first, I thought he didn't trust me."

"I promise you've no need to worry on that score, Ellie if I had time I would take you all out to dinner, but time is tight I must get back to the Airport to Corrina, she doesn't know I'm here."

"it's really lovely to see you again Henry."

"it's lovely to see you Ellie, take care."

Henry called for a taxi to take him to back to the airport.

Forty minutes later he stood in the arrival lounge of Edinburgh Airport waiting for the most important person in his life. When she came through customs dragging her overnight case, tired after the ten-hour Journey, Henry stepped in front of her, for a moment she couldn't assimilate who had invaded her space, taken aback by the intrusion she scanned the smiling face standing before her. Suddenly her intellect absorbed that face, her own face began loading into a smile, finding her voice, querying, "Henry what on earth are you doing here?"

Henry cloaked her in his arms, neither uttering words, only sighs as their mouths closed together affixed by desire, tongues interlacing, hearts in concert drumming the same heady beat, they were oblivious to the throngs of people rushing to and fro. Disappointment came when Maggie interrupted them, offering her usual disparaging aphorism. "Corrina I hope you're not going to get his sea squirt out here? you'll get us all locked up."

Consequently their spell was broken to be replaced with shaking of their heads ensued by fractious laughter.

Corrina getting her breath back wagging her finger at Maggie and grinning, threatened her friend. "Ye heald yer horses ye bugger, ah hud juist arrived in heaven."

Cupping Henry's face in her hands, she repeated the question she asked before he engulfed her in his firm protective embrace, rendered in her soft Scottish vernacular. "Hendre whit urr ye dean' 'ere?"

"Blue eyes, surprise surprise I've come to see you, what else would I be doing here."

"Wow, whit a bonnie surprise!"

Maggie interrupted again apprising. "I don't know about you pair but I want to go home, Corrina I'll see you on Tuesday, goodnight both."

"Henry I think we should be getting home, I want you to meet my family, Elliot his wife Sadie and my niece Becky, they will be delighted to meet you."

"Corrina I do hope your right."

"He is a lovely brother he will love you, they all will."

"Where am I going to sleep?"

"Where do you think?"

"On the sofa?"

"You will be in my bed, nut case."

"That's nice of you but where are you going to sleep?"

"Henry Swan Jenson I'll be in the shed."

"You'll be cold out there, furthermore that's not going to do anything for my stiffy can't I sleep in the shed with you?"

"Henry sometimes you're a right Richard Cranium."

"Well that's better than being called a dick head; I suppose?"

Grinning she advanced her reply, "I'm not giving you an answer to that."

Corrina introduced Henry to her family and he could not have been made more welcome. Sadie hugged him, Becky said hello, Elliot shaking his hand nodded his head towards Corrina, he gently chided, "Henry It's nice to meet you, but it is about time we were beginning to think you were a figment of Corrina's imagination."

Corrina taken aback quizzed, "Why would you think that."

Sadie chipped in advising, "Take no notice of him Corrina he's pulling your leg."

Elliot put his arm around his younger sibling admitting, "I'm only joking I'm really pleased for both of you."

Eleven-year-old Becky, a little shyly asked Henry, "Are you going to be my uncle?"

"I will as long as Corrina doesn't dump me for a handsome airline pilot."

"I don't think that will happen, she talks about you all the time it gets boring."

Henry smiling, diffused any possible admonishment from her mum and dad, with his gentle answer, "Do you know what Becky, everybody thinks I'm boring because I talk about Corrina all the time, because I love her and want to marry her."

Becky's next mouthful nobody foresaw, "You live together in America how come she's not pregnant?"

Before anyone could upbraid her, Henry answered, "If you live together it doesn't mean a woman will get pregnant."

"You must have sex though?"

Corrina and Henry had to turn away to stifle their mirth.

Sadie however remonstrating loudly, construing in no uncertain terms her dissatisfaction at Becky's inappropriate question. "Becky Phelps what is it with you, you can be so cheeky, apologise now to Corrina and Henry otherwise you will not be going to America for their wedding?"

"But Mum that's not fair I wasn't being cheeky, at school they tell us if we want to learn ask questions, I only asked a question."

"Becky sweetheart it's not the kind of question you should ask, those things are personal, now say sorry and we will forget it, go on say sorry."

"Sorry Corrina, sorry Henry."

Henry again coming to her rescue, "Becky sweetheart you are just like my sister Lindy, she always says the wrong things at inopportune moments."

"Does she get into trouble?"

"She does, all the time."

Her question was forgotten and forgiven, when she asked, "What does inopportune mean?"

Two days with Corrina lifted some of the anxiety and testiness which had settled on Henry's normal placid mien. The time together afforded them the opportunity to discuss their wedding plans, Henry also used the occasion to broach the sensitive subject of finance concerning the trip to New York.

Elliot and Sadie both worked in retail, Elliot in a menswear shop which was closing down due in part to the decline in high street shopping, mainly the result of online shopping, he would soon be unemployed. Sadie worked in a local grocery shop most of their earnings went to pay the mortgage, and all the other bills leaving them little money for luxuries like holidays. The very reason why Henry was so concerned and eager to assist…

Taking Elliot to one side his opening line was, "Elliot you can tell me to mind my own business but Corrina is very worried, you may not be able to travel to New York to give her away because of the cost."

"Henry I'll be honest, it's going to be a strain on our pockets but there is no way I'm going to let her down, we will manage."

"Look Elliot don't go borrowing from wherever, If it's too much we will get wed here in Edinburgh."

"I have already promised Becky we will be going to New York; I have to say we are all in need of a holiday, especially Sadie."

Henry put his cards on the table in an effort to help, "Elliot I don't know what Corrina has told you about me, unlike yourself and Corrina, I was born with a silver spoon in my mouth, I have led a privileged life, undoubtably endowed with a loving family, and It's fair to say they are more than affluent, they are very wealthy. Personally with their help I have made my own mark, I have a wonderful life in New York; happily, my luck is set to continue I'm going to marry your beautiful sister. There is another plus, I can get discounts on virtually everything from work boots to air-line tickets."

Elliot answered and posed a question, "Corrina has told us expansively about you, when we shook hands it was as if I knew you, so where is this leading?"

"Elliot what I'm trying to say without causing you any embarrassment, is there in anyway me and Corrina can help to hopefully, allay any financial worries there may be for you?"

"I'm not sure I understand."

"Can we pay for your airline tickets?"

"Henry I'm not embarrassed, I'm grateful of your offer but I feel I should do this myself."

"Look if you are borrowing any money why don't you borrow from me and Corrina? interest free, no timeline for repayment, repaying when you can afford it also while you are in New York, you can stay with us in the apartment."

"I don't know what to say, I'll need to discuss it with Sadie."

"There's no rush."

"Henry whatever we decide thanks for the offer."

Elliot and Sadie although surprised and extremely grateful of Henry and Corrina's fabulous, furthermore, heartfelt offer of financial help, were disconcerted, unsure and worried for a number of reasons wondering would it be the best way forward for them. They were faced with a dilemma, which therefore had to be considered carefully; reasoning that borrowing money from a relative can cause conflict within a family. They were a small but close family unit, the thought that money could possibly effect strife within the family unit, was abhorrent to them. Elliot loved his younger sister, anything that might cause friction between them would be a non-starter.

Elliot and Sadie, after careful deliberations came to a decision which suited both of them, agreeing that by accepting Henry and Corrina's offer, it would take the initial financial strain off them. They were however, concerned as to how and when the loan would have to be repaid, Elliot expressing, he and Sadie were grateful, but Henry would probably have to wait a while before he would get the money repaid. Henry again reassured them there was no timeline, they could pay only when they were in a position financially to do so, no matter how long that would be. He put their minds even more at ease, suggesting the best option would be to open an account in his name, to which they would have sole access enabling them to save when they could, and if they needed money they could use it, Henry and Corrina would have nothing to do with it until the time Elliot and Sadie were in a position financially, to repay them. While Henry was discussing with Elliot his financial situation, knowing Elliot would soon be out of work he made a suggestion to him, advising because of his undoubted experience in retail, dealing with the public, would he be interested in working for his dad's company? if so, he should contact Jenson's, on the off chance there might be an opening. He explained although he was not employed by (Jenson's of Scotland) now, he would have a word with his friend and general manager Ellie Crane to see if they could accommodate a new employee, he also explained clearly, he would have to have an interview, obviously, only if a vacancy became available.

Something was confusing Henry, for some reason when he was in the company of Elliot he experienced, notIletelu, just a feeling that they had met before. Broaching the subject to Corrina, she thought it impossible as the distance between Birmingham and Edinburgh must be close on 500 Km. As far as she was aware Elliot had never been to Birmingham therefore, she too wondered why he should think he had already met Elliot. Henry racked his brains but he couldn't remember anything conclusive from his usually fluid memory bank.

Two nights with Corrina and her family was the analgesic he required, restoring the brighter side of his demeanour, putting him in the mood to be more positive. He flew back to Birmingham not exactly euphoric, nonetheless, he was ready to help his family; he was more than ready to help his dad Frank. Whatever in the future, they might have to face…

Chapter 34

At home for a few days, Henry was unable to settle into any form of holiday mode as he was curious as to whether his dad would require any assistance. A delighted Frank sat grinning at his son who was back in the fold albeit temporarily, Frank understood Henry was there to assist him but Henry had an ulterior motive, he wanted to make sure Jenson's staff were organised in the event Frank might be absent when having treatment. Nobody understood the workings of Frank's business more than Henry who gained his knowledge from advancing the company first into Wales, then Scotland.

Considering the possible severity of Frank's illness there was the probable likelihood he might not be allowed to drive, so he set in motion a protocol whereby each time Frank needed to visit one of his shops, he would be accompanied by either Frank's PA Imelda, or with Frank's old enemy turned best friend; Barney Phillips, added to the mix of willing helpers, Frank's fiancée Elaine, his former PA and Barney's partner Cherry stone. A good team who between them set up a strategy whereby each would combine their own jobs and do whatever was required if and when required. If they encountered any problems they couldn't solve, Henry would fly back from New Yorkio8uio.

Barney Philips was devastated at the news of Frank's illness, he had only met Henry a few times previously but, he needed him to know what his dad meant to him, in tears he reiterated. "Henry your dad was the only person who held out his hand in friendship when I came out of prison, in spite of the preceding animosity between us especially when you consider me and my brother nearly killed him." Taking a breath he continued, "The opportunity Frank gave me has changed my whole perspective on life, thanks to him I have a good job, a loving partner and I have made friends, friends who care, friends who like me for myself not because they are frightened of me oh, and your brother Myles, I love him like my own son, to be honest I will do anything for Frank if it helps him, anything at all." It was at this point a tear trickled down his cheek, continuing to give his thought, "I have a multitude of regrets the worst I must live with, is my wife walking out, divorcing me and taking my son with her. I don't not blame her, I was to put it bluntly, a shithole."

"Barney that's a coincidence my Fiancée Corrina has a brother called Elliot."

Barney enquired, "They're Scottish aren't they? would you believe I have never been to Scotland, never had need to."

"Barney they are a lovely family, they live in the beautiful city of Edinburgh, I'm so lucky to have met her. Have you any Idea where your son Elliot and wife might be?"

"Not a clue they wouldn't want me and I understand why, however I would love to see them, especially my son, just to say sorry, sadly for me it's never going to happen, there aren't any excuses for the way I drove them out of my life. One thing I am sure of is your dad and Cherry are special to me, I have a lot to thank them both for."

"I'm glad you feel that way because I have something to ask of you."

"If I can help, ask away?"

Henry like his dad could see something he liked in Barney, therefore taking a chance just as his dad had done, he asked. "If Dad needs treatment, would you look after the associated companies of Jenson's in Wales and Scotland, if ever either of the general managers are on vacation or off sick?"

"Henry, if he needed me to go to Alaska in midwinter I would go."

Out of the anxiety came humour from Henry, "Bloody hell don't mention Alaska to him, he might think about opening another branch of Jenson's."

"Hopefully not, but he has set his eyes on locations in Ireland that is both sides of the border."

"Jeez Ireland, hasn't he got enough to contend with?"

"Henry there's nothing wrong in being ambitious, it's something I am only just learning."

"He needs to concentrate on his health not expanding his business, he'll kill himself."

"Don't worry, it was only a suggestion he made in case you ever decide to come home."

"Barney there is not the slightest chance of that ever happening, when I can I'm going to apply for American citizenship, I love America and the Americans."

"I sincerely hope it works out for you, you're a chip of the old block and no mistake."

"I hope not I'm a one-woman man."

Barney chuckled, "I meant the way you work."

Three days after his temporary co-option to Jenson's, whilst enjoying a family dinner Henry enlightened Mary of Frank's suggestion to Barney of maybe spreading his business wings further afield, perplexed she asked.

"Where?"

"Ireland, apparently both sides of the border if I was ever to come back."

"Would you?"

"No way Jose, Mum there is nothing that would bring me back, I love my life in America."

"Sad as it makes me, I know that son, bet your life he hasn't said anything to Elaine she'll be the last to know."

"Mum, it won't happen so you don't need to say anything."

Henry, Caro, Mary and Elaine all accompanied Frank to the hospital where he was to have the scan. Frank appeared to exhibit his usual outgoing gregarious persona, though Henry could feel tension hiding behind his normally affable communicative self, there was something not quite resonating. Henry realised for the first time in his life Frank was unsure of himself, he had lost control, other people were taking over, so for once in his life he would be taking direction from others.

From his teen years into his adult life, Frank had fought to overcome anything, furthermore anything that resembled an obstacle that stood before him, he always climbed up and over whatever obstruction opposed or hindered his quest to succeed. His industry and single-mindedness alongside sheer determination would inevitably come to the fore, proclaiming him victor, the one exception being the breakdown of his marriage to Mary, the one and only time he was unable to contrive the outl of which his mettlesome, swashbuckling charismatic presence usually achieved. He couldn't regain her love, sling he always regretted, he had never before experienced the sense of loss which totally surrounded him; sad times all of which were his own making, Frank always believed it to be his only true failure.

Colon cancer however, was a different proposition for him to deal with, it was going to take more than persuasive words to fight, as he called it 'the fungus' which had decided to infest part of his body. Henry felt saddened, knowing there was no magic wand or potion with which he could alleviate his dad's Illness, they could only hope the medics could conjure up a spell, not to just to repair the damage but dispel the damage caused by the hostile parasitic growth invading his large intestine.

Despite the disquiet, Henry perceived that behind the smiles and jocularity expressed by Frank when he emerged from the X-ray department, Henry was convinced his dad was worried, extremely worried.

Henry enquired, "How did it go?"

Frank replied in an uncertain tone, "It seemed to go alright I think, you can't tell because you just lie there, they don't say much just tell you to lay still, a couple things were said, I don't remember though, it seemed to be over before I realised."

Elaine wrapped her arms around him comforting him, "Frank my darling I'm sure you will be come through this, it's just a distraction."

Frank acknowledged Henry's intuitive perception of his dad's inner turmoil commenting, "I hope so, but I'm not going to build my hopes up, somehow I get the feeling this may be the last chapter of my life, the last page."

Elaine burst into tears while Mary remonstrated with him. "Frank Jenson behave, this is not like you! Don't let yourself slip into morbidity, you are stronger than that, be more positive this is just one more challenge to face, it's another of life's battles, a battle I know you can win and will win as you have won every other battle."

Mary's castigation dragged him out of his melancholia advocating, "Mary this is bigger than any battle this is a war I'm fighting but you're right I can defeat this enemy within."

Henry marvelled at his mum's outburst even though she was his ex-wife Frank was still a friend, Mary knowing him so well, knew how to handle his rare show of despondency, she had put him firmly in his place, incredibly despite the divorce Mary was still the only one who could make him see sense, deep down he still carried a torch for her.

Caro wiped a watery emotion from her eyes, sad advising, "Dad please be more upbeat, be my dad, the one I know and love." Frank responded to Caro's unfeigned entreaty by putting his arms around her, assuring her, "Caro sweetheart, I promise to do everything the medical staff ask of me, I have the determination to overcome this unwelcome, uninvited intruder attempting to take over my body."

Caro and Henry in concert asserted, "Now that's the dad we know."

The anxiety pervading all of the family slowly began to dissipate with smiles lighting their faces, relaxed because Frank had decided against 'giving up' which for Frank, throughout his life had never been an option; his resourcefulness and determination always found an answer. This was the first time he needed his family to encourage him, dysfunctional as they were, they all adored him. Over the years his mistakes were many, however they didn't detract from the care, time and warmth he afforded not just his family, but anybody he came into contact with. The women with whom he had fathered children, would without doubt give testament to his concern for everyone: they were a very close-knit family. Frank had brightened the atmosphere, nevertheless, behind the smiles lay a great deal of concern, the worst part of the medical protocol for the family, waiting for the result. They had been told not to expect an answer for at least two weeks, two weeks waiting time seemed like forever.

Henry unsure as to where Corrina may be in the world, they might even be at opposite ends, but ignoring the time difference he facetimed her. He got an answer from his bleary eyed fiancée, despite the time, her soft blue eyes sparkled, her face broke into a smile that lit up Henry's I pad, his own face returned a smile wider than whatever distance was separating them.

Her opening words set his heart racing, "Henry my darling I was dreaming about you my special man."

"Corrina sweetheart, likewise, whenever we are apart my nights are spent dreaming of you, trouble is when I wake up, disappointment is my companion."

"Henry you're making me sad, when are you coming home? I miss you so, our bed is too big for one I feel lost."

"Oh you're at home, for how long?"

"Arrived yesterday evening, back to Edinburgh tomorrow; how's your dad?"

"He's had his scan, it'll be a couple of weeks before he gets the results then they will decide on the treatment he will need."

"When will you be home?"

"I'll stay for two more days then I'll get a flight home, when you get back home I'm not letting you out of our bed until you have to fly back."

"Oooooh Henry Swan Jenson, I wish you wouldn't I won't be able to sleep, you've got me so worked up, I like it though, keep talking."

"Corrina Jade Phelps you little madam you're getting me worked up. I'll be walking with a limp seeing you in that nightie, it doesn't hide much does it, what are you doing?"

"What does it look like? I am taking it off."

"Corrina, you cruel bugger you're making it worse by showing me such a licentious, brazen, immodest, shameless but beautiful display of sexual venality, It's really working, I'm yours forever."

"If I knew what venality meant, I would probably agree with you?"

"It's everything a man dreams of, to be corrupted by his lover."

"Hmmm, corrupting you am I, somehow I think you corrupted me the moment you kissed me."

"Who cares; looking at your nakedness, I want to be corrupted."

"It's so you don't forget what I look like."

"Corrina Jade whatever happens in our lives I would never forget your beauty, your face is etched permanently in my minds-eye, what are you doing now?"

"I'm putting my nightie back on."

"Meany."

"Henry my darling I don't want you having problems with your sea squirt."

"Too late I'm already having problems it's strangling me."

"I wish you were here so I could rescue you."

"Blue eyes I wish you could rescue me, I'll let you go back to bed we will talk tomorrow, hopefully this rising appendage will have subsided."

Corrina laughing, advised him, "Take a cold shower, that should lessen your eagerness somewhat."

Shaking his head but grinning, he countered, "You're not very nice to me, I thought you loved me? Cold shower indeed, Brrrrrrr."

"I will love you until the man up in the clouds decides otherwise, never forget that."

"Blue eyes I love you too, good night."

"Good night my special man, I will return to my dream of making love to you."

Henry remained in Birmingham for two more days in order to tidy up a few loose ends. Once his and Frank's opinions were in harmony, ideas were put in place to cover all possibilities that might appear over the next few months in case Frank's treatment might incapacitate him completely.

Henry was still quite apprehensive, his dad seemed distant and withdrawn he was certainly not his usual responsive and sociable self. Frank had fallen into a dark place hiding behind the smile used to conceal his true feeling. Melancholia appeared to be another invasive unwanted enemy. Frank's quiet mien weighed heavily on Henry's heart, he wanted to reach out to make him whole. Reluctantly resigned to the fact he hadn't the wherewithal to perform a miracle, all he and the rest of the family could do was offer encouragement, moreover, put their faith in the medics entrusted with the task of looking after him.

Family ties or not Henry wanted to get home he was getting homesick for New York, though there of course was a far more compelling reason in the shape of his bride to be Corrina.

Two days later Henry returned home, as he put the key in the door to his surprise it opened, Corrina smiled a smile of utter pleasure, her soft blue eyes glowing she pulled his head into her hands engaging in an unrestrained frenzy of lubricious kissing; they remained on the landing locked in a forceful embrace which neither of them wanted to relinquish.

Their hello, although unspoken testified to their undoubted need for each other, still entangled in their potent embrace they somehow found their way to the bedroom, the way they touched, the way they sighed, the totality of giving themselves to each other showed their deep innermost feelings, their carnal needs had to be indulged. An hour later their animalistic instincts satiated by their amatory union Henry smiled broadly admitting. "Corrina coming home excited me however, while inserting the key into the door, for a moment loneliness beclouded me. The idea of entering our home thinking you were somewhere else in the world left me feeling quite gloomy, oh I have missed you Corrina, that was the most wonderful welcome, now I know I'm home."

"My special man I have missed you more than I can ever put into words."

"Blue eyes how long have we got, when did you get here?"

"An hour before you arrived, so we have two nights."

"Wow fantastic."

"How was your dad when you left?"

"Worried, he tries not to show it but I see it in his eyes, if the results of the scan are positive the consultant will decide the best treatment for him."

Corrina advised him, "Henry you must be positive, I know what you are going through, its gut wrenching watching the people you love hurting. When my mum's illness was diagnosed, it was far too late, but your dad hasn't been so silly."

"I'm not so sure, apparently he hid the symptoms from Elaine, bless her she noticed things weren't right but she still had to badger him, then Mum and Caro got on his case, in the end he acquiesced to their rather aggressive arguments."

"Well at least he has accepted he needs treatment, what I will suggest is we leave the wedding until he is able to travel, it's a long journey."

"Sweetheart I think we will need to talk about it some other time, but that is an offer of an angel."

"I'm not an angel, just realistic, are you hungry?"

"Only for you."

"Mmmmm crafty bleeder lets go for Dinner first, you've already had your starter I haven't eaten all day."

"Oh I'm glad that was only a starter can't wait for the main course and the pudding."

"Henry, you're incorrigible."

"I'm, not I'm C of E."

"Come on or you won't get that pudding."

"You mean bugger."

They enjoyed a wonderful two days, Henry watched with sad eyes as Corrina flew back to Edinburgh, at least they had their daily chat on facetime to look forward to, happily she was working the New York flight for the forceable future, the only thing blighting their happiness; waiting for the results of Frank's scan. Ten days later Henry received a call from Elaine buzzing with her news, "Henry the cancer has not spread to anywhere else in his body, they are going to operate on Saturday."

Henry absolutely delighted asked, "How long will he be in hospital?"

"If all goes well about four days, while he is in there he will receive enhanced recovery practices to promote faster recovery, at the same time reducing the risk of complications such as blood clots in his legs."

"Blimey that's fantastic, I suppose he'll have to rest up for a while after."

"They have told him if he feels up to it he can resume normal activities like climbing stairs, he can even drive as long as he doesn't lift anything weighing more than twenty pounds."

"That will please him as long as he doesn't overdo it."

"Henry, I will make sure he doesn't."

"I hope so but you know what he's like I don't think it would be advisable to drive, he'll do something stupid like buggering off to Wales, you know what he's like; obstinate."

"I can assure you I will go to work with him, I was his PA so I know what he's Like, I won't let him get away with anything."

"Elaine that news has cheered me up no end, I can relax and, we have Christmas to look forward too."

"Yes and Frank will be fit and ready to enjoy it, he really hasn't been well, I have never seen him so withdrawn."

"Elaine keep me posted, if he starts going against medical advice I'll have to fly back."

"Hopefully for once in his life, maybe, he will listen to his family."

"We can only hope, thanks Elaine for letting me know I'll facetime him on Sunday see if his optimism is coming to the fore."

"Henry I hope to see a different Frank not the one who has been hiding behind the fascia of sanguinity, he couldn't and didn't fool me."

They said their goodbyes.

Henry buzzing, rang Corrina to tell her the good news, she didn't answer so he left her a message, she rang back later that evening and was delighted for the family especially for her special man, while conversing Henry asked if she could get some time off in January explaining he wanted her to see New York in winter extolling its beauty, offering, "It is almost as beautiful as you blue eyes."

"Ooooh Henry I'll see if I can."

"Then when we get home, I know a way we can warm up."

She replied, "I love you my special man, bye-bye."

"Bye-bye blue eyes bye."

All his anxiety banished, Henry that night slept the sleep of the blessed, the sandman indulging him with Corrina laden dreams.

Chapter 35

In a more relaxed state of mind, Henry watched and marvelled at New York's changing flora and fauna as the weather began to chill, winter was on the doorstep. October and November had occasioned a beautiful colourful autumn efflorescence of red, orange, caramel and yellow leaves which had gradually replaced the glorious green and vibrant colours of spring and summer before fluttering gently to the ground, creating a carpet of nature's maturity. December arrived bringing its dark icy mornings to greet the irascible shorter days, the occasional flurry of snow was expected, New York on the threshold of Christmas. It was Henry's second Christmas in New York, Corrina hoped she would be by his side to enjoy the idiosyncratic New Yorkers who made Christmas very special.

To be in New York at Christmas is indeed something different, it has a charm and flavour of its own, a distinctive quality with an intangible unique ambience. When you walk down the streets, the cold wind is dismissed by the warmth Christmas seems to generate from within the community. Holly wreaths are hung on every door, Santa clause collects for various charities on every street corner, the locals, for the most part smile and are friendly as they go about their business, brass bands play and choirs sing carols. Freezing cold air magnifies the feeling of goodwill, ruddy faces glow through that freezing air, children stand excited in queues of stores to see Santa Clause their eyes coruscating at the attractive, colourful tempting displays of toys and candy in shop windows…

Christmas eve and Henry had an added pleasure when Elaine informed him that the medics attending to his dad believed his cancer was in remission, his chemo treatment though painful continued to nullify any unwanted anxiety. Another plus, Corrina would be joining him for Christmas, she had expressed her request to secure two weeks annual leave over the Christmas holiday, which was rewarded, they allowed ten days,

Henry and Corrina shared a really wonderful Christmas, their first as a couple. Henry woke up early on Christmas morning hoping to surprise Corrina, only to find her wide awake and leaning over him smiling sunnily, her eyes incandescent with happiness, her welcome words, "Happy Christmas Henry Swan Jenson my very special man."

Rubbing his eyes, focusing through the darkness observing the radiance of Corrina's blue eyes whispering huskily, "Happy Christmas Corrina Jade Phelps my blue eyed lover."

Corrina reiterated her greeting of, "Happy Christmas my special man," advancing her excitement, "shall we look out of our window, I want to wish Mum a happy Christmas. Christmas was her favourite time of the year, despite being a single mum she did so much for us, this is my second Christmas without her, last year was awful, coming to terms with the fact she wasn't with us anymore. I wish you could have met her she would have loved you, she would have been so happy for me, just like she was when Elliot met and married Sadie, oh and she adored her granddaughter Becky."

"I feel like I know her, even though we never met."

"Henry I feel she has sent you to look after me."

They stood as they always did, naked, looking out of the window at the night sky; sadly, clouds hid the stars but it didn't deter them from expressing their thanks to her.

Back on the bed Henry reached underneath for an envelope which he handed to Corrina, she looking puzzled and asked him. "What is it?"

"Sweetheart unless you open it you will never know."

Upon opening the envelope, she Stared at the contents open mouthed, unable to assimilate fully what lay in her hand. Henry had to explain, "Really it is a present to both of us, It's tickets for our honeymoon."

Teary eyed she whispered, "Henry where are we going?"

"Well my darling, we will be cruising round the Caribbean for two weeks, then a further week in St Lucia staying at Sandals hotel, lazing round the pool."

She burst into tears, "Henry I don't know what to say, except you never cease to amaze me I'm overwhelmed, but we still haven't fixed a date."

"When we know we will change the dates on those tickets, anyway Corrina that is for our honeymoon this is your Christmas present."

She looked at him speaking quietly, as another tear ran down her cheek, "Henry I don't need anything else, this is already special and just being in our home on our first Christmas together is wonderful, I'm so happy."

"My blue-eyed lover, If ever there comes a time when I can't indulge you in the good things in life, I promise, you can be sure you will always have my love, come what may."

"I know when you kiss me heaven sighs, when we touch I'm weak at the knees, when we make love I feel the whole world is mine."

"If I could give you the world I would."

"Henry you are my world."

"My darling its Christmas morning, I want to make you week at the knees but Open your present."

"I'll open it later."

Light began to filter through the part drawn curtains, they finished making each other weak at the knees, the outside world temperatures freezing cold and damp. The inside world had produced passion, correlated to nuclear fission so hot so wild, akin to an electrostatic attraction, their energy enriched with a desire to give themselves to each other. Exhausted by their celestial fusion they lay still for a while, holding hands breathing in the heady exotic redolence filling the air; before both drifting into a much-needed dormancy. They believed their love was indubitable, their love was infrangible, a love so strong nothing except God could create a situation to separate them that would ever be stronger than their love.

Coming out of his dream laden somnolence, Henry lay gazing at his naked fiancée listening to her gentle rhythmic breathing, his mind completely at peace, the most important person in his life. Allied to the news that Frank's surgery to remove the malignant neoplasm from his Colon had gone very well, to all intents and purposes the cancer was in remission, Henry's Christmas was complete. Later Henry would be speaking to all his family via facetime, there was a bonus for Corrina too, she was expecting to be able to facetime Elliot. On cue, Henry's I pad flickered into life, Elliot's face came into view smiling, but at the same time he admonished Henry, "Henry you have given us far too much! I was and still am dumfounded, but thank you so much for the I pad, Becky is over the moon, if that wasn't enough you added the I phone for Becky as well, you and Corrina are not just family you are friends."

"Elliot I'm glad you like them do you want to talk to your little sister, she is in dreamsville but I'll wake her." Henry gently woke her with a soft kiss;

Her eyes opened rapidly, she proposed.

"Happy Christmas Elliot how is Sadie and Becky?"

"Happy Christmas Corrina, the girls are here waiting to talk to you."

Both Sadie and Becky came into view shouting, "Happy Christmas Corrina we miss you, Happy Christmas, Henry," Sadie added, "this is the first time we have been able to talk, and see you at the same time, while you are so far away, thank you so much."

"Sadie I'm chuffed, we'll be able see as well as talk to each other, as often as we like, I do miss our chats."

"Corrina we will give you and Henry's presents when you get home, have a lovely time, speak tomorrow, we all love you, bye for now."

"Bye Sadie, bye Elliot and my lovely niece Becky bye, bye."

Henry and Corrina spent the next hour talking to the rest of the family, it was good to hear Frank was back to his best smiling and being the perfect host as all the family were having dinner at the 'High Chaparral'.

Conversations with both sides of the family concluded, Henry and Corrina sat on the bed with Corrina grinning from ear to ear, a salacious look on her face at the same time displaying her feminine charms, huskily she voiced, "Henry My special man, I'll go and put the Turkey in the oven?"

"The turkey can wait."

"Christmas dinner will be late," was her croaky reply.

"Who cares?"

Dinner was going to be very late…

Turkey would have to wait until Boxing-day. That evening they dined on fried eggs and oven fries followed by pancakes served as a sweet, not exactly Christmas fayre. They opened a bottle of wine which was followed by another then another. Whilst drinking wine and they listened to 'Radio country live of New York' and they exchanged Christmas presents. Corrina presented Henry with a small box wrapped in festive paper of red decorated with Holly leaves, Upon opening the box, there lay inside a gold St Christopher with a gold chain. "Henry I will always know you are safe when you wear it."

"My darling you will be with me always, thank you it's beautiful."

She also gave him a bottle of 'Joop! Eau-de Toilette' his favourite, in addition because of his sweet tooth she gave him a large box of hand crafted 'Vosges' truffles another of his favourites. Henry while grinning told her, "I don't know whether to eat chocolate or make love to you what do you think?"

"I should eat chocolate after last night Henry Swan Jenson you will need to rebuild your strength."

"Corrina Jade Phelps cheeky bugger are you intimating I'm a weakling?"

"Not at all but it was a long day I'm knackered so you must be."

Henry Reached behind the sofa for Corrina's gift, he handed her a small box wrapped in festive paper, her Jaw dropped and her eyes widened the width of a Cinerama screen as she unwrapped a stunning pink and white diamond cluster ring set in nine carat rose gold. Henry explained that diamond was her birth stone for April, he also gave her a bottle of her favourite perfume (Beautiful), enclosed in the box was a note stating 'because you are so beautiful'. He then he handed her a plain envelope, inside was an old 1959 vinyl record by Gene Pitney (I wanna love my life away) he explained, "Because my blue-eyed lover, I really want to love my life away with you."

As tears began to trickle down Corrina's face, Henry although a little mystified, wrapped her in his arms asking quietly, "Hey blue eyes, why the tears?"

Slipping into her Scottish vernacular, "Hendrie A hae ne'er felt sae wanted or loved sin maw died."

Something Henry very rarely did, he responded in the same way. "Corrina mah blue chocked burd a'm wantin 'n' wull loue ye 'til th' jimmy 'boon th' clouds decides otherwise."

Corrina open mouthed was staggered at Henry's bilingualism, she had never heard him speak the Scottish vernacular, astonishingly he rendered his speech perfectly. Reverting back to plain English lauding his ability she queried. "I knew you understood the lingo, but I never thought you could speak it so well, honestly you never fail to amaze me my special man, I love you so much."

Boxing day arrived, Corrina dismissed Henry's entreaties to stay in bed a little longer, rose early to prepare and cook their overdue Christmas dinner, Henry feigning annoyance to keep her next to him, dutifully followed to help in any-way she wanted. They celebrated their first Christmas dinner together by imbibing a bottle of good Californian sparkling wine, deciding against a second bottle. With dinner over, they snuggled up on the sofa feeling content, both a little tipsy from the wine, lapsed into a state of absent minded daydreaming.

Outside snow was falling, needing to shake of their drowsiness they went for a stroll in the snow covered streets of Greenwich Village, returning cheery hellos from strangers as they passed by, warming to the ambience of the streets, it was all a child's dream, a white Christmas.

More snow fell as they made their way back to their apartment, the day had been the start of a very happy Christmas holiday creating so many memories, memories that would be warmly thought of every Christmas thereafter.

Henry had promised he would show Corrina why New York was so spectacular in winter and why it was so special to him, which he did, when showing her Central Park covered by a carpet of snow. She clung to him in wonderment at what filled her senses, the sounds and smells as they walked through the park.

It can only be described as truly wonderous, throughout the park there is exuberance, furthermore, joyfulness radiating from the glowing faces of families, adults and children alike and yet it offers peacefulness.

Family groups were Ice skating over the Woolman and Lasker ice rinks also across the beautiful Conservatory water, but only if the ice is deemed to be thick enough. They decided to give the ice a try, Henry was quite an accomplish skater, as a young teenager it had been one of his favourite sports, Corrina however had never ice skated before. After a number of bumps and crashing falls, ultimately ending up on her backside resulting in some very painful bruising, Henry sporting a cheeky lascivious grin promised to kiss and massage them better. Bumps and bruises aside, she possessed an inherent sense of balance, in a very short space of time she was competent enough to be considered quite a proficient skater, however riding a sled was a different proposition, there were too many people on the hills, she wasn't frightened for herself but feared if she lost control she might crash into somebody, her biggest fear it might be a small child.

Corrina fell in love with wintered Central Park the same way Henry had, sadly she was due to fly back to Edinburgh on new year's day nevertheless they would see in the new year together, hopefully in Times Square. Cornelius recommended they get there early, as early as they possibly could, because the viewing areas begin to fill up early afternoon, furthermore, they should make sure they wear as many layers of warm clothing as possible, despite the crowds it gets damn cold. They took his advice.

Welcoming the new-year for millions of Americans begins with all the American glitz and glamour at the emblematic Centre of New York; known as the Times Square New Year's Eve Ball Drop. It is estimated one million people attend each new year to be entertained by the Dick Clark New Year's Rockin'

Eve Show, hosted By Ryan Seagrave. It starts at 8 pm going through to midnight, featuring entertainment with performances by popular musicians, concluding on the stroke of midnight with the ball drop. The anticipation rises as the minutes count-down to midnight, when the ball drops at eleven fifty-nine pm it falls one hundred and forty-one feet in sixty seconds, then followed by 1,400 kilos of confetti showering down on the party goers which heralds a simply stunning pyrotechnic display. The crowd singing along with a million of other joyful participants, all giving their rendition of (auld lang Syne) at the very top of their voices, partying in all its unabashed extravagant excitement, furthermore its rumbustious dazzling flamboyance it is truly magnificent, is American at its finest...

After ten hours partying in Times Square, they were exhausted, what's more frozen to the core but extremely happy. When the Times Square ball dropped to welcome the new-year, they exchanged a long lingering loving kiss, the love flowing between them created a river of desire bringing the life back to their equally frozen libidos. Back home in their apartment Henry made coffee most of which they left in the pot going cold, the last few hours of their first Christmas together before Corrina flew back to Edinburgh, had to be a special. Unsure how long they would be apart, tiredness deserted them, love was on the menu and young love will have its way. Their amative coupling, reached a sensual furnace of fierceness so hot it likened to molten base metal extracted from the ore, liquefied and flowing white hot from the smelting furnace to the mould. Sheer exhaustion induced sweet and much needed dormancy.

Henry and Corrina had never experienced the like of it, Corrina Scottish through and through reckoned it was the best Hogmanay celebration she had ever been part of, telling Henry. "What a fabulous way to ring out the old and ring in the new-year."

"Corrina my blue-eyed lover it has been fabulous, believe me from here-on in we will welcome every new year together."

The holiday came to a conclusion all too quickly, over before it began or so it seemed. Henry sat on the bed watching Corrina pack her case for the flight back to Edinburgh voicing his innermost feelings, "Corrina Jade Phelps, soon to be Corrina Jade Swan Jenson when I look at you, it brings to mind a quote by Gilbert Chesterton."

She interrupted him, "I have never heard of him but knowing you he must have said something profound."

"Oh he did, he said (the way to love anything is to realise that it might be lost) when I look at you I am frightened I might lose you."

"My special man, there is no way on earth we will be lost to each other."

"I'm glad you feel as I do, anyway if you finish packing I'll drive you to the airport you don't want to miss your flight."

Henry remained in John F Kennedy airport to watch the plane take off, his thoughts caressed by the images of the wonderful Christmas he and Corrina had shared, how they played, how they talked, laughed, and loved. Their love making, the resin compound binding them together creating the very quintessence of romantic bliss.

Back in their apartment he lay on the bed, his musings of the previous ten days set him smiling, but suddenly for no apparent reason he was seized by a sense of disquiet, shaking him sharply out of his reveries. He stood up looking out of the window at the grey sullen clouds, black thoughts began to prevail anxiety was uppermost, he was scared. In his mind, it wasn't beyond the realms of possibility that something might happen to the flight carrying his future bride back to Edinburgh. He called Elliot who promised to call back as soon as Corrina's plane landed. Henry's all-consuming afflicting thoughts meant he couldn't settle, he spent the night staring continuously through the window at the mackerel starless sky, his mind swirling in a state of flux, relief eventually came, when true to his word Elliot called informing him Corrina's plane had just touched down. Half an hour later Corrina called too, her smiling face lighting up the phone. "Hello Henry, Elliot said you were worried."

"Stupid I know but I had a moment, I've been looking out the window all night unable to put my mind to anything else."

"We didn't experience a single second of turbulence during the flight, I slept most of the way dreaming of you, so I'll let you get some sleep special man."

"Bye blue eyes, see you next week."

"Bye, Bye, love you."

A very relieved Henry lay back on the bed smiling to himself, a heavy storm cloud had been erased from his worried mind, he was happy: sleep came easy.

Chapter 36

Awaking from his slumbers Henry, wholly unfettered by dreams of fear, horror and distress, was refreshed once again, enthusiastic about his future; furthermore he was ready to take on the world. Later in his favourite Diner he took a breakfast of bacon, eggs over easy and grits, hot, heavily buttered rye bread toast, all washed down with numerous cups of black coffee. Fully relaxed his thoughts drifted sweetly to Corrina, remembering the first time they met In Cardiff, his mind recalled how struck he had been by her appearance wearing a short skirted red and green flowered dress with her blonde hair worn down on her shoulders. He remembered how effortless their converse had been, especially when he later walked her back to her hotel, as though they had known each other for years, the very hotel where he was residing at for some two months. He really liked her, however because she lived in Edinburgh precluded any thoughts that their paths would one day traverse the distance of 250 miles between Birmingham and Edinburgh. Nonetheless the impossible had come to pass, the consequence of which had endowed them with an unbreakable love. Henry remembered something he had read by Nathanial Hawthorn (the inward pleasure of imparting pleasure that is the choicest of all) he fully understood the sentiment.

Henry's love for Corrina without fear of contradiction would be described as devout, his love was fervently passionate, his adoration of her ecclesiastical. By the same token, Corrina's love for Henry could only be defined as reverential she was besotted with him, consummately intoxicated verging on a delirious devotional divine desire. Their love was a truly complex set of variations which were interwoven accordingly furnishing a total belief, furthermore strength of trust afforded of each other, they shared everything. Secrets never came into the equation, they were able to discuss anything and everything without fear of hurting each other. The apartment was their home, even their personal bank accounts had been merged into a joint account, such was their commitment to each other.

After the wonderful time, they enjoyed together over Christmas, Henry realised their love was a love blessed by a higher presence, combined with the wonderful news from the medics, Frank's cancer was now, thankfully, in remission. Henry decided to propose again via face time, Corrina giggling, replied, "Of course I will, silly sod, when were you thinking?"

"How about becoming an April bride?"

"Henry, how wonderful."

"When you get back home, we will set the wheels in motion, what do you Think?"

"I do love you Henry Swan Jenson, I'll tell Elliot and Sadie."

"Ok blue eyes, give them my love."

Corrina chuckling said, "Hang on a minute," she disappeared from the (I pad) for about five minutes, during that time Henry could hear distant shouting, she returned with her face all flushed, she giggled and said, "Henry I told the family we are planning to tie the knot as soon as possible, Sadie and Elliot send their love and congratulations to us, however cheeky madam Becky asked. "Why, so soon have you got a bun in the oven?" Sadie has gone ape, demanding to know why she would be so disrespectful asking such an impertinent question, she's in big trouble and no mistake."

"Blimey sounds just like a mordantly abrasive comment, my darling sister Lindy would voice, but to be honest 'she' would probably have more to say on the subject. What will happen to her, if Sadie is so angry?"

"I would imagine she will be grounded for a few days."

"Ah well We've all been there."

"Oh, by the way I forgot to tell you Elliot has got an interview at your dad's company next week, they have a vacancy."

"I'll keep my fingers crossed for him."

Corrina cheered him, "It's late my special man I'll say goodnight, I'll be home on Saturday though, all being well."

Henry replied. "Mmmm roll on Saturday, goodnight my blue eyed darling goodnight."

Henry excited as always because Corrina was coming home, collected her from JFK Airport. Every time she came through from security her entrancement moved him to fall deeper in love, she was by then the flame that ignited the fuel that drove his passion for life. Anyone watching would have thought they had been separated for an inordinate amount of time, not less than a week their hello unrestrained. They went back to their apartment together feeling very happy, over dinner they began to make plans for an April wedding.

Corrina was raised in the Catholic faith, the importance of marrying in a Catholic church was paramount to her however, Henry although christened in the Anglican Church, was a non-believer, they understood there might be problems to be confronted. Google came to the rescue; reading the text concerning the marriage ceremony in a Catholic Church both of them sighed with relief at the findings. It stated marriage is one of the seven sacraments of the Catholic Church nonetheless to be sacramentally married in the Catholic Church both parties must be baptized but at least one of them must be a Catholic. Smiling cheekily Henry voiced a paradox, "I don't believe in God but thank God I was christened."

Corrina grimacing, shook her head at his spoken anomaly, wagged her finger at him asseverating, "Henry Swan Jenson you will never be allowed through the gates of heaven."

Still smiling he offered his thoughts, "I won't need to I'm already there, in heaven that is."

Looking puzzled she queried, "What do you mean you're already there."

"Well Corrina Jade Phelps my little cherub I'm in heaven because I have you to love." They kissed a heavenly kiss.

The weeks that followed were a blur as trying to arrange a wedding in a short space of three months presents a whole set of complications. The first disappointment they encountered; every Catholic Church within Greenwich Village area was sadly, unable to accommodate them, many of them explaining they were fully booked for the rest of the year and beyond. Corrina was deeply disturbed, she believed that the catholic religion did not recognise and would not recognise her future marriage as valid.

Google again came to the rescue, Henry researching the subject read a report posted in the magazine (The Catholic world) it denies Catholicism does not regard civil marriage as a real marriage, furthermore they insist it is binding, adding marriage between all baptized persons is a sacrament.

Henry digested the article before showing it Corrina hoping it would be enough to lenify her, he also promised if they had a civil wedding they would have a full ceremony in the hallowed environ of a Catholic Church; as soon as their situation gave them the opportunity. Henry even suggested perhaps her local church in Edinburgh would be a possibility, then told her he would marry her every week if he could. Corrina's discomfort desisted she was relieved, the thought their marriage would not be recognised in the eyes of the church had troubled her greatly.

Nevertheless, they were still left with another dilemma, finding a venue in time for April, If they couldn't have a church wedding they wanted somewhere special, something a little different. As promised Henry's colleague and friend the one a[nd] only Dusty J Upthegrove 3RD came to the rescue, his motto 'I'm on the case and if I can't do it nobody can. He surprised them by offering his own majestically capacious house set amid an imposing myriad of indigenous, rare and imported flora and fauna. To the rear of the garden stood a small but imposing pavilion, Dusty gave Henry and Corrina a full guided tour, they couldn't believe their eyes, the place was stunning. Dusty suggested, "If the weather is warm. You could wed in the garden under the pavilion, what do you think?"

Corrina's eyes moistened she was enchanted, she threw her arms around Dusty declaring, "Dusty you are a star, it is beautiful thank you, and yes please I can't think of anywhere as beautiful to get married, thank you so much."

"Give me the date and I'll organise the justice he's a friend of mine, how do you fancy a band, country of course?"

Henry for once was at a loss, "Sir if there is ever anything I can do to repay you, just ask?"

"Henry son it's my pleasure, come inside have a look around and meet my wife Avalina."

Dusty with a proud smile on his face introduced them to Avalina his wife, a lovely petite Mexicano, born to a wealthy family, and to their six children, all girls, Abril, Adonia; Angela, Amanda; Alyss and Analee, ranging in ages from five to seventeen, all as gorgeous as their mum. Avalina invited them to dinner revealing. "Henry, you and Corrina are the first people Dusty has invited here from work, he sees a lot of you in himself: that is apart from his dress sense of course. To be perfectly honest he trusts you, you are like the son he would have liked and wanted. Sadly, it wasn't to be, here we are with six beautiful daughters and he adores them all equally, adoration which is requited, he is a wonderful dad and a wonderful husband."

Strangely, although Corrina was brought up in a relatively poor background, completely at odds with the very affluent lifestyle Avelina was used to, she still thought in many ways they too, were alike. Both were intelligent, both were family orientated, furthermore both had a wicked sense of humour. They quickly became very close friends. Spending time with Dusty and his family Henry understood what Avalina meant to him, Avalina equated Henry as a younger Dusty, they were both filled with ambition and both a one woman man.

Corrina and Henry were invited to stay for food, what really surprised them was Avalina serving up a roast beef dinner, including Yorkshire pudding, she admitted they had acquired a taste for British cuisine after living in Britain for three years. Dusty's favourite was the full English breakfast, which meant having a regular order of black pudding and pork sausages sent over from England. Avalina commenting, "Our girls love the food too, they miss England."

Corrina by-passed cloud nine, riding cloud twenty-seven, such was her excitement thanks to the generosity of Dusty and Avalina availing their beautiful home for their wedding venue. Other news lifted her spirits, her brother Elliot had joined (Jenson's office supplies Scotland) the week after his previous employment had terminated due to them closing. She and Henry were able to begin planning for their special day.

Although the venue was sorted, Henry's preferred month of April for the wedding was proving difficult coordinating family mums, dads, children and grandparents. Therefore, after many discussions they settled on the alternative date, Saturday the twenty first of May twenty sixteen. Frank organised the flight for all of them, except for Corrina's brother Elliot, his wife, Sadie, their daughter Becky and three of Corrina's friends and their partners. Henry had the task of finding hotel accommodation for all of the family and friends once he knew how many would be making the journey, all of whom would be arriving five days before the wedding, giving them time to settle in. Thereafter everything went swimmingly Dusty and Cornelius helped with arrangements, Corrina conversed a lot with Avelina discussing how they could make the pavilion special for the ceremony, hoping the weather was warm enough.

The big day drew closer, Elliot, Sadie, Becky, Maggie and Corrina's best friends and colleagues from Edinburgh, flew out ten days before the wedding to help with the preparations. It gave Henry and Corrina a chance to spend time with them, they could showcase their life in New York. Elliot was stunned by Henry's Ford Fairlane, shaking his head he commented. "Wow I have a Ford a Focus. It's a fifteen plate but wow I have never seen anything like this, wow Henry it's fantastic."

"Would you like to drive it?"

"I would but not just yet, later maybe."

When they entered the apartment, Sadie was also stunned. "Corrina it is massive, I have never seen a kitchen so big, you could fit the ground floor of our house in here."

"Sadie I am so very lucky, I wish Mum was here to see it."

"Yes, your mum would have been chuffed for you."

"Also, I have Elliot to give me away, I'm so happy."

Elliot joined the conversation commenting, "I am really proud to do so, I just wish we would have had a dad to do what dads are supposed to do."

"Elliot, Mum will be watching over us I'm sure, that's all that matters."

"Little Sis don't you sometimes wonder where our dad is, for that matter who he is? Someday, I'll go looking for him," wrapping her in his arms he continued, "but it doesn't really matter he's the one missing out."

Corrina's face reflecting sadness replied, "Thanks big Bro but I never think about him, he didn't want us so sod him, Mum never once said anything nice about him, he was a bully."

Henry interposed, delivering his own thoughts, "Corrina I'm with Elliot, obviously there were problems but I think if I were in the same position I would probably be curious."

Becky also had her say reflecting on the fact she only had one grandparent, her maternal grandmother, "It would be nice to have a granddad."

Sadie lightened the talk, "Corrina! Let's see your wedding dress I bet it's special?"

Corrina's mood changed, a smile illuminated her face, "Sadie I fell in love with it the moment I saw it, but first Becky."

A puzzled Becky asked, "What?"

"Come into the bedroom with me I have something for you."

"For me?"

Sadie and Elliot also puzzled followed into the bedroom, Corrina grinning, pointed to a dress on the bed, "That's for you, if you'll be one of my bridesmaids; will you?"

Becky, wide eyed exclaimed, "You want me to be a bridesmaid?"

"Of course I want you."

She sang, "I'm going to be a bridesmaid," then tearful, she hugged everyone adding, "can I try it on now?"

Sadie, so excited for her daughter shooed the men out of the room, "Come on Becky try it on, let's have a look at you."

Becky normally a defiant know it all twelve-year old, with a predisposition for opening her preteen mouth giving unintentional, hurtful, aphoristic comments without thought of the consequences, showed off the dress and commented kindly, "Corrina its lovely to see you so happy, when Nan died I didn't think you would ever smile again." Then back to her normal self, cheekily added, "I wonder what Henry has got, that keeps a smile on your face?"

Sadie and Elliot looked astounded at what their daughter was intimating, both were about to explode but she was saved when Corrina and Henry burst into intemperate laughter. Sadie who couldn't contain her own mirth had to join the hilarity shaking her head remarked, "Becky, cheeky monkey I don't know what to say, just give me and everyone else a hug, we'll will say no more?"

Henry still grinning added, "We are in for a rocky time when Lindy gets here, the two of them will be a nightmare together, they are so alike."

When Becky and Lindy met a few days later, a friendship was forged very quickly, their puerile attitudes to everything, were matched, two twelve-year old pretentious girls giggling constantly, giving out cheeky but subtle derogatory implications, usually aimed at their parents.

Up to no good, while their parents were out, Lindy sporting a witting face enquired of Becky, "Last night did Henry and Corrina keep you awake with all that ooohing and aahhing<"

Smiling smugly Becky's riposte, "Yes they must be worn out, I know I am."

There appeared to be a competition between them as to who could display the rudest, discourteous aphorism furthermore; they both lacked any form of respect for authority. Nevertheless, discipline was restored when Corrina took them aside expressing her dismay at their antics revealing, if they didn't curb their rudeness and insolence she would not have them as her bridesmaids.

Peace reigned.

Two days before the wedding Frank, Elaine and Henry's brother's Jude and Myles along with Cherry arrived, later than others because of Frank's business commitments. Barney Philips who by then was his best friend and right-hand man remained home, with the responsibility of steering Jenson's on a steady course.

Frank and Elaine were introduced to Corrina and her small family on the eve of the wedding, welcoming them all into the Jenson family, they could not have been more genuine and loving, hugging the girls. However, when shaking hands with Elliot, Frank experienced an uncomfortable awareness that something didn't quite fit. Nonetheless putting his disquiet aside, he began to be the man everyone knew him to be; the life and soul of the party: back to his best.

Henry who normally coped with any business complications, for the first time in his life, his mind was stretched to its limits, so much so he had an attack of nerves on the eve of the ceremony, the ceremony he longed for.

He wanted to see her dressed in white, he wanted to lift the veil and gaze into her soft blue eyes he wanted to love her forever and longer, his love stronger than the surging overwhelming waves of an ocean tsunami.

He wanted the perfect day for his Corrina Jade…

Chapter 37

The eve of Henry and Corrina's nuptials arrived, Henry and his best friend Cornelius, whom he had asked and who had been delighted to accept the role of best man, were busy with wedding arrangements. Henry, always meticulous in his preparations whatever he was involved with, made sure everything was on hand ready for the morning. Henry and Corrina had agreed both of them should be dressed in white, although Corrina couldn't, in her mind's eye foresee just how he would look. However, with Dusty's help, Henry embracing his love of America chose a western cowboy style suit consisting of a white frock coat, pants, white double-breasted shirt, a white Kentucky Bow tie, and white boots all topped off with a white fedora Stetson hat. Cornelius also chose a copy of the suit: a duet.

A little worried of how Corrina might perceive his wedding apparel Henry posted her a video via (WhatsApp) she replied with a face-to-face chat. "Henry my darling, if you turned up naked I would be just as proud of you."

"Blimey do I look that good naked I'll take the suit back."

"I don't want the rest of the girls getting Jealous of your sea squirt, It's for me alone."

"I'll keep the suit then."

From the background, Maggie's obtrusive voice intervened, "Sod the suit let's see the squirt."

"Henry, take no notice of her."

"Corrina, I think we had better sign off before her crudity degenerates down to barnyard indelicacy."

"I take it you mean filth?"

"That's the term, filth."

Both choking with boisterous hilarity, said their goodbyes with Maggie adding her own reply, "You cheeky pair of bastards."

Henry ended the conversation with, "I rest my case; see you at two o'clock tomorrow blue eyes."

All the men went to a bar for a quiet drink so they could get to know each other, Avelina, Dusyi's wife, accompanied them purely to make sure no unsavoury incidents would detract or spoil any part of the proceedings on the morrow. Elliot and Frank got to know each other, Elliot informed him he was one of his employees at his Edinburgh branch, they chatted for a while and Frank enquired how Ellie was while extolling to Elliot his high admiration for her managerial ability. Frank for some reason, out of the blue told them, "Me and Mary, Henry's mum had a friend called Susan Phillips who lived in Birmingham not far from us, in fact she used to babysit for us, she had a son called Elliot, she had a daughter as well, I didn't know her name."

Elliot replied, "Mum died nearly two years ago and as far as I know she had never been to Birmingham, neither have I, and I don't think Corrina has either, anyway our surname is Phelps, similar but that's all."

Once everything necessary for the wedding had been put into place the women settled down enjoyed a few glasses of wine and played cards, the kids played Scrabble, a pleasant evening was enjoyed by all. Avalina did her job admirably, by ten o'clock every single member of the men's party had gone back to their hotels, the women and children too, in preparation for the big day…

It was the early hours of the morning on the day of the wedding, both Henry and Corrina had experienced sleepless nights effected by a mixture of excitement allied with worry, hoping all their work over the previous three months, which was on the cusp of fruition, would go as planned. Henry after a couple of hours fitful sleep, facetimed Corrina, her smiling face lit up the screen, hair all tousled and draped over her left shoulder he whispered, "Hello my blue-eyed sweetheart."

"Hello my special man I was hoping you would ring, I couldn't sleep."

"I've been the same, never mind It won't be long, about ten hours and you will make me the happiest man on earth."

She spoke with her voice rising, "I'm excited I'm going to be Corrina Jade swan Jenson, I wish Mum was here because she had such a bad time with her husband, 'my so-called dad', I never believed it was possible to fall in love and be so happy."

"My sweet love I will never do anything, to make you unhappy."

Maggie's voice showing a touch of vexation interrupted their converse, "Will you two keep the noise down, Corrina let me get some sleep before you start talking about his squirt again."

Grinning at Maggie's illation Corrina offered a riposte, "There is far more to my man than his bits, as good as they are."

Henry chuckling assumed an intervening position reminding them, "Hey you two have you forgotten I'm here?"

"Henry don't take any notice of her but I do love your bits."

"See Henry I was right she's sex mad."

"Maggie I think we should all try and get some sleep goodnight my darling."

"Shouldn't you be saying that to Corrina?"

"Maggie, bugger off."

"Charming," he heard her shriek with laughter.

"Goodnight Corrina sweetheart, see you in a few hours."

Henry switched off, tiredness caught up with him.

Despite his sporadic sleep, he woke refreshed, excited and very happy, showered, he enjoyed a breakfast cooked by Cornelius then they both took the opportunity to rest for an hour prior to dressing, for what Henry considered the best, most exciting, moreover, important day of his life. As time moved on Henry's nervousness and excitement began to manifest, at one stage he couldn't get his breath Cornelius thought he might have a panic attack. He calmed him by giving some news of his own, reaching into his suit pocket he produced a small red velvet covered box containing a ring. "Henry after the ceremony I'm going to propose to Maggie what do you think?"

Henry laughing offered, "You're very brave, but by the same token she is a lovely girl."

"I'm nervous she might turn me down."

"Cornelius she would be barmy to refuse, but she won't I promise, honestly according to Corrina she adores you, what more can I say except to go ahead; propose."

The same nervous excitement lifted and revivified Corrina from her drowsiness making her whole body effloresce, her smile lit up the morning.

She, Maggie and Sadie rose early and had breakfast, eventually Elliot and Becky dragged themselves out of bed to join in the hustle and bustle of the preparations. Elliot got dressed and ready to go quite quickly, so he sat watching reruns of the sit com friends until the women were ready. When Corrina came out of the bedroom, Elliot normally a man who had difficulty in showing any emotion stood agape, he had difficulty finding an expression with which to comment, nevertheless his mouth did find an utterance. "Corrina you look stunning."

"Awwww Thank you Elliot."

Elliot still staring at his beautiful sister, took her by surprise when he revealed to her his innermost thoughts. "Corrina to think when you were little, you were a real pain in the arse, a real irksome little oik of a tomboy, Seeing you in that dress makes me so proud, our dad is missing out big time, whoever and wherever he is."

"Elliot don't make me cry I'll have to do my makeup again."

"Mum bless her, would have been absolutely chuffed with your choice of husband, she would be so happy for you, just as I am." Elliot continued, "Corrina I have had three special moments in my life, when I married Sadie and when Becky was introduced into this world, this is the third, you really do look lovely, Henry is a lucky man to have you on his arm, I have never said this before, but I do love you my baby sister."

Corrina burst into tears, reciprocating his emotion, "Elliot I love you too, I would love to give you a hug but I don't want to crease my dress, and now! I will have to do my makeup again."

Corrina's happy tears were shelved temporally, and her makeup restored immaculately, they made their way to the wedding car. While in the car Elliot reiterated how lovely she looked and how Lucky Henry was, which brought another tear. "Elliot stop being so nice I'll have to do my makeup again."

Elliot stood tall as they stepped from the car into the warmth of the day, one very proud brother escorted his baby sister Corrina into Dusty and Avelina's house: thereto, espouse the man she loved and would love all her life. They entered the garden, Friends and family sat either side of the aisle leading to the pavilion, to which an arch covered in white roses had been erected, under which the ceremony would be conducted. They were followed by a video cameraman there to record the whole of the nuptial proceedings.

The band struck up the wedding march, Corrina on Elliot's arm was followed by her entourage of bridesmaids Maggie, Lindy and Becky, all slowly approaching the pavilion. Henry's heart was beating louder than a jet plane breaking through the sound barrier, he turned to watch her walk down the aisle.

She walked towards Henry with sweat running down his face, 'courtesy of the cowboy attire he had opted for', his eyes glazed over mesmerised by the sight of his angel walking towards him; she was a sight that took his breath away. Henry was transfixed, rendered motionless with awe, he was experiencing a state of hypnotic induction. Cornelius, his best man said something which Henry didn't quite hear, but it drafted him out of his mesmeric state, his beaming smile replacing the gape. Corrina at last stood beside him, gently he lifted her veil gazing lovingly into her soft blue eyes. Her soft sparkling blue eyes gazed back into Henry's tearful eyes, her smile lighting up like a beacon fire welcomed and guiding Henry into her heart, into her life: forever. The ceremony, for both of them seemed to evanesce before it began, culminating when reaching the zenith of celestial love with the exchange of rings. When the Justice pronounced them man and wife, they shared a kiss that tasted of astral born honey: the sweetest of concoctions.

As Corrina and Henry walked back down the aisle, Gene Pitney's record (I wanna love my life away) played, requested by Henry, the guests began clapping and cheering, rice and confetti rained down on them. Henry as they walked whispered in his occasional use of the Scottish vernacular. "You keek pure dead brilliant in th' dress bit a can't haul dyer horses tae tak' it o' ye fer Iv git a stiffy a real boner."

Giggling she whispered back. "Sadly, it wull be a few hours afore ah kin dae anything' aboot that."

Maggie showing a disapproving face interrupted. "Mah god ye nae doon th' aisle 'n' effter his sea squirt yer throwing a sausage up a close mad."

Corrina stopped turned to give Maggie the evil eye before doubling up with mirth railing. "Maggie my best friend it's a good job me and Henry are the only ones who understood what you have just said."

Becky chimed in. "I ken whit she said; and if I had a boyfriend lik' Hendrie I'd be throwing a sausage up a close mad." The term (throwing a sausage up a close mad) Interpreted as Scottish for 'sex mad'.

Corrina was astonished at her niece's preteen testimony, while attempting to hide her amusement she gently scolded Becky, earnestly requesting that in future it would be wise to think before opening her mouth. "Becky if yer maw ever heard ye say hings lik that she wid gang barmy."

Lindy though she didn't understand the full text of what Becky had said, added her own attestation, "She fancies Henry big time."

Realising her wording were inappropriate, looking decidedly worried, Becky cast a supplicating expression towards Corrina, "Ye won't say anythin' tae ma maw wull ye."

"Becky darling' I don't tell tales, especially aboot ye."

Her face brightened acknowledging she had escaped any form of punishment for her outburst, by giving Corrina and Henry a hug, all was forgotten. It was time for the photographer to take charge, however with so many people to marshal it took over an hour before they could enjoy their wedding breakfast.

During the ceremonial splendour of the wedding Breakfast, one of the speeches was orated by Henry's very proud father Frank, his opening began by quoting Lucy Maud Montgomery when stating. "There is so much in the world for us all, if we have the eyes to see it, and the heart to love it, and the hand to gather it to ourselves." He furthered, "My son Henry has achieved all of that, he is farsighted, he Is able to foresee future developments. He will give himself completely to everything he attempts, the proof of the pudding lies in the success he has garnered. To be fair he has more than proved his ability in the tough world of commerce and I think Dusty will vouch for that. Friends, you only have to look at his new wife Corrina, she is beautiful, hardworking and intelligent, they are a special couple, I hope, no I believe they will always be happy. Therefore, it is with the greatest of pleasure, that I welcome with open arms Corrina Jade into the Swan Jenson Family: welcome Corrina."

Wedding protocol denotes the bride and groom take to the floor for the first dance to which the newly married couples shuffle rather than dance…

Henry's eyes glazed over at last he had Corrina back in his arms he was spellbound as they danced their first dance as man and wife. The spell was broken when Corrina started to giggle, a little perplexed he queried. "what's funny is it my Terpsichore?"

Her giggling got louder. "I don't know what Terpsichore is."

"Dancing."

"Henry not at all I was just thinking about Becky."

"Go on, explain then."

"I'll have to watch the little bugger."

"Why?"

"She is not even in her teens and she fancies you."

"Come on what woman wouldn't fancy me I mean, I'm very handsome, and charismatic; no I'm kidding myself, why would a little girl fancy me?"

"Henry my darling husband I love you and I fancy you big time and I'll show you later when we finally get to our room."

"You minx I'm getting a hard on again I wish you wouldn't threaten me with such a shameful display of coquetting."

"Henry if you don't like it, I'll find someone who does."

"I'm a broken man, just married and I'm being dumped."

Giggling even louder she wrapped her arms around him but managing to Whisper, "I hope that stiffy stays that way I'm in dire need of it."

"Oh I'm not being dumped then, you still want my body."

"More than ever, I wish we could go to bed now this has been the most exciting day of my life, but it will be crowned when we make love."

"Corrina my beautiful wife and hopefully in the future you will be the mother of my children I love you."

"Henry making them will be fun, I think we had better get changed husband."

"I think we must wife."

"Henry I mean get changed nothing else."

"I don't know what you mean, nothing else?"

"I take it there is a hint of finality expressed in your answer?"

"HENRY! Our guests will be wondering where we are."

"Maggie won't."

"Come on my special man get changed, we can have a drink."

There didn't seem any point in furthering the discussion, he changed out of his suit then watched his new wife take off her wedding dress making his heart skip a beat when she revealed her underwear.

"Oh I see something blue ay, I'll have the pleasure of taking them off later."

"It'll be my pleasure, my special man."

Later that evening Henry stood up with Corrina by his side to address the assembled guests. "Friends and family first, we have to express how much we are indebted to Dusty and Avalina, for kindly allowing us to use their beautiful home for our special day. I have lived a dream since she consented to be my wife and now that dream has come true she is my wife. We also have to thank each and every one of you for joining in our celebrations, some of you have journeyed three and a half thousand miles to be with us," he paused before adding. "I have something else to tell you," there was a distinct undercurrent of suggestive murmuring and giggling from by then, quite bibulous friends and family.

Grinning he furthered. "Sorry to disappoint, but we are not expecting, if we are, I have not yet been informed."

Corrina interrupted, grinning, tongue in cheek reminded them, "How could we, we are only just married."

There was much louder giggling from the partygoers, Henry continued amid the mirth. "Cornelius and Maggie come up here please."

Both looked puzzled, but did as they were asked. "Cornelius I think you have something to say to Maggie, so why don't you do it now."

Cornelius shocked, visibly shaking fumbled in his pocket, producing the red velvet covered box out of his pocket, still shaking he proceeded to get down on one knee, in a quivering voice, he supplicated, "Maggie my darling would you do me the honour of becoming my wife?"

Maggie with hands on hips, a reproving look on her face, held back on her answer. Cornelius sweating profusely waited, Maggie suddenly broke into a rapturous smile at the same time shedding a tear, "Cornelius yes, yes, yes." Enthusiastically telling him, "I thought you would never ask, I honestly thought I would have to wait until a leap year to ask you."

Cornelius still visibly shaking, managed to put the ring on her finger she looked at it with pleasure, her face beaming with joy, then she showed it to everyone. Throwing her arms around him she buried her tongue in his mouth before gasping, "Cornelius you have made me so very happy."

"Maggie you have made me even happier."

The party erupted in spontaneous clamorous applause, clapping and cheering, the music got louder and the party also got louder. Cornelius still a little dazed furthermore embarrassed, shook Henry by the hand to thank him. "Henry I have been trying to build up the courage to ask her all day but every time I got close my courage deserted me, my friend you gave me the push and the courage to ask."

Stern faced Henry apprised him, "You know that is only the first part over with, you will have to go to Edinburgh to ask her dad that could be more traumatic than anything you have ever experienced."

A worried frown spread across Cornelius's face asking Henry, "Why what have you heard?"

Managing to keep the same stern face Henry imparted to him, "You know Maggie is not afraid to speak her mind well he is ten times worse, not only that he's not averse to using his fists."

A crestfallen looking Cornelius nervously expressed, "What have I done, what if he doesn't like me?"

"That's a difficult one, from what I've heard he's a member of the Edinburgh Mafioso and he adores Maggie so you will have to be careful."

"Bloody hell I was looking forward to meeting her family, now I'm not so sure, nonetheless, I love her and he will have to accept me for what I am."

Henry couldn't hide his deception from his best friend any longer grinning broadly he admitted, "Cornelius my best friend I'm pulling your leg I have never met him, but Corrina reckons he is a very friendly man, he, is where Maggie gets her sense of humour from."

Cornelius visibly relieved shook his head, "You bastard you got me going there and no mistake." They man hugged, both laughing like Hyenas. "Time for a drink I think Henry?"

As usual there came a robust comment from Maggie, "Bloody hell Cornelius you have just proposed to me and now you're trying to shag your best mate."

Cornelius uttered an expression Henry had never heard him offer before, completely out of character, "Maggie my darling there is only one person I want to fuck and that's you."

"Oooh Ooooh hark at Cornelius the tiger, we'll leave that till later."

Amidst the hullabaloo, Frank for some reason managed to find time and space away from the party to converse with Mary, he seemed concerned pointing out how Corrina was the spit of Susan Phillips, "She could have been her doppelganger don't you think?"

"Frank I'm not sure what you're getting at, yes she does look very much like her but they are Scottish and her surname is Phelps."

"I know but I get this feeling when I look at her."

"Frank, I hope it's not the same feeling you had for Susan Phillips?"

"Don't be daft, I have regretted that part of my life ever since."

"Frank it's in the past you have Elaine and I have Mathew."

"Don't get me wrong I love Elaine, however I am sorry I hurt you, I have been a bloody fool in fact a real bastard; It was always a stupid ego trip, as I say I regret it. Mary I'm glad you are happy Mathew is a nice guy."

"Frank just leave it, let's have a dance for old time's sake, the past is the past."

"Mary that would be nice."

Henry watching his mum and dad dance, his mind wondered what if? Despite the heartache surrounding the divorce his mum had found a man she adored furthermore, the adoration was reciprocated, he was glad. He believed he had found in Corrina the same love his mum shared with her husband Mathew, whereas his dad had sown his wild oats scattering his seed far and wide the products of which were; all there at the wedding.

The night was long and boisterous the hour of four o'clock struck before the last of the partying guests wended their way back to their hotel rooms. Henry and Corrina both the worst for wear from over imbibing too many potations, expressed their virtually incoherent utmost thanks again to Dusty and Avelina, before retiring to their room which Dusty and Avelina had kindly set aside for them. Opening the door a heady sweet redolence greeted them, there was a surprise, the room had been decorated with red roses and scattered across the bed, red rose petals. Corrina garbled. "Isn't it lovely, I love you Henry Swan Jenson but I'm so tired, I feel like I've been awake for a week." Clasping Henry's face in her hands she kissed him, he returned her advance, his eyes were closing, like Corrina he was physically and mentally drained. Exhausted lying locked together in each other's arms, still fully clothed entering the world of the sandman they slept the sleep of the venerated, such was the fullness of their love they would wait till morning for fulfilment.

A soft kiss brushed his lips waking Henry, still exhausted It took a while for him to focus, through blurry eyes, gradually there appeared an angel smiling like the sun in a cloudless sky. Corrina whispered, "Hello my special man you are my husband, so I'm telling you I love you."

"Hello blue eyes you are my wife and I'm telling you I love you."

"I'm not sure of the time but It must be quite late, we should be to getting up, we need to get out of our party clothes."

"I think it's time for a shower don't you?"

"Ladies first, my special man."

"No way have you forgotten we share everything, we may be dirty but I can be really dirty."

"You're not going to be rude are you Henry?"

"Would I be rude with you Corrina Jade Swan Jenson?"

"Henry Swan Jenson, I bloody hope so."

Lovemaking which can only be described as emotionally all-consuming and profound, verging on intemperate; giving of themselves totally consequently arousing a flood of exquisite fulfilment from their fervent coupling. Their body's satiated from the greatest intensive force of nature it can release, left them trembling with sheer exultant happiness…

Stepping into the shower stimulated their erogenous zones, bodies and minds revived by the hot steamy shower and the warm sensation derived from embracing, then with the softness of the towels they gently dried each other. Their honeymoon began in earnest, the first kiss sweeter than nectar, their touching non-restrictive, advancing to delicacy and eroticism of foreplay, thereon softly eliciting the intensity of their lovemaking.

Avalina made them a late breakfast, contrary to her protestations Henry and Corrina aided by Dusty and their six daughters helped to clear up the mess from the previous day. When Henry thanked him again, Dusty put his arm around him, In his southern Texan drawl he offered some advice. "Son it ain't my first rodeo, so I will give you some advice for a newly married man. There are two theories to arguing with a woman, neither one works, therefore never miss a good chance to shut up."

Henry looking quizzical asked him, "Dusty sir I don't know whether to laugh at your analogy or take it seriously?"

"Whatever and whenever, son."

After leaving dusty and Avalina's, the next two days were lost in a continuous blur of celebrations with the family. Luckily the newlyweds had the foresight to prepack their luggage before any of the family had arrived from Britain because as expected, there followed two days of riotous all-day imbibition; partying which left everyone to put it mildly in a state of disrepair. Nonetheless before they could turn round it was time for all the family to say heart-breaking goodbyes. Suddenly sadness and silence prevailed, the apartment felt decidedly chilled, now free from the strident confusion that surrounded the hullabaloo which was deemed necessary by the women whilst preparing to make ready Corrina and Henrys nuptials. Corrina shed a tear observing. "Henry my special man I'm so glad we are going away."

"Corrina Jade Swan Jenson my darling wife, tomorrow at ten o'clock we will be enjoying our first in-flight gin and tonic, a couple of hours later we will be enjoying a gin and tonic in the beautiful island of St Lucia, however a little later I think we may have to lie down?"

"Henry I hope we won't be sleeping…"

Chapter 38

Though Henry and Corrina had been living together for nine months, the longest time they had spent together was a total of ten days at Christmas, as Christmas is such a busy time for family and friends there is little chance of a time alone so that they could really get to know each other. Apart from Christmas day and new year's eve they were never a couple, just part of a circle of friends. They were in love, looking back, both had been in love from the moment they first met in Cardiff five years earlier Married at last their honeymoon in St Lucia was a chance to do their 'courting'. They were able to gaze into each other's eyes, hold hands, dance close, dance so close they become one and whisper fervent words of love to each other. They were in the grip of an incontestable, indestructible love which was expressed every night. Each morning Henry would wake and stare at his new wife, bewildered by his luck, he had fallen in love with someone so stunning, Someone who had a mind which he understood to be untarnished by a wicked world full of the most unfavourable and most undesirable of humankind. She believed everyone and everything should be given a chance furthermore she loved him. Their honeymoon, was Idyllic. Three weeks of rest, sun over indulgence of food together with an immoderate amount of drinking in all forms of alcohol, you name it, they tried it, beer, wine, cocktails, Corrina's particular favourite white sands, a rum cocktail.

St Lucia is how anyone would imagine a tropical island should be, green, Palm trees, soft white sandy beaches, hot sunny days complimented by a gentle but permanent warm but cooling breeze reducing the strength of heat from the sun. Two thirds of St Lucia is covered in natural rainforest there is also the majestic Piton Mountains...

The newly-weds took time to explore, visiting the stunning Rodney Bay, on the coast of St Lucia, its beauty astonishing. Some afternoons they sat in the cool bars of Castries, the capital city, drinking local brewed piton pilsner beer usually followed by one or three rum punches.

One of those astonishing anomalies is you spend months excitedly planning, looking forward, full of expectation to a special occasion, you feel you are never actually going to reach that particular event you have circled on your calendar then in the blink of an eye it's over, disappeared like vapour blown away by a fierce gust of wind, sadly time has overtaken, you are homeward bound, with only photographs and memories left.

Honeymoon over, after arriving home, Corrina had very little time to get unpacked as the following day she had to fly back to Edinburgh, to prepare for work. They had decided to carry on as normal for the foreseeable future. Henry described each time Corrina came home as experiencing another short but exceptionally pleasurable honeymoon.

Chapter 39

One November evening, for Henry, very early morning Corrina facetimed Henry, when her face flickered into view, Henry was taken aback because she looked worried.

"Hello blue eyes what's the matter are you feeling unwell?"

"Hello my special man, why do you ask?"

"You're not beaming the gorgeous smile that normally greets me."

"I have just been sick but honestly, I'm not unwell."

"Been on the pop have you?"

"No cheeky bleeder I most certainly haven't and I won't be partaking for at least nine months."

"Go on, you haven't signed the pledge have you?"

Shaking her head, she started to laugh, "Oh Henry haven't you caught on yet?"

"Caught on to what?"

"Henry you have given me something special."

"Corrina jade Swan Jenson what are you talking about?"

"Henry you are the cleverest, most educated man I know in fact I have ever known, and still you are none the wiser."

"What do you mean?"

"Henry you are going to be a dad."

His mind was still in a fog, "You're pregnant honestly?"

"I'm glad the penny has finally dropped, of course I'm pregnant."

Stunned but grinning from ear to ear his acknowledgement, "Corrina I'm going to be a dad."

"My special man, yes you are going to be a dad."

"Blimey, I'm going to phone everyone, I'm going to be a dad, I'm going to be a dad, I'm going to be dad, wow; Corrina I never asked are you pleased?"

"Henry I can't wait to be three of us, I'm so very happy, happy because you're happy too."

"Happy I'm ecstatic, I'm going to be a dad, I'm going to be a dad."

"Henry now you know I'll let you get back to sleep."

"I'll never get back to sleep, I'm too excited."

"My special man I'll be home tomorrow afternoon, I mean…we will."

"Great I'll pick you up from JFK I love you my darling wow, wow."

"I love you too, see you tomorrow bye."

There was no way on earth Henry would be able to sleep, he rang his mum, his dad and sister Caro to give them the glad tidings, they were all delighted for both of them. Mary, as soon as Henry put the phone down rang Corrina to tell her how excited happy and delighted she was to becoming a grandmother. Corrina who now called Mary mum cried, "Mum I'm so glad you rang we will have so much to talk about, Henry is going absolutely barmy he is so happy."

"Corrina when he spoke to me he was euphoric, on cloud nine, so happy."

"I know, wait till baby arrives I'm sure he will be the best dad ever."

"One thing for sure is, he won't be like his own dad, I'm not saying he's a bad dad, nonetheless he has had his 'mischievous moments' but he has always been there for the children, all his children love him, and he loves them."

Henry and Corrina were set for one of the happiest times, for once time did not drag, they lived every moment together, including Corrina's continual sickness. Henry watched as her lithe figure changed shape, her tummy gradually gaining a bump and sharing the joy of feeling baby kick and Corrina's expanding breasts. He would tell her, "They're out of control I don't know about a bra you will need a pair of hammocks, one thing for sure, baby is not going to go hungry."

Their causerie ritual was never recited with malice always delivered with humour usually incurring exuberant merriment. Their minds were fully in tune they had very few moments when irritability would cloud their sunny horizon.

Despite the obvious excitement, babies can bring with them problems to be solved, their apartment only had two bedrooms, fortunately they were both very large so they had the spare room converted into two rooms. One was a small nursery for baby, the other big enough for a double bed. Another problem, twelve weeks into her pregnancy Corrina had to relinquish her position as a flight attendant for BA because of her sickness when Corrina was twelve weeks into her pregnancy because of her sickness she had to relinquish her position as a flight attendant for BA. Providentially, the powers that be found her a job in JFK in departures check in desk, which meant she and Henry were able to enjoy for once, their new-found, fulltime home life.

Henry was the consummate father to be, he revelled in shopping, choosing with Corrina everything parents require for their new-born. Cot, pram, car seat, a sit to stand learning walker, buggy, toys for the pram/cot, and of course baby's first teddy bear. Choosing a name for their offspring presented no problems, Corrina wanted Denni for a boy and Danni for a girl.

During the Nine months leading up to the birth, Henry took time out from work to go with her to the hospital for check-ups. A picture from each scan 'Boy or girl' he placed into an album, he wanted to be a part of the baby's life from the inception to birth and beyond. Neither of them wanted to know its gender, they were just happy baby was healthy.

The best laid plans of mice and men oft go astray is an idiom that very often bears fruit, and so it proved when baby was expected to make his or her entrance into the world. Arrangements had previously been made for Mary to fly over to help out when Corrina and baby left hospital, however one week before Baby was expected to arrive, Henry received a call from Corrina, sounding excited but frightened, "Henry my waters have broken, baby is on its way, Avalina is here, she is going to drive me to hospital."

"My darling, I'm on my way I'll be there as quick as I can."

Henry could hear Avelina the voice of experience advising Corrina, they had better get going unless she wanted to have her baby in the car.

Henry arrived at the hospital in the nick of time, just as baby arrived, a mixture of excitement allied to anxiety and overwhelming joyous emotion when they said it's a healthy boy, he fainted. When He came round, he was sat in a chair next to the bed, his baby son Denni cradled in Corrina's arms, grinning she offered in her Scottish dialect, so no one else could, understand what was being said, "I'm th' yin wha shuid be fainting ye muckle wuss."

Still befuddled he conjured up a grin answering likewise, "Ye gallus sod ah hae ne'er felt sae excited 'n' drained afore 'twas just tea muckle," gaining his mental equilibrium he continued, "how are you feeling blue eyes, you look absolutely beautiful?"

"Thank you, my special man, it was all over before I knew it, I'm just a bit sore and tired otherwise I'm good, aren't you going to hold your baby son?"

Henry stood up, sat on the edge of the bed and took his baby son in his arms saying, "Hello Denni," then suddenly burst into tears garbling, "I'm a dad, isn't he handsome he's my son, he's my son."

"Henry he is your double, there is no way you could deny him."

"I can't wait to tell everyone about the present my beautiful wife has given me, my son Denni."

"It's not all down to me, you played your part as well."

"Corrina I am so happy I have you and now I have Denni, I am so lucky."

"Oh Henry we do seem to have everything, we are lucky."

"I forgot, I'll must tell Mum she is a grandmother."

"Tell her not to rush I'm sure we can manage."

"Do you honestly think she won't be on the first flight available?"

"Do you think she will? I'll be so glad of her help. I only wish my mum was here as well, but still; I can't dwell."

"When does he get his first feed?"

The nurse intervened, "You should try now while he is awake, after that Mum you can have a rest, Dad can come back in a couple of hours."

"I don't want to leave but I do have calls to make, I'll leave you to feed the little fella and I'll see you later, bye blue eyes, bye Denni." With a smile on his face, he joked, "I hope you like what's on today's menu son."

Corrina chuckling pulled a face, "See you later Henry Swan Jenson."

The nurse at first giggled but on seeing Corrina's reaction burst into full throttle of hilarity.

Henry was on an emotionally aroused high at becoming a father he spent the next hour phoning his mum and dad. Mary, just as excited and happy for him said she would be on the first possible flight.

Corrina and baby Denni were discharged from hospital the following day, Henry proud as punch drove them home in his ford Fairlane, where Maggie who had just arrived from Edinburgh and Cornelius were waiting to greet them. Later that evening Dusty and Avalina with all six of their girls arrived all wanting to hold the 'little fella' as Henry called him. Once the first few days had elapsed and the never-ending stream of well-wishers had reduced to a trickle. Mary, to coin a very overused adage, 'was over the moon' she was on the doorstep just sixty hours after receiving the call from Henry, declaring she was much too young to be a grandmother. When Henry opened the door, she stood grinning and bearing gifts, including a case full of baby clothes all in blue. When Mary was introduced to her grandson, her smile lit up the room observing, "My God he looks like you Henry when you were first born, I am so proud, if you get fed up of him can I take him home."

Corrina obviously wished her own mum could be with her, however her answer to Mary's supplication, "Mum I couldn't think of anyone I would trust with my little man other than you, thank you for getting here so quickly."

For some reason, humankind believes nature has decreed and foreordained for the female of the species that nurturing and raising of a child or children by a mother comes naturally. To an extent that may be a fact, nevertheless for a young new mother, to have a more experienced mother to help and guide them through the early days of motherhood is special...

Mary was an angel to Corrina, helping, watching and guiding her through the early stages of motherhood, she stayed with them for two weeks allowing Henry to return to work. When Mary went home, Corrina was ready for the task of coping with the strains and stresses of raising her first child. They were a young couple in the throes of learning the why's and wherefores of parenthood they always seemed tired, so there were moments when they had to think carefully, before irrationally stepping into arguments over silly things that were really unimportant, they never entered into large scale out and out riotous discussions whereby they would hurt each other verbally, their love was indubitable, deep rooted and stable. They were not just an item their love, one would class as conspicuously unparalleled.

Henry to this day, could still remember hiding under the bed linen to drown out the arguments that were raging downstairs between his mum and dad, at the time, he had no idea the shouting was all about: but it frightened him. It was only some years later he understood the cause of the rows which led to their divorce. There will never be a time he would let Denni be frightened in the same manner. Henry would only impart love and pleasure to his wife and son, he would never deliberately cause them hurt or displeasure, he loved them both too much.

Henry and Corrina had grown even closer together, if that was possible, as Denni grew from a baby to a toddler. Denni brought them more joy he was an added attraction, a very important added attraction to their romance. From the day Denni came into this world, he unified their love into an unbreakable force; their love was unassailable.

Chapter 40

When Denni was eighteen months old, the family were out shopping, looking for clothes for each of them, Henry received a call from Elaine. Elaine was imparting news, which was about to change the whole direction in which their lives had previously been focused, great sadness was about to crash down on them leaving their happiness in catastrophic ruins. Elaine informed him that his dad Frank, had been feeling unwell for a while but hadn't told anyone. For once, he was intelligent enough to understand his body wasn't feeling right thus, paid a visit to his doctor, who, referred him back to the hospital where his surgery for colon cancer had been performed. The shock news, the cancer had spread to his lymph nodes, meaning he would have to undergo chemotherapy, and possibly more surgery Henry very disturbed at the news said, "Give me half an hour, I'll ring you back?"

Corrina knew exactly what Henry was going through, she understood how difficult it is to alleviate the shock you feel when someone you love and admire is seriously poorly. Back in their apartment she managed to calm him before he returned Elaine's call, his opening question. "How is he can I speak to him?" Elaine passed the phone to Frank. "Hi Dad how are you?"

"Not too good son, I start chemo tomorrow."

"Hold on in there, Dad I'll be over as soon as I get organised here."

"I know it won't make any difference if I say there is no need?"

"Dad I'll see you as soon as, so go and rest, bye for now."

Making a decision to go back to Birmingham took them two minutes, Corrina knew he would need her by his side to keep him calm, therefore all three of them would travel. Henry rang Dusty who told him to take as much time as he required. They Landed in Birmingham two days later and took a taxi straight to Frank's house, Elaine was overjoyed to see them the strain on her face dissipated like vapor, especially when she saw Corrina and Denni, it was the diversion she needed. Elaine was worried he wouldn't be able run Jenson's furthermore

Barney, his right-hand man was honest enough to say it was too big a job for him to even consider. They had a discussion resulting in an exposition whereby Henry would on a temporary basis assume control of Jenson's.

Frank was abed, he was exhausted from the side effects of the Chemo. Chemo drugs can be debilitating in their own right, the time schedule of each cycle of treatment two to four weeks, Frank's was expected to last three to six months: he had a long way to go, his health was in far more trouble than he first recognised, any illness befalling him in the past was, as he often described it, just a distraction, nothing which would affect him enough to reconsider his lifestyle. This cancer was a different proposition, he was advised to change his eating habits to a vegetable enriched diet and minimally processed dairy foods, such as milk, cheese and yoghurt. For a time, he would have to do without fish and chips! He was warned of the whole series of the effects chemo might cause, these included hair loss, nausea, mouth sores, diarrhoea, and fatigue. The only time Frank had ever felt fatigued in his life, happened only when too many alcoholic beverages had been imbibed the previous evening. Chemo allowed alcohol to be drank only occasionally, instead water had to be the preferred drink and to be consumed often, to keep him hydrated.

On waking, regarding his portentous circumstances, Frank managed a weak smile, but the sight of Denni his grandson ignited his face, expressing a more cheerful acceptance of his condition. He had seen Denni via facetime but now for the first time he was able to hold him. However there appeared to be a problem, each time family were together Frank experienced a strange physical sensation which invaded his thoughts, a very uncomfortable feeling. Corrina was completely unaware that Frank's eyes would involuntarily be drawn to her, something bothered him whatever that worry was he couldn't fathom it, nor could he shake it.

That same evening Henry and Corrina visited Mary and Mathew to assure them, just as they had Elaine, Henry would take control of Jenson's until Frank was in a position both physically and mentally strong enough to return to the day-to-day politics of business life. Usually they would stay with Mary, however on this occasion everyone agreed the better option was for them to stay with Frank and Elaine, so Henry could keep his dad in the loop regarding the business. Elaine was overjoyed, as previously she had difficulty keeping her own lucidity from slipping into a downdraught of mind destroying depression.

From there, they took time out to visit Caro who understood that everything and every discussion had to be about their dad, it was natural, however although Caro was upset about her dad, she broke into a radiant beaming smile. She had some special news of her own, she was pregnant. Corrina queried, "Mum never said anything."

"I have only just done the test, half an hour before you came I will have to have it confirmed by our doctor."

Giving Caro a hug Corrina asked, "Oh that is lovely news, fantastic, what about you and Lindsay are you happy?"

Corrina, "We are ecstatic whatever, boy or girl we don't mind he or she will be loved."

Henry commented, "I think you should let both parents know, it will take our mum and dad's minds off his illness, lift the sadness infusing our family for a while at least. Corrina, shall we leave so Caro and Lindsay have the joy of telling everybody their wonderful, exciting news?"

The following day, Henry took charge of Jenson's, aided by Frank's PA Imelda plus the ever-helpful Barney Phillips. It took a while for Henry to establish total control of Jenson's, retail is notorious for its quick turnover of staff therefore Henry to alleviate any worries, visited all eleven stores in England. His primary intention to introduce himself to all members of staff, from managers to part time employees, informing them of who he was and why he was assuming temporary control, furthermore assuring them their jobs were safe, all the company policies to remain in place. Subsequent conversations with Jenny King and Ellie Crane, the general managers of the Welsh and Scottish divisions of Jenson's respectively, whom he had personally employed, left him in little doubt they could continue without any interference from him in the future.

Ensuing from his conversation with Ellie Crane there arose a problem, Frank had understandably forgotten to forewarn him Ellie would be taking maternity leave, unrealistically leaving him two weeks to find a suitable temporary replacement, given the time he had, it was a, big ask. Ellie had stayed on despite the fact that she was only three weeks away from giving birth, Henry felt she should leave immediately, nonetheless, she insisted she would give him time to find a temporary replacement. Henry wondered momentarily, maybe he should use an agency employee then ultimately deciding against such an idea, Henry went through all the Scottish employee's personal files instead. He hoped to find someone who had the wherewithal to rise to the challenge of maintaining the smooth operation Ellie had achieved, his brother i-law Elliot came to mind, but he lackedIce as Henry perceived Ellie Is almost indispensable. She had been instrumental in establishing Jenson's in Scotland, her perceptive and shrewd approach to business had enriched the stability of the company, he believed she was worth her weight in gold. Another problem presented itself to Henry, whoever he found to assume the role of general manager and more importantly could be trusted, would be required to live in Edinburgh for at least six months.

He Sat at Frank's desk deep in pensive contemplation, considering the dilemma to find a new manager for Scotland, the stark reality was, there was nil time to advertise, or even invite candidates for interviews. Miraculously, who walked through the door but Barney Phillips, Henry remembered he had asked him to avail himself if required when Frank was first taken ill, his answer had been affirmative therefore, keeping his fingers crossed, he asked, "Barney, do you remember me asking, that on the off chance we might need a temporary general manager in Wales or Scotland? You advised me, you would do anything for Frank?"

"Henry I do, and I still will, why?"

"Barney it's a big ask but we need a general manager in Edinburgh, are you game? It will be for at least six months."

"When do you want me to go?"

"Shouldn't you ask Cherry first?"

"Yes I should do, if she agrees, when do you want me to start?"

"Next Monday Ellie Crane will be taking maternity leave the week after."

"I'll discuss it with Cherry tonight."

Cherry and Barney's former problems were no longer an issue they embraced whole heartedly their togetherness, as far as Cherry was concerned she would prefer to have him at home, not working away, nonetheless reluctantly she gave her blessing. Barney worked tirelessly to put his previous uncontrollable, unruly, lifestyle behind him. That same evening, he proposed to Cherry, whose answer came with a reflection, "Barney when I think of what we went through before, you have turned your life round, you are thoughtful caring and loving, I would never have believed I would ever feel the way I do now, Barney I love you and yes I would love to be your wife."

Barney's elation spilled over like a shot glass filled with a magnum of champagne. From his pocket, he produced a box which he opened, inside lay a solitaire diamond engagement ring, Cherry was shocked.

"Barney how long have you been planning this."

"I bought the ring six months ago, but never found the courage to ask you, all things considered given my previous record with my ex-wife and you Cherry stones, I would have totally understood a refusal, I can't believe you have said yes."

"Barney shall we go to bed I'm not going to see you very often?"

"We're not going to sleep are we?"

"Only if you're tired."

"I think I've got some mileage in me yet Cherry Stones."

"let's see how much?"

Henry left Frank's PA Imelda in charge while he and Barney, who was still on a high left for Edinburgh, accompanied by Corrina and the little fella Denni, they were going to stay with Elliot. Elaine and Mary assisted Imelda as much as they could, as a new unit, they managed to keep things running back home.

Henry reserved a room for Barney at the Edinburgh East Hotel where He had resided for a short time when he first moved to Edinburgh. During the next three days they visited all four stores so Barney could be introduced to all the staff and explain the different protocol of those Scottish stores which Henry had established. During the introductions, there was a curious moment when Henry introduced his brother in-law Elliot, Barney looked querulous as if he had a question to ask him, but he didn't put voice to his look.

Once Barney was settled and understood the way Jenson's of Scotland functioned, if he was to make his mark, he would have a lot to learn about the courtesies, furthermore, the humour of Scottish people. Barney was amazed at Henry's fluency of the Edinburgh dialect. Barney set about his new job albeit temporary with enthusiasm, he wanted to repay the trust shown in him by Henry, his determination to succeed was akin to both Henry and Frank. He had been given a chance and wanted to repay the faith they had shown in him. Every time he visited one of the stores, he talked to all the employees, managers and staff alike. His conversations helped him evaluate, moreover solve any problems quickly. His congenial manner quickly endeared him to the staff who at first had been ambivalent as to who might replace Ellie, he became very friendly with

Elliot, and came to the realisation that he, was future management material. His enthusiasm to do well stood out, furthermore he was intelligent.

One evening going through the routine of locking up for the evening sharing a joke and talking about family, Barney mentioned he had a son called Elliot.

In his strong Scottish accent, Elliot remarked, "Have you? I was the only Elliot at school I thought my mum had engineered the name."

"I named my son after the American prohibition agent Elliot Ness."

"Did you, perhaps he's in the police?"

"To be honest he might be but I haven't a clue."

"How, come?"

"Elliot it's a sad story I'm not sure you would want to hear it, for that matter I'm embarrassed to tell anyone."

Elliot puzzled was curious to know more. "Why now you've wetted my nosey appetite, I'm interested to know more?"

"Let's finish locking up I'll set the alarm, you need to get home to your family."

Elliot took Barney by surprise inviting, "Barney why don't we go for a drink one evening?"

"Do you know that would be good there are people in the hotel I speak to, but it still gets lonely, every night I facetime my Fiancée Cherry and her son Myles, whom I love like my own, and I will be going home every two weeks, but it's not the same I miss them."

"Ok I'll check with Sadie to make sure we have nothing planned."

"I look forward to it, I have to warn you I'm tea-total so if they haven't got alcohol free beer, I'll be on the squash."

Next day Elliot advised Barney, "I will be free tomorrow evening, so if you would like to go for a drink I know just the place."

When they closed up the following evening, Elliot told him, "Peely-wally tak' ye tae mah yin o' ma fave waterin' holes."

"Smiling and shaking his head Barney asked, could you speak in English I get the watering hole what's the rest?"

"I'll take you to one of my favourite watering holes, you'll catch up with the lingo one day."

They sat in the Sheep Heid Inn, apparently a place frequented by the local buskers, one such review describes it as 'a braw, we place with bags of character' and so it proved. Luckily, they did serve alcohol free beer, Barney glad of the company got them in.

Barney asked Elliot. "How's your family?"

"They are good thank you Sadie my wife and my fourteen-year-old daughter Becky have gone swimming, they're on one of those fitness crazes, I can swim but I don't like it I find it really boring."

"How are your family?"

"They are good I spoke to Cherry this morning, sadly there are two people I don't know the whereabouts of and I don't blame them for that."

"Why is that?"

"Elliot I count myself extremely lucky to have Cherry however; I had all this before and blew it big time."

"How, what went wrong?"

"To be honest I didn't go wrong, I was never right."

"How do you mean?"

Barney initially reluctant to explain, decided he would. "It's not easy to admit but during a large part of my younger days I developed from a school bully until my vitriol ego, drinking and drugs, landed me with a well-deserved prison sentence."

"Blimey and here you are general manager."

"I'm only temporary but I owe everything to Frank, Henry's dad, he is a true friend and my saviour."

"Why what happened?"

"It all started at school, me and Frank we were sworn enemies, a story that continued for a number of reasons for many years. It came to a head one night when me and my brother attacked him, we put him in hospital, we hurt him so bad he could have died, those injuries we inflicted were so bad, I went to prison and deserved to."

"Wow and now you are friends."

"Yes the best of, I would do anything for him."

"This is some story what happened to your son?"

"Sadly I haven't a clue, his mum my wife Susan walked out on me taking Elliot with her, after she divorced me it's as though she just vaporised, as I say I don't blame them I was an egotistical self-obsessed drunk, who cared for nobody else but me, to put it bluntly I was a bastard."

"How long were you in prison?"

"Two and a half years, never again I had to change, luckily for me when I came out Frank held out his hand in friendship, he offered me a job for which I will be eternally grateful he is more like a brother."

"Are you looking for your wife and son?"

"I've tried but wherever she found to hide, she did a good Job."

"Barney I hope you find her."

"Maybe, you never can tell, mind you if it did happen, in her position I wouldn't have anything to do with me either, you've heard my story would you want to be reconciled with the idiot I was in my previous life? I wouldn't. Anyway that's enough about me, tell me about you and your family?"

"Well I have my lovely wife Sadie and my daughter Becky and you know my sister Corrina, that's it."

"There must be more surely?"

"Mum died of breast cancer three years ago, she was a single mum, we know absolutely nothing about our father, all she ever said was he wasn't very nice. She divorced him he obviously didn't want us, he never once sent us a birthday card or Christmas card."

"What about Grandparents, uncles, aunts and cousins?"

"None just the four of us, no that's not true we have Sadie's mum and dad she also has an elder sister Megan."

"It's strange we have similar names I'm Phillips and your' Phelps, I had a son Elliot but not a daughter."

Barney was surprised with himself he had opened up to someone who was really a stranger, nonetheless, he enjoyed the evening it was good to have someone to talk to, sharing his story gave him the impetus to abide by the rules he had set himself. Back in his room Barney lay on his bed ruminating, the main features of his retrospections of which were his lost family, or as he himself would admit, had been driven away out of fear for their own safety. His evening with Elliot had reawakened his desire to find them, hopefully if possible be reconciled. He snapped out of his musings realising they were nothing more than abstractions, why would they want to re-establish a close relationship. In his mind, he could not envisage any form of harmonious or sympathetic rapport with an Individual brute of a person who had blighted their lives: himself.

One Saturday afternoon, couple of weeks after Barney's night out with Elliot they were closing up for the weekend when out of the blue Elliot asked. "What are you doing tonight?"

Puzzled, Barney replied. "Dinner in the hotel followed by a few alcohol free drinks and then bed why do you ask?"

"Would you like to have dinner with me and Sadie?"

"Elliot I would love to, are you sure Sadie won't mind?"

"Sadie is inviting you as well not just me."

"Thank you, give me ten minutes I need to speak to Cherry otherwise she will be worried, give us your address and I'll catch up with you."

Barney was a little later than ten minutes, when he arrived he was bearing a huge bunch of flowers for Sadie and a bottle of Champagne, not forgetting a bottle of none alcoholic wine for himself. Sadie was astounded at the bouquet thanking Barney, informing them both you'll have to wait for dinner I need to put these in water. The evening for Barney was thoroughly enjoyable just chatting, getting to know Elliot's family and making Becky blush telling her, "Becky you are so pretty all the boys will be chasing you and you will probably break a few hearts I'm sure of that."

Dinner every other Saturday with Elliot and Sadie became a regular feature, however; one particular Saturday Barney was laying the table for dinner when Elliot asked him into the lounge remarking. "Barney I have something important to tell you, well I think it is very important."

A querulous Barney asked, "Is there a problem?"

"To be honest Barney I don't really know where to begin."

"Is there something bothering you, have I upset you or Sadie?"

"No, no, nothing like that."

"Mmmmm I think you had better tell me."

"Ok I have had a bit of a problem in fact I have thought of nothing else for the last few weeks. Sadie and me have talked of nothing else and I'm still in a quandary whether I should say anything at all."

"Elliot I'm curious at the same time worried."

"I don't know where to start."

"That bad is it?"

Sadie listening from the kitchen joined them in the lounge. "Barney, I think it might be a good Idea for you to sit down."

He sat down enquiring, "What is going on, what is wrong?"

Sadie spoke quietly with a question, "Your surname is Phillips?"

Even more puzzled by her question he just replied. "Ye—s."

"This has been a difficult decision for Elliot to make, however, I will explain. Elliot's surname used to be Phillips, when he reached sixteen he changed it by deed poll to Phelps to be the same as his mum, who had changed her name thirteen years earlier, just before Corrina was born, Corrina doesn't know that."

"I'm sorry I don't understand what you're telling me?"

"What we are trying to tell you is we think you are Elliot and Corrina's dad."

Barney looking directly at Elliot was at a loss for words eventually stammering, "Wwwhaat on earth makes you think I might be Elliot's dad."

Sadie took some photos from a draw in the coffee table for him to view explaining, "These are photos of Elliot's mum Susan, take a look."

Barney looked, gulped, his eyes bulged as he stared at the photos. "Oh my God that is Susan the one I treated like shit, the one whose life I made miserable, I don't understand why am I not the object of intense hostility, the least I expected is to be called a bastard, my actions probably contributed to her death. Elliot if there is any way I can say sorry, I will I am so sorry."

As Frank had done some years before, Elliot too, held out his hand, expressing. "Barney you had nothing to do with Mum's death, what went before is gone." The biggest surprise was Elliot put his arm round him and hugged him.

Tears welled up, he was emotionally drowning, he had found his son and he had a granddaughter.

Barney then asked, "How old is Corrina?"

Elliot replied, "She is three years younger than me why do you ask?"

Barney stunned them, advising, "There is no way in on earth that Corrina could possibly be my daughter because she would have been born twelve months after Susan, your mum finally escaped my bullying."

"That must be why the father isn't named on her birth certificate."

"Has it bothered her?"

"Not really I gave Corrina away, I did talk to her about you, but we always believed we had the same father."

"Blimey over the years I have caused so many problems and heartache, most of all to my family and now this, Corrina will never know who her real father is."

Elliot looked troubled. "Me and Sadie have a mountain to climb, we will need to find some way of telling her, at least she is my sister."

Sadie quite emotional herself said, "I think it's time we told Becky, she has another Granddad she is in her room probably on zoom to her friends."

Elliot called up the stairs, "Becky can you come down please I have something to tell you."

Becky her eyes conveying a look of curiosity asked her mum, "What's going on maw?"

Elliot called her over to him quietly explaining, "Becky sweetheart, me and your mum have been wondering and discussing something we believed to be true for some time, and tonight we have our answer."

"What do you mean?"

"Barney is your granddad."

If you were to describe the facial gesture of a gaping grimace, open mouthed astonishment unable to assimilate the news which had just been imparted to her, completely stunned without voice, an answer would be 'goggle eyed'.

Sadie confirmed, "Becky he really is your granddad."

Barney explained, "Becky it's as much of a shock to me and your mum and dad as it is to you."

Sadie thoughtfully put an arm round Barney's shoulders whispering, "Say hello to your granddaughter."

Barney felt like a king responding to Sadie's supplication, though a little embarrassed when expressing, "Hello my granddaughter Becky."

Becky who's shocked white face had regained its rosy colour, with a huge grin giggled, "Hello my granddad Barney."

Barney kept looking at his son and granddaughter, a tear in his eye realising his exaggerated sense of self-importance, his indifference to the thoughts and needs of others including his own family: wasted years. His contrition was deep seated, the moral anguish arising from past misdeeds had tormented him from the moment he became a guest of her majesty's prison, and the tremor he experienced when he first heard the cell door banged shut behind him. Because of his arrogance the authorities rightly labelled him as someone who rehabilitation would be impossible. Despite the prognosis of all his detractors, he worked hard to put the past behind him, he had been a model prisoner earning him an earlier than expected release, then his real rehabilitation began with a simple handshake offered by Frank. For the first time in his life, he felt he had everything, he had a good job and was liked and respected by his colleagues, he had regained the trust and love of his fiancée, to cap it all he was reunited with his son. There was however sadness impinging on his happiness while looking at his son, his wife Sadie and granddaughter Becky had an adhesive that bonded them: love. Barney understood something about his makeup, realising it prevents him from giving even canonical love, namely affection for anyone. For a while, sadly even his loving parents had disowned him, his dad once stated. "I think there must have been a mix up in the hospital we were given the wrong baby."

Time and patience from all of the family would be required if possible to totally reconcile and repair lost years. He stood at the dawn of a new chapter of his life his cerebrum, trying to comprehend the evening. There appeared little, in fact any recriminations his son Elliot and his little family may have held, it seemed they had been consigned to history. There were two moments of sadness trespassing on his happiness which heretofore he would have considered unimportant; the death of his ex-wife Susan however more importantly how Corrina would respond to news she and Elliot had different fathers. Later that evening one of the sweetest moments Barney ever experienced occurred as he said his goodbyes, Elliot grinning declaring, "See you on Monday Dad."

Hearing Elliot express the word 'Dad' brought another tear to his eye, his choked reply, "I will son goodnight, goodnight, Sadie, goodnight my beautiful granddaughter."

Sat in his hotel room he facetimed Cherry, when she answered she looked at his smiling face querying, "Had a good evening have you?"

"Cherry my darling I have some wonderful news, what I'm about to tell you, you're not going to believe."

"Calling me darling, it must be good."

Barneys, excitement was so intense he could not hold his news back any longer burbling, "Elliot, Corrina's brother is my son, the one I never thought I would ever see again."

"Barney calm down and tell me clearly."

Taking a breath he reiterated, "Elliot, Corrina's brother is my son."

"Are you sure?"

"Absolutely on hundred percent positive and I have a granddaughter as well how about that?"

"Barney if it's true I am so chuffed for you."

"Oh it's true! Cherry can you come down next Friday and meet them?"

"Of course I will, remember I have already met them in New York at Henry and Corrina's wedding."

"Cherry don't tell anyone yet, there is a problem concerning Corrina, which needs to be addressed, I'll tell you more when you get here on Friday, just don't say anything to anybody."

"What about Myles?"

"Bring him as well, of course he also knows Becky they met in America at the wedding, apparently, they got on very well just ask him if he wants to come, if he does I'll book an extra room."

"I'm gobsmacked, how am I going to keep that a secret?"

"You will be the soul of discretion I'm sure, By the way I love you."

"Barney I love you too I'm so happy for you, I'll speak to you tomorrow."

His emotional converse with Cherry was understated considering the sheer exhilaration racing through his veins, his head spinning trying to apprehend the implications, the expectations and conventions befitting of a father and grandfather towards his family. Barney lay on his bed reflecting on one of the best days of his life, he was a granddad he kept hearing his granddaughter giggling, "Hello my granddad." Despite that, nothing could compare with his son saying, "See you on Monday Dad."

His ruminations continued into the early hours; his mind still indulged in self-questioning. He wanted to do so much for his new-found family. He was extremely happy, nonetheless in his mind he was at a loss as to what he considered lost years. Incapable of understanding why he had spent so many of those years unable to say sorry for the indiscretions he had perpetrated. What on earth had possessed him to be a law unto himself, for which he ultimately paid the price—dearly.

When pride is rubbed into your face; when disavowed by so called friends, and laughed at by people not as deleterious as yourself, it's hard to readjust. Barney had surfed those dangerous waves fighting the surging tide, which in no small measure had engulfed him through which he had capsized almost drowning him. Miraculously Barney had, because of a handshake of friendship offered to him by Frank, survived. He had never been a believer, however that evening for the first time in his life, he offered a prayer thanking everyone who had helped him turn his life around.

Chapter 41

During Barney's temporary placement as general manager in Edinburgh, the family became the focus of his life, Cherry became an integral part of that focus as did Frank's son Myles. Myles and Barney's granddaughter Becky, appeared to get on very well. There still remained the problem of how to address the complex circumstances equating to Corrina's paternity, the dilemma of explaining to her that she and Elliot were from a different paternal lineage, out of that another dilemma arose, which had to be considered, namely Myles who was obviously fully aware of the situation. Cherry had to convince him that under no circumstances must he bring the issue into any family conversation. He wasn't wholly aware of the nature or significant of the circumstances of why he was asked not to say anything, but acceded to their entreaty. Fourteen years old he was more interested in Becky he was really quite taken by her, she was the same age as him and felt the same. Cherry and Sadie were worried there might be a burgeoning teenage romance which they would have to watch closely, mindful that it might get out of hand.

For more than a week, the family engaged in many earnest conversations whereby thoughts and feelings were exchanged as to how and when Corrina should be informed. At a loss for an answer, they determined Henry would probably be the only one who could resolve their dilemma. Barney spoke to Henry via facetime conveying a sense of pressing importance that he needed to talk to him as soon as possible. Henry puzzled, replied, "Okay I'll come this weekend Corrina will be delighted to see her family we'll bring the little fella he's growing so fast."

Barney quickly dissuaded Henry from bringing his family revealing. "Henry I know this is a strange request but we need to talk to you on your own."

Confused, he queried. "Why, what's the problem?"

"I can't say anymore, trust me, Elliot and myself need to talk to you in private, all I can say is, it is a family problem."

"I don't understand."

"I know I'm asking a lot, but if you come up we can explain fully."

"This is going to be awkward Corrina will want to know why she can't accompany me and see Elliot and Sadie."

"I understand it's difficult, but what we have to say is very important."

"Blimey that important, you've got me worried and baffled."

"Look Henry all I can tell you is that it concerns Corrina, we need your input we think you are more suited to deal with this problem."

"I really am worried here! but if it's that important, I'll see what I can do."

"Henry what I will say there is nothing physically serious, by which I mean nobody is ill."

After their converse, Henry was perplexed but to a small degree relieved because Barney's rhetorical assertion indicated illness was not the problem. He was devoid of how he could explain to Corrina that his presence was required as a matter of urgency in Edinburgh, but she wouldn't be able to accompany him.

He sat at his desk trying to conceive an answer to the puzzle placed upon him. One person who he thought might shed some light on Barney's request, was Cherry. Cherry looked startled when Henry paid an unforeseen visit to the warehouse she managed, from where they operated the online business, curiously she asked, "Hello and to what, do we owe this unexpected pleasure?"

"It's alright Cherry don't worry I'm not checking up on you."

Chuckling she responded, "It never entered my head, but I am surprised, is there a problem?"

"I have just spoken to Barney, do you know what's going on? he seems very worried and he wants me to go up there as soon as possible but he won't give me a reason."

"Henry I'm not supposed to say anything, and quite honestly, I'm not sure if I should, but I think you had better come into the office because it's a very private matter and I will put you in the picture."

"Yes please if you will?"

"Henry this is going to come as a huge shock, as it did to all of us." Taking a sharp intake of breath before disclosing to Henry, "Barney is Elliot's dad."

A look of sheer disbelief spread across his face, "NO."

"I promise you he is."

Realigning his thoughts he asked slowly, "Barney is Elliot's dad, are you sure?"

"Yes he couldn't be more pleased, he's over the moon at finding his son."

"If he is happy and obviously he would be, what is the problem?"

"Corrina is not his daughter, that is why he has not broadcast it to all and sundry, we have been trying to find a suitable opportunity to tell her. She is probably going to find the situation distressing. Henry the saddest part in all of this is, nobody knows who her dad is, he isn't named on her birth certificate, in the space where it says father, its blank."

"Bloody hell!"

"Yes I know, it's one hell of a problem we have landed you with."

"Thanks Cherry my God I have to find an excuse, how am I going to explain why I need to go up to Edinburgh?"

"If there is any-way I can help just ask?"

"Thanks Cherry."

Henry sat in Cherry's office his creative mind processes clattered into gear, attempting to find a workable solution, the thought of telling Corrina an outright lie was contrary to his natural integrity. It took a while but an idea finally settled across his thoughts not exactly a eureka moment, nevertheless an idea, which required the able assistance of Cherry. He asked her, "I know it's a big ask but do you think it would be possible at such short notice to arrange a girls weekend away?"

"It's possible, I could ask but where?"

"I don't know somewhere like Blackpool or Weston what do think?"

"Henry leave it to me I'll see what I can do."

"I will be so grateful if you can, don't forget the kids."

"As if I would?"

"Oh by the way Cherry congratulations on your engagement I look forward to the wedding, when is it likely to be?"

"Thank you, as soon as Barney finishes in Edinburgh this problem with Corrina is far more important."

"I'll ring him and make him aware of our plan."

"That's good, he's been so worried. Anyone who knew him a few years ago would find difficult to believe, he's changed, he is a lovely man."

Cherry somehow persuaded the women to go to Blackpool for the weekend, something the teenagers would enjoy too, although Myles was a bit miffed as he wanted to go to Edinburgh, Becky was a bigger draw. Cherry had to do some manipulating, how she worked that problem was a mystery to Henry, but he was extremely grateful. Friday morning as soon as the family, that is the women and kids left for Blackpool, Henry flew to Edinburgh where Elliot picked him up from the airport. Henry noted both Elliot and Barney were extremely apprehensive, worried for Henry but more concerned for Corrina, Sadie greeted him with a hug and a cup of tea, "Henry it's a mess I don't envy you having to tell Corrina she has a different father than her brother."

Henry enquired of Barney, "What in the first instance made you aware of, or thought you and Elliot might be related?"

"Mmmm I think it started when we spoke about family, why I told him about my previous life I don't know, Elliot himself broached the subject actually, telling me his thoughts, then Sadie showed me some photos of Susan, Elliot's mum, there was no mistaking, in the photo was Susan my ex-wife. Elliot is my son. Henry I have caused so many problems in my time but hell, this beats the lot."

Barney as far as I'm concerned everything happens for a reason, we will find the right path to follow.

"Do you think so?"

"We will, I promise you."

Later that evening Henry spoke to Corrina via face-time, her face illuminated the screen and warmed his heart, like always she started their long distance exchanges and feelings, "Hello my special man had a good day?"

Trying to give the impression everything was satisfactory but pulling a peevish face. "Wish I was with you and Denni, instead of covering for Cherry, are you having a good time?"

A little face appeared on the screen. "Hello Daddy."

"Hello Denni what have you been doing?"

"Making sandcastles Daddy."

"Who have you been making sandcastles with?"

"Myles and Jude and Mummy and Nanny and Caro and Elaine and Cherry!"

"Have you been to the fair?"

"Mummy what's the fair?"

Corrina laughing, answered her son's question. "You know when we went on the bumper cars and we had ice-cream?"

"Daddy we went on the bumpy cars."

"Who was driving?"

"Mummy she kept bumping into everything."

"No changed there then."

Corrina's response, "Cheeky bleeder."

"What's a cheeky bleeder Mummy?"

Henry choking with hilarity, queried. "How are you going to explain that?"

"I think I'll say good night my special man, before I say anything that might cause me anymore problems."

"Good night Denni good night Blue eyes."

Henry filled with guilt sighed with relief when they said good night, it was the first time he had ever lied to his blue eyes. Solemnly vowing it would never happen again whatever the problem.

They had a prolonged and lively exchange of opinions, whereby the net result of which was to say nothing, until there was no escape from the reality of the situation, Elliot was in despair he loved his younger sibling they were very close. Sadie encouraged him to stay strong until Corrina was aware that she and Elliot were sadly the product of different paternal lineage, advising him. "You will need to be there for her."

Henry was back home when Corrina rang him, opening with her usual causerie. "hello my special man what's it like managing a shop?"

"Hello blue eyes I didn't today, I left it to the staff they are perfectly capable, I'm missing you how are you and the little fella?"

"I'm ok but Denni keeps asking for you he's a proper daddy's boy, otherwise we are having a great time. The kids are loving it to be honest, us girls are as well especially when they are abed."

"Too many beverages imbibed I suspect?"

"We have one or two but the girly talk is lovely."

"I bet I'm getting a roasting from you?"

"Of course that's part of the fun."

"I'll give you some fun when you get home."

"Don't tell me your sea-squirt is playing up?"

"Of course just thinking of you naked gives me a real boner I'll need to go ten rounds with Jose Cuervo to get some sleep."

"Who on earth is Jose Cuervo? Obviously not a friend."

"It's a country drinking song by Tracy bird, the ten rounds are ten shots of tequila drinks to drown his sorrows, I'll need something to put me to sleep."

"Ah didums."

"I'll give you ah didums!"

"I hope I'm going to get more than that?"

"Now whose a cheeky bleeder, give Denni a big hug and a kiss from me and I'll see you tomorrow my beautiful blue eyed lover."

"Goodnight my special man."

Henry sat ruminating on how the problem concerning Corrina's paternal parentage could be resolved, taking into account all that had been discussed as a family, the original decision was not to say anything, that is until it was necessary, however in his heart he knew he had to find the courage to explain all that had been said, there was no alternative, he had to tell her the truth. Henry's relationship with his wife was a love imbued with trust which he understood to mean there were no secrets between them and certainly no lies. He was facing the highest mountain he had ever had to climb…

Chapter 42

Sunday evening after they had put Denni to bed Henry was actually trembling. He invited Corrina to sit down before commencing his declamation, of which he considered to be a wilful betrayal of fidelity towards Corrina: a true perfidy. Corrina sensing there was something amiss enquired gently, "Why what has Happened?"

He put his forefinger to her lips shakily admitting, "Corrina my blue-eyed lover since we first met I have never lied to you, that is I'm ashamed to admit until Friday night."

She looked startled at his confession, "When, how, why and what have you lied to me about?"

"The first thing I have to admit is, when I spoke to you on Friday I wasn't even in Birmingham."

Corrina stammered, "W——-w-here were you?"

"My darling I was in Edinburgh with Elliot, Sadie and Barney."

"Why what's going on?"

"Well I'm not using it as an excuse because I know I should have told you what was going on. However, Barney had called me asking if I would go up to Edinburgh because he and Elliot had a problem to which they did not have a solution, he didn't want to expound on the reason until I was able to meet them."

Sadly, furthermore anxiously, she again queried. "Why what has Elliot, Sadie and Barney to do with whatever you had to go up there for?"

"This came as a complete and utter shock to me as it will to you, the reason they wanted me there was so they could tell me that Barney is related to Elliot."

"How?"

"Barney is his father."

"What! I don't understand, does that mean he, is…?"

Henry interjected before she could complete the question, "Corrina he is not your father, Barney is adamant he and your mum were separated nearly two years before you were born."

Her face held a look of astonishment, "If Barney is Elliot's Father who is mine does anybody know?"

"Thereby hangs the question, nobody has a clue, you yourself know your mum changed her name to Phelps hoping to deny her ex-husband Barney ever having any chance of finding her, however why she didn't give the name of your father is somewhat of a mystery."

Henry too was gobsmacked when she articulated her own admission, "To be honest I don't really care, because providentially I have been endowed and blessed with you and our little boy Denni, I consider myself very fortunate. I also have a caring brother, mind you I was always curious of the veracity of why on my birth certificate the place for father, was blank. I always believed because she suffered severe and emotional distress received from, as we now understand to be Barney, she didn't want him on the birth certificate, nonetheless there was never any intimation I had a different father."

"There must be some other logical perhaps even persuasive justification why she refused to admit who your father is, really, there must be."

"Henry how is Elliot coping with his newfound estranged father, is there any indifference or hostility towards Barney?"

"Strangely there doesn't even appear to be any resentment, I think Elliot is quite pleased to have met him, though he is very concerned of your feelings."

"I'll ring him he has often spoke about meeting his father, I'm pleased and happy for him and for Barney I like him a lot."

Corrina spoke to Elliot and Barney wishing both of them every happiness, then furthermore assuring them as far as she was concerned they needn't worry, disclosing. "I have lived till now without knowing who my father is, to be honest there must have been a good reason, I'm happy I have my loving Henry and my adorable little fella Denni, and of course I have you Elliot, Sadie and Becky."

Communication completed Corrina looked at her husband, steely eyed glowering, Henry's eyes lowered focusing on the floor, head and heart full of guilt he was bearing the weight of complicity, in a contrived untruth which could be construed as downright equivocation. He waited for the onslaught of tongue-lashing which he believed he richly deserved, nonetheless it never materialised, her face broke into a warm smile, she wrapped her arms around him kissing him, then gently chiding him, "Henry my special man you daft nana, not for one fleeting moment did I ever believe you would genuinely lie to cover for some improper, unseemly or adverse secret, you my darling are implicit in steadfast adherence to a moral code. You are my special man unable to cheat at anything, let alone wilfully lie to me, you love me too much, furthermore that love is returned one trillion fold."

Later lay in bed Henry once again apologised to Corrina for what he perceived as a negative episode. Corrina, predetermined his dispirited thoughts, they were ill-founded, Corrina would have none of it, reiterating her previous attestation, "Henry I would know instinctively if you were hiding something untoward that would jeopardise my happiness, your love fizzes through me, every time we touch, every time we kiss, every time I hear you speak, every time you look into my eyes and every time we make love."

Henry still feeling a remorseful sense of guilt, snuggled up spooning Corrina she whispering softly, "That's more like it, my special man, you've got me fizzing again."

"Blue eyes, if you're fizzing, I'm going to uncork your voluptuous body by caressing it until your sensual nerve endings effervesce and bubble over."

"If you keep talking like that, I'll blow my top before you start uncorking, my special man I don't know what I would do without your love."

"My darling Corrina Jade you will never be without my love whatever obstacles life launches in our direction. Now where was I? oh yes, about to uncork that voluptuous body until it reaches a rhapsodic elevation to a euphoric conclusion."

"Mmmmmm giggling her reply, she made Henry rupture into side splitting laughter when expressing. "It's a good job Maggie's not around to hear your figurative prose, she would probably say, "Corrina he's going to shag the arse off you."

With great difficulty garbling through his immoderate mirth at Corrina's discerning assertion, he voiced his reply, "She would be right, come here blue eyes let me get you uncorked, but know more of Maggie's homely aphorisms, not tonight please my sides are hurting."

Chapter 43

Frank's recovery from that mutinous, malignant neoplasm invading his large intestine was slow. Happily the Chemo was defeating the baleful cancer, forcing it into remission, what it couldn't do was take the strain of his emotional turmoil. Unexpectedly for a man who's self-imposed predetermined destiny and strength of character which lay in his tenacity, on occasions would drift into moments of melancholia. Depressingly the chemo treatment left him fatigued to the point of exhaustion, furthermore mentally unable to concentrate because he felt so ill. Frank always believed his body had the resilience and capability to resist attacks from outside interference to germinate, fortunately he had never had flu, the sum total of anything nearing an illness which dared to impose itself on his physicality was a persistent cough allied to a runny nose, even then he wouldn't admit he had caught a cold. Like most humans he never entertained or envisaged the prospect of cancer, its evil influence spreading dangerously through his body, he knew it was fighting a battle: a battle he was determined to win. In order to cope, he had to drum up all the resolve he had shown over the years to overcome any problems he was faced with.

For a while, Henry had to assume complete control of (Jenson's office supplies) insisting that it would only be on a temporary basis until Frank was fit enough to resume his role as sole proprietor and chief executive of the enterprise he had started. It had expanded quickly over a period of several years becoming a significant business empire.

Henry and Corrina despite the enjoyment of being with family in the UK, missed their American way of life. Particularly their apartment, the nights when they would stand in the window of their bedroom enwrapped in each other's arms looking up into the night sky, captivated by the beatific vista, amid the towering multistorey buildings of the city. Their chats to the celestial bodies emitting their twinkling points of light, perceived by them as recognition of their love by Corrina's mum, Corrina would talk to her mum and Henry would thank her for allowing Corrina to love him. Weeks turned into months Henry began to worry they wouldn't be home for Christmas. Christmas in New York in central park with the little fella was where he and Corrina wanted to be, it was special to them.

By mid-October, Frank's course of Chemo was completed, the medical staff who nursed him through his often painful protocol concluded his cancer was in remission, therefore gave him the green light to return to the workaday world. Henry on the other hand, refused to let him return to full time work until he was considered fit enough, insisting he did a phased return gradually letting him retake control. Father and son, one afternoon were taking a coffee break, their conversation turned to Barney and how circumstances can affect your outlook on life. Henry cited, how Frank by holding out his hand in friendship to Barney had achieved the similar effect of acting as an uninterrupted flow of Diamorphine into his veins. Barney, previously had always been hostile, his manner contentious, who on his release from prison was a dispirited wreck, unsure of himself, his future clouded, he had visited Frank to apologise for his actions.

"Henry I was shocked when he came into the office, wondering why and readying myself for further confrontation."

"Dad he's a different man to what I was led to believe."

"I know we are the best of friends he's a grafter, his demeanour has transformed, when I say he's affable I mean approachable, gracious and obliging, as you know all that is required of a manager. There is another aspect of him I would never have thought plausible, he has integrity I would trust him with anything, whatever."

"Dad I think the same, you know when Caro was in New York she took me by Surprise, relating how he and Cherry were an item again. I was also delighted for him when it came to the fore, he had found his son and they were reunited."

Henry was open-mouthed when Frank questioned. "Where, when, who is he? Nobody told me."

Puzzled that Frank was unaware, he asked, "You didn't know Corrina's brother Elliot is Barney's son."

"Blimey when did this happen?"

"A few months after he took on the job as temporary general manager in Edinburgh, which I have to say he has taken to like a Duck to water, really well."

"So Corrina will be pleased she knows who her dad is? And Barney has met his daughter."

"Sadly she still doesn't know who her dad is, Barney is adamant he and her mum had separated at the very least, twelve months before she was born and never put forward his name for the birth certificate, where it denotes father it has been left blank."

"What your telling me is that Susan, his mum, changed her name to Phelps similar to Philips in order Barney wouldn't find her?"

"Dad you knew their mum, was she Scottish?"

"No she was from Birmingham a proper Brummies' the same as all of us."

"Blimey Dad this is some story, you couldn't write it."

Frank suddenly went quiet his thoughts travelling elsewhere, which Henry detected that his mind was embroiled in an argument with itself one to which he obviously couldn't find a solution.

"Penny for them Dad?"

Frank snapped out of his preoccupation giving Henry an ambiguous answer.

"It's nothing really at least I don't think so, that is I hope not."

"That's a trifle cryptic for a coffee break?"

Frank still displaying a confused expression as though he had something to say shook his head iterating, "It's nothing honestly son."

Henry decided against delving deeper into Frank's thoughts, knowing when he had fully digested and clarified the questions swimming around his dad's head, in due course he would avail him of the answers.

Chapter 44

Late November Henry, Corrina and the little fella were packed and ready to fly home, their excitement growing, at the thought of being home for Christmas. Meanwhile Mary, unbeknown to them had organised an early Christmas dinner for the family in her favourite restaurant 'hotel De' Grande' the very place where Mathew had proposed to her. All the family were invited including the Scottish members Elliot, Sadie and Becky, Barney and Cherry were now classed as family so they were invited too. For the family, it was a very happy occasion, a time to celebrate, with the added bonus of Frank's remission, from that virulent growth. He was very much on the mend, almost back to his best, everything on the home front appeared good.

During the celebrations Corrina was talking to Elliot and Barney, she suggested they should all fly out to New York and spend Christmas with them. Disappointingly, Barney could not take up the offer as his placement as general manager in Scotland kept him far too busy over the Christmas period. Elliot also refused for financial reasons he reminded Corrina that he still hadn't repaid all the money he had borrowed to go to the wedding, Corrina was disappointed but not wishing to make him feel uncomfortable accepted his refusal.

As the evening wore on Mary sat talking to Frank, who again pointed out how much Corrina resembled her mother Susan, then curiously added, "I'm told she doesn't know who her father is."

"Why what's it to you, what are you saying?"

"Nothing really, just wondering."

"Wondering what?"

"Honestly nothing."

Mary looked closely at her daughter-in-law. "She does a bit I suppose, she would do being her daughter, you were closer to Susan than me. Much, much closer, she was the beginning of the end for me and you."

"I know I was stupid, it's all in the past, over done with."

Something was obviously bothering him though, however whatever it was he put to the back of his mind when the little fella Denni, came to sit with his nanny and granddad.

The celebrations continued into the early hours of the morning, it was a joyous affair to all, which however was tinged with sadness because disappointingly, part of the family would be flying back to New York, although Henry and Corrina loved their family, after six months the thought of going home excited them. When Henry left New York, he was unsure if they would keep his position at MSIA open, if not he would need to start looking for employment. Dusty had originally given him unlimited furlough, nevertheless Henry considered six months an awful long time to keep his position open so emailed Dusty regularly, concerning the progress of Frank's illness.

Before they boarded the flight home, Henry Emailed Dusty and received an immediate reply which read, 'welcome home son, your desk is waiting for you' That Email lightened the sadness of their goodbye's considerably, Henry carried Denni in his arms while Corrina dealt with the formalities of checking in and receiving boarding passes.

Their flight took ell hours which seemed like an eternity but at last they reached the front door of their apartment. Henry opened the door then he picked up Corrina who was holding Denni and carried them both over the threshold. Placing them down he kissed Corrina voicing his innermost thoughts and feelings, "Corrina Jade I am so happy when we are together, home at last."

Corrina put Denni to bed and she herself was so tired when her head landed on the pillow she slipped into dormancy before Henry had even slipped under the bed linen. Henry lay ruminating over six months of working in Birmingham, running the family business was the easy part but watching his dad Frank fighting his illness took its toll leaving Henry at times, mentally drained and despondent. He turned his head to look at Corrina her hair tousled across her face, breathing gently he wanted to make love to her but she was under the spell of the sandman, he smiled to himself. His dysphoria about his dad's illness dissipated, while travelling with his loving family across the pond from Birmingham.

Henry was awakened by Denni jumping on him shouting, "Daddy, dinner, five minutes."

With one fuzzy glance at the clock, eleven, it was never Eleven was It? rubbing his eyes his head slowly demisted, he stretched, finding the wherewithal to hug his son and the voice to answer, "Hello little fella."

Henry stretched again, picked up Denni and while hugging him, walked a little unsteadily towards the kitchen where Corrina stood wearing the radiant smile that always melted him. She giggled and said, "Hello my special man sit down we'll have breakfast."

"Why didn't you wake me, where did you get the food?"

"Me and the little fella went shopping, I didn't wake you because like me you needed sleep, only more so you were knackered, how are you feeling now? you look brighter."

Stretching again, "My darling Corrina Jade I am ready to take on the world."

"Feeling that good ay?"

Quickly regaining his sanguinity he had a sudden thought. "Corrina we didn't rechristen our bed did we?"

"That Henry Swan will have to wait; there's a lot to do."

"What have we to do that's better than that?"

"How about the washing and ironing, it doesn't do itself, not only that we have all the shopping to do?"

"I thought you'd been shopping."

"Only for breakfast or should we say brunch."

"Point taken, can I have fried eggs sunny side up?"

"Yes milord and don't say anymore."

Cornelius and Maggie paid them a visit, Cornelius was overjoyed Henry was back; for two reasons. 1 his best friend was back, 2. Cornelius and another guy called Guy had been covering for him during his leave of absence, Cornelius admitting, "Henry I don't know how you put up with all that shit, complainers, whiners, the ill-mannered, discourteous, unpleasant and often offensive people who think you are there to wipe their boots and asses for them."

"I have done it for so long it's like water of a ducks back, it doesn't have any significant impact on me, they can be as abusive as they like if I can sell them an igloo to build on the Arabian Peninsula."

"Where the bloody hell is the Arabian Peninsula?"

Life in the American household of the Swan Jenson family regained its Idyllic status. On returning to work, Henry had a meeting with his CEO and friend Dusty P Upthegrove 3rd who welcomed him back, "Henry son, Cornelius and Guy have done well enough between them however it has been a strain for them," then Dusty used a word Henry had never heard before, continuing, "they found difficulty to deal with all the constant 'Kvetching' from customers and staff alike so welcome home."

Meet concluded, Henry sat back at his desk the word kvetch intrigued him, he checked dictionary, laughing when he read it's definition, Kvetch: Yiddish, pinch; squeeze: a chronic whining complainer, customers can be contrary and maybe a trifle awkward but never kvetch.

Henry then called a meeting to thank all the staff in his department for keeping the ship afloat during his absence, picking out Cornelius and Guy to give them special praise for all their hard-work.

Chapter 45

Their Christmas was very special, the first time they would fully watch their darling son become aware of the magic of Christmas and what was happening. The build-up gave them so much pleasure, which included taking Denni to see Santa Clause for the first time. He was timid at first, however a little gentle coaxing from Mum and Dad and he was persuaded to talk to the man with the long white beard, Mum and Dad's enthusiasm, moreover excitement transferred to Denni, he wanted to talk to every Santa in every store and every street. Denni was agog when the Christmas tree was decorated, his face expressed a wondrous look especially when his dad switched on the fairy lights.

Christmas Eve, they waited until Denni was abed before putting presents under the tree, later that evening when they were sure Denni was asleep, Henry, alias Santa accompanied by Corrina, alias Mrs Santa crept into his room placing his presents at the bottom of his bed before going to bed themselves.

Henry and Corrina as new Christmas parents were far too excited to sleep, they lay talking about the first Christmas's they could remember. Henry thought he was three years maybe four, remembered his mum and dad sitting on the bed while he opened his presents, Corrina agreed she must have been about four too, only it was just her mum and brother Elliot, no Dad. Then she said something which saddened Henry. "As I got older I used to wonder who our dad was, Elliot now knows who his dad is but I'm still in the dark, It's got me wondering who my dad is."

Henry wrapped her in his arms encouraging. "Blue eyes it's his misfortune, if I had a child somewhere I would want to be part of its life, come on let's go to the window and wish your mum Happy Christmas."

They stood clinging to each other looking out into the dark leaden sky no stars to wish upon but it cheered Corrina. "Mum happy Christmas! I will say happy Christmas to Denni for you and tell him how much his Nanny loves him."

Henry added his own felicitations, "Happy Christmas Mum, thank you for giving me your daughter and Grandson I will always look after them I promise."

Corrina staring at night sky gasped. "I think it's snowing it is, it's snowing." Henry squinted into the darkness and concurred. "Blue eyes it is, it's snowing, wait till Denni sees it."

Lay back in bed snuggled up to each other Corrina feeling loved and happy giggled, "I can't wait for little fella to wake up, I'm going to sit on the bed ready to help him unwrap his presents."

Corrina shed a tear when Denni woke early morning, commenting, "Our little boy will always have his mum and dad on Christmas day."

"Corrina my darling nothing will ever stop us being with him at Christmas, his birthdays, first day at school, when he graduates, when he gets married and we will always be there to help when he has problems, whatever they may be."

Corrina let the tears roll down her face which prompted Denni to cuddle up anxiously pleading, "Mummy don't cry."

"Denni little one, I'm not crying because I'm sad, I'm happy because you are happy and Daddy is happy."

When Corrina opened the blinds to show him the snow, still gently falling, Denni surrounded by toys, candy and torn wrapping paper was unable to comprehend what was going on. He pressed his nose up against the window staring intently, only coming away when Mummy picked him up hugging him she told him, "Breakfast little one," sitting him down at the table.

Turkey safely stowed in the oven, the vegetables prepared, they ventured out into the cold for a walk Denni wearing his wellingtons, between them holding hands. Henry remarked, "this is family life and I love it, I'm out with my beautiful wife whose eyes light up the sky when she smiles and my adorable toddler son."

It was a typical happy laid back family Christmas lunch, Turkey with all the trimmings and a Christmas pudding Corrina had made, the little fella wasn't keen but settled for ice cream. That evening Henry and Corrina cozied up on the sofa watching television while the little fella played with toys. They considered themselves to be in paradise.

Chapter 46

Christmas over Corrina and Henry were looking forward to seeing in the new year, they decided Denni was much too young to take to the Times Square ball drop, concerned the crowds would frighten him, they determined they would watch it on television.

Tuesday twenty seventh of December 2016, one date that will always stick in both Henry and Corrina's memory banks when out of the blue they received a letter from Mary, which was unusual as customarily they would converse via Face time at least once a week. The letter contained an ambiguous explanation, revealing only that she needed to talk to them, it was very private matter, one she couldn't discuss over the phone, therefore she would be on the first flight out of Birmingham after New Year. Perplexed by his mum's vague furthermore worrying text, in which she gave no clue as to the reason why, she would travel three and a half thousand miles just to talk to them. Henry and Corrina stared at each other Corrina echoing Henry's thoughts, "What on earth is going on, why is Mum flying here to talk to us?"

"Corrina Jade I just don't know, reading that letter confuses me, it must be very important for her to travel three and a half thousand miles to tell us the reason."

"Do you think it might be because your dad is ill again?"

"I think she would have said, however, you can bet your bottom dollar he is someway involved in whatever it is: you mark my words."

"Henry, let's not dwell on it, we will find out soon enough."

"Easier said than done where my dad is concerned, I just know he will be central to anything that is about to unfold. Mum will be just the messenger; I just hope the message isn't unfavourable."

"Henry Swan Jenson don't be so pessimistic, whatever the problem we have each other and our little boy, we are so lucky."

"Corrina Jade Swan Jenson you're right we will worry about it when Mum arrives and not before."

"That's more like it I didn't marry a pessimist, I married a special man who will find a solution to any problem which attempts to derail the status quo."

Drawing her close he put both his hands up her skirt pleading. "I have the answer what is Denni up to?"

"Why do you ask?"

"Well if we have a quicky that would take my mind of Mum's letter."

"Henry a quicky indeed we'll have to wait until he has his nap."

"I'm not sure I can hold out that long."

"My special man as soon as the little fella is having his afternoon nap then we will see what might happen."

"Wow afternoon delight aye, I like it."

Denni was a very tired little boy therefore the invitation for some afternoon delight was irresistible.

Henry rang his mum later that same evening hoping she would explain the contents of her letter, she was not forthcoming with any explanation, However Henry asked her. "Is it something to do with Dad? I bet it is, has he been up to his old ways I haven't got another brother or sister have I?"

His assumption seemed to throw her a little by going quiet for a few seconds then she changed the subject. Using the same charismatic technique learned from his father He tried to wheedle information out of her, but she was having none of it all emphasising it was too private to disclose anything over the wire. Closing his I pad down he was disappointed, he had gleaned nothing from either the letter or the phone conversation he would have to wait until Mary arrived in the new year.

Corrina tried to ease his troubled mind insisting. "It can't be that bad otherwise she wouldn't wait until the new-year to tell us."

"Blue eyes you're probably right but I get this uneasy feeling it's something to do with Dad, I remember when he was causing problems for Mum, she always hid the worst from me and Caro."

"I thought he was a reformed character."

"Does a leopard ever change its spots? Somehow, I don't think so, why couldn't Mum tell us what is going on."

"Whatever the reason might be, we will see it through together."

"Corrina Jade I can't express how much I love you."

"Henry Swan Jenson you do, I see it in your eyes all the time, I feel it in the way you touch me, I feel it even more when we make love."

A new year was on the doorstep, despite Henry's worries concerning his mum's letter they put those thoughts to the back of their minds, which enabled them to enjoy the build-up, as new year approached. There wasn't much snow left which pleased Corrina because she was insistent Denni would not be allowed to go sledding on the slopes of central park, even with his dad protecting him, nonetheless it didn't stop them all going ice skating. They bought skates for the little fella, wrapped him warm against the cold making sure he wore a helmet at all times, then they introduced him to the ice. It took three sessions, a lot of falls bumps and scrapes accompanied with a lot tears, nevertheless after careful and sensitive encouragement from Mum and Dad combined with gaining confidence in himself which belied his tender years, to Mum and Dad's joy he accomplished the balance to skate in a straight line.

Denni got the bug, a little boy who wanted to skate all the time. So keen that when he did fall, he forgot to cry but laughed instead, he laughed even louder when Mum or Dad ended up on their backsides.

New year's eve arrived, Henry and Corrina and Dennie went skating, then took the little fella to Ample Hills Creamery Ice cream parlour, a favourite of theirs, to finish. Treasured days, which for Henry and Corrina their idea of utopia and having the little fella with them, made it all the more special. Back home in their apartment all cozied up on the sofa they watched some DVDs, notably the little fella's favourite film 'Frozen', they had watched it a dozen times before, yet they endured it twice more. Denni, dog tired from skating ultimately fell asleep on Corrina's lap, luckily she had dressed him in his pyjamas; carefully so as not to wake him she put him to bed.

Henry and Corrina watched the new year's eve fun filled razzamatazz of the Times Square Ball drop on television from the comfort of their sofa, quietly celebrating, kissing and whispering happy new year to each other, then singing Auld lang sine along with the throngs of people in the streets in and around times square.

Chapter 47

With the new year celebrations over, anxiety began to beset Henry, his normal pragmatic approach to life began to desert him, in his mind he knew something was amiss, he was sure a storm was brewing, he also believed somewhere down the line his dad Frank would be the cause of any disruption to his family life. He shared his unease with Corrina, they talked at length about what could be so serious furthermore so private, that it required Mary to fly three and a half thousand miles to explicate her dilemma.

They didn't have to wait long, Mary arrived on the fourth of January. As she entered the arrivals lounge her face was pale; showing concern. After the initial causerie and hugs, they drove back to Greenwich Village, Mary wasn't her usual bubbly self, she was obviously very disquieted. What little conversation offered was stilted, Mary barely managing to smile and chat to Denni. Henry felt his heart sinking into his stomach which was grinding like a cement mixer, as they got closer to their apartment his apprehension manifested to the point where he felt sick, he loved his mum dearly, but he was actually wishing she wasn't there.

Inside the apartment Corrina made Coffee. Mary sat opposite them with the cup in both hands visibly shaking. Corrina could see she was virtually unable to give the reason for her visit, so quietly she questioned her, "Mum, you look worried, I think you should tell us why you are here."

Mary's face was ashen with a trembling voice she opened up. "I really don't know where to start."

"Mum, start at the beginning."

"Henry, Corrina, this really is the most awful thing I have had to do."

Henry was getting more agitated, "Mum, please tell us what is going on?" Henry's mind was working overtime, "What are you trying to tell us?"

"Henry, Corrina, this is so difficult, I just don't know where to start."

"You know Barney is Elliot's father but not Corrina's," she hesitated.

"Mum, please explain?"

"Okay son, look Corrina, the person who believes he is your father has come forward."

Henry realised what his mum was trying to say, "Mum, are you telling us that my dad is Corrina's dad as well? Are trying to tell us is we are brother and sister?"

"There is no actual proof, he only thinks he could be."

For a minute, Henry lost his temper, angrily venting his feelings, "I knew he would be involved somewhere down the line, the bastard."

Corrina remained silent unable to apprehend what she was hearing, staring at the ceiling a tear beginning to trickle down her cheek, she put her head on Henry's shoulder struggling to talk. Finally finding her voice in the Scottish vernacular. "Hendrie thare mist be some mistake how fur could it be?"

Henry replied, "My darling Corrina Jade I don't ken bit ah suspect Mum wull be able to clarify whit she means."

Henry queried, "Mum how can this be I thought Susan was Scottish."

"Let me explain the possible circumstances, Susan was a true Birmingham girl a friend of both mine and your dad, she was going through a bad time with Barney, and here it gets painful for me, I found out he was having an affair with Susan. Corrina trust me, I'm not blaming your mum, she was very vulnerable at the time and Frank took advantage, as you both know he could charm his way round any woman."

Corrina posed a question. "I don't understand, Mum's Scottish accent was stronger than mine?"

"Corrina sweetheart, she must have worked at it, perhaps moving to Edinburgh and learning the accent gave her the confidence to feel safe."

Henry addressed another question, "How did you find out Dad was having an affair did you know Susan was pregnant?"

"No not at all and Henry, you! told me about the affair."

Puzzled Henry asked, "How?"

"When you were three, Frank would take you to the park to play on the swings and roundabouts, but, he would often visit Susan. One day you asked me why was Daddy kissing Susan; that was the start of the end of the marriage, then suddenly Susan disappeared off the face of the earth as though she had never existed."

"Mum I have to ask the question why does Dad think he is Corrina's father there must be some evidence, has he said anything, anything at all?"

"This is the only reason he has given, when you were six you fell of your bike and you created such a fuss we believed you had broken your arm, as a precaution Frank took you to the hospital, while you were there he came across Susan. Why she was there he didn't know and he didn't ask but she had Elliot and Corrina with her, she didn't introduce Corrina to him she just said this little girl is your daughter, then he got distracted by you and Susan left in a hurry, he reasoned to himself that because she had never contacted him, it wasn't true and he tried to never think about it again."

Corrina still with her head on Henry's shoulder another tear trickling down her face trying to control the tremor in her voice asked, "What happens now?"

Mary continued, "Corrina there isn't any actual proof, the only way to really find the truth is by DNA testing, do you want to do that?"

"I am a Catholic girl, I don't want to know but I need to know."

Henry equally as worried wanted to know, "What happens if Frank is Corrina's father, where do we go from there?"

Corrina gave a tearful reply, "Henry you are the only man I have ever loved but our marriage will have end, it's over, we can't be together if we are brother and sister."

"Where does that leave Denni in all this chaos?"

"Henry my love, he is still our little boy, mine and yours, nobody can take that away from us."

Mary interjected, "now hold your horses we don't even know yet, we will have to wait and see, can I make a suggestion?"

In unison, they pled, "Please Mum."

"Nothing is proven, and you could always just stay here and no-one would need to know."

Corrina beginning to get upset again reminded Mary, "Mum I'm a Catholic I could never give up on my faith."

Henry a none believer would have loved to quote Mark Twain (Faith is, believing what you know ain't true) but resisted the temptation because he loved Corrina so much, he gave his own suggestion, "Corrina we should have the DNA test but we must stay together at least until we receive the result, whether it is positive but hopefully negative, in which case we don't have a problem. What do you think?"

Putting her arms around him tightly her voice sounding stronger agreed, "Henry, yes okay but I'm dreading It," slipping back to her Edinburgh Scottish she continued, "Hendrie we wull hea tae bide ilka moment th'gither juist in trial it's a positive result 'n' we ur brother 'n' sister."

Henry understood their love was so strong he just answered, "We wull we wull fur sure we wull."

Mary managed to grasp most of what had been said, adding how she felt about the problematic circumstances confronting them, "I will be here to support you both because I love you both, so much."

Corrina's reply, "I don't know where you found the strength of courage to give us this news but I thank you for being so honest, whatever the outcome of the test we will have to face the music whether it's a dirge or a rock and roll classic."

Henry had to ask Mary what his dad had to say about the situation and why hadn't he come over himself to explain.

Mary explained. "He's still not in a fit enough state of health, otherwise Elaine would have insisted he told you personally, by the way they send their love so does Caro and Lindsay."

"Do they know why you are here?"

"Obviously Mathew does, but we haven't told Lindy why I'm here, but we will have too soon."

"Listen Corrina and you Mum, I know we have a lot to talk about but let's go out to dinner, there is nothing we can do tonight or the next few days, so I think we should have an hour or two of respite from what may be, to come."

Later that night alone in their room, Henry said, "Blue eyes I sincerely hope Dad is losing his mind with his misguided assumption you are his daughter, without you, life will never be the same. My lover whatever happens, there will never be anyone else."

"Henry I feel the same, our love, our marriage, our partnership has got stronger and stronger. It's a good job we have Denni because if the result of testing comes between us, Denni will be the only reason I will have to keep going, honestly I could never even imagine life without you either. You are the only man I could ever love you Henry Swan Jenson are my special man."

After Mary flew home, the significance of their distressing news, hit them as if they had been trampled by a herd of rampaging African elephants. They had tried to remain as calm as possible while Mary was with them, but her disturbing postulation and its implications for the rest of their lives left them bereft of any sanguinity. Henry's usual practical outlook on life deserted him, optimism evanesced, furthermore pessimism weighed heavy on his mind, yet he encouraged Corrina to think of a rainbow after the storm, how fresh and heart-warming its colours are against the clearing sky. Both of them had the same idea on their minds, knowing Frank's history as a man without moral restraint, a philanderer who throughout his life indulged in what Henry described as libertinism.

The outcome of DNA testing would clarify their true marital status, the possible outcome unwanted, although necessary, they would go back to the UK to undertake the testing as soon as possible.

Chapter 48

By the end of January, they were ready to fly back to Birmingham, Henry had spoken to his immediate superior and friend Dusty P Upthegro^{ve} 3rd to discuss the possibility that he may never return to New York, therefore would he accept his resignation. Dusty refused explaining in his slow American Southern drawl vernacular. "Henry whe-yn ya gitt' thuh bottom auf what is appenin' eend ifin kay-un be resolved the-yn we will address the situation and not befo-wr," taking a breath he continued, "Ma partner ah hope ya git thuh long and short yu ahr lookin' for."

Cornelius was heartbroken. "Henry you are the best friend I have ever been fortunate enough to know, I really hope everything works out for you and Corrina, whatever happens we will meet in Edinburgh when me and Maggie get married."

"Raining always bloody raining," lamented Henry when they landed in Birmingham, his bemoaning continuing, "why is it, when it rains in New York it never seems so wet."

"I know it's daft but it does seem soggier here in the UK than it does at home" Corrina concurred.

Mary and Mathew accompanied by Henry's youngest sibling Lindy were there to welcome them, however because of the very emotional nature of the reason for their return to Birmingham, the journey from the airport to Mary and Mathew's house was quiet, the conversation was sparse. The atmosphere brightened somewhat when Mary served up dinner Henry's favourite, sausage and mash, but it was only a matter of time before the reason for traveling three and a half thousand miles came to the surface. Mathew broached the subject of the DNA testing, "When are you planning to have the test done?"

Corrina explicating dolefully, "Sometime in the next couple of weeks, to tell you the truth I don't want to and I am frightened of what it means if Frank is my father, very, very frightened," tears trickled down a her cheeks as she added, "I love my husband, I don't want to lose him."

At Corrina's response, quietness was deafening, filling the room with an eerie perception of morbidity which brought more tears. Henry could feel his own eyes moisten, a single tear tricked down his cheek he expressed, "Corrina if the worst comes to the worst, and the church exorcises cannon law moreover, the laws of what our national sovereignty decree we have to separate, you will always be my wife, no one will ever convince me otherwise."

"Henry I am so frightened I swear if Frank is my father, I will never have anything to do with him, I don't want him near me, he will have taken away my husband the man I love, I could never forgive him."

Henry went to see his dad to arrange for the testing, Mary advised Corrina not to go, she was in a state of melancholia her head drowning in a quagmire of heart-breaking thoughts and fears for her future, for the first time in her life she began to doubt her faith. Frank was not at his best either, Elaine was quite worried about him so persuaded Henry to leave getting the test for a few days until he was better. Henry returned to Mary's, Corrina's relief was palpable for all to see, her demeanour actually lightened awhile.

It was the beginning of March when they finally took the test, Corrina cried as Henry took a small swab of saliva from the inside of her cheek, Elaine did the same for Frank, with both samples labelled, they were dispatched to the laboratory two copies were requested one for each of them. Anxiety increased with every day while they waited for the results, each day seemed drawn out longer than the preceding day. Corrina and Henry found themselves sharing a mental turmoil both morose unable to find any inner contentment; sadly, they would only achieve a valid quietude if the testing proved negative. They talked endlessly of the consequences of a positive result, each day inwardly their thoughts became cloudier and colder, which to both of them signified a portent that all was not well. Henry managing to hold up during those depressing days but was profoundly concerned for Corrina's health, she would slip into bleak, depressive funereal thoughts, waking up in the middle of the night sobbing and garbling incoherently in her Scottish vernacular, "Och Hendrie how come is this happening tae us whit ur we aff tae dae ah don't want a da ah hae ye mah guidman th' jimmy ah loue the ainlie jimmy a'm waantin tae loue, th' ainlie jimmy ah wull ever loue." Though distressed himself, desperate to console and comfort her, he enclosed her in his arms gently caressing her whispering, "We must hold strong for Denni my darling, all we can do is hope, my love for you will be as strong in fifty years' time no matter what."

Through sheer exhaustion she would usually cry herself to sleep, it was all getting too much for her to cope. The waiting became almost unbearable.

Every day they waited nervously for the post to arrive, nearly four tension ridden weeks had slowly dragged by, before that unwanted manila envelope bearing results, dropped through the letter box. Corrina was shaking violently, she did not want to open it, she felt the devil had conspired to break her heart, furthermore take the most important person in her life away from her, her special man, her husband Henry. Henry, discomposed fearful of what possible tumult might be in that envelope, aided by Mary tried to calm Corrina down, coaxing her to open the envelope. Corrina drank a black coffee made by Mary in an attempt to steel her nerves, after several minutes still shaking violently, inhaling heavily, she tore open the envelope. It took her several more minutes to cautiously remove the contents and several more minutes to unfold the paper containing the results. As Corrina read the text her eyes clouded, she began to shiver convulsively screaming she slumped forward pummelling the kitchen table with her fists, thereon crying hysterically. Henry took the letter from her hand he didn't bother to read it. He pulled her away from the table gently and quietly whispered, "I don't care what the results say, there is something wrong, there must be a mistake somewhere down the line."

Taking the letter from Henry still shuddering, she put her head on his shoulder then she found her voice, a voice cracked, lacking cohesion, "Oh my God Henry, according to this you are my brother, but you are my Husband! where do we go from here?"

His head in a tormented whirling chaotic jumblement he desperately searched for some way to soften the enormity of the heartrending reality that lay before them; his own heart was breaking. He was totally at a loss, his mind confused, devoid of any capacity to conjure up some magic words that might ease an impossible situation: he just held her tight. Corrina was his life, she was indispensable, all-encompassing, she and their son Denni made his every waking day worthwhile.

Corrina was sobbing quietly in Henry's arms when the phone rang, Mary answered it there was a pause it was Elaine. "Mary, I guess you have had the results can I speak to Henry."

Mary passed the phone to Him, "Henry how, has Corrina taken the news?"

Henry's anger spilled over yelling, "How do you think, she is broken, heartbroken as I am, is there anything else you want to know?"

"I'm so sorry but your dad wants to speak to you."

"What the bloody hell for, his selfishness has ruined our lives all because he couldn't keep his cock in his trousers, and NO! right now you can tell him I do not want to talk to him if ever, you can tell him to fuck off."

Slamming the phone down he couldn't hold himself together it was all too much, to his mind his dad the man he looked up to, even idolised had betrayed him, Henry felt his eyes well up and the saltwater ran down his face.

Difficult is an adjective that underplays another adjective, unbeatable, they faced an unassailable mountain, despite their despair Henry and Corrina were trying to calm themselves, brother and sister they may be, nonetheless it could never defuse their deep love for each other. Nothing would ever change that and of course they had Denni to consider, he was even more important than the problematic circumstances in which they found themselves. How those circumstances would be resolved at that moment in time was too challenging to contemplate, they would need a lot of time...

Chapter 49

Corrina and Henry were both overwhelmed, they read that hideous letter a dozen times, their wounded hearts sank further down to the pit of their stomachs they were emotionally hurting and mentally bereft of any hope. They sat motionless, neither giving voice to their thoughts staring vacantly, their glazed eyes without clarity of focus. Corrina started crying again lamenting, "Oh Henry this is a mess, at this moment I don't want to live but I have Denni to think of."

Corrina's sad vociferation snapped Henry out of his mesmerism, "Corrina my beautiful wife, which is who you are, we both have Denni to think about. At least, he will know who his mum and dad are, but I don't think the test is right."

Tears wiped they calmed sufficiently, to begin addressing the situation in a quiet controlled manner.

"My darling Henry I wish with all my heart you were right, but the science tells the true story," she wrapped her arms around him giving him a passionate kiss advising him, "Henry that is the last time I will ever kiss you like that. My faith determines because we are brother and sister we are not married, I will move into the spare room, despite that, I have to reassure you the depth of my love for you is like a never-ending circle, you are my sunrise and my sundown, how I'm going to cope I do not know. Henry I desperately want to make love to you but I can't it will be a sin."

Her saddened eyes looked to the floor, she postulated something more heartrending, "I will have to go back to Edinburgh and see if I can get a job, will you return to New York? I honestly think we should stay as far apart as possible."

"Corrina Jade you have nothing to worry over, we have not committed an original or mortal sin, In the eyes of catholic church it is a venial sin, we were unaware we are brother and sister there won't be any condemnation of our life together, nevertheless you will need to speak to a priest to get the churches reaction, meanwhile I will speak to a solicitor."

"Henry if what you say is true then my conscience is clear, but we still can't be man and wife the laws of the country insist we have to separate."

"I fully understand but there is no way I can return to our home without you, I'm living a nightmare I need to be able to see you and Denni! Blue eyes I love New York but I will move back here, I need to see the little fella on a regular basis he is not going to miss out on having his dad in his life, he needs to know me, moreover, I want to be there for him I want him to be a big part of my life, I want to watch him grow up. There is another reason."

"What?"

"To be close to the one woman I have ever truly loved, you my darling Corrina Jade. You will not have to worry about finance, whatever the law say's as far as I am concerned you are and always will be my wife, there will never be another Mrs Jenson."

"My God Henry, this is so unfair."

"I know, I know."

Over the course of the next few weeks, they laid their plans for the future. Their solicitor dealt with paperwork for the painful annulment of marriage, on the grounds it was not legally valid. Unfortunately they hit a problem, for the annulment to go ahead one of them had to have permanently resided in England or Wales for twelve months or owned a house in England or Wales for six months, they could have gone to a Scottish court, however they do not recognise annulment only divorce. Because of the love they held for each other they decided to live for twelve months in Birmingham, Corrina wanted to stay married to Henry for as long as possible, he felt the same…

Henry and Corrina chose a house in a quiet residential area of Four Oaks in Sutton Coldfield, away from Frank. Corrina moved in with Henry into the new house, just glad to be with her special man. Her Catholicism forbade her to sleep with him, thereon they had separate rooms. Sadly, the strength of their feelings for each other reached a point where Corrina felt she couldn't live in the house without being able to share the intimacy of love. So with a heavy heart she decided she would return to Edinburgh. She made plans to stay with Elliot and Sadie until she could find her own place.

That was a sad time for both of them, neither could fully face a time when they would be unable to talk like lovers do, sharing their hopes and aspirations, their fears, their love, laughing making fun of each other, giving and receiving in equal measure. They had cried together celebrated together…

They found a house to rent in Edinburgh on the same street as Elliot and Sadie, a few doors down. Henry drove up and carried Corrina and Denni across the threshold kissing Corrina softly on the cheek.

Sighing heavily Henry advised, "Any problems call Barney he will look after you."

She started to giggle, Henry hadn't heard her giggling in a long while, he asked, "What's amusing you blue eyes?"

"It's ironic, from what Elliot has told me he is a lovely man, a good dad and grandfather, I wish he was my dad."

Henry gave her his own observation, "I know how you feel but if he was, we would never have met, not had our wonderful time together in New York and we wouldn't have the little fella."

"You're right we have had a good time, a wonderful life together, it's been exciting, now, what are you doing about work?"

"I'm flying out to New York to see Dusty, I'll hand in my resignation and have a beer with Cornelius, while I'm there check everything is ok in our apartment."

Puzzled Corrina queried, "Are you keeping it on?"

"Of course why would I let it Go? it's our home we can't be together as a married couple, but we can use it for holidays, I'll be up to see you in about two weeks."

"Take, care my special man, I love you, Denni give Daddy a kiss." He clasped the little fella in a loving embrace and said goodbye. In a dark depressive mood, he drove back to Sutton Coldfield, to his empty house.

They were both suffering from severe emotional distress their sensibilities balancing precariously on a knife edge, their hearts feeling as though they had been summarily hacked out of their chests with a meat clever. Even though they could not be a family in the true sense of the word, they both needed to be strong for their son, every moment spent together as a pseudo family was of great importance to them. They spoke to each other every day, to an extent their lives were not completely empty there was one source of enjoyment they had Denni.

Chapter 50

Henry cut a lonely figure when he flew back to New York, the flight reminded him of the first time he crossed the pond to start a new life in New York, he was also alone then, but it was a happy exciting time. Oh How circumstances can forge a change in the whole panoramic life you hopefully expected and in his case ultimately achieved...

Arriving at JFK international, rain was bucketing down, unlike his first tantalising sight four years earlier when he arrived on a warm day full of excitement, his aspirations for the future firmly fixed and his expectations for the American dream rising with each searching look. He hailed a cab, his journey through Greenwich Village affected him even more, his mood pensive as he passed the café's, bars and their favourite Diner, where He, Corrina and the little fella would breakfast: his heart was broken; Spirits at an all-time low. Sadly and silently he walked through the apartment reliving ghosts of the most important, moreover happier times of his life. He stood in the window of their bedroom; dark grey clouds hid the sky causing more despondency to filter out of the surroundings into his being. Nothing could ever shake the foundations of his life in such a calamitous, dispiriting, atmospherical manifestation his father had managed to conjure from a twenty-five-year-old infidelity.

Though technically the condition of social order disavowed his and Corrina's espousal, Henry still regarded Corrina as his wife refusing to accept precepts of statute or ecclesiastical law. Time zone difference between New York and Birmingham UK is about five hours six o'clock in New York, eleven O'clock in Birmingham, it was late, but Henry needed to speak to Corrina. He called her via facetime, when she appeared on the screen her smile lifted him out of his dolefulness she asked, "Hello my special man how are you feeling and how is our home?"

Returning her Smile, he admitted, "Blue eyes New York is bloody lonely without you when I walked into our home, I was in despair Sylvia Plath hit the nail on the head when she described despair as 'like an Owls talons clutching my heart' I felt so low."

"Who is Sylvia Plath? I understand her feelings because I have been there."

"She was an American poet and novelist."

"Are you ok, you've got me worried?"

"I'm good, honestly talking to you has given me a lift."

"Are you sure?"

"Honestly: I'm good."

"How long are you staying?"

"Only a few days, just to get our home in order and say goodbye to everyone, how's the little fella?"

Corrina started giggling a rare occurrence over the last three months which made Henry's smile get wider, "What's tickling you? It's good to hear you laughing."

"Me and you talking as if we were still married."

"Corrina at this point in time we are still married. In my heart, I will always be married to you."

"Henry my special man I have only ever loved one man, I will only ever love one man as long as I live, that man is you."

"Don't you'll get me all bleary eyed, Is Denni asleep?"

"I think he must have heard you, he's supposed to be in bed asleep but here he is, come on Denni say hello to Daddy."

Henry's face radiated love when his son, "Hello Denni my lovely boy, are you being a good boy for Mummy? Daddy will be home soon, shall we go ice skating, what do you think?"

His face lit up turning to his mum, "Daddy said we can go ice skating."

Henry spent a little while talking to Corrina and the little fella before saying goodnight.

Sitting staring out of the window feeling lonely and sorry for himself, he called Cornelius keeping his fingers crossed his best friend would be available for an evening on the town, he rang him to ask, delighted when he said yes. Only two people had been privy to his and Corrina's marital status, they were Dusty P Upthegrove 3rd and of course his best friend Cornelius. Cornelius arrived, Henry had, had a surprise, he was accompanied by Dusty. Dusty as unlikely as it seemed to Henry hugged him, and In his usual laid-back drawl, "Good to see you son."

Henry during the course of very pleasant evening, thanked Dusty for being so patient by allowing him time to consider his future, nonetheless he informed him, with much sadness he would be handing in his resignation. Dusty though disappointed understood Henry's commitments lay elsewhere, asked him to hand in an official resignation letter so he could start looking for a replacement. Following their night out Henry visited head office to meet with Dusty who, looking serious sat him down and questioned him, "What are you going to do when you get home?"

Henry explained, "I'm not going home, New York is my home, what I am doing is going back to my family Corrina and Denni, I know we are not Legally married but I should get back to them as soon as possible."

Dusty's serious face broke into a grin, "How would you like to carry on working for MSAI?"

"I'm sorry sir I can't see how, as I have explained I really do need to be with my family."

Dusty leaned on his elbows, chin resting on hands with fingers interlocked queried, "Henry where did we first meet?"

Henry perplexed by the question replied, "When you first interviewed me."

"Yes, but where?"

"West Bromwich, West Midlands why do you ask?"

"At last, we are on the same page Henry, there is an opportunity for a COO at West Bromwich, if you think you're capable?"

"Chief operations officer, there's a vacancy?"

"If you want it, you will need to have an interview though, what do you think yes or no?"

"When and where do I go for the interview here or West Bromwich?"

"Son you have just had your interview your hired, when you get back to Birmingham you will find a letter confirming your appointment. Mr Jones the CEO will be expecting you."

"Dusty sir, I'm at a loss for words, I'm bewildered by your offer."

"Henry we need to keep a hold of our best people."

"Wow I feel wanted, leaving New York and all you guys is one of the hardest and saddest times of my life, I speak for Corrina too, we have had a wonderful time, thank you all, thank you."

"When are you leaving?"

"As soon as I find someone to look after the apartment, Corrina's faith won't allow us to be together full time because loving your brother is a no-no, in the eyes of the law 'obviously' but more importantly for Corrina is her stance on Cannon law, for which I have to respect."

Dusty unexpectedly displaying a softer side to his usual brusque hard-nosed business exterior, in a low guttural voice asking, "Henry son come and see us next time you are able to visit, don't forget to bring Corrina and Denni we are going to miss you."

"I will sir, thanks again, oh and say thank you to Avelina and the girls."

Driving back to his apartment in his beautiful ford Fairlane car, sadness befell him disappointed at the final outcome of the life he and Corrina and their toddler son Denni had once embraced. His world seemed to be falling apart shattered unintentionally into a billion pieces by his father whom he always loved, respected furthermore wanted to emulate his success. He had the same insatiable appetite to achieve the goals he had set for himself. Always striving to attain the maximum reward from any enterprise to which he set his determination to attain success, despite any barrier he might encounter. However, that is where the similarities ended. Henry's loyalty knew no bounds in direct contrast to his dad's philandering ways, there was no way on earth he could violate the rules and sanctity of his marriage which now, had been supplanted by his dad.

Later that afternoon he rang Corrina to tell her his news about the offer of a job in Coventry, whilst in conversation with her and the little fella the front doorbell rang, "Blue eyes I'll ring you back, there's someone at the door."

To his delight Cornelius and Maggie stood bearing gifts, two bottles of wine and pizza. Maggie gave one of her usual comic sermons, "I always knew there was something dirty about you."

Henry guessed what was to follow because she often indulged in comical usage of indelicate language when he riposted, "What do you mean something dirty about me; Maggie May?"

"Pumpin' yer sister 'n' don't ca' me Maggie Kin gallus bleeder," Cornelius shaking his head but laughing interjected, "don't take any notice I think she would like to shag her own brother."

They both fell about at their own mirthful banter."

Henry showing a wry expression on his face, just shook his head.

Maggie changed her tone showing a more caring side to her character, reverting back to English telling Henry, "I'm so sorry, Corrina is in bits I know how much you love each other."

"Thanks Maggie but there isn't a thing we can do, regardless we will still love each other albeit a platonic love."

His answer let Maggie in again, "She's going to miss that dirty mouth of yours she will have to buy herself a battery-operated rabbit."

Sporting a grin Henry riposted, "Why, don't you lend her yours?"

"No good I've worn it out anyway I've got Cornelius now."

"Cornelius you're a lucky man," Henry opined.

Maggie obviously worried for her friends asked, "When will you be seeing Corrina and Denni again?"

"O bloody hell I was talking to them when you rang the bell I'll have to ring them back you can speak to her she will be chuffed."

Corrina's smile lit up his I pad offering, "Oh there you are, I thought you had forgotten me my special man."

"Hey blue eyes that will never happen just look, who was at the door."

"Hello Corrina."

"Maggie how are you, you look great it must be all that sex."

"Oh yes, It does keep you fit, enough of me how are you keeping?"

"I have some good days especially when Henry is with us, when he isn't which will probably be more often when I move back to Edinburgh, it's not too good. I miss him so much."

"You and Henry's story is the most bizarre moreover saddest I have ever heard, it elicits disbelief it would make a good book."

"I know I always wondered who my father was now I wish I didn't know, me and Henry were so happy we had and still have so much love for each other, to think we can never make love again hurts I would find it impossible to love someone other than Henry."

Maggie was visibly upset remarking, "I know I can't help but I really wish I could" her tone brightened when asking, "is Denni there can I say hello to him?"

Corrina called Denni over, "Denni come and say hello to Maggie and Cornelius?"

He said, "Hello" but he was upset and started to cry he wanted his daddy to come home. Henry with a few quiet words managed to mollify him enough to put a smile on his face. Making him laugh pulling faces when blowing kisses to him, furthermore promising he would be home very soon, then they would all go skating as long as he was good for Mummy. That did the trick which pleased Corrina, she explained, "Henry he has been really miserable he's missing you so much, I'm worried now what will happen when I move back to Edinburgh."

"Blue eyes that's something we will have to consider, nonetheless I'm certain we will work something out which will benefit the little fella. Blue eyes I know I shouldn't declare my love for my sister, trouble is I love you more than ever and always will."

"Henry I feel the same about you."

"I think we should say goodnight we are embarrassing Maggie and Cornelius,

Goodnight blue eyes see you in a couple of days."

Before Henry was able to close down his iPad, Maggie interrupted with a huge grin spread widely couldn't help herself when saying good night she added, "Do you want to borrow my rabbit?"

"Sod off Maggie" or words to that effect was Corrina's expressive riposte.

Maggie couldn't catch her breath, emitting unarticulated sounds like a Hyena in distress, eventually calming enough to reply, "Goodnight My best friend."

"Goodnight Maggie, goodnight, Cornelius, and a special goodnight to my special man."

Henry went quiet which caused Cornelius to ask, "You've gone quiet and you look worried, what's the matter?"

"I am worried, extremely worried about Denni. I've only been away four days and he's upset It reminds me of when my dad first left home. I didn't understand at the time that it was because of his philandering, I couldn't cope with the fact he didn't want us, I slid downhill emotionally into a melancholic haze, only re-emerging back into the light from the hurt and anguish, when he came back."

"Henry my friend if anyone can find a solution you can, it's obvious you need to be close to both Corrina and Denni, and Denni needs to be with his dad, I'm going to miss you, you are a true friend."

"Thanks Cornelius I'm going to miss New York, most certainly Greenwich Village and especially you my very best friend."

Maggie had to chip in with one of her pithy but humorous declarations, "Ah if you two start kissing I'm going to puke."

Both of them expressing annoyance in unison told her, "Sod of Maggie."

"Huh get of your high horses I was only joking."

Cornelius put an arm round her, "We were joking as well." Whilst waiting for a cab to take him to JFK airport Henry sat in his and Corrina's bedroom looking out of the window on the New York skyline, reflecting on trials and tribulations they had faced over the previous six months when uncertainties began to proliferate. Their lives together had never before been subjected to such stormy clouds, their horizons had always been sunny from the moment they had met in Cardiff. Three years later they shared their first kiss, followed by a sunny day when they exchanged their vows of love, that wonderful day was only exceeded when Denni made his first appearance into the world to be held in the loving arms of his mum and dad for the first time. Those times had been exciting, warm, stimulating, ardent, loving and above all happy. They doted on each other and their son Denni. Sadly, throughout the last six months their dreams for their future had fragmented lying in a heap the consequence of which precluded any hope of ever piecing them together: a jigsaw with the most important piece missing. Henry and Corrina were still very much in love and both would admit always would be. However; the moral moreover legal bounds of their predicament highlighted the immensity of the personal decisions that now lay before them. A family ravelled, the knots of which were impossible to undo. Henry's sang-froid had on occasions been sorely tested, his pragmatic approach to life replaced with scornful jaded negativity.

The bodeful onrushing of the annulment of their marriage, was raising its singularly painful heartache, dispensing insomnia and an inability to experience pleasure, caused by their separation. Henry and Corrina necessitated one another, their main consideration being son Denni. If they couldn't be espoused, they had to remain involved and share fully his upbringing for his benefit and welfare. Corrina understood the bonds a boy builds with his dad, exactly the same as she had with her mother the proof of which brother Elliot was building with his dad. Henry the man she loved would have to stay in their lives despite what they considered unjust; they would have to abide by the law of the land.

Locking the door to the apartment fully aware that unless there was an unforeseen change in their circumstances it would remain closed for the foreseeable future, if not the rest of their lives. Dispirited, Henry wiped a moistened eye, he was closing the door on a home, their home, his, Corrina's, and Denni's home, a home once blessed with love.

Chapter 51

Alexander Dumas wrote, "Only a man who has felt ultimate despair is capable of feeling ultimate bliss." Henry was on the downside teetering on the brink of ultimate despair. Ultimate bliss once the prime importance of his existence with Corrina and son Denni, though not intentionally or wilfully it had been ruthlessly ripped from his grasp by the man he once aspired to be like; his own father. Henry was caught between the devil and the deep blue sea he loved his dad but he loved his sister more than life itself, therefore refused to talk to him. He wanted no part of the family business or his father…

Henry arrived at Birmingham international airport, his mum Mary met him and tried to persuade him to stay with her and Mathew, he refused preferring to be alone with his discursive problems which required a lot of thought. Disappointed but understanding, she drove him to his house in Four Oaks, Sutton Coldfield. She watched him go inside, as a mum she was feeling his pain she wished there was some way she could alleviate that pain. Again he felt hurt, the home held memories where he and Corrina had shared for a short time, before their situation forced her to move back to Edinburgh. Stood looking around the lounge introspectively his thoughts pensive, loneliness began to take a strangle hold, he missed Corrina and Denni he wanted both of them in his arms, he wouldn't see them for ten days, so he called them via facetime. His heart lightened when Corrina's smiling face lit up the screen voicing, "Hello my special man where are you?"

"I am home blue eyes."

"At Mum's?"

"No, our home in Vicarage drive, I'm lonely without you and the little fella where is he?"

His head popped up in front of Corrina, "Hello Daddy, are we going skating?"

"When I get home Denni and we'll have Ice-scream and sweets."

"Can I have a chocolate milkshake Daddy?"

"If there is any room left in your tummy, you can."

Corrina stepped in enquiring, "When do you think you will be with us?"

"A week Friday, I'll fly up, I start my new job on Monday I can tell you all about it then, Corrina, I know you are my sister, but I love you and I always will."

"Henry, don't call me sister, as far as I'm concerned you are my husband."

"Corrina I know I shouldn't admit this but I get aroused every time I think about our love-making it was to say at the very least unrestrained always exciting, always so very loving, always special."

"Oh stop it Henry I get the same thoughts, and then I go to pieces the tears flow because we will never be able to make love again."

"Blue eyes at least we have some wonderful memories we only have to look at Denni who is the result of our love."

"Henry my special man, my husband I think we should say goodnight."

Reverting to his black country dialect which always made Corrina giggle, in fact she marvelled at his ability to speak the different dialects, "bostin se ya layta I'll see yaouw soon I cor wait."

Denni's head popped up again, "Bye Daddy."

"Bye bye Denni, bye Corrina."

"Bye, love you Henry."

By then, tiredness and loneliness had sapped his creative mental awareness he couldn't comprehend any of his desultory thoughts: a visit from the sandman was his only escape. Nevertheless, sleep sadly didn't show any mercy, his mind seemed resistant to dormancy allowing only spasmodic but welcome unawareness, equally those sporadic moments were, interweaved with abstractions eliciting intense distress. Henry was glad when morning had broken, he could at least speak to Corrina sometime later, his night had been shrouded in gloom and despondency, for the first time in his life he shuddered at what his and Corrina's circumstances might portend. As the morning broke it was bright, warm, furthermore sunny, sitting in his garden drinking coffee he listened to the bird singing, he pulled his thoughts together realising self-pity was not the answer, getting his act together was a more realistic approach. That sunny Morning changed his outlook on life, remembering as he grew up his single mindedness, his relentless drive and his commitment to everything he attempted, had born fruit In more ways than one. He cleared his head of all negative thoughts to concentrate on how he would always be part of his family who, to all intents and purposes had been exiled to Edinburgh.

Enjoying a second cup of coffee in the warm sun he hoped his new position at MSIA, would give him the freedom, whereby each Friday evening he could fly up to Edinburgh and return to Birmingham Sunday evenings. Although happy and determined to follow through with the plans he was formulating, doubts began to beset his thoughts. Realistically they would never be able to enjoy a full family life because he felt there was never going to be any quantitative easing of the distress and loss he and Corrina had experienced. This continued to hold their lives captive, in what Corrina described as her idea of purgatory. Despite Henry's belief, something would rise to the fore to expiate their dilemma, it was refusing to show its smiley face. Nonetheless whatever it took he would do his best for the woman he loved to distraction and of course their son Denni. He in fact, had loved her from the very first moment they met.

First things first new responsibility followed with his new position as Chief Operations Officer or (COO) at the West Bromwich Office, his position meant he was assistant to Mr J Grieves the (Chief executive officer). Henry met with his CEO to discuss his role within the company, Henry's first impression of the man he would be working for was, shall we say stilted. The first words he sarcastically offered to Henry were, "Oh you're Mr Upthegrove's blue eyed boy," then made it clear he was CEO and insisted he be called Mr Grieves. Henry withheld his anger at Mr Grieves disparaging articulation preferring to wait until he could appraise the reason behind such an acerbic connotation, however, all did not bode well for a harmonious working atmosphere as Henry could foresee problems, the CEO came across as a man with limited ability to interact with his staff. Henry considered his affected pompous attitude towards his senior staff as ill-mannered and discourteous wondering if he should give him a salute. He was appalled at his downright over-bearing authoritativeness which Henry considered unpleasantly forceful towards his junior and younger personnel; he had to withhold his anger. One incident that made Henry wince in embarrassment occurred when a young girl Debbie brought them a cup of tea, visibly nervous and shaking she spilt tea into the saucers, demonstrating his Hitlerite lack of empathy towards the youngster he vented his displeasure in no uncertain terms when calling her a stupid girl. Nevertheless, in spite of Henry's uncertainty he would bide his time because hopefully, perhaps Mr Grieves was just giving it large to impress Dusty's 'blue eyed boy' to show who was boss: only time would tell.

Mr Grieves had replaced Dusty when he moved back to New York, therefore he certainly had the wherewithal, therefore, Henry gave him the benefit of doubt realising they were both experienced in their field, which would or should allow them to explore, hopefully interrelate their ideas for the mutual benefit of the company. He believed, if they both produced elements which appropriately combined, they could establish a relationship of mutual trust. Now he was having second thoughts; still he would wait and see.

Mr Grieves straight faced then proceeded to outline what was expected of his new COO, his remit was exactly the same as had been required of him during his vice presidency at the New York office. As COO he would be expected to take responsibility for the daily operations of the company, to oversee the development and the cascading of the company mission statement to the lower ranking staff. Another factor was planning and prioritising customer, employee, and organisational requirements, to generally align personnel with company goals. Obviously, Henry was well versed in all these aspects of management having been CEO at two of Jenson's family companies which he himself, had established, building them into successful enterprises and more importantly they had achieved a high level of profitability, which had been sustained since he left.

Henry confused at his CEO's arrogant and domineering disposition wasn't sure if he wanted to work with him, he couldn't apprehend what would warrant such animosity he was so unfriendly, in fact quite hostile for some obscure reason it was obvious he didn't look favourably on his new COO. In spite of his doubts, Henry would give it a month then if they couldn't have an amicable and workable relationship, he would leave.

As always when Corrina's smiling face lit up his laptop orating her welcoming words, "Hello my special man." He put the cares of the day where they belonged, behind him.

"Hello blue eyes, had a good day?"

"Boring really I need to find a job, if you were here it would be different."

He could hear Denni shouting something to Corrina, she replied, "Hang on Denni leave that, come and say hello to Daddy."

The little fella climbed on his mum's knee squealing enthusiastically, "Daddy are you coming home so we can go skating?"

"Denni I'll be home on Thursday then we'll go skating."

Turning to his mum he asked, "When is it Thursday?"

"Two sleeps and Daddy will be home."

"Daddy when is two sleeps?"

"You go to sleep tonight, then you get up in the morning, then that night you go to sleep again, then when you wake up that day, I will be coming home."

"Daddy then can we go skating?"

"Denni we will, I promise."

With that, he went back, Henry could only presume to his X-Box game. Henry was a little concerned, "When you say find a job what do you mean? You don't have to worry about money."

"Oh Henry I need something to take my mind of the heartache I'm feeling, I know we will never be able to make love but that won't ever stop me loving you, you are my life."

"Corrina Jade Swan Jenson I know you think I am daft, however, I just feel deep down something isn't right, whatever it is I'm sure it will come to the surface eventually, hopefully and I say this with tongue in cheek God willing."

Corrina giggling, "You're turning religious."

"I don't think so, one thing is for sure they can never take the Jenson name from you, you really are a Jenson."

"Henry I only want to be a Jenson because I am married to you, not because my father is a Jenson."

"Blue eyes I still believe there is something in all of this that doesn't sit right."

"Oh, I wish that could be true."

"Ah well we shall see we shall see."

Before signing off, they sat talking for an hour with interruptions from the little fella, both declaring how they would always love each other come what may.

Chapter 52

Henry arrived back from Edinburgh after spending a few days with Corrina and Denni, he had just unpacked his case when the doorbell rang, he looked at his watch, it was eleven o'clock, he looked at his security monitor and saw his mum Mary, his dads fiancée Elaine and sister Caro stood at the door, mystified he let them in. "Nice to see you all but what's going on? I don't usually get half the family visiting so late on Sunday evening."

Caro looking decidedly down, answered his question, "Its Dad he has got to have surgery, the cancer has spread."

Henry went ashen, hardly able to speak wanting to know, "How bad is he?"

Elaine struggling to hold herself together explicated, "We won't know the full extent of his illness until they operate, he has been going downhill for a couple of months but as usual wouldn't see his doctor, bloody fool."

Henry despite his antagonism towards his dad, asked, "What, are you asking of me?"

Mary explained, "Henry nothing for the moment, but I'm sure we will be asking for your help depending on the prognosis."

Elaine then said something that made him feel not just uncomfortable, but sad in its extremity, "Frank is beside himself with guilt he understands why you don't want anything to do with him, but will you please find it in your heart to forgive him, at least try?"

"Elaine you are asking me to forgive him, when his outrageous libertine lifestyle, has left me bereft of any chance of being with the woman I love?"

Caro who hadn't said much commented, "Henry everyone makes mistakes he has been a good dad to all us kids over those years, please help him if you can."

Exasperated and getting angrier at their attempts to justify Frank's free living, Henry expressed his anger, "Everyone makes mistakes? He is a serial womaniser, his affairs have spawned three children out of wedlock and those are

294

the ones we know about! How many more children are there lined up waiting to show their faces, he has no moral restraint."

Mary who Henry would always take advice from, quietly expressed her own observations, "Henry son sit down and calm down, anger isn't going to make any difference, all it does is cloud your thinking and may cause you to make the wrong judgment. We all empathise with your anger, he can never atone for the legacy of emotional unhappiness he has endowed you with, but I know he would forgive you of anything, please go and see him or at least speak with him."

"Mum, he broke your heart, how can you stick up for him?"

"He gave me a lot of happiness as well, he gave me you and Caro he cares for all of us, if any one of us has a problem he is there for us."

"That's for sure," Elaine agreed.

"I really don't know what am I going to say to Corrina, she refuses to acknowledge he is her father she will be mortified if I help the one person who has imploded our lives."

"Why don't you just try, ask her?"

They watched him slump forward with his head in his hands unable to decide if he could do what they were asking of him. None of the women said anything further, they waited. It was only a few minutes, but to them time stood still, sighing loudly Henry responding by nodding his head, advising them when assenting on one condition, "Okay I will do whatever is required, however I will have to speak to Corrina if she is in the slightest way upset then it's no go."

Mary smiled and hugging him said, "Thank you Son, just you talking to him will give him a lift, Corrina is a beautiful person she won't object."

Elaine also thanked him with a kiss and Caro volunteered, "Henry he is lucky to be blessed with a son like you. I have some other news!"

"What would that be then, no more trouble I hope?"

"Absolutely not, you are going to be an uncle."

Henry's face lit up, throwing his arms round her he expressed his delight, "Congratulation my little sister, when is this happy event expected is Lindsey pleased?"

All three of them in chorus answered, "He is over the moon."

"Oh Caro I'm so chuffed for both of you, that really is some very good news."

The news his sister was pregnant snapped him out of the despondency, the whole atmosphere in the room brightened. Henry, though very tired made coffee for everyone before asking them to leave, explaining it had been a long day and he was starting his new Job in a few hours, he needed to get some rest. Before they left, Mary advised, "Henry your dad has been so down, you speaking to him will lift his spirits and take the pressure off Elaine and your brother Myles."

"Mum I'll speak to Corrina tomorrow."

"Henry I honestly don't believe she will be angry; she is too nice a girl."

"We shall see Mum, good night Mum, good night Caro, Elaine, good night."

Early Monday morning Henry dragged Corrina out of her date with the Sandman, opening up her I pad smiling, she queried, "Hello my special man what's the matter is there something wrong?"

"Hello blue eyes when you ask if there's something wrong, it depends on how you perceive what I have to tell you."

A worried frown replaced her smile, "That sounds ominous, tell me."

"Late last night Mum, Caro and Elaine paid me a visit."

"Why what's wrong?"

"They came to tell me Frank, our dad, has been diagnosed with a pernicious secondary cancer, they came to ask me to help them and him, but after what he has put us through I'm unsure, what do you think?"

"Henry my special man unlike you I can't comprehend that he is my biological father, you have to do what you think is best, I know and recognise how much he loves you and how much that love is reciprocated. Henry you must do everything you can to help."

"Thanks for your input I'll think long and hard, don't forget I start with MSAI this morning that's why I'm calling you so early."

"Special man you can call me anytime, I hope everything goes well what I will say is, you will have a lot on your plate, new job, now helping out in the family business. I'm not being awkward when I say we as a family will have far less time together, Denni needs his dad."

"I know it will be difficult."

"My special man, I'm with you all the way, you have to do what is necessary."

"Enough of that, blue eyes. I have some good news, Caro is expecting!"

"Fantastic I'll give her a ring and send her and Lindsay a congratulations card."

"She will love that, thanks blue eyes, I know I shouldn't be saying this, but I love you."

"Henry I love you too."

"I'll say bye for now I'll ring tonight let you know how my day went."

"Bye, Henry Bye."

Chapter 53

Henry started his new job, but within a couple of hours he knew he had made a mistake...

His CEO MR J Grieves dictatorial direction to all his staff, including Henry. It was as he understood, company policy to be impermissible behaviour, the man exercised intolerable bullying particularly to the junior staff, Henry at times had to hold himself back from interfering. For some reason, one of those junior staff, the young girl Debbie, who he had given a rather malevolent upbraiding when they first met, he was exceptionally unpleasant whatever she did, it was wrong.

Overcoming his first unsavoury day, he decided after all to visit Frank, they met at the 'High chaparral' his face brightened like the morning sun when he saw Henry.

"Henry son come in, I honestly thought you would never have anything to do with me again, how is Corrina?"

"Dad what do you think? she is devastated, we both are why you had to open your mouth I will never know. She refuses to accept that you are her father, I'm sorry but I don't think she will ever forgive you, but putting that aside she encouraged me to visit you to see if I can help, how are you?"

"Tired son, always tired which given the nature of the illness is only to be expected, who knows what the future may bring us."

"Dad don't be a defeatist it's not like you, when you have had surgery you will be back to your irrepressible self, you mark my words."

"Son, I wish I had your optimism."

Henry, alarmed at Frank's unusual dismalness, attempted to cheer him a little more, telling him, "Dad don't worry about the business I'll take care of It," grinning adding, "I promise I won't run it into the ground."

"Henry son you have put my mind at ease," then slipping into his Churchillian mode, "I will fight this invasive force, I will fight this malignant neoplasm, I will never surrender to this pernicious spreading evil, I will never give in."

"Dad that's more like the man who raised me, adventurous, fearless, and above all, loving to me and Caro," he continued, "I'm just so sad you found it necessary to take your love elsewhere."

"Henry I am so very sorry."

"Dad I will call over every night while you are in having treatment, I'll see if Barney can come back from Edinburgh, that's if Ellie can return early from maternity leave."

"Son, I can sort all that, thanks, you are the one person I can trust to keep the whole thing running smoothly thank you."

"Dad, I'll do whatever it takes, I won't let Jenson's go down the pan."

"Henry just be careful you have your own job to worry about and Corrina and Denni, I know you will do your best and that's all you can do. Thank you for caring."

Just a few days into his employment, Henry came across the young girl Debbie, a quietly spoken girl she was crying in a corridor the same girl whom Mr Grieves had severely chastised for spilling some coffee into the saucers a few days previously. Since joining the company Henry had taken a protective interest in her, very concerned he asked her to meet him in his office at lunch time. When she entered his office, her worried face showed she was very nervous, he calmed her with his opening statement, "Debbie there is no need to be nervous, honestly what is said in here will go no further," Which brought a slight smile to her face. He brought a more pronounced smile to her face when he explained, "I've asked you here because we all know Mr Grieves is well, shall we say awkward but I can't for the life of me understand why you seem to be the main target of his awkwardness." Said while using his fingers as inverted commas. "Debbie I need to know what is wrong why does he pick on you?"

Henry needed to find out what possible reason there could be for treating her so venomously. Henry encouraged her, emphasising, "Debbie you are not in trouble but I need to get to the bottom of this animosity towards you and everyone else for that matter, including me." Debbie starting to cry again, opening up she revealed, "He said I would get the sack if I said anything, apart from the travelling every day, I like it here, I can't afford to lose my job the money is too good."

Henry bewildered by her declaration queried, "Why would he say that? Whatever it is, I think you should tell me why he would threaten you with the sack."

Her worried look returned, still a little reluctant to give a reason she began to mumble a reply, Henry asked her to speak a little clearer, she suddenly found her voice, "He tried it on with me, I pushed him away and told him I was going to report him."

Henry was gobsmacked, "What did he do?"

"We were in the staff room I was making tea when he grabbed hold of me pushed me against the wall and put his hand up my jumper, he thought it was funny, it upsets me to think about it."

Henry astonished at this disclosure, had never had to deal with a problem of this magnitude, but immediately deciding higher authorities would have to be informed, however; he wanted to find out if he had abused any of the other women and be sure of the facts, "Debbie has there been any more women complaining?"

"I don't know I was too frightened to say anything to anyone."

"Mmmm, Debbie don't say anything for the moment, but whatever happens I promise you your job is safe, where do you actually live?"

"I live on other side of Birmingham, Hollywood."

"Wow that is some distance to travel, to West Bromwich by bus every day.

If I can find you a job closer to home, would you be willing to at least consider it as an option?"

A wider smile came to her face whispering, "If you could, I would certainly be interested thank you Mr Jenson."

"Debbie, I will see what I can do."

That same evening he spoke to Frank about Debbie's Dilemma, Frank's face lit up advising, "We have an opening in the Haslucks Green warehouse for someone to train up to work in the on-line business which is booming, I'm not sure what wage she would be expecting, but she will certainly save money on travelling expenses. I'll have a word with Imelda my P.A. Bring the girl in for an interview," he continued, "Cherry is running it and Jude is helping out learning the trade like you did, he's doing well."

Henry from the moment he introduced himself to Mr Grieves, noted he subjected all his staff to what he believed to be invalid criticism. He also noted he would assail the younger personal, particularly young women with cruel insulting and hurtful words, designed to demoralise them. He sat in his office at a loss wondering how he would approach Mr Grieves, regarding young Debbie's worrying exposition. Henry did not like Mr Grieves, he would have to tread warily there had only been one accusation, which needed to be substantiated. As no other accusations had been bought forward, he decided not to interview any of the women yet, he would wait until the CEO was taking leave. His chance came three nauseating weeks later, when his majesty as Henry called him, Mr Grieves had decided to take a couple of day's annual leave. Henry took the opportunity to speak to each of the female staff in his office to ask them directly if any of them had been abused by the any of the male staff. Four of the women though reticent to admit they had been subjected to what they ultimately recognised as sexual harassment, did eventually present him with their experiences. All of them agreed Mr Grieves had wandering hands always touching them inappropriately. Henry listened to their appalling stories of sufferance which included threats of losing their jobs. One of the women admitted if she was unaccompanied, would refuse to occupy the lift with him such was her nervousness of him. Like their colleague Debbie, because they were well paid, all four of them did not want to jeopardise their jobs by complaining.

Henry promised them they would not lose their positions within the company, he gained their trust and got their consent to take the matter further, but asked them not to discuss their complaints until he had spoken to Mr Grieves about their grievances. Henry rang his mentor Dusty that evening specifically to impart the information he had gathered concerning the women's accusations, however he had to admit he had no actual proof, just their word. Dusty shocked and disquieted by Henry's distasteful postulation. He acknowledged that the substance of the allegations had to be investigated. He advised, "Henry son leave it to me I will inform Jerry Styne the chairman of the board, I'll leave it to him to deal with as he sees fit. Henry, I'm grateful to you for bringing this to my attention because there ain't no room in this day and age for harassment of any kind!"

"Dusty sir I never imagined I would ever be called on to take action of this nature, especially regarding a superior member of staff. I'm not quite sure how to confront Mr Grieves."

"Henry you have handled the situation very, Well it's the type of reaction I fully expect from you, that is why you have the position of COO."

Ending the business side of their converse they exchange pleasantries, Henry asked how Dusty's wife Avalina and his six daughters were keeping, Dusty in return asking how Corrina and Denni were keeping, he was saddened to learn they lived so far apart.

When Henry stepped into his office on Monday morning, he was surprised to find Chairman Jerry Styne sat at his desk, furthermore an even bigger surprise ensued, when he informed him Mr Grieves had resigned, without giving a reason. He proceeded to ask Henry if he would assume the responsibility of chief executive officer on a temporary basis, until they found a permanent replacement. He explained, "Henry, Dusty thinks you are very capable, call him I'm sure he will ask you to apply."

Before he spoke to Dusty, he called Debbie into his new office, she looked pensive but it didn't take long to bring a smile to her face, "I thought you would like to know Mr Grieves has resigned, I am taking his place on a temporary basis. I have some other news, if you are interested a company I know in Hasluck's Green has a vacancy for a trainee to work in their online business, however, if you want to stay here I'd be very happy for you to do so?" While he was talking her smile got warmer, "Hasluck's Green? that's on my doorstep, to be honest I like my job here but I would like to know more, but would they think me suitable for an interview?"

Henry withheld from her that he was related to the owner, purely because he wanted her to be given the position on merit. If she was to Join Jenson's, she would in due course find out who he was, therefore he continued, "Debbie, I have received very good reports from your immediate superiors, in fact they have all been impressed with your attitude and attention to detail and notably your work ethic. I'll give you their phone number the company is called Jenson's, give them a ring for an interview but don't leave it too long."

"Thank you, Mr Jenson, I will ring lunch time."

"Debbie we don't want to lose you, but I think you will find there aren't any Mr grieves types there, and as you say it's on your doorstep, good luck. Don't forget you will need to give us one month's notice."

When he mentioned Jenson's, she looked at him quizzically, but never queried his involvement.

She left the office with a huge illuminating smile.

His converse with Debbie concluded he rang New York to speak to Dusty, laughing dusty expressed his thoughts, "Hi Boss man how are you?"

"Dusty sir I thought you might have something to do with this, I'm honoured to have been given the chance so soon, I've only been here five minutes."

"You still have to go through the rigorous adherences of the established rules, which I would assume will be a formality for someone of your experience."

"Sir I take it you mean I have to apply and have an interview?"

Laughing again he added, "Henry go for it son, it's a position made for you."

"Thank you, sir."

"Any time you have a problem son, just ask."

Throughout his career Henry just like Frank considered his working life to be paramount, allowing nothing to prevent him achieving all the goals he set himself. During those earlier years he would have been excited at the prospect of being CEO of a large company, though, to some extent his goals had changed. His working life was still important but he viewed Corrina and son Denni to be the most important: nothing would ever distract him from looking after them, they were without doubt his life.

The following Tuesday morning, Debbie asked Henry if she could have some time off, stating Jenson's had invited her for an interview. Smiling he replied, "Debbie you go for it, don't forget if it doesn't work out you still have your Job here, in the meantime I'll keep my fingers crossed for you, I'm sure they will like you."

"Mr Jenson thank you again."

The following day, Henry was settling into his new office, got called into the board room to meet the directors. Firstly, they thanked him for stepping into the breach as it were, then proceeded to inform him they were required to advertise the position of CEO in accordance with company policy. Nonetheless they expected him to apply. He thanked them for the opportunity that had arisen in such a short space of time.

That same afternoon when Debbie walked through Henry's office door her facial expression said it all. There was a glow to her cheeks Henry guessed, "I take it your interview went well?"

"Mr Jenson very well I have been offered the position of trainee manager of their online business it was too good to refuse." Enthusing with her excitement growing, explicated, "Branch manager Cherry and assistant Jude showed me round explaining what they expected of me, while making me feel wanted, to be honest I never realised how big a company they are."

Henry really pleased for her reminded her, "Debbie don't forget you have to give one month's notice."

Giggling she made a joke which tickled him, she handed him an envelope, "Here's one I made earlier," adding, "thank you again Mr Jenson."

"Debbie I am really pleased for you but I haven't done anything you have obviously been offered that position on merit, I can assure you it has nothing to do with me."

She looked at him quizzically, "Thank you again Mr Jenson."

That same morning Henry submitted his own application for the position he was currently holding temporally, that of Chief executive officer on a permanent basis, However, he had nagging concerns. Coping with the politics and responsibility of the position he knew would never be a problem, his worries stemmed from supposing he was actually appointed CEO, he had the added burden of his family business, which looked increasingly possible he would have to do more, than just oversee Jenson's.

Henry's working day was long, far too long. Taking into account the daily running of MSAI, his evening administration of Jenson's moreover his daily visit to see Frank, the mental effort required to cope with the strain began to stress and fatigue him, this meant he had to give up his weekends in Edinburgh. His only outlet was speaking to Corrina and son Denni each evening.

When they said their goodbyes, it was not unusual for him to shed a tear, they were no longer married. Nevertheless, emotionally they were still entwined sharing an indestructible love. Corrina aware of the problems he faced, encouraged Henry to do whatever he considered best for himself, as much as she missed him. Even if it meant he had to forgo travelling to be with them in Edinburgh. Nonetheless the decision was taken out of his hands when Frank, due to his failing health asked Henry to take over his position as head of Jenson's until he was fit enough to resume the mantle.

Chapter 54

Whilst waiting for a cab to take him to JFK airport Henry sat in his and Corrina's bedroom looking out of the window on the New York skyline, reflecting on trials and tribulations they had faced over the previous six months when uncertainties began to proliferate. Their lives together had never before been subjected to such stormy clouds, their horizons had always been sunny from the moment they had met in Cardiff. Three years later they shared their first kiss, followed by a sunny day when they exchanged their vows of love, that wonderful day was only exceeded when Denni made his first appearance into the world to be held in the loving arms of his mum and dad for the first time. Those times had been exciting, warm, stimulating, ardent, loving and above all happy. They doted on each other and their son Denni. Sadly, throughout the last six months their dreams for their future had fragmented lying in a heap the consequence of which precluded any hope of ever piecing them together: a jigsaw with the most important piece missing. Henry and Corrina were still very much in love and both would admit always would be. However; the moral moreover legal bounds of their predicament highlighted the immensity of the personal decisions that now lay before them. A family ravelled, the knots of which were impossible to undo. Henry's sang-froid had on occasions been sorely tested, his pragmatic approach to life replaced with scornful jaded negativity.

The bodeful onrushing of the annulment of their marriage, was raising its singularly painful heartache, dispensing insomnia and an inability to experience pleasure, caused by their separation. Henry and Corrina necessitated one another, their main consideration being son Denni. If they couldn't be espoused, they had to remain involved and share fully his upbringing for his benefit and welfare. Corrina understood the bonds a boy builds with his dad, exactly the same as she had with her mother the proof of which brother Elliot was building with his dad. Henry the man she loved would have to stay in their lives despite what they considered unjust; they would have to abide by the law of the land.

Locking the door to the apartment fully aware that unless there was an unforeseen change in their circumstances it would remain closed for the foreseeable future, if not the rest of their lives. Dispirited, Henry wiped a moistened eye, he was closing the door on a home, their home, his, Corrina's, and Denni's home, a home once blessed with love.

Chapter 55

Frank's operation to remove the cancer according to the medics treating him had been a success, they assured the family the prognosis was good, his next procedure would be to undergo a course of Chemotherapy. Even before he began that debilitating course of drugs, Henry wasn't sure Frank was strong enough, he appeared gaunt and hollow eyed, in fact to Henry's eyes he looked like death warmed up. Frank's illness was taking its toll, his outlook on life like his body, began to fade.

Henry's nettle since returning from America had moderated, Henry felt duty bound to do whatever he could for the family, determining he might have to resign his position at MSAI. Corrina was saddened by the decision he had to make, possibly giving up on the path he had forged for himself, nonetheless fully understood Henry's feelings, Frank was his dad. However; any feelings she herself held for Frank were still negative refusing to accept him as her father, she found it difficult to forgive him; he had broken her heart. Even so she encouraged Henry be the son a father, who despite his philandering was a very good father to all of his children. Henry felt obligated to do the best he could to take the worry and strain off his dad's shoulders, he would assume responsibility for his commercial interests, but however willing he was, in a very short space of time it dawned on him, he could not commit himself, moreover divide his time and attention between two business enterprises.

Henry spoke to Dusty apprising him of the dichotomy troubling him, he really wanted, nothing more than to advance his career within MSAI but the prevailing compassion he felt for Frank overruled his own ambitions, consequently his definitive decision was to concentrate on helping to keep the family business running like it always had been: like a well maintained machine. Dusty was disappointed, he wished him well, but at the same time recognised MSAI were losing a valued member of staff. Dusty believed he would have been the future of the company especially if he ever moved back to New York. Sadly, Henry sat down to write his letter of resignation.

The next day It was with a heavy heart he informed the board of directors he was withdrawing his application for the position of CEO and at the same time handed in his resignation, detailing his situation. He thanked them for the opportunity afforded him, furthermore trust and support they had given him. They in turn expressed their regret but thanked him when warmly acknowledging his sensitive handling, given the exigent circumstances prevailing, when highlighting the abuse apportioned by his predecessor to his female staff.

Henry completed his one-month notice, but on his final day the women who had been abused by the previous CEO thanked him by taking him out to lunch. Leaving MSAI was a wrench, nonetheless his once lost pragmatism came to the fore, accepting everything happens for a reason.

Before taking over the family business, he flew up to Edinburgh to spend a few days with Corrina and Denni. Their meetings were quite unreal proceedings two people still very much in love with each other nevertheless, their hellos were subdued: just a hug and a kiss on the cheek. They would never be able make love again, no one would regard Corrina as a puritan but she did not want to be damned and despite their marriage annulment she vowed never to remove her wedding ring.

Henry's love transcended his own needs and desires, if the powers that be demanded sibling cannot be lovers, he would do the next best thing, look after his sister Corrina and their son Denni. Just being close to his disconnected family, affectively lifted both their spirits.

They shared a lovely, few days together, Denni loved to go skating with his mum and dad they spent hours at the boardwalk ice rink, back home a film was the order of the day usually a cartoon. After Denni went to bed Henry and Corrina enjoyed a glass of wine together, gazing devotedly into each other's eyes, desperately in love but emotions sadly handcuffed by protocol.

Henry flew back to Birmingham knowing his next visit might be months away, only when circumstances would allow. In spite of receiving a lot of support from all his family, brothers, sisters and mother he was facing a period of loneliness. He knew how Frank worked; none stop, all hours, therefore he felt duty bound to continue in the same way, preferring to work rather than sit at home watching television on his own. His only consolation came by way of the wonderful I pad and I phone, he could converse every day with his family. Every day heartbreakingly, Denni would ask, "When are you coming home Daddy?"

"When Granddad gets better," was the only answer he could give his little one; always said with a smile but with his heart bleeding. Separated by law nonetheless Corrina and Henry constantly expressed their love both rejecting the thought they needed someone else. They were both heartsick neither of them could envisage a time when if not physically, but mentally, and emotionally their lives and their love would always be entwined. They shared a love which was unbreakable however at times it seemed intractable. Continuing his converse with Corrina he said, "Corrina thank God we have technological communication I haven't a clue when we will have a weekend together, Dad is poorly the chemo is having a dreadful effect on him at the moment he is a broken man I have never seen him looking so ill, so despondent, truly seriously depressed. Corrina began giggling which prompted Henry to ask what it was she found funny," she replied, "Henry I'm not being callous or indifferent or unsympathetic I really do want your dad and mine for that matter, to fully recover, but since when did you believe in God."

"What made you say that?"

Still giggling, "You saying thank God for technology, Henry I'll make a believer of you yet."

"Corrina love of my life if we are ever able to be man and wife again I will thank your God."

She reproached him sternly advocating, "Henry Swan Jenson he's not my God he is everybody's God. Henry my love, whatever you say or think my faith holds me together."

"Corrina Jade I'll say good night and I'll speak to you tomorrow, give Denni a big hug from me tell him how much Daddy loves him."

"I do every morning when he wakes up, Henry he does miss his daddy, he cries after you have said good night to him."

"I miss him so much, as I miss you, I too feel like crying, you are both continually in my thought, I'll say goodnight before I start blatting, goodnight Corrina."

"Goodnight my special man."

Despite his frustration furthermore anger at the architect of the emotional and physical breakup between him and the love of his life Corrina, Henry, Initially seething moreover raging inside, arousing a great deal of resentment towards his dad. He discussed the situation at length with Corrina ultimately there was probably only one course of action he could follow to abnegate his own ambitions: after all blood is thicker than water.

Chapter 56

Henry spoke to all the family informing them not to say anything to Frank about resigning his position at MSAI as he would more than likely insist that he would find someone else to run Jenson's. Henry walked into head office of Jenson's only to find Frank looking tired and facially drawn, surprised but pleased to see Henry he asked, "It's Great to see you son, but what are you doing here?"

"Dad, I'm here to cover for you until you are well enough to return."

"Son, it's good of you but you have your own job, you can't do mine as well."

"I'm taking leave for as long as it is required so don't worry. I think you need some rest, it will help you fight the enemy."

"That's one word for it, yes it's an enemy alright, Son you must work for a good company allowing you to take time out to help someone else."

Grinning like a Cheshire cat Henry informed him, "I'm not doing it for nothing, I'm hoping you will put me on the payroll?"

Frank's face suddenly lit up, "Henry it will all be yours when my time comes."

"What about the rest of your nestlings?"

"They will be looked after, don't you worry."

"What about Elaine don't you think you should get married?"

"As soon as I beat this carcinomas malignancy invading my body, I will do the honourable thing and make her my wife, if she will have me!"

"Have you told her? I think you should ask her as soon as possible."

"Will you be my best man?"

"Dad. I'd be honoured."

"Thanks Son, now I have work to do."

"Dad go home I will take over you need to rest, I know Jenson's inside out go on let me take over, temporarily of course."

Frank surprised him when he asked, "Are you sure?"

"Yes Dad, now go home and get fit."

"Okay, to be honest I do feel tired, Chemo hurts and drains you, thanks Son." Henry watched Frank drive away, he took a deep breath it was time for him to make his presence felt. He spoke to Frank's long time PA, Imelda, who was pleased Henry was looking after the business while Frank took time out to focus on getting through the treatment he was receiving. Imelda knew Henry well, having worked with him before he followed his dream and went to New York. Now their conversations were entirely about Frank, his work ethic moreover the time he allotted to his business. Imelda had been his PA for a number of years and from the off had admired his impregnability, furthermore his mental application to always overcome challenges set before him invariably with a smile and a twinkle in his eyes. She had watched the drugs depleting his body of strength moreover his humour, she was upset by Frank's general demeanour his lack of piquancy for life sadly annotating, "Henry over the last few months your dad has become a shadow of his former self, his attitude has been unusually sour, stripped him of his customary flamboyance, the fun has drained from him and yet he was still working all hours. He looks so ill Henry, I'm so pleased you decided to help."

"Imelda you will have to go through everything with me whose who, the ifs and buts, the could and should haves, the whys and wherefores, everything! let's keep it working properly for when he comes back."

"There's a lot of work to get through."

"Imelda, I think as soon as Ellie Crane is back from maternity leave, Barney can come back from Edinburgh, I also think you should have an assistant someone to do the filing and typing."

"Frank won't like that, you know what he's like."

"Imelda, you can't be doing it all, I need to get to grips with everything, you will be able to manage things easier, especially when Barney is back. I'll speak to Cherry she will be glad to have him back home."

Despite his prolonged course of chemotherapy, enervating him, Frank had kept Jenson's running smoothly to date? but by burning the midnight oil to an extent whereby he was putting his health in further jeopardy. Henry determined when Frank had made a full recovery and was able to return to work fulltime he would require more staff so working closely with Imelda instigated a strategy whereby Frank would remain the owner, chairman of the board and chief executive, the undoubted top dog, the difference would be having someone else to execute the day to day running of the business. The business he had worked so hard to build over many years, so they both agreed Frank required a general manager. Adverts were placed in local papers for the position of manager. Nonetheless they would have to be extremely careful who they employed because Frank would more than likely interfere with any decisions he believed would be detrimental to Jenson's viability, whatever any manager introduced it would have to be workable, ensuring the continued success of Jenson's. This left Henry with a slight problem, namely Frank, Henry had the unenviable undertaking of convincing him it was the right avenue to go down, Jenson's required a capable administrator.

Henry called in to see Frank on his way home to explicate his concept for Jenson's going forward, which would alleviate the pressure Frank had been under. Frank was at his lowest point looking tired and frail when Henry talked of the changes he was about to make, suspecting Frank would reject his proposals with distain, in spite of his considered unease concerning how to approach his dad with his recommendations, Henry was taken by surprise when Frank accepted when he considered his proposal without any angry debate while posing the question, "Why don't you do the job?"

Henry shaking his head his reply unequivocally expressed, "DAD I'm doing your job, but only until you are strong and fit enough to return, however long that takes and but! you can be sure I will do it my way."

"Just a thought."

"Dad my home is in New York when the circumstances are right I will go back, I still have my apartment there that is my home."

"Ok Son I'll leave it in your capable hands."

Handed Carte blanche to exert his own influence, Henry thanked Frank, Frank countered, "No Son, thank you from the bottom of my heart, Elaine told me you have resigned your position at Mighty sales to look after Jenson's for me, once again thank you, I'm lucky to have a Son like you."

"Stop it Dad you'll have me crying into my beer tonight, to be honest I have already advertised for a general manager."

"Hmmm you don't mess about do you?"

"Like father like son aye, well maybe not quite."

They were inundated with applications for the post of general manager, Henry left Imelda to organise the interviews while he planned visits to every shop, all seventeen of them including the Welsh and Scottish branches and the

Haslucks Green warehouse which operated the online sales. It had come to his notice many employees were concerned they may be made redundant so he set out with a strategy to allay any fears of such a possibility, by speaking to all employees.

For obvious reasons, the first port of call would be Edinburgh. He spoke to Corrina apprising her of his plans, she cried with a smile on her face, "Oh Henry I thought it would be months before you would be up here," she called Denni, "Denni it's Daddy, come and say hello he's got something to tell you. Leave your game, he's playing Kart Racers on his Xbox, come on Denni?"

"I don't know that game."

"He takes after his dad, too clever by half, come on Denni."

Denni dragged himself away from his game, a little peeved, "Hello Daddy."

"Hello little fella I'm coming home tomorrow."

His face lit up like a beacon, Henry knew what was coming next, "Can we go skating Daddy?" he was skating mad.

"Denni we will, and have sweets and milkshakes, then we will have fish and chips, and then we can go to the pictures and have Ice cream and popcorn."

"Mummy we are going to the pictures, Daddy can we see frozen?"

"Again, you've seen it five times."

Corrina interjected, "You are spoiling him."

"Corrina I'm allowed, I'm his dad, I love him like I love you."

"Henry I will always love you."

"Corrina Jade I dream of those nights when we used to stand in the window of our bedroom looking out at the night sky after making love."

"I also dream of those nights constantly our love is strong, but depressing as it is, it is never, ever, going to happen again, we have to remain friends."

"Corrina Jade I still can't believe the love we have shared is going to be nothing but a memory."

"I know, it's as though I have cut myself and the bleeding will never stop, if we didn't have Denni I don't think I would be able to face life without you."

"Look Corrina we will just have to make the best of situation in which we find ourselves, I'll fly up tomorrow."

"Oh Henry I've got some news I've bought a new car I will pick you up from the airport."

"Fantastic what have you bought?"

"I've got a ford KA, a little bit smaller than your Ford Fairlane, Elliot helped me choose it, oh and by the way he's paid off the loan, you can close the account."

"We didn't really want the money, still I'll thank him tomorrow where's Denni? Time to say goodnight."

"The little bugger is playing that game again, Denni come and say goodnight to Daddy?"

"No leave him play, I see you both tomorrow. Goodnight Corrina give Denni a kiss from me, love you."

The following morning Corrina was waiting for him, proudly showing off her new car, in light of the circumstances they hugged more than a brother and sister should, the little fella asking, "Are we going skating Daddy?"

"As soon as I come back from work we will go skating."

Though Corrina informed him before they went skating they would have to buy him some new skates as his old skates are pinching his toes; he's growing so fast.

Henry spent a total of five days in Edinburgh, during which time he and Corrina took the little fella skating each evening. Corrina commenting gloomily, "Why oh why did this happen to us? We should be a proper family we should be able to be together all the time, stupid laws."

"Corrina we are a family, we love each other, difficult as it ma-be we have to live with our situation."

In the daytime, he visited the four shops and reorganised the staff at the Edinburgh branch and he was able to persuade Ellie Crane to return from maternity leave a little earlier, to resume her position as general manager. He recalled Barney back to Birmingham, much to his disappointment. Disappointed because over the months he had grown very close to his son Elliot and his family, especially his grand-daughter Becky, nonetheless Barney who held great respect for Frank and considered him to be the man who gave him an opportunity for which he will be ever grateful. He gave no opposition to the request from Henry to return, Barney was asked to revert to the position he held previously, work closely with Imelda while Henry visited the remaining thirteen shops starting with Cardiff.

Henry Arrived at the Welsh capitol Cardiff, booked into the Ramada Hotel where he used to reside while supervising the opening of the very first shop 'Jenson's of Wales'. While sat in his room before visiting the shop, his thoughts drifted to the night he met Corrina, he remembered the night like it was happening. He pictured her blonde hair, her soft blue eyes and the red and green flowered dress she wore, it brought a lump to his throat. A lot of water had run under the bridge since that evening, some of it sparkling and crystal clear some of it clouded with sewage.

After three days in Wales, he returned to Birmingham where he had interviews to conduct. Imelda had chosen candidates who she believed were suitably qualified, arranging the Interviews to suit Henry's heavy schedule. Henry then continued to visit each of the other ten shops throughout England. His next port of Call the warehouse at Haslucks Green from where they operated their online service, managed by Cherry Phillips, this being a fairly new divergence from the usual retail outlets introduced by an idea put forward by Cherry's husband, Barney. Henry as experienced as he was, when it came to online sales could only guess at the way it operated, hence the real reason for his visit.

Cherry was in the hot seat, until they were certain Debbie was ready to assume the role as manager surprised by his visit, but welcomed him warmly commenting, "It's lovely to see you Henry," then queried, "is there something wrong?"

Replying he assured her, "Cherry there is nothing wrong, I wanted to see how the online service functions, you seem to be busy?"

"We are, extremely so."

Jude came into the office, grinning he said, "Hi Bro haven't seen you for ages where have you been hiding?"

"Probably because you're always out, I hear you've got a girlfriend."

"I have she's lovely, I'll ask her to come and meet you."

When his girlfriend entered the office, her face showed a mixture of surprise and puzzlement stuttering, "Hello Mr Jenson are you, Jude's brother? he talks about you all the time, I never gave it a thought, but I should have, Jenson the name gives it away, you were the boss at Mighty."

"Hello Debbie how are you keeping, I hope you're keeping him in check? he's a bit of a sod."

Jude riposting: "cheeky bleeder."

"Mr Jenson thank you so much, I am very happy I love the job and yes I am keeping him in line."

"Debbie I'm so glad for you, and by the way call me Henry," smiling he continued, "okay Cherry show me how this arm of the company works?"

Chapter 57

Frank was worn out, which made him more vulnerable to his illness, therefore taking over from Frank albeit on a temporary basis, Henry began to understand why his dad agreed to his request to employ a general manager. Three months into his role in charge, Henry realised how stressful being the sole proprietor of such a large countrywide enterprise, a corporate body of three companies, comprising of seventeen retail outlets and a warehouse. He was working the same number of hours and using the same amount of energy Frank had expended throughout his adult life, some days he was so late getting home it was too late to speak to Corrina and Denni, which made him more determined to find a manager who could take some of the strain off him and Frank, when Frank recovered to full fitness. Frank had always resisted Jenson's becoming a limited company, he was in sole charge of every aspect of his business, believing he was, the company.

In between visiting Jenson's various shops, Henry had the added burden of interviewing applicants for the position of general manager, He perused the list of applicants Imelda had carefully vetted. One applicant caught his eye, Mr J Grieves, surely it could not be his CEO from Mighty? Henry spoke to Imelda who said he was very qualified and was charming when she invited him for an interview. He was unconvinced by her enthusiastic assessment, he explained to her why he was uneasy at the prospect of meeting Mr Grieves. On examining the CV of Mr Grieves, the words waved a red flag, one of his previous employments was listed as CEO of Mighty Sales of America Incorporated. He asked Imelda to inform Mr Grieves they were extremely sorry, but the position had been filled. His interviews with other candidates proved fruitless too, he was at a loss, they would have to advertise again.

Sat in his office feeling a little deflated, Barney walked in to discuss a problem with a delivery which hadn't arrived. Henry looked at him, his mind juggling and doing somersaults, then a light switched on. The one person who knew the business almost as much as Frank and one of the most trusted and loyal of his friends stood in front of him. "Barney, sit down for a minute please, I have something to ask you."

Barney looking puzzled but joked, "That's sounds ominous."

"Well that depends on which way you look at it."

Barney smiled replying, "Now I'm really curious."

"Barney, you know I've been looking for a general manager to take the strain off Dad when he's well enough to return."

"Yes I guess from your question you have had success."

"Oh I think I have, if he accepts the job."

"Why do think there will be a problem?"

"I hope not."

"When will he be starting?"

"Immediately if he says yes."

"Who is it then?"

"Barney, I'm offering you the position what do you think?"

Barney's expression one of total surprise answered, "What did you say?"

"Barney will you take on the job of general manager for the whole of Jenson's?"

Barney still looked flabbergasted, "I'm in shock you really want me to be general manager?"

"Barney will you accept the job?"

"Of course I accept, wait till I tell Cherry."

"Barney I have to warn you it's hard work."

"Henry I don't care one iota, I will do anything for Frank, he is a special friend, I can never repay him for the chance he gave me. Henry I can't wait for him to get well."

"Barney I'm glad you feel that way, I'm having a new desk and computer sent over for you, I thought we could share this office."

"Henry I'm totally stunned! I've come from being a loser, an abusive arrogant pernicious thug, to a happily married man with a family and a fantastic job, not only that, I have friends. It's all down to Frank I can't thank him enough."

Henry felt the weight of the world was off his shoulders, he trusted Barney. That evening he went home early so he could speak to his own little family,

Corrina's glowing face flickered onto the screen, almost in tears he croaked, "Hello blue eyes I'm missing you so much, you look so beautiful."

"Hello my special man I've missed you too, Denni keeps asking when is Daddy coming home, now I'm asking. Any time soon?"

"I'll be able to come up more often when Barney, who is now general manager has settled into his new position within the company. Corrina I don't know how Dad worked so many hours I'm shattered after only three months."

"You look brighter than you did last week, you say Barney is now general manager?"

"Yes I realised he was the best man for the job, he's a grafter."

"Henry I'm so glad you've got some help, it'll take the strain off you."

"Yes I'm relieved, no wonder Dad is ill, where's the little fella?"

"I'll get him out of bed you can have a chat."

Corrina collected Denni from his bedroom, Henry knew what he was about to ask, "Hello Daddy can we go skating?"

Corrina interrupting, explained, "I don't know, if he's not playing that bloody computer game he wants to go skating, he is skating mad! I've taken him twice this week and it's only Thursday."

Henry made Denni's face light up, informing him, "Denni as soon as I get home we will all go skating."

"My special man I'll say goodnight, it's time the little fella went back to bed, Denni say good night to Daddy."

"Goodnight Daddy."

"Good night Denni."

That night, for the first time in ages, Henry slept the sleep of the venerated; waking early with a smile on his face, he thought his workload was going to be less demanding now he had Barney by his side. However, sadly his workload was about to increase quite substantially. Two months after Barney took up his position as general manager, one Wednesday afternoon he received a call from Elaine asking him to meet with her, they arranged to meet at his house in Sutton that same evening. He knew something was amiss when she arrived, Elaine was accompanied by Mary his mum, both wearing sombre faces forcing him to query, "What's wrong is it Dad again?"

Elaine started to cry, Mary also on the verge of tears answered, "It's your dad he is very ill, in fact his illness is terminal."

"But I thought he was in remission."

"He was but its spread, the prognosis is six months maybe nine."

Henry dazed by the emotional impact of the news, slumped into a chair he sat stupefied trying to assimilate the words screaming through his befuddled brain. Elaine and Mary sat down next to him, waiting for him to rationalise his muddled thoughts. They knew despite Frank's appalling record as a philanderer whereby he had unwittingly broken Henry's heart, his son still loved him, admired and aspired to be successful like him. It took a while for him to regain his composure, slowly emerging from the initial shock he asked, "Elaine how has he taken it?"

"He has been quite strong, when we were driving home from the hospital he said, all that work and I'm not going to enjoy any retirement, then he told me he loved me, which made me cry."

"I'll come and see him tomorrow, I need some time to get my head round it, I don't know what I'm going to say to him."

Mary interposed, "Whatever you do, do not treat him as an invalid, he will tell you how he feels, just let him do the talking."

"Do the other kids know?"

"Caro does, she is heartbroken especially as the baby is due in about six weeks, we haven't told Lindy but we have told Jude, Cherry will tell Myles, you will have to tell Corrina."

"I'll tell her when I speak to her later, the strange thing is I detect she is beginning to accept him as her dad, whatever; she will be upset for me."

"Henry I would feel the same if it had happened to me."

"I'll go and see Caro this evening before I speak to Corrina."

"Henry son, she will need your support she adores her dad, we will say goodnight we need to get back to the kids."

"Ok Mum, Elaine, I'll see you tomorrow."

As soon as Henry returned from visiting Caro he called Corrina, her usual welcome, "Hello my special man," was said with a sad tone, "Barney called earlier to tell me the sad news. I'm so sad, despite everything that has gone before, I wouldn't wish that on anyone."

"Blue eyes I'm trying to get my head around it I always thought he was indestructible he would go on forever."

"I thought exactly the same when Mum was ill, so I understand what you're going through mentally; it's painful. Henry my special man you have got to be strong for him, easier said than done I know, but you must."

"I Know, I know, but how are you blue eyes?"

"I'm sad, so very sad, that news brought memories flooding back."

"Where is Denni?"

"He's in bed I took him skating, he is worn out, he fell asleep in the car."

"Never mind, can you pick me up from the airport on Friday evening? it might be a while before I can get up there again."

"I'll be there with the little fella, he will be a happy boy when I tell him Daddy is coming home."

"Corrina Jade, I shouldn't say it but I love you as much now as when we married."

"Henry my special man I feel exactly the same I will always love you but it's an arm's length love and will have to stay that way."

"Sadly, I know but it doesn't make it any easier, I'll say goodnight blue eyes, see you on Friday."

"Goodnight my special man, goodnight."

The weekend Henry, Corrina and Denni spent together was special, they knew they wouldn't see each other for quite a while…

Chapter 58

Frank had decided he was not going to give in to the malignant neoplasms proliferating and consuming his body, his medics encouraged him to continue with the chemo and radiation treatment. For a while, six or seven weeks he seemed to be holding his own, showing all the determination he had throughout his life, nonetheless that malevolent destructive growth began to get the better of him, his health deteriorated fast, furthermore he was beginning to experience pain. Watching his dad suffer disturbed Henry greatly. He required considerable unfaltering effort and mental strength in order to hold his emotions together for the sake of the family, However, each evening when he spoke to Corrina he would pour his heart out and shed a fountain of tears.

Out of the blue Frank made a strange request, asking if he could stay with Henry as Elaine and Jude couldn't cope with what was happening to him, he was saddened because he could hear Elaine crying maybe say in her bedroom? Or something which was occurring more often. Henry ever ready to help his dad agreed to his request which led to a heated discourse with Elaine who eventually agreed, however insisting on the condition that when Henry was at work she would be there to help. Frank moved into one of the spare rooms, while there he was restless, he missed Elaine and Jude, but he wanted time to think; time to put his house in order.

Barney had taken to his new job like a Duck to water boding well for the future of Jenson's including taking time out every day to visit Frank. When Frank had a bad day, Henry would stay at home with him which meant Barney was left to take over the mantle of CEO. To be honest Henry considered it too much for one man so Henry called a meeting with Barney and Imelda to discuss a possible solution to assuage the workload on Barney, their conclusion was to hire an assistant to share that workload. Barney and Henry were in awe of Frank and wondered how he managed to keep control of his business for so many years with only help from his PA Imelda. The more Henry thought about his dad's workload guilt pervaded his thoughts he was full of self-recriminations thinking maybe he was wrong to have followed his dream perhaps if he had remained within the Jenson fold he might have been able to alleviate the strain Frank must have been under.

Henry bared his innermost thoughts to the one person who would listen and give him some moral boosting support and offer fair criticism, the one person he adored Corrina. Listening to his emotive outpouring she was adamant there was no reason whatsoever, he should feel culpable, "Henry my special man our dad made his own Bed," with a hint of sarcasm, "too many of them."

"I see you called him our dad."

"Biologically he is, but for me that's where it ends."

"If you can find it in your heart to forgive, I'm sure your God will look favourably on you."

"My special man I'll pray for him to overcome this dreadful sickness, for the moment that's all I can do for him."

"Ok blue eyes do that for him, I'll come to see you as soon as, but for now I'll say goodnight."

"I can't wait my special man, By Henry speak to you tomorrow."

Henry felt a touch of relief from Corrina's words of encouragement, nonetheless, he still felt the shadow of guilt dampening his fortitude. Watching Frank's health decline rapidly, Henry knew in his heart the treatment was not producing the intended result; confirmed when Frank refused anymore treatment.

Frank began to get weaker, so much so serious discussions took place between Frank the family and the medics treating him. The consensus was for him to go into hospital whereby they could monitor his progress and give the palliative care he required, however in spite of their entreaties he insisted he wanted to move back to his beloved High Chaparral. His decision pleased Elaine, if he wasn't in hospital then she wanted him home so she could look after him, Henry moved in to help Elaine, Jude just couldn't face watching his dad who he loved and respected dearly being despoiled by his illness, therefore the family shuffle continued when he moved in with Mary and Mathew.

Frank also had something else on his mind, marrying Elaine. He asked her to marry him, to which her answer was, "Frank I love you of course I will."

He explained to Henry the reason he wanted to marry her, apart from the obvious one being he loved her. "I want her to have the house, if she wants to sell it she can, it is probably too large for two people."

Frank then set out to Henry his considered blueprint for the time he perceived he had left. "I have made provision for all my children including Corrina and my grandson Denni, as for you son! Jenson's will be yours, I know you will make changes because you see things differently to me, but hey that's progress I guess."

Henry was too choked with emotion to make any meaningful comment, taking into account over the previous year he had lost the love of his life, and was about to lose his dad the man he admired most in the world, though he knew he had to snap out of his melancholy mood for Frank's sake. He tried to make Frank laugh when joking, "Are there any other brothers and sisters you haven't told us about I wouldn't want to end up marrying another sister."

Frank looked distressed and remorseful replying, "I am so sorry for the overwhelming sorrow I have caused all my family over the years, perhaps you will find someone else and then find it in your heart to forgive me?"

"Dad I'm not in the market for another wife, no one else will ever be in my heart, I know Corrina is my sister but I still love her and she still loves me I'm glad we had a few years together, most people in life don't get to find true love but I have."

"Henry son, there isn't any way I can change what has occurred, I have a daughter who despises me and—"

Henry interposed on Frank's statement, "Dad Corrina doesn't despise you she just finds it difficult to forgive, when I spoke to her the other night she referred to you as our dad."

Frank's face lit up at Henry's remark his pallid smile gained a luminosity not seen by Henry in a long while, he responded, "Honestly, she doesn't hate me?"

"Dad when we received the DNA result, we both hated you, it was an outcome we dreaded, the full implication of the words painfully erupted out from that letter piercing our hearts, we have bled ever since. Both of us have to live with it: it is what it is. Dad, at least me and Corrina can always be close, we have Denni. So we will share long-distance emotion but remain at arm's length. Neither of us hate you, if we did I wouldn't be here."

"Son, I feel humbled by your remission."

"How could I hold any malevolent enmity towards you, you are my dad, I love you?"

Henry took Frank and Elaine to the local register office to give notice of their impending wedding. While they were driving back to the High Chaparral, Frank settled a sombre atmosphere on what should have been a happy occasion when with a hint of a tear in his eye, said, "It won't be long before you come back here to register something else."

Elaine and Henry both saddened by his obvious and deep sadness could not find a suitably reassuring reply, they remained silent.

The Jenson family over the years had become ravelled into one tangled knot mostly caused by Frank's lack of moral restraint. However; all the people who had been hurt by his libertinism loved him, his children his ex-wife Mary and each of his lady friends who had carried his children all forgave him, even Corrina who was coming round to the fact she had a dad. Corrina even sent Frank and Elaine her congratulations in a card saying 'love from Corrina and Denni'. That card made the day brighter for Frank, he felt he had been forgiven, telling Henry, "I wish they were here so I could hug them."

The family ensured Frank and Elaine enjoyed a memorable day, Henry was his best man, who made the comment, "I must be the only person who has had the honour of giving his mum away, best man at his dads wedding and married his own sister."

Henry noticed everyone who attended the wedding dichotomised equally into happiness and sadness. He also watched Frank struggle to hold himself together, his health had declined rapidly over the previous month which reflected in his eyes; that said he tried to make light of his dire situation not wishing to spoil Elaine's and his day. Their time together as a married couple would be short but Elaine would do her best to make it special for both of them.

Frank in pain, feeling very weak told everyone he and Elaine would be leaving the party, joking, "Will, you excuse us but we are off on our honeymoon."

Henry left at the same time to drive them home in order to help make sure frank was comfortable. When they got to the High Chaparral, he called Corrina who smiling gave her usual happy causerie, "Hello my special man how did it go?"

"It went well but Dad is not well at all, would you do me a special favour?"

"My special man anything at all what is it?"

"I know I'm asking a lot, maybe asking too much, but would you speak to Dad and Elaine, especially Dad."

"Henry, I can't hold a grudge forever but yes I will speak to them."

"My darling Corrina Jade Swan Jenson thank you."

Henry took his I pad into the lounge, "Elaine, Dad, somebody wants to talk to you."

Frank's face lit up reflecting an incandescent shine when he saw Corrina, but he dissolved into a torrent of tears when Corrina said, "Hello Dad hello Elaine."

Frank in shock at her acknowledgment, blubbered, "Hello Corrina I'm so sorry for the pain I've caused you and Henry."

Corrina put him at ease, "At least I know who my dad is, I can't really blame you, the whole thing is one ginormous family knot. Would you like to speak to your grandson? I'll call him over, Denni come and say hello to Granddad and Elaine."

"He won't know who we are?"

"Don't worry I showed him our wedding album and the video, he knows who you are."

Denni's little face came into view which made both newlyweds blubber further, "Hello Denni what have you been doing?"

"Hello. I've been skating with Mummy."

Corrina interposing added, "If he's not skating he is playing with his Xbox, but I don't mind it keeps him quiet, when he's playing a game I don't get a peep out of him." Elaine did not interfere, she let Frank talk to his grandson, she hadn't seen him looking so happy in a long time, she was happy just watching him talking to his grandson; for those few minutes he forgot his pain.

Frank and Denni finished their talk, thereafter Frank continued his converse with Corrina, "Corrina I wish I had known about you, if I had, your life would have been completely different."

"I understand, but honestly I have been afforded Henry's love, I'm still in love with him. Our destiny was set out when my lovely mum sought solace from her abusive husband, and yet look at him now one of the nicest of men you would ever wish to meet."

"Corrina darling all I can do is reiterate my sincere heartfelt apologies for all the hurt you and Henry have endured."

Her answer was a rainbow for Frank, his face lit up again when she called him Dad, "Dad let's not think of what might have been, I never thought I would ever meet my dad but I have, and I'm happy I have."

"Corrina thank you for being so forgiving."

"Dad I have done a lot of soul searching, the circumstances that prevailed and subsequently the manifestation of those circumstances did leave me angry, dejected and heartsick. In my heart, I understand now, there is nothing to forgive."

Elaine interceded earnestly expressing her delight at the converse between Frank and Corrina, enthused, "Corrina I am so glad you feel comfortable knowing Frank is your dad, I saw his face glowing when you called him Dad: he has been so down."

"Elaine he is my dad science has proved that, so there is no way I could possibly turn my back on him, he didn't know I existed, that's not his fault."

With a gladdened heart, Henry had listened to Frank and Elaine's happy interchange, with his sister Corrina, his thoughts rising to a bubbling cauldron of unrestrained love for her, there would never be a release from the turmoil in his head.

Frank had to admit he was too tired to carry on, but his face lit up again when Denni said. "Nigh night Granddad, nigh night Elaine," finishing with, "night night Daddy."

Corrina concluded with good night Dad, good night Elaine but left nobody in any doubt about her feelings for Henry, "Good night my special man, I'll see you as soon as."

Corrina spoke to Frank every day until two weeks before he died, as he was too full of pain killers to concentrate on anything. Elaine believed he only stayed with his family as long as he did, because of Corrina.

Chapter 59

Henry called a board meeting purely to assess how everyone was settling in to their new positions, he gently eased back into the stresses and strains of business life, any irksome problems were sorted with a smile on his face. After watching his dad suffer such pain in his last few weeks, Henry was of the opinion spending your life working all hours was a negative proposition. It was his nature to be ambitious and he would always provide for his family and he would always need a project to satisfy his fertile brain but in spite of his desire for success, time spent with family would be his focus, vowing to spend his life looking after Corrina and Denni.

Reading the letter Frank had left with his will, highlighted Frank and Henry's different personalities this allied to the story of which his mum was totally unaware he had overheard. Henry shall, we say was hopeful. Because of that girly chat thereby lay a sensitive question to ask his mum, as to whether or not she would be forthcoming with her reminiscences of her hen night he noted his mum had dismissed her friends account and it's possible significant consequences as preposterous, relating to her conduct that evening. Henry understood it was a rather delicate question to ask her which she would probably find rather disrespectful, in all probability too embarrassing to even listen to, more likely she would stonewall him. He had to think long and hard of how he could approach his mum with such a personal, highly charged interrogative question, reasoning he had two options. One, he could ask his mum outright, however stumped on how he would propound such an intrusive question, two, he would have to employ a devious tactic of having his DNA compared to Frank and Corrina's without her knowledge. He decided going behind his mum's back was an unqualified no, she had always encouraged him to be ingenuous being a man without affectation there was no chance he would pursue that deceitful avenue. He was wary, heedful that he might cause animosity between them, he would have to tread carefully, asking your mother if she wouldn't mind checking his lineage is strange request, all because of a conversation he had overheard, but he had to know, it could mean that Corrina was not his sister. If Corrina was his sister all well and good, if not his world would open, he would remarry her tomorrow if he could.

When a marriage is dissolved by a civil annulment, the law declares that a marriage had never taken place, never happened. This definition set Henry excitedly reminiscing of when and how he proposed to Corrina in J F Kennedy international airport, New York and if his hopes came to fruition how he would propose again, he would take her back to New York and propose in the airport lounge as before. But first he had to find out if he and his blue eyed Corrina Jade were indeed biological siblings. He concluded enough time had elapsed since his dads passing, his desire to have a definitive answer could not be held back any more he would have to ask for the truth, carefully though because of the embarrassment he may cause his mum.

Two days of umming and ahhing Henry eventually found the wherewithal to seek an answer from his mum whether it would be propitious or unfavourable, whatever the answer, he would live with it, at least he would know and not spend the rest of his life wondering. He made a surprise visit to her house, chuckling she asked, "To what do we owe this unexpected visit, have you come for dinner, fed up of fish and chips are you?"

Pretending to look hurt he riposted, "No Mum I've come to ask something personal of you, I warn you it's very personal."

Sporting a querying expression, she asked, "Why what's the matter?"

"Mum, I have a difficult question to ask you, but I must because it is really important to me."

"Henry I think you had better explain, if I can help I will?"

"I don't know where to start."

"That's not like you, you are usually able to elucidate on any subject, the most widely read person I know, so come on spill the beans?"

"Mum," he took a troubled sigh, "it's about you and Dad."

"Why, what do you want to know?"

Inhaling a deep breath he stepped in where he didn't want to go, "Mum towards the end of the reception at Dad's funeral."

Puzzled she answered with a drawn out, "Ye-e-e-e-s."

"Well," taking another deep breath he continued, "you were talking to your friend about the night of your hen party before you married Dad or should I say your friend was, I think pulling your leg."

Her jaw dropped, "You heard what she was saying?"

"I'm sorry Mum but I have to know was she telling the truth?"

"In what way?"

"Is Dad my biological father?"

Mary was completely stunned stammering, "Henry darling of course he's your biological father he is your dad."

Henry was determined to find out the truth of that night continuing, "Mum Dad is my dad he raised me, he gave me everything including love, even if he wasn't my biological father he would still be Dad." Pausing while he collected his thoughts furthering his questioning of that night, "Mum will you tell me the full story of that night, I need you to understand because if he wasn't my biological father Corrina is not my sister please tell me what you remember?"

Mary was as white as a sheet, she sat down, stammering she tried to explain, "Okay son, I'll tell you all that I can remember of that night."

"Thanks Mum, I'm sorry but it is important to me."

She was embarrassed and worried of how Henry would receive the story she was about to unfold. "It was a Thursday night my Hen party, a crowd of us misbehaved not stupidly, just enjoying being out on a jolly," she stopped for a minute to think, resuming she admitted, "I remember this good-looking guy joining us at the table, he bought us all a drink, we couldn't get rid of him he persisted and he kept buying drinks." She stopped again, "The memory gets hazy in fact I don't want to remember."

"Mum I won't think any less of you, try to remember."

She shook her head, "Henry son I woke up about four in the morning, my head was spinning turning over I realised I was in bed with someone, as I got out of bed I was naked I couldn't remember anything, or if anything had happened, I got dressed and fled. I don't even remember his name, I have never seen him since or been back to that hotel."

"So what you're saying is that guy could well be my biological father?"

Nodding her head with tears in her eyes, "I'm sorry son but yes, possibly, maybe? I really do not remember and I'm ashamed."

"Mum there is no need to feel ashamed you are the best mother in the world, I just need to find out for sure because if Dad isn't my biological Dad, I can be with Corrina."

"What are you going to do?"

"Mum if you don't mind we have Dad and Corrina's DNA results, I think I should get them checked out against mine, in fact I only need to have my DNA compared to Corrina's DNA."

"Have you told Corrina?"

"No I don't want to build her hopes up."

"Mum this for me is really awkward, a dichotomy."

Mary was perplexed by his statement which prompted her to ask, "Why is that son?"

"Mum on the one hand I desperately want to be with Corrina as a loving couple in the real sense, however I'll be sad if Dad isn't my biological father especially for you."

Smiling warmly she wrapped her arms around him voicing words he didn't expect, "Henry my lovely boy I want you to be happy, honestly if you are not Frank's son it's too late to worry about any outcome. Mind you how I'm going to explain it to the rest of the family I do not know?"

"So you are agreed I can go ahead with the DNA test in spite of what the consequence may be or the embarrassment it will cause you."

"I have to tell Mathew what is going on I don't keep secrets from him, I can assure you I never kept secrets from Frank I loved him more than life itself."

"Thanks Mum it is really the only way we will ever know If I'm not a Jenson I don't care who my biological father is, Frank will always be my dad, in fact he will have given me the greatest gift I could ever imagine, my blue eyed Corrina Jade."

"Henry I'll keep my fingers crossed for you, you deserve to be happy but have another slight issue, you will have tell Corrina."

"Mum if the result is positive in my favour, I'll shout so loud she will hear me yelling in Edinburgh."

"I mean this son I honestly hope it goes in your favour."

"Thanks Mum I love you."

"I love you too, son."

Chapter 60

Henry contacted the same laboratory who had produced the comparison DNA of Frank and Corrina which confirming Frank was Corrina's Biological, father. Henry's DNA could be compared with either of their DNA, both would give the required answer and the result he was hoping for. To make sure there could be no mistake, he asked his doctor to draw some of his blood which was placed on a small phial; Henry delivered the blood to the laboratory himself.

It would be a few weeks before the result, but for once In his life his thoughts were indeterminable, nervousness began to take hold, he vacillated unsure of his feelings. In his heart, he wanted Corrina more than knowing who his father was.

Henry's heart fluttered when the manila envelope carrying the letter that contained his future life and possible future happiness dropped through the letterbox. His reactions were a mixture of excitement, anxiousness in the extreme, heart pounding hands trembling, he placed the envelope on the mantelpiece and sat on his sofa staring at it. However curious to investigate what might be written within, the trepidation gripped him, whatever annotation was enclosed held his future but he needed to think seriously of the repercussions it could possibly pose his mum. Henry decided to call his mum to inform her to be ready for whatever spilled out of that envelope. Her reaction, "Henry, thank you son for calling, but you must open it. Don't worry about me I've told Mathew and Caro."

"What was their reaction?"

"Mathew hasn't stopped laughing Caro just said MOM out loud with a look of disbelief, then she started laughing querying have we got the same mother? the cheeky bugger!"

"Mum I'm nervous, I think I will leave it till I've calmed myself down."

"Why don't you bring it over here and we can read it together?"

"Mum if you're sure you don't mind, that will be good?"

Henry and his mum Mary both sat looking at the envelope both curious but both nervous, at last Mary advised, "Open it Henry we both need to know, and the sooner the better."

"Ok Mum let's do it."

Trembling with anticipation, his hands sweaty he ripped the top of the envelope and slowly extracted the report that lay within. It took him a few more minutes before unfolding the report, and only then when Mary encouraged, "Go on son read it."

Henry studied the list of numbers on the report which to him were irrelevant, however, it was the notation printed at the bottom of the list which read...

The alleged father is excluded as the biological father of the tested child. Based on testing results we obtained from the analysis of the DNA loci listed the probability of paternity is 0 %. This means the possible father is not the biological father, because all data gathered from the test, does not support a relationship of paternity.

Henry read and re-read the report setting his emotions running wild, confused at first unable to grasp fully the words jumping off the page. He read it again and again, Mary's voice suddenly dragged him back out of his disorientated state.

"Can I read it?"

Henry passed it to her, as she read it she put her arm around her son and with her face breaking into a warm smile said, "Henry my lovely boy this is the news you have been waiting for, and most certainly hoping for, you and Corrina can be together you can get married again."

Henry's feelings were strangely mixed, ecstatic for himself but mortified for his mum, shaking his head he quietly answered, "Mum I'm sorry for you and how you must be feeling."

"Son, I'm good and so should you be, the only thing is you will never know who your father is."

"Mum, my father, my dad was Frank Jenson, I don't give a fig for who it might be I'm just glad Dad didn't know, he suffered enough in the end."

"Yes he was a special man."

"Mum I know he let you down."

"Son it's all in the past, when are you going to tell Corrina?"

"I'll see if I can get a flight tomorrow. I don't want to tell her over the phone."

"I don't suppose we will see you for a week or two, are we invited to the wedding?"

"Of course! everyone is invited to the wedding that's if Corrina still wants me."

"I don't think there is any doubt on that score, she adores you Henry."

"I hope your right Mum."

"I'd bet my life on the answer she will give you, why don't you go home and pack, then get yourself up to Edinburgh. Go and give her the news and then take the little fella skating."

"Thanks Mum I'm on my way."

Henry managed to get a flight the next day Corrina picked him up from the airport with her usual smiling face and her welcoming line, "Hello my special man, I've missed you."

Henry picked up Denni who was shouting, "Daddy, Daddy."

"Hello Denni, Hello blue eyes I've missed you too."

"We were not expecting you for another week or two."

"The reason I'm here Corrine Jade is I have some very important news to tell you, but it can wait till we get home give us a hug after all we are brother and sister we are allowed to hug."

Their brother and sister hugs were always characterised by more of a romantic attachment than most brother and sister relationships they were, embraces that stirred emotions siblings should not share. On the way to the house, they rented, she asked him, "What's suddenly with the little sister address?"

Henry was beginning to enjoy the dissembling of the situation preferring to make it clear though contrary to the truth he and Corrina would always be brother and sister, explaining, "Corrina I love you more than ever but it can never be therefore, I have to accept we are brother and sister calling you little sister makes it easier."

"Henry I wish you wouldn't talk like that, it makes me so sad."

"Yes we were good together, as man and wife it was special."

"Henry leave it now anyway what news is so important that you have come all the way up here two weeks early to tell me?"

By then hardly able to contain his excitement and keep a straight face, he advised, "Listen little sister when we get home I'll tell you."

"Are you always going to call me little sister I don't like it, are you going to give me bad news?"

"it depends on what prospective you view it I think it's good, we will see what you think over a cup of tea."

It was late so Henry put Denni to bed while Corrina made tea. Tea In hand Corrina asked again, "Henry what is this important news you have to tell me I really am curious you are not usually this secretive in fact never ever, what is going on?"

"Blue eyes I have something to show you."

Giggling Corrina advised, "Don't you dare we are not married."

By then, Henry could barely restrain himself from bursting into unrestrained, overmuch laughter, finding it really difficult to withhold the mirth which was almost bursting forth, unable to keep a straight face he turned his face as he reached into his jacket pocket to produce the envelope containing his DNA report, he passed it to Corrina. She took the report out of the envelope, he carried his charade a little bit further telling her, "I think you should read this very carefully."

Puzzled she opened the envelope and began to read. Henry's face even more twisted tried to stop laughing, he watched her face intently as it metamorphosed from puzzlement to incomprehension to incredulity as the text found its mark in her head, stuttering she asked, "Does this mean what I think it means?"

"Blue eyes what do think it means?"

"You are not my Brother you are not my Brother?"

"No, I'm not your brother Frank was your Biological father but not mine."

"B-b-b-but how, I mean how on earth did this come out, how on earth did you find out?"

Henry by then calm but extremely buoyant proceeded to explain to a very excited Corrina Jade how it all started and his worries of approaching his mum, after overhearing the story at Frank's funeral. Subsequent talks with his mum encouraged him to get the DNA test.

Corrina, her head in a complete whirl said. "I am having difficulty trying to comprehend this story, so when we were married it was legal in every sense of the word?"

"Absolutely we were legally married, no doubt whatsoever."

"You are absolutely sure?"

"Corrina Jade would I lie to you?"

"Henry my special man I know you wouldn't, who else knows, how many of the family know?"

"Probably everyone we know, once a story of this nature gets out it doesn't stay secret for long." Then he concluded his story with the widest grin when suggesting to Corrina, "Do you realise you can be a shameful and sleep with a man you are not married to?"

Giving him a sultry-look she grabbed hold of his tie pulled him to her, taking hold either side of his head she proceeded to pull his face to her face, they enjoyed what seemed like their first kiss of love. She whispered, "Let's go to bed before I burst, I want you to love me now; I want to make love to you. Henry my special man my body is waiting for love and Henry only you can give me that love."

That was the moment neither of them had ever imagined would happen again, their first real kiss since receiving the unpleasantly negative news that Frank was Corrina's biological father. It was a nectareous kiss, ambrosia sweet, melting their mouths together. What followed that kiss was a night filled with powerful erotic sensuousness enriched with tenderness and bounteous amounts of love and affection, a night of passion in its entirety, receiving and giving to each other totally. Their bodies satiated by the physicality of their amorous union they lay in each other's arms, both drifting into paradoxical sleep, filled with well born dreams.

Darkness filled the room, Henry dreamily stretched in the warmth of the bed clothes reaching across for Corrina, she was missing. Puzzled he tried to focus his eyes, moreover realign his thought processes croakily voicing, "Corrina where are you?"

She whispered, "I'm over here at the window my special man."

His eyes focused fully, there was an interstice in the curtain allowing enough light from a street lamp to just make out her slender naked figure in the darkness he sleepily asked, "What are you doing?"

"I'm looking up at the night sky thanking my mum for bringing you back to me, she will be as happy as I am."

Henry joined her at the window putting his arm round her, Corrina putting her head on his shoulder recreated a memory of the first time they had made love he commented, "I never thought I would talk to your mum again, thanks Mum I will look after her for you I promise."

His eyes moistening, he furthered, "Come back to bed blue eyes I want to make love to you."

"Henry as many times as you want, I think this is the most wonderful night of my life I have my lover back with me, Henry I love you so much."

"My blue eyed Corrina Jade Swan Jenson this is the most wonderful night of my life as well you know nothing can ever come between us again."

Leaving the window, back in bed every touch released the longing that had built up over the time they had been separated, forced apart ultimately through no fault of their own, thus creating a force of nature so explosive their tumult woke Denni.

Denni ran into their room hysterically shouting, "Mummy Daddy stop it stop it." Henry extricating himself from Corrina's arms reached down lifting him into bed with them, he was a very upset little boy, tying not to laugh at their predicament mum and dad calmed him while reassuring him they were not fighting they were just playing, he lay happily between them, the sandman came quickly for all three of them. Peace and quiet did not reign long Denni woke and wanted to play with his dad, six o'clock not even light, however such was their infinite night of passionate fulfilment, both were physically fatigued. Henry was back with his family in every sense, while Corrina made a cup of tea he sat playing Denni's favourite X Box game but try as he might, he could not get the better of his son the little fella knew the game inside out.

Corrina brought the tea into the bedroom with a grin querying, "How are you doing, beating him?"

"No he's too good," said with an irksome expression.

"I could have told you that for nothing."

"I don't know, he stops us in mid-stream so to speak, then he beats the pants off me on the X box, It's a good job I love him."

"Henry what's going to happen especially now you're the boss of Jenson's?"

"Blue eyes I haven't had time to think about it, Corrina it's not what I want it's what we want, we have to decide together, we are a family. I want to spend as much time with you over the next couple of weeks before we make any decisions on our future."

"Henry we have to tell Eliot and Sadie."

"We'll go after breakfast, they might know, I'm sure Barney would have told them by now."

337

"I'm going to phone Maggie she will go ape; I dread to think what effluent dictum is going to emanate from her unrefined mouth."

"Whatever, for sure, it will make us laugh."

Maggie did not disappoint, her expansive unrefined unsophisticated crudity, computed, "Bloody hell, I suppose you'll be shagging all night dirty lucky bastards?"

Elliot and Sadie were gobsmacked when they read the report, Sadie gathering her thoughts together tried to understand the situation, she commented, "So, we have proof Frank was your father, Corrina, but you, Henry, weren't his son?"

"Exactly; it's a sort of role reversal. Corrina didn't know who her dad was now I don't know who my real dad is, but I don't care who my real dad is, Frank was my dad. What is important to me is that I have Corrina back. I might even ask her to marry me."

Grinning from ear to ear, waving her finger, "I might be married to someone else."

Grinning and waving his finger back at her, Henry's answer to that reply, "Well, you little slut, if you are and he finds out about last night, I can see a divorce on the horizon."

Gasping, Corrina riposted, "Henry! Shhhhh, my brother and sister-in-law don't want to know that," she continued, "anyway I will only ever be a slut with you."

Sadie, barely able to control her mirth, remarked, "It didn't take you pair long to reacquaint, did it? mucky sods."

Corrina still giggling added, "I'll have you know we had to wait nearly half an hour until Denni was in bed."

"Corrina, I am so chuffed for you both, are you going to get married again?"

"If Corrina will have me, then we most certainly will."

"Henry, I can't wait, Denni can be pageboy."

When Henry and Corrina remarried, it brought about the end of entanglement of the family which Frank, through his indifference to moral restraint, had over the years conjured up a ravelment of many women and children. Some came to the fore, others according to his detractors he kept secret, if nothing else his reputation for promiscuity gave him notoriety. Some of those women had borne him offspring, all of whom loved him. His antics produced extraordinary consequences, some broken hearts and strangely, a lot of happiness; he was admired and loved. Henry and Corrina's wedding undid the tangled mesh of romantic intrigue that had followed Frank throughout his busy life; the family was finally unravelled.

Henry and Corrina moved back to New York and became American citizens.

It wasn't long before they introduced into the world a daughter who they named Mary Susan (Mary Sue), after their two mothers. Henry remained head of the family business, flying back to Birmingham four times a year to chair the board meetings; he also maintained his ambition away from Jenson's and returned to work for Mighty where he was now CEO. He and Corrina opened a small bookshop by way of a hobby, which opened three days a week and was managed by Corrina. Denni played for a local youth ice hockey team.

Henry had never wanted to be away from his ménage—they were his life. He always admired and aspired to be like his dad, except for his dad's predisposition for women—there was only ever one woman for Henry: Corrina Jade.

Printed in Great Britain
by Amazon

43083760R00190